THREE ROADS

A Sequel to:

Hoofbeats in the Wind
Coffee With Cowboys
The Legend of Bijou Bay

GRANGER:

Fifteen-year-old Granger Miller's mother moves them from the city life to a rural life. Although he has never been around horses, new friends invite him to a saddle bronc clinic. His destiny is found, and dreams come alive. His road is filled with years of learning on the rodeo road, life-long friendships, heartbreak, and a bucking horse stallion that becomes his nemesis.

SAMMIE:

Growing up and competing in the cutting horse industry, Sammie switches to barrel racing. Her parents believe in her goal of becoming a champion barrel racer and gift her with the horse that could help her fulfill those dreams. Her road is rocky with questionable friends, wrong decisions, and doubts. The pressure to succeed begins to tear her down.

ACE:

When he was three years old, his world champion team roping father was killed in an accident. With his younger brother at his side, Ace's life is filled with roping and family. His road is filled with the ghost of his father which leads to success and tragedy. What will it take to come out of the shadows of his father?

This book is fiction. The characters, properties, and dialogues are from the author's imagination and are not to be construed as fact.

ISBN- 978-1-7339528-7-3

ACKNOWLEDGMENTS

A huge thanks to the following for their willingness to answer all my research questions for the last few books. That research led to this book.

Tracy Hammond	Lindsey and Chad Hutsell
Crystal Longfellow	Brady Portenier
Devan Reilly	Roscoe Jarboe
Kirk & Katie St. Clair	Tate Owens
Brody Cress	Johnny Espeland
Ike Sankey	Martee Pruitt
Cody Yates	Lori Smith
Lewiston Roundup Association	Darryl Kirby
Trenten & Maria Montero	Rylee Potter Hansen
Jessica Gates	Kim Grubb
Dillon Holyfield	Amberleigh Moore
Ty Roberge	Sierra Schoenfeldt -Phillips

THREE ROADS

Dreams are fulfilled at the end of a long road.

by

Gini Roberge

CHAPTER ONE

SAMMIE PARKSTON

My heart was pounding in my chest as my hand slid down the dark bay horse's nose as if he were an illusion. I couldn't believe he was there…that I was now the owner of a horse that had run in the Thomas and Mack arena at the National Finals Rodeo. My dream of earning the right to be there was even closer.

"What a nice young woman," Mom said as we walked to the outside door of the indoor arena.

"I've heard nothing but positive comments about her," Dad held the door open for us to walk through. "Her dad is an honest cowboy, and she is obviously one hell of a horsewoman."

"She answered all my questions about him," I nodded excitedly with the horse walking by my side and to the horse trailer. My voice was high-pitched and fast. "She was so patient as I rattled off every question I could come up with before she left."

Her truck and trailer pulled away from the arena and Delaney Rawlins waved with a smile as she drove away.

"She answered all my questions about Pepper and running for the NFR," I added. "She really loves Memphis, too. He is going to have a big career with her."

"Just like Pepper will with you now," Dad nodded in clear amusement.

"I cannot believe you two kept this from me," I opened the back gate of the trailer and stepped the horse into it for the first time. My horse…Pepper was now MY horse. I giggled and jigged my feet again as I slid my hand down his dark brown back before closing the partition. I danced out of the trailer and into my parent's arms. "I cannot tell you how happy I am and so thankful that you two are my parents."

"You have big dreams, and we just wanted to help you any way we can," Mom squeezed tightly with tears in her eyes.

"We gave you the tool, but it's up to you to put in the hours and the work," Dad added.

"I will not let you down," I declared.

It was January with snow and freezing temperatures outside, so Pepper and I spent the first few months riding in our own personal arena and down the snow packed roads surrounding our family ranch in Madras, Oregon. When I wasn't working with Pepper to keep him in shape, I was in the gym getting myself in top shape, so we were both fit and ready.

My parents raised, trained, and competed with cutting horses, so we had dozens of foals that were due in the spring. The foals and the yearlings were my favorite while my brother, Mason, excelled in training and riding the show horses. He spent most of his time in Oklahoma.

Mason called right after I had loaded Pepper into the trailer on our way to our first official jackpot barrel race.

"What are you doing, Corn Flakes?"

My giggle of happiness echoed in the cab of the truck, "Taking Pepper to our first race in Redmond."

"About damn time."

"I know! But with winter, and then foaling, it's been busy around here."

"You need to focus more if you're really setting out to go to the NFR."

"The qualifying year started last October so it's too late this year. I start up in June and will get my permit. Hopefully, I can earn enough to fill it by the end of September so I can hit the ground running the first weekend in October. We'll start close to you in Tulsa."

"Keep me posted so I keep a room in the bunk house for you."

"You're going to make us stay in the bunk house?" I chuckled.

"Yeah, it's only a one-bedroom manager's apartment and that would be for me and my new girlfriend, Angie."

"Oohhh…must be serious if you're looking that far out into the future."

"So far it is."

"Well, I'll have the three-horse living quarters trailer for us, so I'll be taking my home on the road with me so my friends and I can stay in it. There are rodeos all over Texas in October and November and we plan on hitting as many as possible for a strong start."

CHAPTER TWO

GRANGER MILLER

The house was quiet, which meant Mom didn't come home again. I glanced out the window to confirm her car was gone. She must have a new boyfriend which meant it could be days before I saw her again. I opened the refrigerator to see the shelves full. She stocked up for me, which meant she didn't even plan on coming back for a while. Some 15-year-old kids would love the freedom of having a house to themselves; the independence and freedom. But it bored me.

I grabbed a paper bag and threw in food for lunch then dropped it into my backpack. I hurried out the door to make it to school on time; it was a fifteen-minute walk I had to make in sixteen. We had just moved from Bellevue to Walla Walla, Washington in time to start the spring quarter of the school year. The bell was ringing as I jogged up the steps to the old building.

"Hey, Granger!"

I turned to see Leo Wallens and Alder Spence hurrying toward me. The duo was in most of my classes but had never talked to me before. They were in a different circle of friends than me; they had a group of cowboy friends and for me? It was just me.

"What?" I huffed.

"You ever do any fencing?" Spence asked.

I looked at them like they had lost their minds, "Like, with swords?"

They stopped, looked at me in confusion, and turned to each other. After a moment, they both started laughing. I rolled my eyes as my stomach gurgled in embarrassment and irritation then turned to walk into the school.

They were quickly at my side.

"Sorry about that," Leo said hurriedly. "You caught us off guard."

"We're just around people that automatically know what we're talking about," Spence added.

"What are you talking about?" We dodged between other students hurrying to class.

"Putting up barbed wire fence for cows and horses," Leo explained.

I stopped and looked at both and thought of my 'swords' answer. It made me laugh and they both grinned and chuckled. "No, I haven't done the swords or the barbed wire."

"We have a job this weekend and it would go a lot faster if there were three of us," Leo added. "You're bigger and stronger than both of us, so we're thinking, if you're up to earning some money, that you would help us out."

Three days later, I was standing on the flatbed trailer at the back of Leo's truck with 600 metal fence posts and at least a dozen spools of barbed wire.

Spence jumped onto the trailer and handed me a pair of leather gloves, "Don't ever try to do barbed wire fence without them."

"Hurts like hell," Leo chuckled. "And by the time we're done, if you're not careful, your pants and shirts will have holes in them."

What had I gotten myself into?

After pounding in the fortieth fence post, I knew, and I loved it. My arms were scratched, muscles ached, neck was throbbing, and energy was building. This was physical and heart pumping. I turned to Leo as he prepared to pound in the next post.

"Leo, look at the guide wire," I shouted in disbelief. "You're six inches off."

"Who the hell cares?" Leo laughed. "It's only for cows."

"Come on, man, it's going to be out here for years," I shook my head and walked to him to move the post. "Keep it straight, pegs out, and follow the guideline. That's why we took all that time to string it out. Take some pride in your work."

Spence tossed the next posts onto the ground, "Your dad harp on you about that, too?"

"No," I huffed and felt the heat form in my stomach. "He left a few years back and we haven't seen him since. Just do the job right."

"Oh," Leo exhaled. "I didn't know that."

We finished another hundren feet of posts and wire in silence.

Leo turned and looked back, "I have to admit, it does look good."

"Yeah, it does," A deep voice said from behind us.

I turned to see a tall, older version of Leo.

"You must be Granger," The man stretched out a hand.

I nodded and shook his hand, "Yes, sir."

"You can call me, Dale. I've seen how these two run wire, and so I'm guessing you're responsible for it coming out straight and the wire is level instead of up and down the posts," He gave Spence and Leo a teasing grin.

"Yeah, he is," Leo nodded. "And, he's never fenced before."

"Well, you must be a natural at it," the older man nodded. "If you're interested, I have some friends that need some line run, too. You have enough money with this job to get you to the clinic?"

I looked at him in surprise, "What clinic?"

"These two are earning money for the bareback and saddle bronc clinic in a couple weeks. You're going with them, aren't you?" Dale asked.

I didn't know what he was talking about and was a bit embarrassed, so I just stared at him.

"It's riding bucking horses," Spence explained with a grin, and he bounced in excitement. "Man, nothing gets your heart pumping like sliding on a horse that is going to try and buck you off."

"You have anything better to do?" Leo asked. "You're sure welcome to come with us. Dad used to ride when he was younger, so we started with calves and little ponies."

"We're ready for the bigger horses now, so we're going to the clinic," Spence added.

"I can call and get you signed up," Dale offered.

I looked at the older man then back to my new friends. Riding horses sounded a lot more exciting than sitting around the house watching television. "OK, I'll go, but I've never been around horses before."

"Well," Dale grinned. "You're in for a real awakening then."

CHAPTER THREE

ACE CONNERS

I backed the horse into the box. The second his butt hit the box pads; the bay roan stood frozen as a statue. Only his eyes moved as he watched the judges and men in the arena. Then I nodded. The rattle of the roping chute had my legs squeezing, arm lifting the rope in the air, and the horse bolting after the steer that ran out into the arena. Two swings and the throw had the rope swirling around the steer's horns and we turned to the left. Taylor's rope captured the heels and with a 4.2 second run we captured the High School Rodeo National Championship.

"Yeah!" Taylor yelled and threw his end of the rope in the air as we trotted after the steer and down the arena.

The crowd roared, but over all of them, I could hear our mother screaming in excitement. When I finally found her in the crowd, she was jumping up and down with the proudest grin any son would want to see from his parents.

Taylor rode to me with a hand in the air, and we came together in an elated high-five then trotted out of the arena to be met by all the members of our rodeo team.

When the initial celebration eased, I was pulled aside by Lori Ann Marker, a reporter.

"Congratulations on your second straight team roping title at the National High School finals and your third place in tie-down," Lori Ann grinned. "Tell me, Ace, as a senior this year, what's on the horizon now?"

My heart was pumping in excitement, stomach still tumbling from the nerves, and my grin was wide. "I'm headed home to Texas for a bit then we'll go from there."

"This is your last year in high school, which college rodeo program piqued your interest?"

"There were a couple of them," I nodded. "I'm going to rope for a year, until my brother Taylor graduates, and then we'll go rope at college together."

"What about the PRCA? You're 18 now and can get a permit and follow in the footsteps of your late father, the seven-time NFR qualifier and World Champion team roping header, Austin Conners."

The excited knot in my stomach was replaced by anxiety, "I am not my father." I managed to say without a growl. "He died when I was three. I have my own path."

I started to turn away when Lori Ann grabbed my arm.

Her brows were raised in surprise, "I didn't mean to…"

"Thank you for your time," I yanked my arm from her grasp and walked away. My stride was wide and fast.

At the end of the rodeo and the awards presentation was the announcement of the Horse of the Year. Taylor's red roan tie-down horse, Quincy, had won two years before. I had hopes that my bay roan, Bear, would win one before we were done. He was the finest horse I had ever trained or ridden.

"Ladies and gentlemen, now for the horse of the year," The announcer said. "This gelding is very special. He is out of a mare named Maggie that was the sole survivor of a horrendous accident that claimed the life of his rider's father, seven-time NFR qualifier and world champion header, Austin Conners."

Taylor and I shared a glance, and my mother squeezed my arm tightly.

The announcer continued, "The Conner brothers have never competed on a horse that was not from the infamous Maggie, and I am very pleased to crown this year's gelding ridden by Ace Conners, Maggie's Bear Tracks, known as Bear, as the horse of the year."

So many emotions ran through me as the celebration erupted from my family. I was overjoyed for my horse, but I knew, no matter what, I would never get out from under the shadow of my father.

CHAPTER FOUR

UNKNOWN

I followed behind the tall and wide white dually truck as the line of vehicles pulled down the driveway and under the log opening where a metal steer skull hung announcing the ranch. My small SUV was nearly hidden between two large pickups as we parked in the front pasture between the road and the ranch house. At least a hundred vehicles and horse trailers covered the pasture. Many horses were tied to the trailers as they waited for the team roping jackpot to start after the wedding.

I remained in the car until the music began that indicated the wedding had commenced on the back side of the house next to the arenas and corrals. With the small bag in hand, I walked to the front of the house as if I lived there, then cautiously glanced around me for anyone within sight. I withdrew the tiny camera from the bag and placed it next to the house numbers by the front door. It was nearly invisible. With a push of a button, the camera activated with the video showing on my phone. I could see the pasture full of vehicles behind me. Another camera was placed in the corner of the window but facing inside the house. The video on the phone showed a wide hallway, rodeo pictures, saddles, and trophies, and an abundance of exercise equipment. I could see three doors to the left and one at the far end.

Hurrying down the steps, I made my way around the corner of the house and inconspicuously slid onto an empty chair toward the back of the wedding audience. Tipping my large-brimmed summer hat to hide my face, I constantly watched for anyone that might be looking at me or taking a picture with me in the background, but everyone was watching the bride and groom.

When the newlywed couple, their families, and wedding party disappeared for the wedding portraits, a small band began playing on a flatbed trailer that was parked by the arena fence. The music was upbeat and had the crowd cheering, laughing, and dancing. Over two hundred people were spread-out from the house to the barn, and I easily and stealthily maneuvered between everyone until I was in the barn. A cat turned at my appearance and watched me as I made my way down the aisle and up the stairs that led to the hay loft. Two cameras were placed at the large glassless windows and the video was checked. An overhead view of the arenas was visible on one, and the other showed the side of the house, porch on the back, and the multitude of wedding guests milling around the yard. I could also see the expanse of driveway.   Perfect.

After making my way down the stairs, I listened for any movement before stepping into the aisle. There was no one there…except the barn cat. I smiled at the feline then, very calmly made my way through the crowd and to my car. After sliding onto the front seat, I checked all four cameras and was delighted to see clear videos from all.

Not wanting to look conspicuous as the first to leave, I remained hidden in my car for an hour until the first departing guests started their vehicles. I followed them down the drive.

For ten days, I watched the family come and go, ride their horses, do their chores, and all without knowing the cameras were there. I could barely sleep the night before my plans were put into action. The morning found me a mile down the road pulled over and watching the videos as the attendees of the bucking horse clinic arrived. Two large semi-trucks that had carried the horses to be used during the clinic were now parked in the front pasture where once the wedding attendees' vehicles had been. A few cars and trucks turned down the driveway. The arenas were abuzz with activity.

Once the clinic began, and everyone was in the arenas at the back of the house, I drove down the driveway and parked between the two large semi-trucks.

The sky was blue with not one cloud to be seen and the temperature remained a pleasant 80 degrees. It was a beautiful day. Everyone remained in the backyard and there was no chance to accomplish my goal, so I did not leave my car. The next day, the temperature rose to the nineties and there were no clouds to block the hot sun. Just after the group had restarted the clinic after lunch, the bride from two weeks previous appeared on the video. She walked down the hallway with all the exercise equipment and disappeared into one of the rooms. After a few moments, she walked out the door and disappeared around the hallway. I waited until she appeared on the video walking out the back door and to the arenas. I made my move from the car.   A large rolling bag that resembled a rodeo cowboy bag was carried to the front door. With a deep breath, I slid a gloved hand around the front doorknob…it turned easily. A relieved exhale escaped as I checked the window camera one more time, then the barn cameras to make sure the bride had not returned to the house. She was standing at the corral watching the group of riders.

I slid through the door and down the hall to the second door. I knew the right door to go to since I had watched for ten days as people came and went. There was no doubt a video camera would be in the room, so I watched the video from the corrals until the monitor hanging from the fence was clear. When no one was looking near it, I withdrew the long expanding antenna from the bag and peered inside the second bedroom…into the nursery. Both babies were sound asleep as the antenna was stretched out and pushing the monitor so that it aimed at the closet instead of the cribs.

One more look at the camera view at the corrals…no one was near the monitor…everyone was watching a cowboy on a bucking horse, so I slid into the room and opened the rolling bag.

The little boy was first and didn't stir as I lifted him from the crib and set him on the cushions inside the rolling bag. The little girl was then nestled next to him. I turned and carefully rolled them out of the room, down the hall, and out the front door. I removed the two cameras before descending the stairs and had to keep myself from running across the yard. If I jostled the bag too much, it would wake the twins and might draw someone's attention.

The bag was placed in the back of the SUV before I slid onto the front seat, started the engine, and casually drove away from the house.

CHAPTER FIVE

SAMMIE

"Well, at least he's beautiful."

As I trotted out of the warm-up arena I turned back and looked at Christina. What the hell did that mean?

From the moment the purchase of Pepper was announced on my social media, every word had been positive. *Congratulations, can't wait to see you ride, you'll go far with that horse,* and more had been comments I had received. All of them helped build my confidence.

It was the second summer of traveling with my three friends and we had been to several jackpots, but this was mine and Pepper's first rodeo together. Bertie traveled with me in my truck, and Lynn traveled in Christina's truck with her. Neither of us had a four-horse trailer so we had to take two trucks.

Bertie trotted in next to me as we made our way to the main arena.

"What did she mean by that?" I asked her.

"By what?"

"At lease Pepper's beautiful."

"He is beautiful."

"But what did she mean with the 'at least'?"

Bertie shrugged, "You know Christina. She probably didn't mean anything by it."

"But, her tone was…"

"You're reading too much into it. Just forget about her, go out there, and kick butt in your first rodeo."

I didn't answer as my name was called on the loudspeaker as being third out. My mind went back to the horse, the pattern, and the arena. With a hand stroking Pepper's neck, I visualized the run. I had never felt more confident running into an arena towards that first barrel. Even though our second was just a bit wide, we still finished within two-hundredths of a second behind the winner and took home a check for second place.

At our second rodeo, we won enough to qualify to purchase my Women's Professional Rodeo Association Pro Card. I was elated with my horse.

Pepper's head rubbed against my hip as I opened the gate to his pasture. I chuckled and scratched between his ears before removing the halter. After an hour ride across our property, he still took off at a run onto the green field. Half-way down the hill, he stopped, and sniffed the ground. With no consideration that I had just thoroughly brushed and groomed him after the ride, he still lowered onto the ground and rolled in the grass.

I watched with a contented sigh as he stood and began grazing. I loved that horse more every day and there was no better way to start a birthday than spending it with him. Twenty years old now and no longer a teen-ager I was considered an adult…although I didn't feel any different.

When I walked toward the house, I was surprised to see Dad and Mason standing between their trucks. The old 6-horse stock trailer was attached to Dad's and my three-horse living quarters trailer was attached to Mason's.

"What are you two up to?" I stopped between them and smiled.

Dad's arm slid around my shoulders to tuck me in for a warm hug as he kissed the top of my head. "Happy birthday, my beautiful daughter."

"Thanks, Dad," I grinned and wrapped my arms around him and squeezed.

"Happy birthday, Corn Flakes," Mason grinned.

"Thanks for coming back for my birthday," I said honestly. Although I didn't tell him, I adored my big brother. "So, what are you doing with my trailer?"

"We have to wait for Mom," Mason chuckled with a bit of mischievous joy twinkling in his eyes.

The door to the house opened and we turned to watch Mom step through with a wide happy smile.

"Oh, I love seeing you three together," She lifted her phone and took a picture.

"I want a group selfie for my birthday," I pulled out my own phone and once Mom was tucked in next to Mason, I took the picture.

"Would you like to ride with your father or brother?" Mom asked with a smile.

"For what?" I asked as all three grinned.

Mom answered, "While you were on your morning ride, we cleaned out your trailer."

"What? Even my guitars?" I gasped.

"We were very careful with the guitars...like always," Dad shook his head with a grin.

"It had to be cleaned to trade it in," Mason chuckled. "They didn't want all your crap."

"Trade it in?" I turned to my parents with wide eyes.

"Well, you and Pepper are going to be traveling a lot this year, and we want to make sure you're safe," Dad answered.

"We rarely use the stock trailer so, for your birthday, we're trading in the two trailers for a dependable new rodeo home for you," Mom grinned. "Besides, I want to go with you when my schedule allows, and I want a bit bigger and more comfy space."

"Yeeee!" I laughed and hugged all three.

I walked up the ramp and into the back of the fourth trailer dad had approved for consideration.

"Well, it might be a bit over-kill for just you and Pepper," Dad leaned into the trailer. "But a four-horse will allow room for all three of your friends so you can travel in one trailer instead of two."

"That will save a lot of money," Mason agreed. He was standing at the back of the trailer with the door to the tack room open. "I do like the side loads, so the tack room is the full width of the back of the trailer."

"I agree," I nodded and walked through the trailer. "I love the mangers, flooring, and the padded dividers."

"The covered feed storage barely looks like it has been used for a three-year-old trailer," Mom called out from on top of the roof. "They guarantee the generator and air conditioner." She climbed down the ladder and looked into the trailer as I locked each divider into place.

They were standing at the bottom of the ramp as I stepped out. "I love this layout, so let's check the living-quarters part."

The moment I stepped into the trailer I had that feeling of home. Dark wood flooring, mahogany upholstery, and hickory cabinetry greeted us. To my right were the steps leading to the main bed over the back of the truck. Then the partition that held the flat-screen television and on the other side, another set of steps led up to the bedroom. Straight ahead was the slide-out portion of the trailer which consisted of a couch that folded down to a bed, then a u-shaped bench around the kitchen table. It too could be converted into a bed.

To my left were two barstools tucked under a breakfast counter that led to the kitchen. We walked through the trailer to the door to the back of the trailer which opened to the bathroom with large shower, sink, toilet, storage cabinet and another door that opened to the horse stalls.

My eyes were wide, and heart raced as I looked back at my parents and brother.

"This is beautiful," Mom said softly as she opened the multitude of small storage spaces. "So well taken care of, it barely looks used."

"We'll make sure the tip-out functions properly," Dad nodded with a smile to me. "What do you think?"

"Is it too much?" I whispered.

"If you have your friends with you, then they will need a place to sleep along with the horse stalls in the back," he answered.

"Two people to each bed, you could sleep 6 people in here," Mom said. "That will save them money."

"This gives you room to haul horses from here to Oklahoma for me," Mason grinned. "That will save us money on having to hire haulers."

"As for the length of it," Dad mused. "You've driven my six-horse trailer with a half-million dollars' worth of horses in the back from here to Oklahoma and Texas then back. I'm not too worried about that."

"Me either," Mason and Mom agreed.

"But…" I whispered and looked around the trailer again.

"How do you feel standing here?" Mom asked.

"Like I'm home," I said honestly.

"That is the same feeling when I walked into our horse trailer," Mom nodded with a pleased smile. "It is our second home and I have loved every moment we have lived in it."

"The horse trailer part is perfect," Mason mused. "And the living quarters section has a great layout."

"Sammie?" Dad smiled. "Is this the one?"

My heart raced and tears filled my eyes, "Yes."

Two hours later, the trailer was sitting in the middle of our driveway. While I filled the tack room, Mom was wiping down the living section, Dad was installing the video cameras in the back of the trailer that were linked to the small monitor in the cab, and Mason was removing the unneeded stickers from the outside of the trailer and replacing them with the Parkston Performance Horses emblems. Just below the family PPH brand was a black silhouette of a woman riding a barrel horse and another of a woman riding a cutting horse. It was perfect.

My two guitars were placed in the closet, then Mom surprised me with a dozen boxes of puzzles. Having been a puzzle fanatic since I was little, they were the perfect addition.

By the end of my birthday, the trailer was filled with my tack, supplies filled the kitchen cupboards, and the bed was made. After dinner and birthday cake in the trailer, I decided to spend the night in it.

Cross-legged in the middle of the bed, I typed a message to my friends with a picture of the trailer attached.

Text to Lynn, Christina, and Bertie: My birthday gift from my parents. An upgrade for us so we can travel together and save money.

Text from Christina: Nice, wish I could get birthday presents like that.

Text from Bertie: Beautiful, I can't wait for the first trip!

Text to Christina: I will be hauling for the ranch, too.

Text from Lynn: We will be traveling in style this weekend!

Text from Christina: So, it is a business trailer and your present is the right to use it?

I hesitated before answering Christina. It really was no business of hers that the trailer was in my name and not Parkston Performance Horses. Before starting barrel racing, I was a National Cutting Horse Champion and had won the 3-horse trailer that was traded in.

Text to Christina: It's a beautiful trailer that is going to save us money by traveling together. It is going to be a great summer of rodeos and races.

I scooted down the bed to the top step that led to the main trailer. With Pepper, the trailer, and my friends, the anticipation made my toes tap the floor and hands shake.

I couldn't wait for the adventures and stories this trailer was going to hold in the next year.

Our first rodeo road trip in the new trailer was to Prineville. It was so exciting to have all our horses in the trailer and all four of us racers in the cab. It was a game of rock-paper-scissors that had Bertie riding in the front with me with Lynn and Christina in the back. Although she was smiling, it was easy to tell that Christina didn't appreciate the back seat. She was used to driving her own vehicle. Lynn declared that since it was my family's trailer, I would have the bed up front to myself and two of them would share either the kitchen bed or the living area bed. With another rock-paper-scissors game, Bertie and Christina ended up sharing the larger living area bed.

"Next time we flip for it," Christina grumbled as she slid the sofa down to create the bed. "I'm done with rock-paper-scissors."

Lynn, Bertie, and I shared humored glances but didn't say a word.

I felt like a teenager at a high school rodeo the next morning as we saddled the horses. My stomach was anxious even though Pepper and I had placed in the two rodeos where we had competed. He was anxious and pranced left and right after I mounted.

"You sure you can handle him?" Christina smiled, but the tone was a bit snarky.

"I've ridden all my life, including training," I answered calmly. "If I can stay on nationally ranked cutting horses, then I can stay on this little bit of prancing."

Lynn just shook her head as the four of us walked to the warm-up arena. Bertie pretended she didn't hear the exchange.

When we returned to the trailer, there was no memory of the rude remark. Pepper had run us to second place while the other three had good runs but had not placed. While Bertie and I cheerfully grilled burgers and prepared dinner. Christina and Lynn had disappeared into the mass of trailers and arrived just as the hamburgers were ready.

The next morning, we were on the road to Newport for our second rodeo of the weekend.

"So, you buying the coffee this morning?" Lynn teased me as we drove into the parking lot of a coffee shop.

"Pepper is..." Christina muttered in the back seat.

"He can buy the coffee, I'll pick up the scones and muffins," I said through gritted teeth but a smile hiding the irritation.

When we walked the horses to the arena my stomach was anxious, and smile forced.

"Didn't we run a jackpot here last year?" Bertie asked.

"Yeah," Christina chuckled. "We all placed in that one except Sammie."

My breath caught at the memory; I hit first and second. Why did they have to bring that up?

"Well, maybe Pepper can keep you from hitting them this year," Christina turned her horse away and trotted down the warm-up arena.

Neither Lynn nor Bertie reacted to the comment, they just followed her.

My back was tight as I took a deep breath and nudged Pepper into a trot. They all competed before me and were well off the lead, but they had left all the barrels up.

When my name was announced, my back was still tense, shoulders high, and my anxiety was apparent in Pepper's prancing toward the gate. My heart was in my throat as we approached the first barrel. I hesitated just long enough that he took a stride too many, and we were wide on the barrel. I hit the second barrel with my foot, and the 'ah' from the crowd let me know that the barrel hit the ground. He took control of the third barrel, and it was turned perfectly with a flying run to the end. I stroked his neck as we trotted away from the arena; he was a spectacular horse.

But, even with my love growing for the horse my stomach was churning as I anticipated the comments from my travel partners. It didn't take long as we walked back to the trailer.

Christina turned with a smile that tried hard to hold innocence, "Only one this year. You'll get it next year."

"Maybe Newport just isn't your rodeo," Lynn chuckled.

"We'll see," I muttered and stepped out of the saddle.

"Don't take them so seriously," Bertie whispered. "They are just trying to lighten the mood for you. We teased each other a lot last year."

I took a deep breath and nodded, but it was different last year. They teased me and didn't include the horse I was riding. This time, it always included Pepper.

It was the last rodeo of the weekend, and the next weekend was going to be five rodeos in five days; six days with my companions. I couldn't let them drag me down. I needed to get a grip and focus on just having fun, enjoying my horse, and preparing for October 1st.

"What the hell?" I turned down the road that led to the barn where Lynn and Christina's horses were boarded. Lynn was walking her horse into the back of Christina's trailer. I turned to Bertie who was sitting in the passenger seat. "What's going on?"

Bertie sighed, "Well, I guess she decided she didn't want to be a passenger anymore."

"It doesn't make sense," I grumbled.

"I'm not explaining anything for her," Bertie yanked on the door handle and slid out.

The look on my face as I approached Christina and Lynn must have asked the question for me.

"I like driving," Christina untied her horse from the side. "I have no doubt your father has told you that no one else can drive his truck and trailer but you."

Both were mine, not his, but I didn't correct her. I had no intention of letting her drive my truck.

"We're just taking the regular trailer, not the living quarters," Lynn added. "We'll still be all together at night. It's just the driving."

"It's a waste of fuel," I sighed. There really wasn't any reason to argue with them since their horses were already loaded and they were not going to change their minds.

"Toppenish, Sedro-Woolley, St. Paul, Molalla, and Eugene," Lynn stated. "It's not like we are traveling cross-country."

Right, I thought to myself. Maybe just talking to Bertie between rodeos would be better for my nerves anyway. But, with each rodeo, Pepper and I dropped in our time and standings. There were no more hit barrels but the sharp turns we had begun the summer with, had turned to wide blowouts. Christina's and Lynn's comments had become more subtle but in the back of my mind, I had begun to think how disappointed Delaney must feel about selling me her horse. I was doing him no favors.

After the last race of the weekend in Eugene, I patted Pepper on the rump before closing the partition in the back of the horse trailer, then leaned my head on it and sighed. How in the hell was I going to get past this block?

Voices neared the trailer, "Just because your parents are foolish enough to buy you a NFR horse doesn't mean you have the talent to get it there." It was Christina's voice with Lynn and Bertie's laughter.

"No matter the horse, an average rider is an average rider." That was Bertie; the one friend that I thought had my back.

Tears fell from my eyes. I was making a fool of myself and a joke of my family. I leaned away from the partition and looked out at the three women and Bertie's horse they were walking to load into my trailer. I had known them and raced against them for years, since I had changed from cutting to barrels, and today all three had beaten my time. But I knew they weren't better riders than me, and their horses were not better than Pepper.

A change needed to be made, and I knew what I was going to do.

All three turned when I stepped out of the back of the trailer. Bertie at least had the decency to look embarrassed. Lynn and Christina just smirked, but their eyes narrowed when I shut the trailer door, then lifted the ramp and lowered the handle to lock it in place. It was very clear Bertie's horse was not riding home with me.

Without a word, I stepped to the open doors of the tack room. Any item that did not belong to me started hitting the ground.

"What the hell are you doing, Sammie?" Christina growled.

I didn't answer. When I was done, I just closed the doors on the tack room and walked to the living quarters then opened the door, stepped in, and grabbed a paper sack. Everything in the bathroom that did not belong to me was stuffed in the bag then tossed out the door. Bertie had been walking toward the trailer and the bag bounced off her stomach then fell to the ground with its contents spilling out.

"Sammie, you're overreacting," she huffed.

I picked up every boot or shoe that was on the floor and they landed at her feet.

"You're being a bitch," Christina grumbled.

I opened the refrigerator and began tossing their food.

"Sammie, for heaven's sake, knock it off," Lynn called out as she dodged the bottles of seltzer water.

The storage cabinets were opened and anything that wasn't mine went flying out the door.

A movement behind my three grumbling companions caught my attention. A group of four women were standing on the road watching the commotion. I recognized them but didn't acknowledge them. I just went back to clearing the cabinets as the three women picked up their stuff and shouted insults at me.

One last walk through the trailer to make sure I had nothing of theirs, I stepped outside to retrieve my lawn chair and table. They were calmly set in the trailer then I reached for the cooler. I had purchased everything in it except the bag of chocolate mini-bars. I tossed it high over my shoulder and the little bars flew through the air. All three women swore at me. After setting the cooler into the trailer, I closed the door and locked it.

One last glaring look at the three women scrambling to pick up everything, I turned and walked to my truck. The engine roared to life as I looked down the road. The four women stepped aside, and I put the truck in gear. Of the four women, one of them had ridden at the NFR the year before and the other three were in the top 20 of the standings. As I passed, they smiled in clear approval. I waved.

When I turned out of the rodeo grounds and onto the main road, I felt a huge weight off my shoulders. I should be feeling sad to lose three friends, but I was honestly quite relieved they were out of my life. Traveling to rodeos by myself was going to be more enjoyable than having to defend my family and horse or deal with their negativity.

An hour into the drive home, I was feeling a bit giddy and singing to the radio when the music stopped, and the phone rang.

"Hello, brother Mason," I answered with a smile.

"Have you been on Facebook lately?"

"No, not for a couple weeks, why?"

"Because your tossing those three friends out of your trailer has caused quite the frenzy."

I could hear the humor in his voice, but that didn't stop my mood from plummeting.

"Am I an over-reacting bitch like they called me?"

"They tried to make it sound that way," he chuckled. "Took pictures of all the stuff laying on the ground. You want me to read the original post?"

I sighed, "I don't go on Facebook because of the drama."

"You may at least want to know this one."

"Fine," I sighed.

"OK, so it is from Christina with a tag to the other two. It says, and I quote: This is what happens when a barrel racer hears the truth about her amateur riding and can't handle it. You get yelled at as she throws a fit, overreacts, and tosses your stuff out of her parent's trailer she is allowed to drive. Don't ride with Sammie or you'll become her target, too." He paused. "I take it you didn't tell them it was your trailer."

"It was none of their business and Christina was being snotty that it was my birthday gift."

"Well, the other two commented with snarky remarks then all hell broke loose," he chuckled again.

"What does that mean?"

"Right now, there are about 131…132 comments on it and not in their favor. It started with a couple women that witnessed the event and they are saying they heard what the three 'so called' friends said about you, and it wasn't true that you were yelling at them. You didn't say a word. All of them said they would ride with you any time, then Delaney Rawlins popped in. Her comment, and I quote again, is; Sammie is a true horsewoman with a huge future. I would be happy to ride with her any day of the week. I couldn't have picked a better new owner for Pepper."

"That was nice of them," I sighed, and a knot formed in my stomach. So, I hadn't disappointed Delaney…yet.

"Now we have 156 comments and…hold on…I can't find it," He started to laugh. "It is no longer available. She deleted the post."

"Well, I guess it's not a bad thing I left them in my dust, but I hate losing friends…"

"Sammie, they weren't your friends. They were the fakest people you could have been around."

"But…"

"No buts, Corn Flakes. Everyone could see it the last couple of months since Pepper came into the picture and you earned your pro card; you became a threat to them. But you kept defending them. You weren't going to believe anyone until you saw it yourself."

"Yeah…I guess."

"Growing up we had nothing but positive people around us helping us achieve the goals we set in cutting. You jumped over to barrels and haven't had that same support."

"I thought I did."

"Not from those three. You have to surround yourself with true friends and a support team that stays positive to your face AND behind your back. They did not."

"You're right…"

"Take this as a wake-up call, Sammie. You'll be a bit more careful now who you allow to travel with you. You have big dreams. Don't let them be shattered because of the people you surround yourself with."

I did the right thing, and he was right. My mood began to rise. "Thank you, Mason, for giving me a heads up on the post and a real kick in my backside."

"Kicks in the ass are what brothers are for," he laughed. "Drive safe home and text me when you get there. Love you, Corn Flakes."

"Love you too, big brother."

The music started again indicating he had ended the call.

When I pulled into the driveway of the house, I had come to one conclusion. The post had put a spotlight on me. People would be watching now to see if the three were justified in their tantrum toward me. The four professional barrel racers I had driven by, and Delaney would be watching and judging. Pressure behind my eyes and queasiness in my stomach began. I trembled at the thought of the next race.

Five days later, Mason was calling me again; "Where are you now?" His voice echoed through the sound system in the truck.

"Woke up in Elgin and now in Cheney, where are you?" I countered and turned into the rodeo grounds.

"Cowtown Cutting in Fort Worth."

"Ah, I love that one."

"Mom and Dad just got here. They are really missing you…and I'll admit I miss watching you ride down here."

I parked the truck and turned off the engine. "My family is in Texas having fun without me and I'm here in the middle of Washington by myself." Even to me, the words were pathetic. I wiped away the tears.

"Damn, Sammie," Mason sighed. "It's just this year."

"I'm pathetic, Mason. I was supposed to have three friends with me to make this year easier and fun."

"You're still better off without them. How did you do last night?"

"Pulled a last place check," I sighed. "Pepper is good enough he should be winning these races."

"You'll figure it out. That's why you keep going and why you're still there and not here."

"It's hard, Mason," I admitted and wiped away more tears.

"But you're not going to quit."

"No, I'm not going to quit." I took a deep breath and exhaled heavily. "I can watch you guys compete by the live-feeds in my trailer so make sure you give me plenty of time before anyone rides."

"Where do you go next?"

"Home for a couple days, then Joseph, Oregon then to a whole list of them. I'm working on making the circuit finals, but it has been a struggle."

"You will stay focused, and you will let go of the past, and just look to the next one, not the one down the road. ONLY to the next one...right?"

"Yeah," I sighed and looked out to the rodeo grounds.

Once Pepper was stalled and happily eating his pile of hay, I entered my trailer and sighed at the silence. In an effort to not let myself wallow in pity, I took out one of the puzzles my family had given me for my birthday and got busy putting all the pieces together. My mind relaxed and time flew by.

CHAPTER SIX

GRANGER

"Where are we going?" I asked from the back seat of Dale's truck.

"To the bucking clinic," Leo chuckled.

"No, shit," I mumbled. "Where is it at?"

"Didn't your mother read and sign the papers?" Dale asked with a glance to me through the rear-view mirror.

"She may have read where it was, but I didn't," I had signed the papers. I had seen my mother once in the last two weeks and I doubted she would even know I was gone.

"This one is in Pendleton," Spence answered. "A group from the circuit is putting it on."

"What's a circuit?" I asked.

Leo shook his head, "Damn, you got a lot of learnin' to take in this weekend."

They all three chuckled and I just shrugged.

"Yeah, but you didn't answer the question," I told him.

"The states are divided into territories, but we call them circuits. This circuit is Oregon, Washington, and the top half of Idaho," Dale explained. "Dozens of rodeos are completed during the season and the top money earners from those go to the circuit finals."

"The event and average winners from the finals then go on to the national circuit finals and competes there," Leo added.

"OK," I nodded. "Makes sense but…what does average winner mean?"

They chuckled again.

Spence was in the back seat with me, and he grinned, "You compete twice or three times and add those points or times together. The person with the lowest times or highest points is the average winner."

"Where do they hold all the rodeos in this circuit?" I asked.

My questions and their answers continued until we drove into the parking lot of the Pendleton event grounds. When we walked through the large doors that led to the arena and into the area at the front of the building, a whole new world lay before me.

"What the hell is all that?" I mumbled to myself.

Dale stood next to me, "You'll learn, just take it all in. I'll get you connected with a couple experienced bronc riders that will help you out." We turned back out of the building, and he looked toward the main doors then pointed to a group of men that were standing just outside the main doors. "The guy in the red coat is Evan Rawlins. He's an NFR qualifier in steer wrestling. Didn't win the championship, but he won the average." He turned and looked at me with a wide grin. "Lowest combined time over ten runs."

I huffed, "I was going to ask you what steer wrestling was. Do they actually wrestle steers?"

Dale chuckled, "Let's concentrate on one thing at a time."

"Good idea," I exhaled.

"Evan's son, Brodie, is a bronc rider. Been riding since he was five."

"Horses?" I gasped.

"No, he started with mutton bustin'."

"What the hell is that?"

Dale shook his head with a wide grin, "Sheep…he rode sheep, then to steers, then did some smaller bulls and ponies, and then to the horses. The man next to him in the dark brown jacket is Martin Houston. His son, Craig, is Brodie's best friend. They started riding sheep together and have just finished with high school rodeo. I think they are a couple of years older than you. Evan's daughter, Delaney, is a barrel racer and one hell of a roper. He has another son, Logan. Big guy, 6' 5" or so and he is a steer wrestler, too. So, the whole family is rodeo driven."

I couldn't even imagine the life they had led compared to mine. I was home, riding my bike around the neighborhood, or school. Before Dad had left, we would go fishing or hiking but my mother had hated it.

"Come with me," Dale said, then turned to Leo and Spence. "You two get your bags and saddles and get ready."

Like a lost little kid, I followed Dale and wondered if I had made the right decision.

"Evan? Martin?" Dale stopped and the two men turned to him.

"Dale, good to see you," Evan stretched out a hand.

Dale shook both their hands then turned to include me in the conversation. My stomach ached in anticipation of looking like a fool.

"This is Granger, he is new to broncs," Dale said.

"Never been around a horse," I clarified.

Both men grinned and stuck out their hands. I shook both with a bit of a trembling hand. Hopefully, neither noticed.

Dale continued, "I was hoping Brodie or Craig could help him out through the clinic, but I don't see either of them."

"They are at the back helping get the pens ready for the horses," Evan answered. "They'll be out here before it starts, and I have no doubt they would be glad to help a new rider."

"I'd sure appreciate it, sir," I exhaled. "I'm already a bit overwhelmed at all the terminology."

"Words are easy," Martin grinned. "How did you get wrangled into this?"

"He was fencing with my son," Dale answered. "By the time the job was done, we invited him to try it out."

"Bares or broncs?" Evan asked.

I looked at Dale then back to the two men, "I don't even know what that means."

They chuckled, but I didn't feel embarrassed. There was something about the two men that put me at ease, and I didn't feel like they were making fun of me.

"We'll have one of the boys attached to you," Martin said. "Here they come now."

I turned to see two cowboys walking toward me. They might have only been a year older than me, but they walked tall and with all the confidence in the world. Their grins were broad as they stopped and spoke to another man.

"Brodie!" Evan called out and waved his son over.

"Hey, Dad," He grinned when they arrived.

"The pens are ready for the horses," Craig answered with a welcoming nod to me.

"Boys, this is…" Martin turned and looked at me.

"Granger," I smiled. "It's a unique one."

"I'll get it down," Martin chuckled then turned back to the cowboys. "He is completely green, never been around a horse, but is daring enough to give broncs a try."

"Awesome," Craig turned and looked at me with wide excited eyes. "You're going to love it."

"Leo and Spence tell me the same thing," I smiled, and the excitement began to build.

"One of you take him under your wing for the weekend," Evan ordered.

"I will," Craig nodded. "Brodie already promised to help the Ward's kid." He looked down at my feet then back up. "You have any boots?"

"Nah, do I need them?" I answered.

"Yeah, but I have a pair you can wear. Come with me." He turned.

I nodded to the three men and Brodie then hurried after Craig.

"What size do you wear?" he asked.

"Ten."

"Me, too. You ride with a pair a size larger than you normally wear so if your boot gets caught in the stirrup your boot won't get stuck and you get dragged across the arena."

"OK…"

"I had it happen," he smirked. "Hurts like a son-of-a-bitch but luckily I didn't break anything."

I took a deep breath.

"You'll be OK," Craig glanced at me with a nod. "You're here willing to try staying on a bucking horse; something you know nothing about. That's courage and if you have that…that is a damn good start."

Confidence grew and the next deep breath was more anticipation rather than terror.

"I have an extra pair of chaps, too," Craig continued and handed me a black with white fringe pair.

We walked through the wide doors that led to the arena and stood quietly to watch a cowboy riding on a bucking machine. He was only holding onto a leather handle that was strapped to the machine. "That is bareback," Craig said then we turned to see another cowboy on a different machine that was moving rhythmically up and down, back and forth. The rider was in a saddle with his feet in stirrups and was holding onto a thick rope. "That is saddle bronc. It's the classic event of rodeo. What do you think, bareback or saddle bronc?"

My gut clenched in embarrassment, but I had to be honest, "I don't have much money so which is cheaper to start?"

Craig just nodded, "The riggin' for bareback is cheaper to start, but it doesn't last as long as a bronc saddle. So, in the long run, saddle bronc would be cheaper. But saddle bronc is one of the hardest events to learn and perfect."

Either way I was going to have to save money to start, "Well, since Leo and Spence ride with the saddle, I will, too. I'm starting from scratch either way so might as well start with the hardest."

Craig chuckled and glanced at me as if he was impressed. I felt even more confident. "Brodie and I ride both so we can start you out with saddle bronc and later you can give bareback a try."

I nodded with grin, "I don't have a saddle though. Leo was going to share with me."

"We're almost the same size, you can use my spare. We always bring it to clinics."

Craig stayed with me the whole afternoon; through the group meeting, learning the different equipment, trying the practice equipment and through lunch. His encouragement and energy had my excitement pumping by the time we moved into the arena and on top of the bucking chutes. I couldn't believe I was sitting on top the metal panels listening to a man on a horse that was going to help us get off the bucking horses if we hadn't already fallen off.

"Most these cowboys have ridden before," Craig said as a horse was walked into the chute wearing the saddle Craig had loaned me and had spent the time adjusting it to fit me. "This is a saddle horse, not a bucking horse. You'll slide on and we'll get your feet set, rope measured, and run you through the process. Harrison is the pickup man and he'll talk you through what to do."

Brody appeared and they helped me slide on the horse and adjusted my position. My heart was racing with a bit of fear, anxiety, and excitement. The chute was opened, and the horse was calmly led out into the arena. Craig walked next to me and adjusted my feet in the stirrups and instructed on how to lean back and brace against the stirrups. The pickup man slid in next to me and helped me slide from the saddle horse and over to him.

"Sorry," I whispered as I nearly pulled him from the saddle.

Harrison chuckled, "It's all about learning. You haven't had a chance to learn any bad habits yet, so we'll get you trained right from the start. Never hesitate to ask questions. You don't learn if you keep doing it wrong because you're afraid to ask."

"Thanks," I nodded, and we did it three more times before the clinic ended for the day. We had two more days to go, and I could barely sleep in anticipation.

Saturday morning, Craig and Brodie showed Leo, Spence, and I how to stretch and warm up our bodies for the ride. We spent time on the bucking machines before we went back to the chutes.

I stood on the podium behind the chutes and watched riders prepare their saddles or riggin'. The first gate was opened, and a yellow horse carried a teenager out into the arena with high kicks all the way down to the end. My heart raced and Craig talked me through three more rides; what was right and what they could improve on.

A black steer was loaded into the chute in front of us.

"This guy is going to be your first ride," Craig grinned.

"I thought we were riding horses."

"The steers are closer to the ground and not as eager to get you off their backs," Craig laughed. "It will get you used to being on something live and moving."

Craig showed me how to put the saddle on the steer. My heart was pounding when I slid onto the saddle and my feet instinctively made their way into the stirrups.

"What do you think?" Craig asked with a grin.

"He's warm," I looked at him in surprise. "I guess I never thought of that."

"Can you feel him breathing?"

I paused and felt the calf's breath and his heart beating. My eyes must have shown the surprise because Craig laughed with a wide grin and a nod.

"This is when you learn to read your animal. Listen to him and see if he is calm or he might be fighting. The animal's experience will come into factor, too. They can get so used to the chutes that they are calm and quiet until you open the gate then they just explode."

I nodded in anticipation as a man walked to the outside of the gate and grinned at me. It was Evan Rawlins.

"You look like you're enjoying this," he chuckled.

"So far, I am," I said honestly. This was so much better than sitting on a couch watching television or riding my bike around the neighborhood.

"Well, you let me know when you're ready by nodding, then I'll open the gate and you hold on and get your balance as long as you can." Evan looked up at Craig then down to me.

"Don't forget to lift on the rein," Brodie added. "Lift, lift, lift..."

I set myself down on the steer like I had been shown on the practice equipment and horse. With right hand gripping the rein and the left hand up in the air by my ear, I took a deep breath, then the nod.

Nothing in my life had been as exciting as that gate swinging open. The sound of the handle's clank, the whoosh of the gate and the energy of the steer turning filled my body with an abundance of excitement and a touch of fear.

CHAPTER SEVEN

GRANGER

I was still on halfway down the arena, and the cheering from everyone in the building had my heart pumping hard and the energy gripping the rope. It shocked me when I tipped onto the side and into the dirt. I barely felt the fall and was standing in a blink of an eye. I wanted back on. I wanted to do it again and again.

I ran back down the arena and grinned as I neared Craig.

"Nice job!" he yelled. "Well?"

"Again! I want to do it again!"

Brody laughed, "What do you remember?"

"Not a damn thing, but the rush of adrenaline," I grinned.

Everyone around us laughed. It took all my patience to wait through the rest of the attendees and their turn to ride. I bounced in the boots while Craig stood next to me and helped me critique each person.

Leo did well and stayed on his steer all the way down the arena. Spence's steer took off at a dead run and without a buck. It was exhilarating to watch my friends ride and even when he fell off and rolled in the dirt. He popped up with a grin and ready to get on the next one.

I rode another steer that bucked a dozen times before stopping and laying down. I chuckled and slid off the side.

Harrison rode up next to me and grinned, "Probably the easiest get off you'll ever get."

I nodded with a laugh and ran back to the chutes. Craig met me halfway with a high-five.

"They'll be loading the bucking horses next," he said. "They have a little sorrel outback that I've seen before. He's got a nice little buck and usually goes straight down the arena."

"Ok," I nodded, and we made our way to the back of the chutes again. "But what is a sorrel?"

Craig chuckled, "A red horse."

The horse was loaded in the chute in front of me and my heart was pounding, and my arms gripped the saddle tight. Craig appeared with a grin as he looked at the clear apprehension on my face.

"It's addicting," he warned.

"I'm already there," I laughed.

"Just remember, each time you climb onto the saddle to believe in yourself and that you can ride the horse. If you don't believe it, you'll be in the dirt, and get yourself or someone else hurt."

"Ok."

"Believe."

"Believe," I grinned. "I believe I will end up in the dirt the first time, but I'll get better."

He laughed.

Brodie and Craig were at my side as I lowered down into the chute and onto a bucking horse for the very first time. My whole body and mind were trembling as if coming alive for the first time in my life. Craig instructed me on measuring the buck rein as Evan stood at the gate in preparation of pulling the latch.

"Take your time," Brodie instructed. "Never nod until you are ready."

"Even if they are rushing you," Craig added.

My heart was pounding, but my focus was intense as I listened to every instruction the pair gave me.

"Remember, toes out!" Evan said through the gate.

"It will help keep your boots in the stirrups," Brodie added. "Keep your boots up above the shoulder on the first lunge."

"Don't worry so much about spurring yet," Craig said. "Just move your body and try to stay on like you did on the practice barrel…the rest will come with time."

Nothing could have prepared me for the sudden adrenaline rush, gut wrenching exhilaration, and wave of pure joy when I nodded, and the gate opened.

"Lift, lift, lift!" Craig was yelling and my arm pulled up the buck rein as the horse turned and rolled out of the chute.

Two lunges out, the horse's back hunched under me then seemed to drop out as his back hooves flew in the air. Three times the horse hunched then kicked under me as I pulled on the rope as if my life depended on it. 'Toes out' left my mind as the fourth kick was completed and I began tumbling off the side of the horse. It seemed like a slow-motion dream as I fell to the ground with a thump to my shoulder, but I just rolled and stood and watched the horse buck down the rest of the arena as Harrison and the other pickup man ran after it.

The sound of cheering finally invaded my senses, and I turned back to see everyone celebrating my first ride. I wanted to do it again, and again, and for the rest of my life.

I was hooked.

"Hell, yeah!" Craig yelled and met me in front of the chutes. "You're a fucking natural."

I got to ride two more times before the end of the day.

That night, Craig was at my side during dinner telling me stories of how he started riding and his meeting Brodie and the Rawlins family. The next day was filled with practice, learning the best exercises to get in shape, riding, and stories from everyone. Craig was at my side through the whole day. My mind was full of everything I learned, and my body hurt from tumbling off the horses. Not once, did I have a successful transfer from bucking horse to pick up man.

As we shook hands goodbye on Sunday afternoon, Craig grinned, "I look forward to seeing you in the chutes in the future. You're a damn natural at this."

I just laughed, "My back and every joint in my body would disagree with you."

"You'll get there, and to help," He grinned and walked to the back of his truck to lift the bronc saddle he had let me use and turned to hold it out to me. "This will get you through the first year then you'll need another as you grow."

"Damn, Craig," I hesitated to take it from him.

"Use it to learn and make money so you can buy a new one when you outgrow this one."

I had $26 in my pocket with no current way of earning more. So, I reached out to take it from him, "I'll give it back when I'm done."

We shook hands again.

For the next few months, I put half the money Mom gave me in a box in my room and half to feed myself. The dollar store saw me nearly every day. I also fenced when I could and helped with anything else I could find to do to add to the rodeo fund.

On my sixteenth birthday, I woke to my mother cooking breakfast and two wrapped boxes on the table.

Her smile was hesitant as I walked into the room.

"Good morning, Son."

"Morning, Mom."

"Happy birthday," She slid a pancake onto a plate that was already stacked full and handed me the plate. "I took some time off work this morning so I could make your favorite breakfast."

Taking the plate, I gave her as genuine smile as I could, because I hated pancakes. "I appreciate that."

"Go ahead and open your presents."

I slid onto a chair, pushed the pancakes away, and reached for the larger of the two boxes. There were three smaller wrapped boxes inside. I glanced at her to see a teasing smile.

"Funny," I chuckled and opened the first box to find a gift card for Walmart.

"We don't have much time to shop together, so I thought you could go buy some new summer clothes or jeans. You can take your time that way." She sat in a chair across from me.

"It's cool, Mom," I nodded with another reassuring smile. "Thanks."

The second package contained a gift card for the grocery store.

"Just in case you want something that I don't buy. You're old enough to know what you like." She was watching me closely as if gauging my reaction.

"Two great gifts...let's see what this one is."

The third gift contained a $20 gift card each to McDonalds, Subway, and Burger King."

"Perfect," I smiled at her.

"Sometimes, we just don't feel like cooking," she grinned.

"That is true," I chuckled and placed the smaller boxes and wrapping back into the big box. When I set it on the floor, I glanced at her with a smile. Her eyes were lit with anticipation as I reached for the other present. I very slowly peeled the tape off the wrapping paper and unfolded the paper even slower.

She began chuckling, "You're getting even for the three boxes in one trick."

I grinned with a nod, tore away the paper and opened the box. I exhaled in disbelief and my eyes slowly rose to her. "A phone?"

Her hands clapped together then fingers laced in excitement, "You're surprised! I was hoping you would be. I know all the kids at the schools have them and I wish I could have given you one before you started high school here."

"Mom, that's OK, this is great," I opened the small box and lifted the phone out. "This is perfect."

"It's with my plan so you have unlimited everything. The number is on a piece of paper in the box and there is insurance on..."

She chatted about the phone and presents while cleaning the kitchen and I turned on the phone. Her voice shook with nervousness, and she kept glancing at me. When the kitchen was clean except for the untouched plate of pancakes, she stood next to me with her arms wrapped around her waist. It took me a few minutes of fiddling with the phone to realize she was hoping for any sign of affection. And, for the first time in years, I stood and wrapped my arms around her. Her body was tense, but her hug was strong...almost desperate.

"You couldn't have gotten me anything better," I said truthfully. "I made a couple friends at school and now I can message and call them. We'll be hanging out a lot together this summer."

Her body sighed in relief. Ten minutes after the hug broke, she was sliding into her car. I didn't see her again until the day before school started.

After sliding the pancakes into the garbage can, I poured a large bowl of cereal and sat at the table and played with the phone.

The Walmart gift card bought two pairs of jeans and two western shirts. The grocery store gift card bought the snacks for road trips to the rodeos, and the fast-food cards were used on the road, so I didn't have to use the money I saved for entry fees. I only had to use that money for a cowboy hat and pair of boots I found at a yard sale. Neither fit perfectly, but Craig did say my boots had to be big.

Thousands of saddle bronc videos were watched on the new phone during the summer.

Every Wednesday morning, I woke to find more groceries in the cupboard and refrigerator and a fifty-dollar bill on the counter. Half was put in the rodeo fund and the other half was spent at the dollar store.

My first trip to an amateur rodeo with Leo and Spence, I was on the ground in 2.8 seconds. Not one ride made it to the buzzer that summer, but I was beginning to remember them. Leo's dad recorded each ride so I could analyze them.

In October, I received the first of many calls and texts from Martin.

"Granger?"

"Yes, sir."

He chuckled, "Call me Martin."

"Yes, sir." I grinned.

He chuckled again, "Not sure you know, I am an architect, and have been working on a few ranch homes."

"That's cool...sir," I couldn't keep the humor from my voice.

"Smart ass," He grumbled but I could hear the humor in his. "A couple of homes need some fencing done and I've recommended you. You can work under my business until you get yours going and stay in the spare bedroom at the house with me and Craig. You interested?"

"Absolutely, Boss," My heart soared at the idea. I could earn my own money to get to the next clinic.

"You might be able to get a couple weekends in before the snow flies and we have to wait until spring."

"I don't know how I would get there."

"His name is Craig."

Three weekends were spent in their home before the weather turned. I built fence from sunrise to sunset and in the evenings, Martin taught me how to cook while we watched old westerns.

The first weekend home in the quiet house was depressing.

The first of December, just as I was leaving school, I received a text:

Text from Craig: Just a heads up. Since their mom died, the Rawlins have hosted a Christmas for all the wandering cowboys and cowgirls that don't have a home to land. Don't know your situation, but Evan wanted you to know that you are invited. It is a fun time.

Text from Granger to Craig: Don't know how I would get there. No car yet

Text from Craig to Granger: Aaron comes down from Spokane, he can bring you

Text from Granger to Craig: Thanks, I'll keep it in mind.

December 20th, I answered him.

Text from Granger to Craig: Talked to Aaron, we will be there morning of 24th.

I left Mom a note saying I would be with friends for Christmas and a small, wrapped gift containing a necklace with a turquoise pendant I had picked up at one of the vendors over the summer.

When we arrived, the whole Rawlins and Houston family greeted us. It was the best Christmas I'd had since Dad had left. Seeing their close family connection made it hard to go home to the empty house.

When we arrived at the clinic in March, Craig greeted me like we were long lost friends. It was another full weekend with him at my side and Brodie jumping in when I rode. Every horse I rode on Sunday, I covered a full eight seconds. I went home battered, bruised, tired, and anxious for the year. Leo's dad bought him an SUV we could drive to rodeos when he couldn't take us.

I spent weekends fencing for Martin and stayed in their home while Craig and Brodie were rodeoing in Texas.

The summer of my 17th year, we joined the Idaho Cowboy Association and traveled nearly every weekend through Idaho, Washington, and Oregon. Craig and Brodie surprised me by showing up to a few to help me out. I earned six checks through the summer and bought myself used chaps that fit, and a new saddle and buck rein just before going to the clinic.

During the third trip to the clinic in Pendleton I gave Craig his saddle back. He helped me adjust the new saddle and we practiced every second we could. Every meal was spent with Leo, Spence, Brodie and Craig telling stories and laughing until our ribs hurt and tears filled our eyes.

The middle of June, just days after turning 18, I walked along side of Leo and Spence as we entered our first pro rodeo together as permit holders in Union, Oregon. Brodie and Craig were both there to greet us.

"I knew the first time you got on that red horse at the clinic, I would see you at pro-level," Craig grinned as we sat behind one of the chutes watching Brodie cheering on his brother, Logan, in steer wrestling.

Craig had already taken the lead in bareback; the rest of us competed against each other in saddle bronc.

I laughed, "I really didn't know what I was getting myself into when I told Leo and Spence I'd go."

He turned to me with a wicked grin, "And you haven't regretted a day of it since."

"The only thing I regret is they don't have more."

"Use these next two years of riding the pro horses to improve yourself. Just remember, you're still pretty new to this world. Don't set your goals so high you get discouraged and quit; be realistic."

"This year is to make it in the top fifty. Next year is to cut that in half, then do the same my first card year."

"Good solid plan," he nodded. "Also, if you draw a horse you don't truly believe you can ride, just turn out, no matter the cost. The last thing you need is to get seriously injured."

"Believe," I nodded with a grin. "I believe that is one of the first things you told me."

Craig chuckled with a nod, "Should be on the top of everyone's list."

The clanging of the chutes interrupted our conversation as the horses were loaded. Craig stepped forward with me and was at my side through the whole preparation. Leo was the first rider and he walked out of the arena with a 69-point score.

I slid on the saddle as Spence's gate was opened. I tried not to look and focus on what I was doing, but I glanced up as the horse ran across the arena. Spence's legs were barely moving but he made it through the buzzer. The pickup man, Harrison, rode in next to him and assisted Spence to the ground.

My focus returned to the horse I was on: Iron Jubilee.

"You believe you can make it to the buzzer?" Craig gave me a smart-ass grin.

"Of course, I'm going to make it," I huffed. "Just watch."

I nodded and the adrenaline rush swept through me as the gate flew open. Toes out, lift, heels in the mane, get in rhythm. I did everything Craig and Brodie had taught me for the last two years and my mind was clear enough I could control what I was doing. It was a great ride until the buzzer sounded and the pickup man slid in beside me. I glanced up to see Harrison reach back to unlatch the flank strap then raise an arm out to me. The horse went left as I tried to go right and was inches away from Harrison when I tumbled to the ground.

Just like the other dozens of times I hit the dirt, I stood without a thought and jogged out of the arena. Spence and Leo were used to it and didn't do anything more than smile, but I was met with laughter from Brodie and Craig.

"Seriously," Craig called out as I neared. "You need a better dismount."

"Awesome bounce up, though," Brodie laughed as he climbed over the chute in front of him.

A score of 84 was announced and I grinned and climbed up onto the chutes.

"You would win if they were scoring for the dismounts," Craig laughed and looked out into the arena as the horn blared for the rider that had come off just outside the chutes. "But the important thing is, you're currently leading with one rider left."

"And his name is Brodie," Spence grinned.

Craig turned to assist Brodie as he slid down onto the horse; Blue Blazes.

The nod, the gate swinging open, and the horse lunged with Craig, Leo, Spence, and I yelling. It was a ride that took away my lead and Brodie's dismount with Harrison's assistance was picture perfect.

As he jogged out of the arena towards us, Brodie grinned and pointed at me with both hands, "And that, Granger, is how you dismount!"

Our laughter roared across the arena.

When the five of us had bags and saddles slung over our shoulders, we walked to our rigs but were stopped by a photographer. We cheesy grinned for the picture that posted on social media the next day with a caption that read, 'Brodie Rawlins and Craig Houstin both take the lead at the Eastern Oregon Livestock Show in Union, Oregon'."

We finished the night around a campfire next to Brodie and Craig's truck telling stories of growing up.

"You do that?" Brodie asked.

I had been talking with Spence as a group of cowgirls walked toward us.

"Do what?" I asked Brodie while forcing myself to pull my eyes away from the women.

"Argue at home a lot. Leo says he and his dad argue a lot. Craig and I get along with ours since we have a common passion, and they help us."

"Nah," I shook my head and looked back at the approaching women. "Dad left when I was nine, and Mom's barely home so if I argued it would be with myself." I looked back at Brodie. "And that would be fucking crazy."

We both chuckled and looked up as the cowgirls made it to the campfire. The long-haired brunette on the left wearing tight jeans, white tank top, and fancy blue, knee-high boots strode right to me.

"Mind if I sit?" She glanced at Brodie but turned back to me.

My entire body heated and there was no way I was going to stand so I shuffled to the side of the long cooler I was on which made Brodie and Craig start laughing.

"I saw you ride tonight," she smiled. "Pretty impressive."

"Except that dismount," Craig chuckled before tipping his beer up as a blonde sat next to him.

"Doesn't seem like it hurt you much." I swear her words were a purr and my discomfort in sitting increased.

"No, ma'am," I managed to get out through constricted vocal cords.

"Oh, no, don't call me that." Her giggle chimed. "Call me Angelina."

"Wow, that is a pretty name," I exhaled. "And no, I'm used to it...it didn't hurt at all."

"How many rodeos do you go to?"

"As many as we can, but this is our first pro rodeo."

"So, you have a permit which means you're eighteen," Her smile widened, and eyes narrowed.

"Yes."

She leaned back, crossed one leg over the other and seemed to twist at the waist as she leaned forward again so she was facing me and only me. Her long dark hair fell to the side and a bottle dangled from her fingertips. "How did you get into riding bucking horses?"

We talked for a half hour before I remembered there were other people around the fire. When I turned, Brodie and Spence had disappeared right along with the ladies they had been talking to. Leo had twisted himself away from the girl that was trying to get close to him. As far as I knew, he was the only one with a girlfriend and he was faithful to her. When I looked at Craig, he was grinning like a Cheshire cat at the cowgirl beside him.

"You want to go for a walk?" Angelina stood and reached down to take my hand.

My heart nearly beat out of my chest and my face flushed a deep red. I glanced at Craig who was already standing with an arm sliding around the blonde's waist.

He glanced at me, winked, and mouthed, "Have fun."

Angelina pulled me up next to her and squeezed my hand before grinning, turning, and leading me behind her like a puppy.

CHAPTER EIGHT

GRANGER

On October first I was scrolling through the PRCA standings when I received a text.

Text from Craig to Granger: You made your first year's goal! Fuck yeah!

I read the message and shook my head. I had only mentioned that to him the rodeo in Union. I couldn't believe he remembered.

Text from Granger to Craig: Currently at 46, I even have a little wiggle room in case more $'s are added.

Text from Craig to Granger: Next year, 23, which gets you invited and auto-qualified for a few of the big rodeos your first card year. THAT IS YOUR GOAL AND I BELIEVE YOU CAN DO IT!

Text from Granger to Craig: I BELIEVE I CAN

Text from Craig to Granger: NILE entry is closed, but can you make it to the Chase Hawk Xtreme in Billings?

Text from Granger to Craig: Spence and Leo don't want to go

Text from Craig to Granger: You can ride with us

Text from Brodie to Granger: Come with us

Text from Granger to Brodie and Craig: When can I expect you to arrive?

I was limited to the rodeos I could attend if Leo didn't want to go and fencing jobs I could take because I didn't have my own vehicle. I also needed something to pack the collection of fencing tools I was gathering. I put out requests for fencing jobs and worked nearly every day except Thanksgiving. On that day, I sat in Mom's house alone and watched rodeo videos. It was the first holiday that I didn't see her, although she had put money on the counter for dinner and two pumpkin pies in the refrigerator with plenty of whipped cream. Unlike the pancakes, I loved the pies.

The first of December, I worked every daylight hour I could and watched the NFR all ten nights and cheered on Logan Rawlins. It was fun to see someone I knew win a World Championship. I dreamt of being there and the drive inside me increased. It solidified my need for my own vehicle.

Riding with Brodie and Craig to the rough stock rodeo was different than riding with Leo and Spence. Leo would always talk about his girlfriend and spend hours on the phone with her talking or texting. Spence liked to read when he wasn't driving, and he just looked at the next rodeo, not the future. Brodie and Craig talked, breathed, and dreamed of nothing but rodeo. They had ridden together since they were five years old, and I took in every story and piece of advice they gave me.

With their energy, assistance, and belief, I walked out of the Billings arena in second place; right behind Brodie. I also banked enough money to buy a vehicle for the new year.

When I got home, Martin helped me find an older four-door Dodge Dakota with a canopy on the back. I could use it to store tools and as a bed during the rodeos.

On Christmas Eve, I placed a note on the table for my mother saying I was spending the holiday with friends, left her turquoise earrings that would match the necklace from the year before, and drove to the Rawlins ranch.

With the new truck, Spence, Leo, and I drove to Texas and spent January and February traveling, bucking horses, and playing. When we arrived home, I drove to Mom's house. There were no cars in the driveway, so I walked into the house expecting it to be in the same condition as when I left. It wasn't. The furniture was moved, different pictures on the wall, and dirty dishes in the sink. The only thing that was the same was my bedroom. I sat on the edge of the bed and looked at the world I had left behind.

There was a sense of a lost childhood. Looking around the room, I saw nothing that I missed. I opened the top drawer of my dresser and took out the small box that held what pictures I had of Dad, Mom, and I as a family. That was the only thing in the room I wanted.

I walked out of the room and to the kitchen. Pulling a pen and notepad from a drawer, I sat down at the table to write her a note. I stared at the paper with no idea what to write. After ten minutes of trying to come up with anything, I set the pen down, and walked to the front door with only the small box of pictures. One last turn to look into the house I had basically lived in by myself, I sighed again then opened the door and walked down the walkway. Halfway to the truck, I stopped and turned back to enter the house. I wrote the only thing I truly felt:

Mom, I'm sorry I was such a shitty kid to you. Love Granger

I drove away from the house with the next rodeo in front of me.

The end of March signaled the beginning of the Columbia River Circuit rodeos. It started in Redmond Oregon and with me in 28th place in the world standings. Leo and Spence were barely on the list, but they didn't have the goal of making the Circuit Finals like I did. They wanted to ride and have fun. I wanted to win and achieve my goal of finishing at least 23rd in the world.

Spence went to most of the rodeos with me, but Leo kept holding back because his girlfriend hounded him when they were on the road with phone calls and tears that he didn't love her. It made me sick to my stomach, but I just carried on.

Days after my 19th birthday, the three of us drove into Union, Oregon for the rodeo. We parked beside Brodie and Craig with just enough room between us to start a campfire after the rodeo.

When I stepped out of the truck, all four turned and looked at me as I was looking around the parking lot. They laughed and I was teased all night for looking for Angilena. After placing second in the rodeo and starting the fire, their laughter turned to swear words of disbelief when she strolled toward us and slid on the cooler next to me just as she did the year before. Tall boots over skin- tight jeans, a bright blue tank top, and long black hair flowing over her shoulders and down her back.

"Nice ride, Cowboy." She grinned with brown eyes dancing in joy.

Weeks later, I walked to the back of the chutes of the Hermiston arena to find Craig already sitting on the bench with legs stretched out and leaning back comfortably. He was smiling up at the sky and looked completely at ease.

"What are you doing here so early?" He grinned.

I tossed my pack on the ground and set the saddle on top of it then took a seat.

"Bored waiting in the truck." I answered and he nodded. "Where's Brodie?"

"He's riding with Logan tomorrow. I came with Delaney today…helping some friends move tomorrow."

"Why are you so early?"

"Delaney was meeting with someone about a horse, so, here I am."

"Early and not irritated," I grinned. "What's up?"

He chuckled and his dark brown eyes lit with a warm glow, "Granger…I have met my future. Well, actually met her a few months ago."

My eyes narrowed, "You've been pining for Delaney's friend, Camille."

"Pining, aching, following like a puppy…" he laughed. "Finally wore her down and we've been seeing each other the last couple weeks." He sighed, shook his head in wonder, and grinned. "Last night, we went on our first official date." His cheeks warmed, smile widened, and he sighed again. "Best fucking night you can imagine. I've been sitting here thinking about it…perfect…just fucking perfect. I'm gonna marry that woman."

Happiness radiated from him. "Damn, Craig."

He laughed, "I know."

"She here?"

"Nah, her and her sister, Lacie Jae, went down to California to pack up their parent's house they just sold. When they get back, we're all driving up to Omak."

"Yeah, we ride the same night."

"Neither Delaney nor Logan will let us stay in their trailers so I found a B&B we can stay in just out of town."

I laughed, "I don't blame them. If you're this gushy when she isn't here, I can't imagine what you'll be like when she is."

"I just can't stop thinking about her and last night and this weekend." He glanced over at Leo and Spence who were walking toward us. "Tomorrow night…going to be a fucking long twenty-four hours until she gets back."

"Well, at least you'll be busy and not just sitting around."

He stood with a nod to Leo and Spence, "Let's just win this damn rodeo tonight."

"Sounds good to me," I chuckled.

Two hours later, after he scored an 85 on his bronc and I scored 84 on mine and both sitting in second place, we were back on the benches behind the bucking chutes talking about the rides and waiting for Delaney to run her race.

"Camille and Delaney have been inseparable…I keep expecting her to appear," I leaned a hip on the chute panel and looked at the entry tunnel as the announcer called Delaney's run.

"Me, too," Craig sighed.

Delaney raced into the arena on her roan horse, Gaston. When she ran back out, she took the lead.

"Fucking awesome," Craig shook his head. "They are a hell of a pair. I can see them winning the World this year."

"Yeah," I nodded as we walked down the steps and out to the parking lot. "She is about the only thing that gets me interested in watching can chasers."

Craig laughed, "Angelina isn't a barrel racer, but I've seen you disappear with a few."

I grinned, "That's outside the arena. I've been warned about racers, but I have a feeling Delaney isn't included in that warning."

Craig's eyebrows rose as he looked at me, "You interest in her?"

Shaking my head I chuckled, "Not anymore. Used to have a big crush on her, but she isn't interested in me that way. Besides, she is with someone."

He stopped and looked at me in surprise, "What?"

"I saw her a few months back letting a guy into the back door of her trailer. Looked like they were trying to be secret about it, so I never said anything."

"Well, if that's the way she wants it, no reason to."

"Kind of what I thought."

We arrived at the trailer just moments before Delaney appeared leading her horse.

"Nice run, Rawlins," I grinned at her.

"Thanks, Miller," She grinned and ran a hand down the neck of the horse. "He's pretty special."

"Missing your co-pilot as much as Craig is?" I gave him a teasing grin and he just laughed.

"Sickening, isn't it?" Delaney laughed. "He gushed all the way up here."

I nodded with a wide grin, "And now you have to live with him until she returns."

"And this weekend! Yikes!" She slid the saddle off the horse.

"You guys are just jealous," Craig chuckled and opened the back door of the trailer.

Once the horse was groomed and pampered and walked into the back of the trailer, I stood at the passenger door of the truck as Craig stepped in to slide onto the seat.

"I'm pretty damn happy for you," I shook his hand. "As adventurous as Camille is and as addicted to this life as we are, you two are going to have a great life together."

His smile was wide and eyes content. "Thanks, Granger. Someday you'll find someone as special to you as she is to me." We shook hands, then he closed the door and grinned out the open window. "I'd bet a thousand dollars it will be a barrel racer."

I laughed, shook my head, and waved as they drove away then walked to Leo and Spence who were waiting at the SUV for me. We left the rodeo grounds with Missoula then Cascade, Montana in our future before driving to Omak.

It was five o'clock in the morning when we stopped on our way out of Cascade toward Omak to sleep before finishing the drive. Leo and Spence were in the vehicle as I stood at the front and stared up into the sky. Montana's mornings were always beautiful, and my brain wouldn't stop thinking of the rides and analyzing each one from the last three nights. Besides, Leo was on the phone defending his going on the trip to his girlfriend already and Spence was snoring.

My phone ringing nearly made me jump a foot. I was shocked to see Evan Rawlins calling.

"Hey, Evan."

"Granger…you driving?"

"Nah, we just stopped for a couple hours."

"Ok…I need to tell you…I know you were close…" His voice was low and strained.

"Evan?" I stood away from the vehicle with breath stopped and body fully tense in anticipation.

"There was an accident," his voice quivered. "A car ran a red light and slammed into Craig's truck."

My body tingled, "Is he OK?"

"No…he passed away on the scene."

Disbelief, emptiness, hopelessness swarmed through me before the nausea rose, "He's dead?"

"Yes."

My body fell back against the SUV. "Evan…I…Martin?"

"I just left him with his sister and am driving back to the ranch."

"Brodie…" The word barely escaped as the tears rose and my throat constricted.

"He's at the ranch. Delaney stayed there to tell him and Logan before they found out any other way."

Tears fell as I tried to think of what to say.

Evan continued, "Martin asked me to call you. I'll let him know I did, and I'll tell Brodie."

"Thank you…" The words shook from tears and the hollowness in my heart.

"I'll call when I can." Evan's voice was low as if holding back emotions.

"I can't…I'm so sorry…"

"I know, son. I know. It's going to be a tough time ahead for all of us. Give them a couple days then come over."

The line went silent. My hand lowered to my side, as my eyes rose to the wide Montana sky. My heart hurt, my mind hurt, total helplessness flowed through me as I slowly slid down the side of the vehicle until I was sitting on the ground. My hand grasped my shirt over my heart as the grief tore at me. Tears fell, sobs shook as I crossed my arms over my knees and let the emotions overwhelm me.

Somewhere in the distance, I heard Leo talking, then Spence. My head lifted out of the haze long enough to look at their worried expressions.

"What the fuck happened?" Spence asked.

"Granger…what the…" Leo began.

"Craig…" I whispered and lifted a hand to wipe away the tears.

"What about him?" Spence's eyes reflected the fear.

I shook my head, "Car accident…he's gone."

My head lowered again as the wave of grief gripped my heart again and my body felt as if it was falling down a long dark tunnel.

CHAPTER NINE

GRANGER

The numb disbelief remained for days. We didn't go to Omak; we drove to Leo's home instead and waited for news of the funeral.

I had never lost anyone I knew to death. The pain was worse than when my father told me he was leaving. I was angry at him…but he was still alive. Craig was gone…just gone. No more laughing around the campfires. No more encouraging texts or phone calls. No more analyzing each ride. Just…no more. I didn't know how to handle the emotions.

The day before the funeral, I drove down the long driveway of the Rawlins ranch. Brodie was sitting on the back of the bucking chutes they had in the arena. There were no horses or steers around him. He turned and looked at me as I walked to him. A dark layer of whiskers covered pale skin; no light shone in his eyes that were rimmed with red with blue tired skin under them. His shoulders were slumped. There were no words I could say that would make sense or help him, so I just sat on the chute next to him. Not one word was said as we leaned on the chutes and watched the sky darken.

Hours later, when he slid off the chute and walked to the house, I walked to my truck, slid on the seat and leaned it back. My mind replayed the trip Brodie and Craig had invited me to go to...the Chase Hawk rodeo where I earned enough money to buy the truck. It made my heart hurt.

I woke to a light tap on the truck window. Martin was standing next to the truck and gave me a slight smile. After a deep breath, I stepped out. Tears were already sliding down my face when our eyes met.

"Let them flow, son." Martin pulled me into his arms, and I held onto him until the tears finally stopped.

"I don't know what to say," I whispered to him.

"Just remember, we will see him again when it is our time," Martin sighed. "We have to make sure to live the life he would be proud of so when we see him, he'll be grinning and not shaking his head."

"It's...I don't know how to deal with this."

"There is no rush or easy way to accept it."

Helplessness...the same as the night before with Brodie, there was nothing I could say or do that would help.

"If you need anything..." I leaned away from him, but his eyes were looking out over the pastures.

"I'll let you know," he sighed again then finally turned to me. "It was good of you to sit with Brodie last night. He is a bit lost and angry right now."

"I'll be here for both of you...all of you. Just let me know."

He smiled slightly, "You were a good friend to Craig. He was very proud of you, saw a big future for you. Kept saying you were a 'fucking natural'."

Tears welled as my chest constricted, no words formed as I nodded.

Two hours later, we were on top of the rise in the cemetery standing next to the casket. I couldn't look at it or the pictures that were set up next to it. I stared into the distance and thought of the last time I had talked with Craig at the Hermiston rodeo. When the last 'amen' was chorused across the mass of people, I looked for Camille. She hugged Delaney then turned to walk down the hill.

Without a word, I turned away from Dale, Leo, and Spence and followed her. She looked at me in surprise when she opened the door to the SUV.

"Granger?" Her eyes were wide and questioning.

"I wanted to talk to you," I whispered and took a deep breath. "I want you to know, the last time I talked with Craig in Hermiston, he told me about your relationship."

Tears glistened in her brown eyes.

"He couldn't talk enough about you," I continued even though my own voice shook. "You made him very happy...he was excited for your future."

Her sob shook and hand went to the vehicle to brace herself. "Thank you for telling me," she whispered. "We had such little time together even with the big dreams we shared."

After a slight hesitation, I stepped to her, and our arms wrapped around each other. I held her until her breathing returned to normal.

"He always spoke highly of you." She took a deep breath and exhaled as if to release the emotions. "He really liked you."

"And I him." I looked out to the crowd of people beginning to stand. "I have never lost anyone like this...I don't really know what to do...how to let him go."

"Ride to the house with me." She waved an arm to the passenger side door.

Without hesitation, and without looking at the mourners, I did as she said.

Minutes passed as we rode in silence to the ranch. When she pulled in next to the fence, she shut off the engine but didn't move. I sat quietly and waited.

"My stepfather died last December, right before Christmas," she sighed. "He was not a good man, an alcoholic that didn't spare a fist being thrown at Lacie Jae or myself. The last time I saw him, he was mad at me and stumbling to try and catch me." She looked out toward the horses walking in the pasture. "I felt nothing but relief that he couldn't hurt Lacie Jae anymore...physically or mentally. My stepmother, Lacie Jae's mother, died a few years ago. She was really the one person I knew growing up that really loved me, watched over me, and did whatever she could to help me." Camille glanced at me with a slight smile then her gaze went back to the pastures. "Her death nearly killed me. I was lost...well, I didn't know how to handle it and ended up turning to people I thought were friends to help me get past the feeling of loss, and, well, helplessness."

"That's what I've been feeling. I don't know what to do or how to help."

"Just being there for everyone, like you were for Brodie last night. Sometimes, just being around other people helps, whether you talk or not. Just make sure you're with the right people."

We stepped out of her SUV and walked toward the house.

"As for letting him go?" She sighed. "Don't..."

"I expect a call from him, or expect him to walk up behind the chutes," I exhaled.

"And you will for a while...it will fade. But don't let him go. Remember all the good times."

"That was every time I was with him."

"For me, too."

I opened the back door of the house for her.

"Don't ever let those go," she repeated. "Why would you want to lose those memories?"

"I don't..."

She opened the door of the large refrigerator and handed me a large bowl. "There is a table already setup out back, would you put this on it."

"I can carry another."

She nodded with a slight smile and handed me another bowl.

When I opened the door, I looked back in time to see her wipe away a tear.

She glanced at me as she wiped away another, "Thank you for telling me what he said. It means the world to me."

I nodded and stepped out the door as the first cars drove down the driveway.

Leo and Spence were by my side as I stood on the platform behind the horse in the bucking chute at the Caldwell rodeo. We had all stayed together the last week since the funeral. Both friends worked hard on keeping my mind focused on rodeos. There were only six weeks left in the rodeo year, and I was sitting 31st in the world standings. To reach my goal of making it to 23rd in the standings, I had to focus and ride. I leaned down and stretched my legs and tried to clear my mind.

"You got this," Leo encouraged.

"Just you and the horse," Spence added.

I stood, bounced in the air to stretch my calf muscles and build energy. After checking the cinch one more time and getting a nod from the flank man, I slid over the top of the chute and down onto the saddle. My mind cleared of everything and everyone around me except the horse below me.

I leaned back, lifted the rein, and my left hand rose above my head. I nodded and muscle memory took over as the gate swung open. Ten seconds later I was looking for the pickup man. Just as he approached, the horse stopped and jerked to the side. I took the opportunity and jumped off his back and landed on my feet then fell to my knees.

When my mind cleared, I could hear Spence and Leo hollering at me. As I walked out of the arena, I watched them cheering and pumping fists in the air for the score that put me in second place. I thought of what Camille had said, "Just make sure you're with the right people."

They were the right people for me. I could hang on and make it past Craig's loss with these two friends in my corner.

Text from Martin: Brodie has decided to ride bareback in the Big Four rodeos in honor of Craig. We are putting together a practice session for Monday.

Text to Martin: I will be there.

The practice was solemn at first, but the energy built throughout the afternoon. Halfway through the day, we received the emails with the draw for the Kennewick rodeo.

Brodie read the email then turned and looked at me, "You see who you drew?"

My stomach clenched and heart seemed to tumble. I drew the unridden horse; Destiny's Ignatius. I nodded to Brodie.

"He's big, strong, and unridden." Brodie leaned on the chute behind their ranch house. "You ready for him?"

I took a breath and slowly shrugged, "I need to ride what I can to make my goal this year."

"You need to stay healthy and unbroken so you can finish the year," Brodie pointed out. "Take your time and think about that one. Make sure you're ready."

Thursday night, as I approached the stock pens of the Kennewick rodeo, my heart and brain were battling for control. The large dark stallion, Destiny's Ignatius, was pacing in his pen. He swung a head over to me as I stopped next to him, and we stared at each other.

My heart wanted to ride the stallion in honor of Craig, just as Brodie was riding bareback to honor him. But my brain was repeating the words Craig had told me at the Union, Oregon rodeo;

"Also, if you draw a horse, you don't truly believe you can ride, just draw out, no matter the cost. The last thing you need is to get seriously injured."

Then there were the warning words from Brodie; *"Take your time and think about that one. Make sure you're ready."*

Martin's words: *"We have to make sure to live the life he would be proud of so when we see him, he'll be grinning and not shaking his head."* I knew in my heart; Craig would be shaking his head if I rode the stallion.

It was the words from Craig during the first clinic when I was sliding onto the first horse...the red horse in the chute, that made my decision for me:

"Just remember, each time you climb onto the saddle to believe in yourself and that you can ride the horse. If you don't believe it, you'll be in the dirt, and get yourself or someone else hurt."

If I rode this stallion tonight, I would not be honoring Craig, I would be going against everything he taught me.

I turned to Leo and Spence who had stood quietly waiting for me.

"What did you decide to do?" Spence asked.

"I'm going to honor Craig," I exhaled.

Over the next few weeks, I slowly earned enough money to rise in the world standings. When we drove to Pendleton, I had finally succeeded in breaking into the top 30, but I was still 3 places behind my goal of 26.

As fate would have it, Destiny's Ignatius was in the pen of horses, but it wasn't me that drew him this time.

"You're really going to try and ride him?" Leo said to Spence with a glance to me.

"I'm going to ride him," Spence declared. "I know Granger pulled out, but that was because he wasn't in the right frame of mind after Craig died, but I can do it."

I looked at Spence, "It is your decision to ride or pull out."

"But?" He asked.

"You don't think he can ride him either," Leo smirked.

Spence glared at Leo, "You don't think I can ride him?"

"He is big, powerful, stronger than any horse you've been able to ride before," Leo huffed and looked to me for agreement.

Spence turned to me.

"Two world champions, including Stetson Wright, and three men that have been to the NFR have not been able to ride him." I pointed out.

Spence shook his head, "Somebody is going to ride him for the first time, and if I don't try then we'll never know if I could or not."

There was nothing I could say or do that was going to change his mind, so I just sighed, "I'll be at the chute with you."

"Me, too." Leo parked the car next to the trucks with campers in the rough stock lot.

"Don't worry guys," Spence grinned. "I got this."

Adrenaline hit when the gate was opened. The horse burst from the red chute and leaped out twice before he rose in the air with the first buck. I held my own for the eight seconds as he made his way out to the green grass. As I flew off his side, I knew it wasn't a ride to get me into the finals on Saturday. When I hit the ground, the air rushed out of me, but, as always, I jumped up and quickly made my way to the chutes.

Leo was next. The horse jumped, spun, and kicked within twenty feet of the chute. Leo's feet barely moved the last half of the ride. When he made his way back up to the platform, he was grinning ear to ear.

"At least I made the eight," Leo laughed.

"He was an ugly one, for sure," I chuckled then turned back to Spence.

Even with the height of the chute gate, Destiny's Ignatius was big enough to see over the top. The stallion was looking out to the multitude of riders in the field and seemingly ignoring the stock contractor that was aligning the flank strap and Spence who was tugging on the bronc rein to slide his fingers into it.

"He takes a lot of rein," I told Spence and he adjusted the length again.

"Give it your all," Leo said as Spence slid down over the horse.

"Damn, he's wide," Spence's voice was firm but with a bit of a shake.

I leaned down and helped Spence get his boot in the stirrup and positioned. To brace myself, I placed a hand on the broad shoulder of the horse and felt the heat and strength of him. My gut hurt with the desire to ride him, but my heart was pumping in anxiety and fear for Spence. Even as I helped him position correctly, I wished he had decided not to ride. I glanced at the stock contractor that owned the horse, Adam Westmoreland, he gave me a sideways glance with lips rolled tight. No doubt, he was thinking the same thing.

Spence leaned back, wiggled into the saddle, pushed his hat down tighter, then lifted the bronc rein high. The horse's back rose just inches as he recognized the signal that the cowboy was ready.

The nod and the gate swung open, and the stallion rose in the air with large head and hooves high. He launched himself and Spence at least four feet in the air before flying forward and landing on his front hooves. As the large rump of the stallion flew up, Spence was catapulted from its back and lawn darted into the dirt. I heard a huff, swear words, and a cry out before scrambling down the side of the chute.

The stallion bucked out another twenty feet then took off at a run.

I hurried to Spence's side to see his face writhed in pain as he grabbed at his shoulder. Two men were instantly beside me, and we hovered over him and looked out at the stallion. But the horse was across the arena and racing ahead of the pickup men.

"My shoulder," Spence groaned and tried to sit up. "It's broken, I heard it."

"Stay down," The man on my right said and leaned down to look into Spence's eyes. "How is your head?"

"Fucking fine," Spence grumbled and narrowed eyes looked up at me. "Get me out of this fucking arena."

I looked at the other two men and recognized them from the Justin Sports Medicine team.

To the growled swear words, and groans of agony, Spence struggled to stand. Finally, I wrapped an arm around his waist and helped. By the time the horse had completed his victory lap around the entire arena, we were walking Spence into the Sport's Medicine trailer.

A half hour later, we were in the emergency room of the hospital. It wasn't until three in the morning before Spence's parents arrived and took him home. Leo pulled into the rough stock parking lot as Aaron was just making his way into his camper and invited us in for a beer. Leo was texting on his phone when I leaned my head back against the wall and promptly fell asleep.

"Granger."

I opened my eyes to Aaron shaking my shoulder and grinning. "Damn, you going to sleep all day?"

Through narrowed eyes, and groggy brain, I leaned forward and looked around. "Where's Leo?"

"He stepped out about a half hour ago."

I pulled my phone from my pocket, "Damn, it's already two."

Text from Granger to Spence: Dude, sorry about what happened. How are you doing?

I opened the camper door to bright sunshine and held a hand up to block the light.

Deep breaths and a stretch of the arms, I looked around. Maybe he just left to get something to eat. I visited the closest outhouse, then made it to the rodeo in time to watch Brodie ride. I met him at the back of the chutes and congratulated him for making the championship round in bareback and saddle bronc the next day. He seemed tired and wore out.

"How's Spence?" He asked as he downed a beer before reaching for his bag and saddle.

"Broken clavicle," I walked along side of him as we made our way to the parking lot and trailers.

"That horse is fierce."

"He was determined to try."

Aaron and a few other riders were standing next to the truck and camper when we arrived. We talked for a while before Brodie nodded and walked away.

"That guy has fucking heart," Aaron sighed.

"Yeah, I couldn't imagine going through the rides. Fuck, just losing Craig is mentally hard then he adds the rides to it."

"He's tougher than me."

I glanced around the lot, "Have you seen Leo?"

"Not since I got up."

"You headed to Othello?"

"No, I don't ride until tomorrow night, so I'll stick around to watch the championship round tomorrow."

I looked over at the empty spot where Leo's SUV had been parked. Then, I looked at Aaron's truck. My bag and saddle were tucked under the back by the camper door.

"What the hell?" I whispered and retrieved them and slid them over my shoulder.

Aaron's brows rose and he shrugged as he climbed into the camper.

I walked to the side and down the road to look for Leo. He was nowhere to be seen so I pulled out my phone.

"What?" he answered.

"Where are you?"

"I've been talking to Spence, and he doesn't want to hear you telling him..."

"I am not the type of person to say, 'I told you so' and he knows that. It was his decision."

"Yeah, well, I'm just not sure I want to ride anymore."

"We're supposed to be heading for Othello right now."

"I'm not going. Missy has been crying all morning..."

I did not want to hear about his clingy, annoying girlfriend, "How in the hell am I supposed to get there now?"

"I don't know, Granger. Spencer is out until next year and he's not sure what he is going to do either."

"You mean he's quitting, too?"

"I don't know. I don't want to go through that. I never wanted to ride those horses. I just wanted to have fun, but after watching Spence yesterday...he could have been hurt a lot worse."

"I know. That's why we both tried to talk him out of riding."

"The *I told you so...*"

"Fuck, Leo. That is not what I am saying."

"Yeah, well. You're more driven and goal oriented than we are. Spence just wants to have fun, not make the national finals and I'm not even sure I want to ride again. I'm not that good."

"Leo..."

"Sorry, Granger. I'm already halfway home."

"You're not coming back?"

"No...I'm headed home. I knew you wouldn't understand."

"So, you're just leaving me here without a ride?"

"If I stayed, you would have talked me into Othello, and I don't want to. I'm sorry, Granger. I need to be home with dad and Missy right now."

The line went dead, and my head fell back to look at the sky as my shoulders lowered in disbelief, frustration, and mental exhaustion. The bag and saddle fell to the ground with a thump.

CHAPTER TEN

ACE

"Taylor Conners!"

His name was announced by the principal at the podium. With a bright grin and wide stride, Taylor walked across the stage to be handed his high school diploma.

"About, damn time," I applauded.

"Watch your language in public," Mom whispered with an elbow to my ribs.

I could hear a low chuckle from the other side of her. My stepfather, Rob, leaned forward and gave me a smart-ass grin.

I sighed, "At least now we're free to get on the road."

Mom's arms wrapped around mine, "I hope you don't forget about me."

"We won't," I grinned down at her. "We'll be swinging in for home cooked meals." Her eyes brightened as she laughed. "We'll be spending the next month in Arizona," I reminded her.

"Hopefully, summer won't hit in full force while you're there," Rob said.

My half-brothers, Monte and Liam, twelve and eleven, both laughed.

"It's gonna be hot, hot, hot!" Monte sang out.

"It gets hot here, too," I shook my head at the pair. They were good kids that had occasional interest in riding horses; they were focused on motocross racing with their dad.

"Look who is here," Mom sighed.

I turned to see Barry Wilder, my father's last team roping partner, standing to the side of the crowd. He lifted a hand in a wave and without hesitation, I stood and made my way through the crowd to him. Other than my mother, and cousin Lauren in Idaho, Barry was the first of my childhood memories. After my father's death, he and his wife moved to the property next to my mother's ranch she had shared with my dad. He taught Taylor and I how to ride, rope, and train our own horses. He stepped in where my father couldn't be.

"I knew you would be here," I slid into the crowd next to him.

"Wouldn't have missed it for the world," He was looking out to Taylor with a proud grin. "We finally got both of you graduated."

"And, because of you and your training, we both have full-ride scholarships for college."

"That was the dedication you two had to your horses and your tenacity in roping. I taught you to ride and rope, but you two put the time in to be champions. You have big futures ahead of you and I can't wait to watch."

"You're going to come to some of the rodeos though?"

"Just send me your schedule and we'll be there when we can."

"We'll be in Arizona over the winter, too."

"We'll definitely come visit there."

"And rope with us."

He chuckled, "I'm pretty sure I can be talked into that."

When the graduating class was dismissed, the first person Taylor walked to was Barry.

We celebrated at the steakhouse, and I knew it would be months before we were all together again. But that was OK, because Mom and Barry had raised us to respect each other, take care of each other, and be generally good friends with everyone we met. They would always be a phone call away.

"Why can't I go with you?" Liam asked and kicked the dirt as we walked toward the truck with the camper perched on top; mine and Taylor's home for the next few months.

"Mom will tell you it's because she needs company or you have summer things to do," I grinned at him as I adjusted the pile of bath towels in my arms and opened the camper door. "But I'll be honest and tell you that you're too young to be traveling with us. You might hamper our adventure."

He scoffed, but nodded, "You'd have to take care of me instead of finding girls."

I grinned, "Yes, that is another way of putting it. If you were me, at twenty, would you want an eleven-year-old traveling with you on your first summer of freedom?"

"Nah," he grinned.

"Besides, we're going to be roping day and night, and you don't like roping."

Liam shrugged a shoulder, "I like riding horses, and it's not that I don't like roping, it's more that Dad wants us to ride bikes with him."

"And you love riding bikes."

"Yeah, but maybe, someday, you can come get me and let me spend a week with you on the road?"

"And what about Monte?"

"He can do whatever he wants," Liam smirked. "I just want to go on the road with you."

"Well, I tell you what. Once we get to a place that we might be there longer than a couple of days, then I'll ask Mom if you can come visit."

Liam's grin widened, "Awesome, you're the best brother...way better than Taylor or Monte."

I sat the towels into the camper cabinet then laughed as I stepped back out next to him. "I take it you already asked Taylor if you could come with us, and he said no."

Liam's guilty chuckle gave me the answer.

When we approached the horses that were tied up at the hitching post and waiting to be loaded into the trailer, Monte appeared and looked questioningly at Liam.

The pair had conspired to see if we would let them go with us.

"After they get settled in somewhere," Liam answered the unasked question.

"Rad!" Monte grinned and opened the door of the trailer for me while I untied the first horse.

When the last horse was loaded, and Liam was shutting the gate, Mom, Rob, and Taylor appeared out of the house and walked across the wide driveway to us.

"You checked the propane connections?" Mom asked with an anxious smile as Taylor carried another bag of groceries to the back seat of the truck.

I chuckled and pulled her into a hug, "Of course; and the truck and trailer brakes, the fuel level, the oil levels and everything else."

"And we double checked that the spare tires are full," Taylor hugged her.

"We've gone over everything twice," Rob assured her.

More hugs and handshakes were exchanged, and Taylor and I stepped into the truck and shut the doors. We waved as we drove away.

Mom's last words shouted out to us were, "Stay out of trouble."

Text from Taylor to Ace: I NEED HELP

Text from Ace to Taylor: Didn't you go with the brunette last night?

Text from Taylor to Ace: Yeah

Text from Ace to Taylor: Then what the hell do you need from me?

Text from Taylor to Ace: I woke up when she got out of bed. She's in shower.

Text from Ace to Taylor: ??

Text from Taylor to Ace: Should I just leave or wait until she gets out?

Text from Ace to Taylor: How did it go?

Text from Taylor to Ace: Damn fine, but she's been in there for a while.

Text from Ace to Taylor: She's probably wanting to look her best for you

Text from Taylor to Ace: So just wait?

Text from Ace to Taylor: Or she could be waiting to come out until you leave

Text from Taylor to Ace: Son of a bitch! What do I do so I don't look like an ass?

Text from Ace to Taylor: You want to see her again?

Text from Taylor to Ace: Would not be a bad thing

Text from Ace to Taylor: Leave a note that says you were late in meeting me to head out.

Text from Taylor to Ace: OK, I did…she's still in shower

Text From Ace to Taylor: Then leave. I'll start loading the horses.

Text from Taylor to Ace: I put my number on it so she can decide to call or not

Text from Ace to Taylor: So, she can decide if you were good or not LOL

Text from Taylor to Ace: FU

Text from Taylor to Ace: Where are you?

Text from Ace to Taylor: The blonde took me to her car

Text from Taylor to Ace: Not what I asked. Are you in the building or out?

Text from Ace to Taylor: Parking Lot

Text from Taylor to Ace: Don't come in, get truck, pick me up in front

Text from Ace to Taylor: Why? I'm hungry

Text from Taylor to Ace: Bunch of damn roughies are starting a fight.

Text from Ace to Taylor: Who?

Text from Taylor to Ace: I'm trying to get out without getting hit

Text from Ace to Taylor: Who is it?

Text from Taylor to Ace: Cops have been called. Get out front!

Text from Ace to Taylor: I thought we were 8th out and started at 5:00

Text from Taylor to Ace: Yeah

Text from Ace to Taylor: NO, checked day-sheet we're 1st and it is 32 minutes before start.

Text from Taylor to Ace: Good thing I dropped you off before parking.

Text from Ace to Taylor: Just unload the back two, I just signed us in. OMW

Text from Mom to Ace & Taylor: Watched that run on live feed! You won! Proud of you!

Text from Ace to Mom: Thanks Mom

Text from Taylor to Mom: Thanks Mom

I glanced at Taylor as we replaced the old buckles with the new. "Now, let's actually look at the journal to see what time tomorrow's rodeo starts."

"Now, why would you do that?" Barry asked.

Taylor and I had to lean across the diner's small table to look at the travel journal he was reviewing for us.

"Do what?" Taylor asked.

"You're roping here, traveling all the way over here the next day then going back here the next day." Barry pointed.

"Yeah, so?" I leaned back. "You always said it wasn't about the money we spent, it was about the money we won toward the standings."

"Yeah, but you don't want to waste money either," He pointed to the journal. "These two rodeos are closer to where we are now, and combined they pay more than that other rodeo way over there. You can hit both the closer ones, spend half the amount of money in getting there, and have the chance, between the two, to win more."

Taylor and I looked at the map, then to each other, then to Barry.

"See, that's why we invite you to come visit us," I grinned.

"You know, other than roping with us," Taylor smirked.

Barry laughed, "Let's look at the rest of the rodeo year. What's your goal?"

"Taylor just turned 18 and got his permit," I answered. "So far, we've been just roping jackpots for fun and practice for October first. Then, with the full year ahead of us, we buy our card and make a run for the NFR."

"With a card, we can go to some of the bigger rodeos over the winter," Taylor added.

Barry nodded and looked at the list of rodeos we had planned to travel to.

"You're not going to the Northwest?" He asked.

"Not this year," I answered. "We want to go to Pendleton next year though."

He nodded, "Your dad and I won that one. He always said it was one of his favorite rodeos. Lots of history there, too. Make sure you plan some time to look around and not just rush there then out."

"Okay," Taylor nodded.

"Snake River Stampede in Nampa, Idaho was a fun one, too," Barry continued. "Lauren would be thrilled if you rode in that one."

"Between her and Jamie, they'll be roping and barrel racing there," I added. "As well as their bunk mates; Ryle and Jess team roping."

"Caldwell, too," Barry said. "Work those in. Unless you're pretty high in the standings and feel comfortable you'll make it, you want to hit the big loop of rodeos in the Pacific Northwest in August and September."

"We can always leave a horse down here to fly down and hit the rodeos in Texas," Taylor suggested.

Barry leaned back in the chair and waved the waitress over for more coffee. "That's the end of the year, what's the first of your year look like?"

"Tulsa..." Taylor started.

An hour later, we walked him to his truck. His hand hit the door handle and he turned to look at both of us. "Have fun, be safe, don't do anything I wouldn't do..." We all grinned. "And, unlike I said earlier, NEVER think you have enough money in your standings to not go to a rodeo. Fight to the end...to September 30th. Remember, team ropers have 75 rodeos to count towards the world standings. So, use them wisely."

"We'll keep it in mind," I nodded. As he drove away, I turned to Taylor. "Love that old man."

"Me, too. I feel connected to Dad when we're around him."

"I agree. When other people mention Dad, I get a knot in my stomach like they are comparing me to him or thinking I should live up to his accomplishments. When Barry mentions Dad...it's like Dad is here."

"There's no pressure...Dad is just here with us."

"Somehow, we're going to have to get over that feeling. We can't face reporters and commentators' weekend after weekend and get upset and stressed about it."

We stepped into the truck, and I drove away from the diner.

"Summer is almost over," I reminded him. "We promised the Little Bros we would get them out for a weekend. Have any ideas?"

He opened the rodeo journal and flipped through the pages, "There is the jackpot in San Antonio coming up. We can leave early Friday morning and find someone to watch the horses while we take a day trip to New Braunfels and the Schlitterbahn Waterpark. After roping Saturday, we can drive back to San Antonio and hit the Riverwalk and Alamo. Sunday is the jackpot in Austin then head home Sunday night."

"Or stay in Austin overnight and take them home on Monday while hitting some fun stops on the way."

"Sounds like a good brothers' getaway." He lifted his phone. "I'll send a text to Mom and see what she thinks."

It was only minutes before she replied.

"She says perfect, and the boys will be so happy," Taylor said. "She said to keep each step a surprise so it keeps them guessing all weekend."

CHAPTER ELEVEN

ACE

"Did you have fun?" Mom asked Liam and Monte as they burst from the truck.

The two boys talked non-stop for a half-hour about the waterpark, riding the horses to warm them up, walking down the Riverwalk in the dark, roping again, and every side stop we made in between.

"We even stopped at Gruene Hall where George Strait got his start," Liam announced.

"Garth Brooks, too," Monte nodded with eyes lit with excitement.

"Sounds like a hell of a trip," Rob laughed. "I may have to tag along next time."

"Just us brothers," Liam shook his head with a smirk. "Ace said we can do a trip together every summer."

"And Taylor is going to teach us how to rope," Monte announced. "That way we can rope with them when we go and maybe go on other trips, too."

"For roping," Liam clarified.

Rob's smile faded with a sideways glance to me and Taylor. "We'll talk about that later."

He helped the pair remove their overnight bags from the camper and without another word walked into the house with the excited brothers behind him.

"What was that about?" I asked Mom as she stepped into the trailer and immediately opened the refrigerator door.

"He was a bit bored the last few days without the boys." She shrugged and pulled out the first almost-empty container.

"So, the boys can only ride bikes to keep him entertained?" Taylor grumbled.

She looked around the door and glanced between us, "They are his sons, and he loves riding and riding WITH them. Do not diminish that."

"Alright," I nodded and tried to keep the irritation from my voice. "But, if they want to learn to rope, I'm not saying no because he wants to keep them to himself."

"They are our brothers, and we had a damn good time," Taylor's jaw clenched.

"Well, that was obvious," She chuckled and tried to lighten the mood. "We'll be hearing about it for weeks."

"Mom," I exhaled, and her shoulders lowered. "We aren't going to be around them very much anymore. He'll see them and be with them and can ride bikes with them 90 percent of the year. It's not much for us to ask for what time we can have with them before they grow out of wanting to be with us."

"And do it roping and riding horses if we and those boys want," Taylor added.

"I understand." She nodded and disappeared around the door again.

"Damn, it's 114 degrees outside and it's only noon," Taylor huffed from the comfort of the hotel room bed. He was fully clothed and lying on top with boots off and a tall, iced coffee in his hand.

"Well, I'm glad we decided to get a hotel room instead of sweating this out in the camper." I slid my boots off, crawled onto my bed, and reached for the television's remote control.

"Matt and Brock are in their camper dying of heat."

"Tell them to get over here and watch the Pendleton Roundup with us."

Taylor typed on his phone and received a response in seconds, "They are on their way." He chuckled.

"Tell them to stop for chips and junk food and I'll pay them back when they get here."

"That would be cheaper than the vending machines."

In the next hour, before the rodeo started, there were fifteen people in our room, cases of beer, sodas, and bags of chips and cookies.

Not a healthy item was in sight and the air conditioning was cranked up to the highest level.

Of the people in the room, only Matt and Brock had roped at the Pendleton Roundup. They talked through every team that roped and expanded on the difference between the chute and lane than normal rodeos.

"Didn't one of the Minor brothers break his foot there?" Taylor asked.

"Yeah," Matt nodded. "We roped a few behind him, and I tell ya, it makes it difficult to concentrate when you see something like that happen. I slowed down a bit too much and it cost us money."

"It's the calf roping that will get ya," Brock smirked. "By the time you catch em, you're in the grass and everything is slick. You ever rope there, study Trevor Brazile. He roped a ton there and won all-around championships, too."

"Make sure you have a horse that knows how to get under himself because they will slide," Matt added.

The saddle bronc started, and I was about to turn away to grab another beer, when a cowboy busted out of the chute, made a decent ride, then fell to the ground with a body jerking thud, but hopped up like nothing had happened.

"Damn, that has to hurt," I grimaced.

"They're used to it." Someone in the room said.

Two rides later, a huge horse reared out of the chute and the rider slammed onto the ground with the first buck.

"Nobody can be used to that," I huffed and watched as three men raced to his aid while the pickup men tried to catch the horse. The horse managed to do a complete full-speed lap around the football field sized arena before the pickup men finally caught up with him.

"I bet they are swearing up a storm," Taylor chuckled.

"Impressive fucking horse," Someone in the room added. "I couldn't imagine wanting to get on a horse that size and strength, knowing he was going to try and buck you off."

"Crazy bastards," Someone else added.

Tie down roping started, and I studied each run. I really wanted to be there. When I glanced at Taylor, he was grinning at me with a nod.

Next year, we will be there.

When the rodeo ended with hilarious wild cow milking, the temperature outside was 109 degrees.

"Now what?" Taylor asked.

"Movie and a beer."

Five more people showed up with even more beer and snacks. Laughter drowned out the movie until a loud pounding started on the door.

"Shit, we can't have this many people in here," Taylor turned and looked at the door.

"Everyone, get in the bathroom," I ordered and opened the door.

Low chuckles rumbled through the room as Taylor and two girls started hiding the beer and snack bags in the closet while fifteen people squeezed themselves into the tub and against the walls. Five jumped into the closet with the beer cans and snacks.

"Be quiet until I open the door," I ordered and barely had room to shut the door.

Taylor, myself, and the two girls were the only ones left in the main room when I opened the hallway door.

"What's up?" I asked innocently to the woman that had been at the registration desk when we arrived.

"You're being too loud and the people on both sides have called in twice." She stepped into the room and looked at the four of us.

"Are you sure it was us?" Taylor asked.

The woman rolled her eyes and shook her head, "It was pretty noisy until I banged on the door, then it suddenly became quiet."

"I turned the sound down on the television," I shrugged. "I guess we had it up too loud."

The woman glanced around the room then turned back to the door, "I don't know what the hell you four were doing to make that much noise but knock it off and keep that volume to a respectable level."

She huffed out the door and I closed it behind her, then turned back to the three companions and laughed. I opened the door to the bathroom and the fifteen people emerged from the room as if they were clowns in a tiny clown car. We were all laughing at a "respectable level".

"Ace?"

"Lauren?

"What are you doing?"

"Depends on who is asking."

"Well, let's say I was your mother asking." I could hear her slight chuckle over the phone.

"Just hanging out with some friends."

"And if I was Taylor asking?"

"Whatever the hell I want."

She chuckled again, "And, if I was Jamie asking?"

"Not much, what are you doing?"

"And if Rob was asking?"

I didn't answer.

"Hmmm, that's not getting any better, so, if I'm asking?"

"Just hanging out waiting for my favorite cousin to call me."

"I am your only cousin."

"So, you're my favorite and least favorite...depending on the day."
We both chuckled.

"So, what can I help you with today?" I asked.

"I took a little trip in the pasture yesterday and banged up my knee. Kade is working, Jamie is on a barrel racing road trip with friends for a couple of days, and Pete says he is too old to help me."

Pete was her older roping roommate who stayed in my late father's old room at the Idaho ranch. He was a damn good friend to her. He was also her boyfriend's grandfather.

"I'll help, but first, how bad is the knee?"

"I hyperextended it so it's just a matter of giving the tendons and ligaments time to heal."

"Then what do you need from me?"

"I need you in Idaho."

"How soon?"

"Ah," she sighed. "You're such a good guy."

"Yes, well, tell Rob that."

"It's that bad?"

"This time, he joined a motocross club that allows kids. If Liam and Monte aren't in school, then they are doing some club function. Even the few times we get back in town."

"Are the boys enjoying it?"

"Depends on when you ask them. Sometimes yes, and other times, especially when Taylor and I are in town, they just want to stay home."

"I wish there was something I could do to help," she sighed. "It's one of those times when you just have to wait it out."

I agreed with her, "So, when do you need me?"

"I'll send you a ticket for in the morning."

"Flying out of Phoenix."

"Alright, you must be at Ranch Rio," she chuckled. "Glad you said something."

When I sat my phone down on the side table next to the bed, I rolled over onto an elbow and looked at the pretty blonde that was looking back up at me.

"Hello, Sunshine."

"When do you leave?" She purred.

"Morning...we have all night."

"Ace-man," She sighed and ran her fingers across my bare chest. "Are you sure you aren't going to Georgia this year?"

"I've never been there and honestly, besides you, can't think of a reason to go."

Her smile widened then she sighed again. "Well, I'm sure glad I came to Arizona to visit my cousin for a week and ended up at that barbecue place."

"Me, too." I slid a hand up her hip, then waist, then breast.

She giggled and slid her leg over me and sat up to straddle my hips. Her long blonde hair fell over her shoulders toward me as she leaned down to kiss me.

"If we only have a few hours left of this relationship," She whispered, and my arms wrapped around her waist. "Then we best make some great memories."

"I totally agree." My hand slid into her hair and pulled her down into a deep passionate unforgettable kiss.

CHAPTER TWELVE

SAMMIE

"I appreciate everything you, Dad, and Mason have done helping me get down the road this last month, but you need to focus on Texas and the show."

"Sammie...."

"Mom," I sat on the couch next to her and smiled. "Go to Texas."

Her shoulders slumped, "What are your plans then?"

"I'm not going to lie, it has been a rough couple of weeks, and I have concluded that there is no way I'm going to make the Circuit Finals this year, but I promised you all I wouldn't stop trying. So, I'm leaving Monday morning to finish this year in Pendleton and Othello."

"And the qualifier next week?"

"I have to try," I sighed. "Since I probably won't make the finals, I won't be automatically invited to some of the bigger rodeos. I'm going to have to fight all year, and Rosenburg and Waco rodeos start the new rodeo year in October. I need to run that qualifier in September to make it to the Waco rodeo."

"Then, after you run at Pendleton and Othello, I'll fly home to ride down to Texas with you."

My heart swelled with love for her and the belief she had in me. Even after the rough summer, she wasn't giving up on me.

The Pendleton race didn't go any better than the rest of the summer. The only part that seemed to go well was the long run from the 3rd barrel to the end. It was freeing to fly down the grass field, but it ended way too fast. Pepper's speed helped recover some of the time we lost turning the barrels. We were the 30th rider in slack and already a full second behind the leading rider.

I thought of going home after the race, but I knew the ranch manager didn't need me and I didn't want to be at the ranch without my family. Instead, I spent the next few days in my trailer at the back of the Pendleton property. I watched my family compete in Texas, rode Pepper a couple times a day, and watched movies or pulled the guitar from the closet and played when no one was around. Thursday, I finally wandered out to all the vendors while the rodeo was in full swing.

Friday morning, I stood in Pepper's stall and slowly ran the brush over his back. He was licking the bottom of his grain bucket which made me giggle and the depression eased.

"You're getting a bit bored," I whispered to him. "Maybe we should just go for a walk."

Halfway down the aisle to the main door, I was delighted to see Delaney Rawlins standing in the stall with one of her horses. I hadn't seen her all week, and she was always full of smiles when we would run into each other at a race.

"Good morning, Delaney."

"Morning," She was frowning in worry as she ran a hand over her horse's stomach.

"Something wrong?"

"It looks like he's impacted," She answered and opened the gate to his stall.

"Do you want me to get the vet?" I gasped.

"Yes, please do, but send him to my trailer."

"I'll put Pepper away," I turned and jogged back down the aisle. My stomach ached in worry for her. I had spent many nights worrying and praying over sick horses.

I stood next to the family as the veterinarian examined her horse and was relieved when he proclaimed the horse would be fine.

I was a bit numb when I walked away from their trailer. It was wonderful for her to have her entire family with her, and it made me miss mine that much more. There was no desire to go back to my empty trailer, so I decided to go for a ride. As I saddled Pepper, he continually tucked his head back to me as if asking if I was alright.

"I'm fine, boy," I whispered to him. "Just a bit...lonely, I guess. Seeing that whole family together just makes me miss mine." The tears welled again, but I shook the feeling away and stepped up onto the saddle and leaned forward to run a hand down his neck. "It's just me and you, Pepper. We'll go on a little ride this morning, then drive to Othello for the rodeo tonight."

With a sigh, we walked away from the barn and towards the warm-up arena. As we walked past the encampment for the rough stock riders, I could see Brodie Rawlins and hesitated a moment in thoughts of asking him how Delaney was doing. He was talking to three other bronc riders, and they looked relaxed and enjoying themselves, so I rode away without a word.

The closer to the beginning of the rodeo, the fuller the warm-up arena became so I finished our ride and walked Pepper to the trailer. I knew the stalls would be full of activity, so I left Pepper tied to the side of the trailer with a net full of hay. To entertain myself, I pulled out the guitar and sat on the wheel-well of the trailer and lightly played a few bars. Pepper's head rose and he turned to me with ears perked.

"You like that?" I giggled and played a short song for him. By the time I was done, he had side-stepped himself as close to me as he could get. "Aren't you funny?" I whispered and played another song as I moved closer to see what he would do. He tucked into my side and nudged the tip of the guitar.

"I think he likes your music."

I looked up to see Logan Rawlins on his horse with another at his side. Seven other riders had stopped to watch.

"It seems so," I chuckled. "I've never thought of playing for him before. How is Delaney doing?"

"She'll be fine," He answered with a nod. "Her horse will be fine, and it should be an interesting ride on Memphis."

"He is a good horse, levelheaded."

"That's right, you trained him."

I nodded, with a glance at Pepper; Memphis had been part of the trade my parents had made to buy Pepper for me.

"I did, but he was a bit big for competitive cutting."

"He's worked out pretty well for roping," Logan stated with a bit of a smirk. "She's done well on him in a few jackpots, but it will be interesting to see how he does in this rowdy atmosphere and that chute."

"I'll have to video it for my parents."

"You do that and say hello for me."

"Will do."

With a tip of his hat he rode away. The other riders that had stopped to listen to the music had drifted away so I turned back to Pepper and strummed two more songs as his muzzle played in my hair, snuggled into my neck, and sniffed at my face. Searching my memory for a favorite song just for him, I chuckled to myself and played *Sergeant Pepper's Lonely Heart Club Band*. His lips wiggled in my hair as I played. My love for the silly horse grew.

When I heard the announcement the rodeo was about to begin, I walked him back to the stall, but took my time brushing him and cleaning his buckets and feeders in preparation for our trip to Othello. When I walked toward the arena stairs to the upper level, I caught a glimpse of Brodie standing with a few cowboys. They all looked relaxed and happy. The bleachers were packed with people, so I stood at the top and waited for the breakaway to begin then found an open spot at the bottom seats and asked permission to stay to film a friend.

Delaney was riding Memphis, the buckskin paint, on the far side of the arena. Memphis looked around at the commotion but moved with ease as she walked him into the box. Her run on the horse was near perfection. I was so impressed with the training she had done on him and that her first reaction when the rope broke from her saddle was to reach down and pet him.

We couldn't have asked for a better person to buy one of our horses. In response to the terrible Facebook message Christina had posted after I removed them from my trailer, Delaney had said the same thing about me and Pepper. I hoped she still felt that way.

I sent the video to my parents then walked away with my mood slowly plummeting with each step I took to the barns. I didn't want to be in Pendleton anymore, so I walked into the barns and collected everything in the stall and walked it to the trailer. I returned to clean the stall before sliding the halter on Pepper and walking away.

"Where are you?"

I looked around to find who spoke and saw one of the cowboys that had been with Brodie standing on the side of the road talking on the phone.

"I am not the type of person to say 'I told you so' and he knows that. Are you sure? You're supposed to be picking me up right now to head for Othello. How in the hell am I supposed to get there now?"

His voice faded away as I neared my trailer and loaded Pepper into it.

As I pulled out of the parking space and onto the dirt road, the cowboy was still on the phone on the side of the road. As I neared, his head tilted back, hand holding the phone fell to his side, and his shoulders slumped enough the strap from his rough stock bag slid down and his bag with bronc saddle attached hit the ground.

CHAPTER THIRTEEN

SAMMIE

The debate in my head lasted all of the five seconds it took me to pull up next to him and stop. When I lowered the window, he turned and looked at me with a blank expression.

"I'm headed to Othello, but I'm not in a good mood, so if you promise not to talk to me, I'll give you a ride."

Without hesitation, he lifted his bag into the bed of the truck then returned and stepped into the truck. He didn't say a word and neither did I for the first hour of the two-hour trip.

 As we approached Kennewick, a song came to an end on the radio, my stomach growled, and it echoed into the cab. He glanced at me with a bit of a smirk, and I couldn't help but smile.

"Sometimes, I forget to eat," I sighed. "Can you check to see if there is a Costco around here?"

He pulled out his phone and pushed a few buttons.

"The nearest Costco is 9 miles by car with light traffic," Announced the voice from his phone. "Here are your directions. Turn right..."

Instead of pulling into the Costco parking lot, I drove into the parking lot of the movie theater across the street. "It's easier to get the rig in and turned around over here. Do you want anything?"

He shook his head.

"I'll be right back, then."

When I returned, he was standing at the back of the truck. Having lowered the tailgate, he had set his bag on top and had pulled a spiral notebook from it. He zipped the bag and tossed it into the back of the truck. I lifted one of the bags I was carrying and stretched it out to him.

He didn't take it, but his brows rose.

"As you can probably smell, it's a roasted chicken," I explained. "I stay away from fast food and don't feel like cooking, so I let Costco do it for me. The chicken isn't very big, and I can easily eat one all by myself and I'm not going to sit here and eat a whole chicken in front of you. So, consider eating this chicken a favor to me in return for giving you a ride to the rodeo."

He grinned and stretched out his hand to take the bag and we set them on the tailgate.

"There's water in the cooler in front of you."

He retrieved two bottles and handed me one.

When half my chicken was gone my energy and mood improved, "What's your name?"

I turned and looked up at him. He had just placed a large chunk of chicken in his mouth, and his brows rose as if in question.

"I promise I won't leave you behind if you talk to me," I smiled innocently.

"Ranger." He squeezed around the food.

"Ranger? Like forest ranger?"

He shook his head, "With a g in front of it."

"G-ranger?"

He swallowed dramatically and shook his head, "Granger."

I liked my version better and the funny reaction he had to it, so I smiled, "Well, G-ranger, my name is Sammi Parkston."

"Well, S-ammie, my name is Granger Miller."

I wrinkled my nose with a chuckle, "It just doesn't flow as well as G-ranger."

"True," he chuckled and popped more chicken into his mouth.

I stepped into the trailer to wash my hands and retrieve paper towels for him and returned as he dropped the bags into the garbage can next to the building.

The engine roared to life as he walked back to the truck. I watched him for a moment and wondered why my internal debate to give him a ride was so short. As he reached for the door handle, I hit the lock button even though the window was rolled down. His eyes shot up in surprise.

"I need you to promise me one more thing," I smiled.

"And, what would that be?" He drawled.

"I need you to promise that you will never tell anyone that I picked up a cowboy I didn't know off the side of the road."

He hesitated and his head tilted slightly, "And, why did you?"

"I saw you with Brodie Rawlins a couple of times today, so it wasn't that you were a complete stranger and I overheard you needed a ride."

"You know Brodie?"

"No, I don't believe I have ever spoken to him. I spoke to his brother Logan today. I know Delaney. I trained the buckskin paint she rode in breakaway today."

"You rope?"

"No, my family owns a cutting horse facility. Memphis was too big, so my parents traded him for the horse that's in my trailer, Pepper. He used to be Delaney's barrel horse."

He nodded, "So, because of that, you picked up a cowboy you didn't know off the side of the road."

I smiled at the teasing light in his eyes, "Yes, but no one is to know that but us. My dad would kill both of us."

"Yeah, we can't have that," he chuckled. "So, can I get back in?"

I unlocked the door even though he could have easily just reached in the window and pulled up the knob.

I pulled out of the parking lot, "When do you ride?"

"Tonight, and you?"

"Slack in the morning. I'm nineth out so we can leave early," I glanced at him. "Did you need to go back tonight?"

"Brodie made the short-go, so I just need to be back by noon tomorrow. Did you want me to find another ride back?"

"No, I can take you back, but I don't want anyone telling my dad they saw a cowboy coming out of my trailer."

"I can find...."

"Do you mind sleeping in the truck?"

"This truck?" He chuckled. "No, it's pretty luxurious compared to Leo's SUV."

"You don't have one?"

"I have a broken-down truck. I was saving my money and going to pick up a new one over the winter, but without Leo and Spence driving, I'll need to pick one up before I wanted to. I'm headed to Oklahoma and Texas for the beginning of the rodeo year."

"I'm going to be going back there, too, but might have my mom with me."

"I texted a friend while you were in the store. He offered to take me over with him, so I can save whatever I win for a new rig or fix my current one."

"So, the better you do, the nicer car you can get," I glanced at him to see him nodding. "How did you do in Pendleton?

"Third for the day, but fourteen overall and out of the short round."

"Damn."

"How did you do?"

"The third barrel and the run home were perfect," I sighed. "The 1st and 2nd were wide which took me out."

"That's a hell of a setup though."

"Yeah, Pepper loves to run, so that run home was fun," I sighed again. "I just can't seem to put the rest of it together."

"I'm a big believer in clinics and mentors. That is why I'm on the road. Do you think Delaney can help?"

I nodded, "She agreed to be a mentor the day I got Pepper from her. We've just been so busy. I've done clinics too but it's hard right now with the rodeos winding down for the year."

He nodded and we grew quiet until I got tired of the silence.

"Have you been to Othello?" I asked.

"No."

"Good committee, they feed everyone well, and it is on flat ground with lots of parking available. The fair is going on at the same time. I'll park so we can easily get out in the morning after I run. We'll easily get back in time."

I pulled into the rodeo grounds and once I was parked his hand reached for the door handle.

"You need help?"

"No, but thanks," I smiled across the seat. "I'm well practiced and since is it flat ground and we won't be here more than a night, the only thing I have to do is setup Pepper's pen." I turned and pointed to a small building next to the arena. "That is the secretary's office, and on the other side of those stock pens is where they setup the food."

"OK," He lifted his bag out of the back of the truck, glanced at the arena, then back to me. "You going to watch the rodeo?"

I gave him a teasing grin, "Yeah, I'm going to watch and see if you can get a good check to put in the bank for your new truck."

He laughed, "I'll go check-in and come back and see if you need anything."

I had the panels set up, Pepper released and eating from his hay bag, and cleaning out the back of the truck when Granger returned.

Without a word, he picked up the water bucket and walked away. When the full bucket was placed in the pen, we walked together toward the food stand and passed by the bucking horses and bulls.

"Did you draw a good horse?" I asked.

He nodded and pointed to a horse standing to the side of the pen, "One of their best, Broken Camp."

"Impressive."

"Hey, Granger," A cowboy stopped and reached out a hand. "Heard about Spence, damn thing to happen, but that Iggy is a fucking beast."

Granger shook his hand with a shake of the head, "Yeah, that he is."

I hesitated while trying to decide if I should leave them to their conversation or continue to the hospitality booth. We weren't a couple, so I doubted Granger would expect me to stay but I also didn't want to look rude. Glancing between the two men, I turned to the bulls that were in the pen next to us. They looked so calm, but they were huge. I couldn't imagine who would ever want to slide on the back of one.

"Ready?" Granger asked.

"Yep," I nodded. "You ever ride a bull?"

He shook his head with a chuckle, "No, but then again, I didn't really think too much about riding a bucking horse before the first time I got on one."

We walked back to the BBQ and talked with other contestants in line as we waited.

He only placed meat on his plate, "Anything else before a ride makes my stomach sick."

"I just have a protein bar before I ride, just enough to calm the nerves."

We made our way to the bleachers that were only for contestants and sat quietly as we watched the beginning of the rodeo. It was a late rodeo, and the night was dark, but the carnival and fair lights brightened the sky.

"You like rides?" He asked.

"No, I just like watching them."

"I like the food. You want to walk through it after the rodeo?"

"Sounds like a plan."

"I need to go down..."

"I haven't been around bronc riders," I smiled. "What am I supposed to say to cheer you on?"

"Lift lift lift, toes out, and believe," He grinned and took my plate to toss into the garage can as he walked away.

I sat quietly in the stands with a casual nod to acquaintances until the saddle bronc riding began. I had only known him a few hours, yet I found myself anxious for him. My toes tapped against the bleachers and arms tightened around my waist.

The announcer's voice boomed, "Keep your eyes on chute #4 with Granger Miller and Cougar Country from Big Bend and Flying Five stock contractors. We're coming to the end of the road to qualify for the Columbia Circuit Finals, but this young cowboy has already notched his name into the books and will be in Redmond in just a few weeks. Cougar Country took Tilden Hooper to the win in Reno last year and is one horse every cowboy wants to draw."

The large monitor was aimed into the chute and captured Granger pulling his hat down lower before lifting the buck rein in the air in front of him and right arm above his head as he leaned back. He looked out into the arena then said something over his shoulder to the man pulling the flank strap. The man nodded and Granger turned, leaned back further, then nodded.

My body clenched as the horse lunged out of the chute. A solid, strong kick out the back then down again all the way across the arena before a leaping kick to the side as the buzzer blared.

"That's a solid ride from this cowboy. Way to go Granger!" The announcer yelled just as Granger tipped to the side and flew off the horse to land in the dirt with a thump. "Great ride, but you need to work on that dismount!"

The crowd laughed then erupted in applause when he took the lead with an 84-point score. I clapped and whistled for him as he jogged out of the arena then stood and made my way down the bleachers and to the steps leading up to the walkway behind the chutes. He was leaning over the back of the next rider and helping to adjust the horse who was leaning to the side. When the chute opened, and the horse lunged out, Granger was yelling and clapping for the rider. I stood on the second step to watch the rider and blue roan horse buck their way across the arena and back. The pickup men swooped in and helped the rider dismount, then turned and watched the replay. An 85-point score was announced. He had taken the lead from Granger, but you couldn't tell by the high-fives the men gave each other.

When we first met, we were both depressed and quiet. Slowly we had started talking and gaining strength, but now, looking at him, he looked like a totally different person. His body was taller, energy making him bounce, and grin wide. His blond hair, which just covered his ears, swayed as his body moved. Blue eyes beamed with energy from his ride. This was his 'place'; where he was meant to be.

He turned and looked at me and the grin grew wider. I couldn't help but grin in return.

"Second place isn't bad," I called out. "A bit closer to that nice truck."

He laughed and turned to retrieve his saddle and bag. After placing them in the back seat of my truck, we began our walk to the fair.

"I didn't know Delaney was here," He pointed to the side.

She was riding a dark bay horse instead of her red roan. The horse was beautiful, strong, and looked masculine with a big neck, large rump, and barrel of a chest.

"I didn't either." I wanted to go talk to her about Pepper but didn't want to interrupt her concentration for her ride.

We stood at the gate under the large monitor and waited then watched as she and the dark horse raced into the arena and around the barrels. When we walked away, she was in first place.

We walked through the fair and both bought corndogs, cotton candy, and he followed those with a large caramel apple. We didn't really talk much about anything but food.

Even though the night wasn't cold, I gave him an extra blanket and pillow for sleeping in the truck.

"Thanks for understanding," I smiled as he set them on the back seat.

He turned to me with a grin, "Like I said, this is a whole lot better than Leo's truck."

"Alright, I'll be up early to get ready, but you can sleep in."

"Are you kidding me?" He grinned. "I'll be in the bleachers cheering on my chauffer."

I chuckled and walked to the trailer.

"Wish I had some pom poms," he said as I reached the door.

We both laughed.

Pepper was ready to go, and I was beside him stretching to try and get myself to relax. The thought of the bottle of Pendleton whiskey hidden in the cupboard crossed my mind, but I did need to drive right after the run, so I quickly dismissed it.

I gave up on trying to make myself relax and stepped into the stirrup and rose above the horse. My first instinct was to relax but the closer I rode to the warm-up area, the more my stomach ached. I asked myself the same question I had the dozen rodeos I had ridden by myself: how and why did this happen after such a strong start?

I tried to blame my three 'friends', but it had been months since I had seen them. It was beyond their fault. The announcer called out the first riders and I began taking deep calming breaths. Pepper was warmed up, so I rode to the fence to watch the first five riders. I couldn't help myself and searched the bleachers. Granger was sitting by himself in the stands by the third barrel. I smiled at his pompom comment and felt my body begin to relax. I turned away and, in my mind, pictured him waving pom poms in the air until the announcer called my name.

Pepper pranced to the gate, and I took a deep breath and let him go. The first barrel was good with a sharp turn, second barrel was just a bit too wide, and as I approached the third barrel, I could hear the "GO SAMMIE" yelled from the bleachers as we made a great turn, and I was low to Pepper's mane with reins in hands held just behind his ears I told him to let it all out and he did.

"That's a 17.52, for Sammie Parkston," the announcer called out. "Which puts her in third place as of now."

I leaned down with a smile and patted Pepper's neck, "That felt better." A bit of confidence was back giving me the hope that the trip to Oklahoma to the qualifier for Waco wasn't a waste of time, money, and dreams.

"That looked great," Granger grinned when we reached the trailer.

"I heard ya yell and kind of wished you had those pom poms." I laughed and stepped out of the saddle.

"I recorded it for you. What's your number and I'll send it to you."

A half hour later, we were pulling away from the rodeo grounds, and I was still in third as the slack for barrel racing ended.

"So, what is it you were saying yesterday?" Granger teased.

"Well," I smiled and turned onto the highway. "That is the best race I've had in months, but we were wide on second. Last spring, we would have won that race." I knew it was true and I sighed.

"What's the difference between then and now?"

"I don't know," I sighed again. "Right now, I just want to glow in the some-what good run and not analyze the whys."

"Understood," he nodded.

"How long have you been riding?"

He told me of his journey as a bronc rider for the rest of the ride to Pendleton. His story of the loss of his mentor, Craig, brought tears.

"I remember reading about it," I whispered and wiped away the tears.

"Brodie's last honor ride for him is today, so I wanted to get back and support him."

Most of the competitors had left so there were plenty of places to park. I backed into the same spot I had left the day before.

"Do you need a ride somewhere after the rodeo? I'm headed to Madras."

"Nah, Aaron and I are going down to Texas and try to ride there. I'm a bit short on my goal this year."

I opened my door then turned back to him, "What is your goal?"

"Coming in at least 26th in the standings."

"Where are you?"

"28th."

"Close," I nodded. "But close isn't making your goal. I understand that." We stepped out of the truck, and I turned back to look at him over the seat. "Good luck down south. I hope you make it."

"Thanks," he smiled. "You need help with anything?"

"No, I'm good. You just go help Brodie."

"Thanks for the ride, Sammie."

"You're welcome, G-ranger," I grinned with a mischievous giggle.

He laughed as he lifted his bags from the back of the truck, "I'll see you in Oklahoma in a couple weeks."

"Safe travels."

He smiled again then turned and walked away with the bag and saddle comfortably hanging from his shoulder. It looked so natural to him.

Text to Mom: Decided to stay until Delaney runs in barrels then will head home.

Text from Mom: How did this morning go?

Test to Mom with the video: Left in third, it was OK. I'll let you know when I leave.

After watching the video a dozen times, I laid the phone on the seat and sighed. It just wasn't as good as the spring runs, and I didn't know why.

I made it into the stands in time to watch Brodie Rawlins win the saddle bronc title then waited patiently for Delaney. She won the whole rodeo on her red roan, and I couldn't have been happier for her. After her victory lap, I drove away from Pendleton with the wish, hope, and dream that someday I would make that ride.

It was not going to happen if I quit and had promised my family that I wouldn't quit. I just had to find a way to ride past the problems and do it before going to the qualifier. The thought made my head, stomach, and back ache.

CHAPTER FOURTEEN

SAMMIE

Four days later, I stood in the back of the pickup truck that was parked next to the fence by our back pasture. The phone's camera was aimed at the six horses grazing on the last remnants of grass.

"I'd recommend the sorrel with the wide blaze, the dark grey, and the bay with the longer mane."

"Chappy, Serpent, and McClain," Mason chuckled. "You could have just said their names."

"I just wanted it to be very clear, you've been gone so long I figured you would have forgotten."

He huffed a chuckle, "I was home five weeks ago."

"That's a long time for a male brain," I teased and turned the phone so I could make a face at him.

He responded with a weird face of his own then laughed, "Just bring over those three."

"Alright, we're leaving at four in the morning."

"Drive careful and send updates on the way."

The phone call ended and I leaned back on the side of the truck and watched the horses graze. Hauling the horses to Mason for winter training relieved the guilt I had begun to feel for driving all the way over just to run a race I didn't think I would do good in. The top 60 racers qualified for the Waco rodeo. Over 400 racers were in the draw for the race that could last well past midnight, but I had drawn the 32nd spot. Even after I ran, it would be hours before we knew the results.

I didn't let myself think of the race on the trip to Oklahoma until we dropped off the horses and Mason followed us down to Texas.

Mom and Mason were sitting in the bleachers as Pepper and I circled the warmup arena. The stress made me nauseous and the stress I felt was beginning to show in Pepper. He pranced, fought against the bit, and began to shake his head for the first time. I needed to do something to calm my nerves, so I rode back to the trailer and took two long swigs from the hidden Pendleton Whisky bottle. My body warmed and shoulders relaxed.

By the time we rode to the entry gate, the stress had eased, and Pepper was his normal calm. I watched the five racers in front of me and visualized the race in Othello. Granger's grin and comment of pom poms popped in my head, and it made me chuckle. I chanted "pom poms" until my name was called then we pranced into the arena.

The first barrel was one stride longer than it should have been, the second was a little tighter and the third was always the best with a strong run to the end. The clock stopped putting us in third. By the time Pepper was cooled down and pampered, I was down to eighth.

Mom and I listened to an audible book to keep our minds busy as we drove toward her brother's home in Wyoming as our pit stop for the night. Mason texted every half hour where I was in the standings. Well after midnight the last text came in.

Text from Mason: Congrats Sis, #55, see you next week

Mom screamed into the night, and I laughed at her as the knot in my stomach grew.

"Dad rented you another barn with three more stalls," I told Mason and walked toward the back pasture. "He figured since I was going back there again, I might as well bring you another three horses."

"Well," Mason huffed over the phone. "I won't be getting bored this winter."

"No," I grinned and stopped by the fence. "I can come over and help when I'm not at a jackpot or rodeo."

"Does that mean I can charge you stable fees?"

I laughed, "Only if I can charge you hauling fees." I laughed. "Which ones do you want?"

"Your last three choices were spot on, so I'll trust you on the next three."

"One will be the palomino," Dad walked up behind me and looked over my shoulder. "Branstrom is going to buy that one and is considering McClain."

"But I like McClain," Mason frowned. "He is smart as a whip, down and dirty."

"That's why he is considering him," Dad grinned. "Someone saw you working with him and called Branstrom. Remember, we can't keep all of them."

"Wish we could," Mason and I said at the same time.

"You two have always been that way," Dad laughed. "Now, go ride a horse so Sammie and I can finish checking her truck for the trip."

Mason waved and ended the call.

As per our usual routine, Dad and I walked side by side and checked everything on the truck and trailer: brakes, oil, transmission fluid, antifreeze, tire pressure and anything else he could think of.

When he was finally satisfied, we walked toward the fence and looked out at the horses.

"We leave in the morning for California," Dad stated. "When are you leaving?"

"Couple of days," I shrugged and leaned against the fence.

He nodded, "When you were little and started riding the cutting horses, you were very good at listening to me and taking my coaching."

"Why not learn from the best?" I teased.

He just nodded, "If you were still cutting, I could help you through your slump. But I can't help with barrel racing. I would if I could."

"I know, Dad," I sighed.

"When people buy our horses, we don't hesitate to help them if they have issues. We want those horses to succeed."

"Yeah?"

"Delaney would want to help and offered to help you and be your mentor. Why haven't you called her?"

I exhaled in frustration, "Other than the fact she has been busy qualifying for the NFR and dealing with their friend's death...it's just…confusion…I don't know. I'm just so used to being able to figure it out that I didn't have to reach out."

"Well, if you truly want to hit October 1st at a run and get yourself qualified for the NFR, then you need to just set that all aside, and call her."

I sighed with a nod, "You're right, of course."

He pulled me into a strong embrace, "I know you can succeed. We all do. You have the talent and now you just need the confidence back." He stepped back and waved an arm toward the horses in the pasture. "Now, other than the pali, which two horses do you recommend taking to Mason and I'll go get their traveling paperwork together?"

I glanced at the horses, "Diedra and McBreezy."

A grin spread across his face, "McBreezy…the horse that farts with every turn. Mason is going to love you for that." He laughed again and walked toward the house.

I watched him until he disappeared into the house then pulled out my phone. He was right…as usual. I made the call.

"Hello, Sammi!" Her voice was full of life.

"Hi, Delaney," I tried to fill my voice with more energy than I felt.

"What's wrong?"

Well, I couldn't fool her even on the phone. I sighed, "Pepper and I aren't in sync, and I don't know why."

"Send me your latest videos and I'll take a look."

"OK, but, would you happen to be close to home so I could come work with you in person?"

"No, Hun, I'm in Texas with Ryle."

My sigh was heavy, "OK, I'll just send the videos."

"You know, you live pretty close to a phenomenal trainer. I bought Maestro from her a couple weeks ago and he is working wonderfully.   Lauren Conners; she does clinics all the time. She'll be able to help."

"Is she having a clinic soon?"

"I'll give her a call and get you in there for a one-on-one."

"You sure?"

"She's Ryle's landlady," Delaney chuckled. "That should give us some clout."

I sighed in relief, "Thanks."

"You'll get there, Sammi. Don't give up. We all struggle from time to time. Remember, I took last year off and now I've qualified for the NFR. You'll get there, too."

As much as I tried to believe her, I just didn't feel it in my gut.

"Thanks," I mumbled.

"Where are you headed now?"

"I'm at home now. In a couple of days, I'm supposed to be headed to Oklahoma. I qualified for Waco, barely, but I did and that's a long way to go again and I really want to make sure I do better. I will be going there, then I'm going to hit a few other rodeos before coming home."

"Let's see if we can get you with Lauren while you are home. I'll call you back."

I turned off the highway and down the long drive that led to the Conners 3.3 ranch. Just over the rise in the hill was a wrought iron black gate with the Circle 3.3 brand centered in each panel. I stopped at the panel and keyed in the code Lauren had texted and the gate opened.

Hope swelled in me as I looked out to the home, buildings, barns, corrals, arenas, and horses that speckled the green pastures. An indoor arena was under construction on the far side. It was a beautiful estate.

When I turned the truck and trailer onto the driveway in front of the house, an older man I guessed around eighty years old was walking from the barn with a red roan horse by his side. He waved me over into an area by the fence. When I stopped, he greeted me with a cheerful smile.

"You must be Sammie."

"I am," I stepped out of the truck and stretched out a hand.

He took it with an old trembling hand with knuckles beginning to twist. I shook it gently.

"I'm Pete."

"Nice to meet you," I looked around the area. "This is a beautiful place."

"And I am fortunate that Lauren likes me enough to let me stay here and call it home," he chuckled.

I instantly liked him.

"And this old horse, Barry, kind of likes it here, too. We can just saddle up and go for a ride."

There was a lariat attached to his saddle.

"You rope, too?"

"We do," His eyes twinkled. "Lauren and I made it to the semi-finals at The American last March."

"Damn," I gasped in admiration.

"It was a lot of fun getting ready for it and riding in it; a good adventure for an old man."

I chuckled and walked to the back of the trailer. Pepper grumbled an anxious whinny. He was always excited to see new places. My eyes wandered the property until they stopped at Lauren riding out of the barn on a tall buckskin. She was as beautiful in person as she was on her website that I had perused a dozen times.

"I have three horses with me that I'm hauling to my brother in Oklahoma. Lauren said we could let them run in one of the pastures." I lowered the ramp and opened the trailer door.

"We cleared out the pasture right behind you," Pete nodded and tied his horse to a hitching post then helped lead the younger horses to the pasture.

When I closed the gate, Pete turned to Lauren as she rode toward us. "I best get in the saddle before you leave me behind."

He walked to a mounting block behind a small bleacher. Lauren stopped and talked to him and stayed by Pete's side until he was safely in the saddle.

When I tied Pepper to the side of the trailer, she walked toward us.

"Hello, Sammie," She smiled a greeting. Her long black hair was in a tight braid down her back and a 3.3 logoed baseball cap covered the top.

"Good morning, Lauren," I leaned against the bay horse. "Thank you for taking the time to see me on such short notice."

"Delaney spoke very highly of you."

"I really like her."

"So do I, but we're limited on time so why don't you saddle him, and we'll go for a ride first."

"A trail ride?"

"Yes, it will help relax the two of you."

"Ok…" I turned to retrieve my saddle.

Pete and Lauren sat on their horses and watched the three young cutting horses run circles around the pasture until I was perched on top of Pepper.

"Beautiful horses," Lauren said to me with a nod to the pasture.

"They are pretty special," I nodded with a proud smile. "Born from our own stallion and mares and at home."

"When was the last time you two went on a trail ride?" Lauren asked as we began a walk toward the road in front of her house.

"Honestly, probably a couple months ago," I answered in a bit of embarrassment. "I've been focused on trying to connect in the arena."

"You need to keep his mind anticipating instead of expecting." She said as we started the walk down the road. "Tell me about Pepper."

"I could not believe it when Delaney told me that Mom and Dad had bought him for me. I had watched when she rode him at the NFR and just drooled over both of her horses. She was riding the horse she was buying from my dad, and I rode with her then she told me. I was so shocked and happy and in total disbelief." I was talking fast and overly animatedly, but I couldn't get myself to stop. "I asked Delaney dozens of questions about Pepper and her experience getting to the NFR with him."

"Sammie," Pete smiled with a humored light in his eyes. "Tell us ABOUT the HORSE."

I flushed in embarrassment, "Sorry."

"It's alright," Lauren glanced at me with a thoughtful expression. "Why didn't you rename him when you bought him? Did you consider it?"

"No," I huffed in surprise. "I had watched him as Pepper for a couple years when I watched Delaney ride him, so renaming him never crossed my mind."

"Do you have a nickname for him?" Pete asked and led us off the road and into the trees.

I leaned down and stroked Pepper's shoulder to encourage him. The horse had walked calmly down the road next to Lauren and Pete's horses. Not once did he prance or refuse a command. He had been relaxed and casually looking out into the fields.

"Yes, I love the old Beatle's song '*Sergeant Pepper's Lonely Hearts Club Band*', so I call him Sergeant Pepper." I giggled.

"Ok, now tell me about your Sergeant Pepper," Lauren smiled.

"Like what? What I feed him?" I asked.

"What is his personality," Lauren answered.

"Oh," I chuckled. "When he is in a big pasture and sees me, he'll run and buck to me."

"He likes you," Pete said.

"He likes the peppermint treats I give him," I laughed. "If I'm late to feed him, he'll be standing at the gate bobbing his head and grumbling. He also likes to travel and will load into the trailer if I have the door open; even if I'm just cleaning it and not going anywhere."

"Any hoof issues? Does he stand well?" Lauren asked.

"Yeah, no issues there. My dad has the best farrier in the area work on our horses," I answered. "He also has a chiropractor and an equine massage therapist, and of course we have the Bemer blankets for helping his circulation."

"No, nebulizer?" Lauren smirked.

I laughed, "Yeah, we have one of those, too."

"What is that?" Pete asked.

"It is a cup that goes over their muzzles…it helps with their respiratory," I answered. "We have champion horses and treat them that way."

"So, there are no physical issues with him. Do you have anything wrong with you?" Lauren asked.

"No, I take care of myself physically; running, gym work, and a bit of martial arts. Dad insisted since I travel by myself sometimes. Plus, I eat healthy," I grinned at them. "Most of the time."

They nodded with knowing grins as we rode out of the trees and into a large clearing. It was half the size of a football field and covered in green grass. Two tall trees were in the center and a well-worn path around the parameter.

"This is my conditioning field," Lauren said, and we started walking along the worn path. "Jamie and I use it to condition the horses for the Pendleton race and training for the younger horses."

"Oh, this would be perfect," I glanced around the field again. "I use the fence perimeter in our back pasture."

"So, you've ran it with Sergeant Pepper?" Lauren asked.

"No, not this year. We were at a few rodeos that weekend. I do want to do it next year. I've been working mainly in the arena and not outside."

"You need to open his mind," Lauren sighed.

"Make him anticipate instead of expect," I repeated her earlier words.

"Why don't you take him for a lap and just let him stretch out," Pete suggested.

I looked at Lauren and when she nodded, I nudged Pepper into a trot. He was smooth, didn't hesitate, or even complain when we left the other horses. I had always liked that about him. Half-way around, I nudged him into an easy lope. With the grass covered meadow, aromatic pine trees, and the energy from the rhythmic lope, my whole body relaxed. Pepper's stride widened as he relaxed into the gallop.

As we neared Lauren and Pete, she motioned for me to go around again.

"Get some speed," she called out.

I leaned forward, stretched my arms toward his ears to let him know to run…and he did. Long, heart pounding strides that had my heart racing and lungs searching for air; my body tingled with energy. I felt all the stress of the last few months melting away. The sound of his hoofbeats hitting the dirt made me feel free. "Loving this," I whispered to the horse. "You are such a good boy."

As we neared the pair again, I slowed Pepper to a slow lope then to a trot. We came to a halt next to them with sweat beading and lungs gasping but his hooves pranced.

"Looks like he enjoyed that," Pete chuckled.

"You both did," Lauren nodded.

"Yes!" I laughed and ran a hand down Pepper's sweaty neck. "We both needed to run and let the stress out."

"So, you know he was getting stressed?" Lauren asked. She nudged her horse forward to follow the trail around the meadow. Pete and I followed.

"Yes, and I tried different medications to help with it so he didn't get an ulcer," I admitted.

She was quiet as we walked around the perimeter of the meadow. As we neared the trail to return us to the road, she turned to me.

"I've watched the videos you sent me and a few I found on-line," she started. "Last spring you started well with him, but each race seemed a little more…loose"

I sighed, "I know it was coming from me. When I didn't do well, the next race would be even worse, and I would get so anxious. Delaney rode him so well and consistently, but I haven't been able to get that…connection."

"You are not Delaney," Lauren stated.

My heart dropped, stomach swirled, and tears rose to my eyes. I felt defeated.

She turned and looked at me, "I'm not saying that you aren't as talented as Delaney or that you don't have the experience or initiative to get to the NFR, I'm saying you can't ride that horse like Delaney did."

My lips rolled into a fine line as I tried not to let the tears fall. We rode out of the trees and back onto the road.

"When you think of that horse, are you riding your horse or Delaney's horse?" Lauren asked.

"He was Delany's…" I whispered.

"But he isn't any more," Pete added. "You need to stop thinking of him as her horse."

I looked between the pair, "How do I do that?"

"Stop calling him Pepper or even mentioning Delaney in the same sentence with him," Lauren answered. "He is your Sergeant or your Sergeant Pepper. The more you refer to him that way, the more your mind will accept that you're not riding someone else's horse, you're riding yours."

We rode silently as I tried to grasp what she meant. "Are you saying that my issue isn't the riding but it's my mentality?" I finally asked as we rode back onto the driveway and toward my trailer.

"Yes, exactly," Lauren stopped her horse and turned to me with serious eyes. "You have the talent and drive to go as far with that horse as you can. There is no denying that. You're a damn good rider and a damn good horsewoman. You just have to take control of the run. You're letting him do all the work since you have it in your mind that was how Delaney rode him. It wasn't. She had control and they worked together. You need to take control over him in the arena and work with him."

Take control…I exhaled the anxiety.

"You understand what she is saying?" Pete asked.

"I think so," I nodded with a bit of confidence starting to grow.

"Let's put the horses away and meet in the bunkhouse. We'll review your videos," Lauren stated and rode away from me before I could respond.

Wasn't she going to watch me in person? With the confusion returning, I stepped out of the saddle and tied Pepper to the horse trailer then stood on the front step of the bunkhouse and waited for the pair.

"You can go in," Lauren called out from the barn. "Ace is in there, but the main room is for everyone. We'll be there in a minute."

I stepped into the building, stopped inside the door and looked around. To my left was a large television that faced into the room. To my right was a hallway that led to five doors. In front of me was a large room with four recliners, two couches, a few small end tables and in the back was a dining table that would easily fit a dozen people. A small kitchen ran across the back wall with a window centered in the middle that revealed a back deck.

The floors were real hardwood with a few rugs placed under the furniture. The walls were decorated with old ropes and hand-drawn pictures of cowboys. It was rustic and comfortable. I walked back to the table and slowly lowered onto a chair.

My mind repeated everything Lauren had said. Take control…I exhaled again.

At the sound of footsteps approaching down the hall, I turned to see a tall man appear. He was setting a straw cowboy hat on his head, but I could still see he was my age, dark hair, and angular features like Lauren. He looked up and stopped with a surprised expression.

"Hi," I smiled.

"Hello," He chuckled. "I have to say I wasn't expecting a cute red head sitting at my kitchen table."

"And I wasn't expecting a handsome cowboy to stroll in," I giggled, "I'm Sammie Parkston; Lauren told me to come in, she is helping me with my riding."

"Ace Conners; she told me she was having someone come by before we left."

"You're related?"

"She's my cousin," He walked to the couch and leaned a hip on the side.

"Do you rope, too?"

"Team rope, calf rope, any kind of roping I can get in."

When he grinned, I could clearly see the resemblance to Lauren.

"Then living here must be a dream with all the arenas and chutes."

He huffed with a smirk, "My dad built it for team roping and Lauren has taken care of it since he passed."

"Oh, I'm sorry."

He shook his head, "I was three and have lived in Texas on my family's ranch."

"I'll be heading to Texas next week," I smiled. "First Tulsa rodeo then down to Texas for a couple of weeks."

"Well, I fly out tomorrow to go home then drive to Tulsa with my brother."

Oh, yay!

"Maybe I'll see you there. Are you going down to south Texas?"

"Yup," He nodded with a wide grin. "Let me give you my number in case something happens, and you need some help."

I tried to hold back the wide grin as I handed him my phone.

Just as he handed the phone back, the door opened with Lauren stepping through with a smile, "So, you've met."

"We have," I nodded. "We were just talking about the Tulsa and Texas rodeos the next couple weeks."

"Sounds like we'll be there at the same time," Ace stood and tipped his hat to me. "I need to get the horses ready to go. I'll connect with you in Tulsa."

"Ok," I smiled.

"Safe travels," Ace said just before disappearing out the door.

"Are you going over with a group?" Lauren asked as she walked to the refrigerator.

"Just me; my 'so called' friends didn't turn out to be true friends, so I quit traveling with them."

"Who you travel with is very important," Lauren nodded. "Would you like a bottle of water? There is also apple juice, Red Bull, lemonade, and milk."

"I'm headed to Oklahoma when I leave here so the Red Bull wouldn't hurt."

"Tell that to your kidneys," She chuckled and handed me a can then retrieved a laptop from the kitchen counter. "I have two races to review with you because, I'm hoping, you will see what I mean from them."

"Ok…" I mumbled and gripped the can tightly.

The first race was from Moses Lake in the spring. It was one of the first I ran on Pepper.

"When you're getting ready to go, you look like you're running in to take over the arena," Lauren said and pushed the play button.

I agreed with her.

"Then this one," She started the second video that showed the Lewiston race. "You're not helping him. He takes two strides too far on the first. You should have cued him to turn earlier. Then here on the second, he slips around well but you're just sitting on top of him…there is no energy in that push to third. And there, again, you should have cued him in two strides earlier instead of letting him decide where to turn."

"That was just an awful mess," I exhaled and my whole body shrunk into the chair.

"But, if you're paying attention now, you won't relive that past," Lauren lowered the cover of the laptop. "It's all mental for you. Do you understand that?"

After a hesitation, I nodded, "I have been racing for years and I know what I'm doing. Pep…Sergeant Pepper is a damn good horse that knows what he is doing. We just need to do it together."

"With YOU in charge and in control, not him," Lauren smiled.

I nodded as that bit of confidence grew, "I'm headed down to my uncle's place in Rock Springs, Wyoming tonight and that will give me a good seven hours to wrap my head around it."

"Good," She stood. "Sometimes, off the horse is the best time for thinking what you should be doing on the horse."

"Thank you, Lauren," I followed her out the door. "I'm feeling better about it. Hopefully, by Saturday, when we're in Tulsa I'll be ready."

"You keep telling yourself exactly what you told me about you both knowing your job, you'll get there, and you'll be the team to beat in the future."

Ace and Pete were loading horses into a trailer by the barn, and Lauren helped me catch and load the three cutting horses.

As I drove away from her ranch, the confidence in my stomach grew. I thought of nothing else but the races I had ran for the last six months and how I had slowly lost confidence in myself and let go of control and gave it all to the horse.

"I can do this."

Two days later, I was standing inside the camper portion of the horse trailer with Sergeant Pepper tied to the side and ready to go. Confidence had been building all week, but the nerves and anxiety began to creep in. I knew both Delaney and Lauren would be watching this weekend and my stomach swirled.   The bottle of Pendleton whisky was pulled from its hiding spot. Two shots later, the nerves began to ease, and I walked out of the trailer a bit numb.

The first barrel was overshot by three strides, and we were off angle for the second and it scraped into my knee before tipping over. The third barrel was overshot, and I pulled him back to just lope to the finish line in disgust and defeat.

After tucking the horse into the stall and securing him for the night, I stepped into the horse trailer and reached for the bottle. The decision was made, I wasn't going to Waco.

CHAPTER FIFTEEN

GRANGER

Text from Jack: You in Tulsa?

Text to Jack: Yeah, for about 30, headed south with Aaron

Text from Jack: Didn't I see you with Sammie Parkston the barrel racer in Othello?

Text to Jack: Yeah, she gave me a ride there. Why?

Text from Jack: She's at our trailer sitting in a chair being hit on by a roughie. Dude, she is wasted.

Text to Jack: Where are you?

It was 9:30 when I slung the saddle over my shoulder and lifted the bag from the back of Aaron's truck. I wandered to the horse stalls and looked for her horse. Pepper was there eating from his feeder and at his stall door was a boot I recognized as Sammie's. Hopefully it had fallen out of her bag, and she wasn't walking through the grounds with only one boot. I picked it up and searched for her truck that was only four horse trailers away. I could see the door was slightly opened so I dropped my bag and saddle on the ground and slowly stepped into the trailer.

"Sammie? It's Granger."

An empty bottle of Pendleton whisky lay on the floor alongside her purse. The wallet with money still inside was tossed up onto her bed. I turned and stepped out, closing the door firmly behind me. After a walk around the trailer to make sure it was secure, I tossed my saddle and bag into the back of her truck.

Text from Jack: We're next to the entrance sign.

When I arrived, Sammie was curled into a lawn chair with large glazed blue eyes staring blindly at a cowboy that was slowly running his fingers up her arm. He leaned toward her and whispered something. She rolled her eyes and tipped back in the chair and nearly fell out. My stomach clenched in disgust as the cowboy laughed and reached for her.

"Hands off, Buddy," I grumbled and shoved his hand away from her.

His head jerked toward me with a glare, "Back off."

"Granger is a friend of hers," Jack stepped in front of the cowboy. "He's going to make sure she makes it back to her trailer safe and alone."

I knelt next to Sammie as the cowboy stood with a 'fuck you' and walked off.

She could barely keep her eyes open, and they crossed as she tried to focus on me.

"Damn, Sammie," I muttered.

"Looks like she's missing a boot," Jack walked around the chair.

"I found it by her horse," I huffed with a shake of the head. "Come on girl," I pulled her out of the chair and her legs melted to the ground. "Damn, why did you do this to yourself?"

With Jack on one side and me on the other, we pulled her up enough I could scoop her up into my arms.

"You know where her trailer is?" Jack asked.

"Over by the stalls," I adjusted her in my arms and her head fell to my shoulder.

"Damn, good thing she's tiny," Jack chuckled. "Want help?"

"Nah, I can get her there, but thank you for getting ahold of me." I looked at him in all sincerity. "Hate to think what could have happened to her."

"Glad she landed at our trailer," Jack sighed. "Take care of her; she's a sweet girl."

I started the walk and half a dozen people tried to stop me to ask if something was wrong and why I was carrying an unconscious woman around the rodeo grounds. I just kept walking until we were outside her door. Lowering her legs to the ground, I wrapped my arms around her waist making her head tilt just under my chin. As I opened the door, a warmth ran down my shirt.

"Oh, fuck no," I groaned and gently laid her down onto the trailer floor then hesitantly looked down to brown vomit covering the front of my shirt and trailing down one pant leg. There wasn't a drop on her. "Dammit, son-of-a-bitch." I grumbled as the vomit soaked through the material and stuck to my skin. The rancid alcohol stench made me gag and I had to swallow hard to keep my own vomit down. I hurriedly unbuttoned the shirt and let it drop to the ground.

After glancing around the area, I slid off my boots and unbuckled my belt then dropped the jeans on the ground right in front of the door. I stepped around Sammie and into the trailer clad in just my black boxer briefs and socks.

It was going to be a bitch to try and push her up the steps to her bunk, so I lowered the couch to create the bed and began to drag her to it.

"WHAT THE FUCK ARE YOU DOING?"

I jerked around to see a tall cowboy with the angriest set of eyes I had ever seen.

"She's passed out and I'm trying to get her tucked in for the night," I blurted.

"In your fucking underwear?"

"Take a big whiff," I huffed and turned to pull a blanket and pillow from her upper bed and throw it on the lower converted sofa.

"Holy shit, what the hell is that?" He grimaced.

"She fucking puked on me; brown alcohol vomit," I growled. "It hit my shirt and jeans. I took them off, so I didn't get any on her or in the trailer. Now, help me lift her onto the bed."

He stepped up into the trailer and lifted her knees as I lifted her shoulders, and we carefully lowered her onto the bed. I tucked the pillow under her head as he flipped the blanket over the top of her then pulled off the remaining boot.

Just as I stepped back, her eyes opened, and she looked right at me.

"G-Ranger," She whispered then her eyes closed, and head fell to the side as she passed out.

"What the hell is a g-ranger?"

I turned to the cowboy with a huff, "Just a weird nickname she started calling me." I stretched out my hand to him. "Granger Miller."

"Ace Conners," He shook my hand, then stepped back. "You need to get some clothes on."

I laughed which finally made his threatening stance relax.

"Can you grab my bag from the back of her truck?"

His reaction when he thought I was going to hurt Sammie, gave me confidence to leave him with her. So, after putting clean clothes on, I left him at the trailer and took the vomit covered clothes to the water faucet by the stalls. When I returned, he had set up two lawn chairs in front of her door and was stretched out in one. I had no doubt he was there to protect her.

"How do you know Sammie?" I asked and tossed the wet clothes in the back of her truck.

"Met her a couple days ago at my cousin's ranch and knew she was coming here," he answered. "How do you know her?"

"She gave me a ride from Pendleton to Othello a couple of weeks ago."

He nodded then looked toward the trailer, "You see her ride today?"

"No, she told me she was going to be here, but we hadn't connected yet. I'm guessing that her drinking herself into oblivion is an indication of how she did."

"Blew out the first, tipped the second, and blew out the third…pretty ugly."

"Well, shit. I know she's been stressing herself."

"That's how I met her. My cousin, Lauren, was working with her to figure out what's wrong."

I just looked at him.

He smirked. "They figured it out, she just didn't take control."

"Do you know where she is supposed to be going next?"

"Lower Texas is what she told me."

"If she's running tomorrow, she should be on the road already," I stood and walked to her truck to retrieve her journal. "Damn, she runs tomorrow in Rosenburg, then heads to Waco for the second bracket."

"We're headed south in an hour," Ace stood. "We're still on a permit so we don't qualify at Waco."

"I'm up in Rosenburg tomorrow then over to Waco for the second bracket, too. I was riding down with a friend."

"Can you drive her rig instead?"

I shook my head. "I would if I could, but I've never driven a truck with a horse trailer attached and I'm not starting with a trailer this size on a Texas highway with a prized horse inside."

"Well, fuck," Ace exhaled and looked back toward the arena. "Taylor can drive our truck and I'll drive Sammie's. We'll get her down to Rosenberg."

"Who is Taylor?"

"My brother," He pulled a phone from his pocket. "Hey, bring the rig over toward the stalls so I can get some things out of it. You're driving home tonight, and I'm headed to Rosenberg to help a friend." He dropped the phone and slid it into his pocket without letting his brother respond. "I'll just stay with Sammie and have Taylor meet us in Waco when we get there."

"I can ride with you instead of Aaron," I offered. "If she wakes up before we get there, I can explain what happened."

Ace grinned, "I'd hate for her to think I'd kidnapped her."

I laughed. There was something about him and his Texas accent that I liked. Then there was the fact he was protective of Sammie.

"I'll go get her horse." Ace turned.

"I'll go let Aaron know I'm headed out."

By the time I returned, Pepper was in the trailer but there was no sign of Ace. I stepped up into the front of the trailer to check on Sammie. She was in the exact same position as we had left her. I shook my head and lowered to a knee beside her.

I swept her bangs away from her eyes and took the unobserved moment to take in every freckle, long lash, pink lips, high flushed cheek bones, and envisioned those mesmerizing blue eyes that were now hidden. I loved the color of her hair. "If only I had something to offer you," I whispered to her. "But, sweet, beautiful, funny Sammie, I literally have nothing."

A bang outside the door had me rising and tucking the blanket around her. Ace was carrying the two chairs to the back of the trailer. I climbed up onto the top bed and removed a large comforter and more pillows then placed them on the floor.

Ace stuck his head in the door with a raised brow.

"Just in case she falls out of bed," I grinned.

He chuckled and turned away to a younger version of himself standing next to the trailer.

"You must be Taylor," I stretched out a hand to him.

He nodded, "And you're G-ranger."

Ten minutes later, Taylor was following Sammie's truck out of the rodeo grounds.

In the eight-hour drive to Rosenberg, we checked on Sammie three times while Ace and I talked nearly non-stop. By the time we parked her trailer at the rodeo grounds, Ace had become the brother I always wished I had.

I set up the temporary pen outside her trailer just as she had done in Othello. Ace took care of the horse, and the food and water bucket.

"So, the question is, do we sleep in the trailer or in the truck?" Ace smirked.

"I'm going to say her truck," I looked at my phone. It was 6 o'clock in the morning. "The rodeo starts at two o'clock, so I'll set a timer for eleven in case she doesn't wake up."

We returned to the cab of the truck, leaned the seats back, and I fell asleep instantly.

I woke to pounding on my window.

Through squinted eyes, I looked out the window to a pair of very confused blue eyes.

"What the fuck?" Ace grumbled and his seat flew up and he turned to the pounding.

I rolled down the window.

"What the hell?" Sammie huffed and looked between us. "Ace? G-ranger? You two know each other? How in the hell did we end up here? And, where in the hell is here?"

I lifted the back of the seat and opened the door. "I got a call…"

She stood silently with eyes narrowed and hand on her forehead as we explained the evening and drive. Her face was a bit pale and eyes rimmed red.

When I finished, her shoulders lowered and she sighed as she turned back to her trailer, "I have a headache and need a shower." She disappeared into the trailer.

We glanced at each other with a shrug.

"She didn't look too happy that we brought her here," Ace mumbled.

Pepper had a fresh bucket of water, and his hay bag was full, so she had already taken care of him.

"I'm going to the arena," I lifted my bag and saddle from the back of the truck and walked away with Ace following.

When the rodeo began, I walked along the back of the arena and looked out to the horses warming up. I could see Sammie on Pepper walking along the edge. Ace walked up next to me.

"Well, at least it looks like she recovered enough to ride," I smirked at him.

"We'll see. I've drank the night before a few times, but I'm not sure I could ride after passing out like that."

I chuckled, "I have to admit, I've had a few nights almost that bad and had to get up and ride the next day."

"Me, too...almost that bad."

I didn't see her again before I walked up onto the platform behind the chutes. My horse was already loaded so I focused on him. All thoughts of everyone melted away when I set the saddle down on top of the horse named Harold. I didn't think of her again until I was picking myself up out of the dirt after an 84-point ride. I wondered if she had watched.

It was enough to place second in the whole rodeo. Not bad.

With a satisfied exhale, I gathered my bag, saddle and walked back to her trailer. Ace fell in next to me.

"Nice ride, but that dismount..." he grinned.

"Thanks, you seen her?"

"She was still riding last I saw."

We walked to the arena in time to see her step down off the dark bay horse and lead him to a hitching post next to the barn. She walked to her trailer, and we followed.

The door was open, so I tapped on the trailer and opened the door to glance in. She was on her tip toes reaching up into the tall cupboard, her eyes shot to me as if she was caught with a hand in the proverbial cookie jar. Her shoulders relaxed as she lowered with a bottle of Pendleton whiskey in her hand.

CHAPTER SIXTEEN

GRANGER

"What the hell, Sammie," I mumbled and stepped into the trailer with Ace right behind me.

"Don't do that," Ace shook his head.

"I have a headache, I'm stressed, and it helps me calm down." She mumbled and started to unscrew the top.

I reached out and swiped the bottle out of her hands, "It doesn't help."

"How the hell do you know?" She growled and reached for the bottle.

It wasn't too hard to push her away as I took off the lid and tossed it into the sink.

"You son-of-a-bitch." She yelled and dove for the sink, but I held her away. "Get the hell out." She took a step back and threw something at me. Her phone hit my chest then fell to the floor under the table.

I ignored her demand, and shook my head, "Sammie, drinking isn't the answer, and you shouldn't be riding Pepper when you've been drinking."

"It's none of your business." Her eyes narrowed and nostrils flared as she snarled before turning her back on me.

"Then I'll speak for your horse and your parents," I huffed. "You told me yourself that you're trying to live up to them...for them giving you Pepper to fulfill your dreams. What you're proving now is Christine and those other two friends you left behind saying you didn't deserve..."

She twirled to face me with both hands in fists. Face flushed and blue eyes shining in anger, she hit me full force in the chest, but I barely moved.

"They may have given that horse to me, but I earned every dollar they spent," Her words were full of fire. "From the first moments I can remember I was helping with chores; feeding, cleaning stalls, brushing horses. I have built thousands of miles of fences, scratches from barbed wire, blisters from digging ditches, branding, been pooped on by cows and horses. I've spent thousands and thousands of hours training to compete to be the best that I can be. Barely slept some nights or didn't sleep at all during foaling season or competitions." Her eyes narrowed and glistened with voice tight. "I have held and cried over stillborn foals and dying retired horses that I had known and loved my entire life. I have been bitten, broke a leg and an arm, dislocated shoulder, hundreds of bumps and bruises, and a concussion." She took in a shaking inhale then growled. "I earned that damn horse!"

"Then prove it," I huffed. "Go get on him, run the damn race, show everyone who thinks you're nothing more than a princess on her pretty pony that you are the barrel racer that deserves to command a horse like Pepper."

She bared her teeth at me with fingers clenched as if she wanted to claw my face. "Grrraah…" Furious, she twirled back around and pushed past Ace.

"You're the boss," Ace said firmly. "Don't just let him run the race, YOU run the race."

The door slamming open answered him, and when the door slammed closed, Ace turned to me with wide "holy shit" eyes.

"Glad I'm not you," he smirked.

We both lowered to look through the window to watch her stomp toward the hitching post.

"I'm just going to wait in here until she leaves," I whispered, and we both chuckled.

Sammie mounted the horse, but there was no sign of aggression or anger, but every movement was precise and firm.

Once she disappeared into the mass of vehicles, I retrieved her phone from under the table.

"You didn't really pour out a bottle of Pendleton?" Ace glanced over at the sink.

I lifted the bottle, "Oh, hell no. I tossed it in top up so it wouldn't spill." I placed it back into the cupboard.

Ace shook his head as we stepped out of the trailer, "Damn, she was pissed,"

"I have never seen anyone snarl and growl like that."

"Well, I have a feeling if we hang around that red head, it won't be the last time we see it."

"You mean if we live through the next time we see her," I began walking to the arena and listened to the announcer. "Sounds like tie-down is over so they will be setting up the barrels, we have time to get there and watch. I have her phone, so I can record it for her."

Ace laughed, "Let's record it with our phones and if it turns out well, we can send it to her."

"Yeah, so she doesn't have it on her phone if it's another catastrophe."

"If she is like my cousin Jamie, she'll want it from two different angles."

"I'll go to the bucking chutes."

"And I'll go to the fence by the second barrel."

We separated at the bleachers, and I maneuvered to the chute platform by the first barrel. I barely knew Sammie, but it didn't stop my stomach from tightening in anxiety when her name was called out. I could see her calmly walking toward the shadowed entry lane. She hesitated a moment then leaned forward.

She flew into the arena and whipped around the first barrel so tight I thought for sure it was going over and I caught my breath. I didn't exhale again until she rounded the second and her whole body was pushing the horse to encourage him to run faster. The third barrel was just as tight as the first, but I knew it wasn't going over. Sammie was in control and running her race. When the clock stopped, the crowd roared at the new leading time. She was two one hundredths of a second faster than all the previous riders as she ran out of the arena.

"Hell, yeah!" I shouted and turned to look for Ace.

His fist was in the air as he yelled after her. I made my way around the arena to him, and we both laughed.

"Maybe she won't claw your eyes out now," Ace grinned

We sat on the bleachers and watched the remaining racers, but not one matched her time. Her phone started chiming with alerts.

"She won," I exhaled in great relief.

"Not only won this one, but it qualifies her for the Houston rodeo."

"Which is fucking big."

We both watched the videos we recorded then turned to each other with a grin.

"Damn," Ace chuckled. "I guess it is safe to send them to her."

"Damn, that horse is spectacular. She had every reason to believe in him."

We sent the videos and sat quietly watching the bull riding.

"So, how long do you think we should hide-out here?" I looked out to the trailers but couldn't see her or her trailer.

"Well, she has to cool him down, then she'll pamper him a bit after she gets him in the stall."

"…which she probably has done by now."

"I'm okay with watching the bull riding and see if she shows up."

"That should give her some time to cool off," I leaned back on the bleacher and tried to relax but her phone kept chiming and reminding me I had to face her.

When the last bull rider walked out of the arena, Sammie had not appeared. With a sigh, we stood and walked back to her trailer. There was no sign of her as we approached.

"Let's check on Pepper before we go to the trailer," Ace suggested.

"Yeah, if she is still with him, she'll be in a more forgiving mood."

Ace looked at me with a shake of the head and a grin.

The horse was in his stall, blanket on him, and head in the feeder. But there was no new bedding on the ground.

"She have the stall for another night?" Ace asked.

"I don't remember reading that in her journal," I shrugged then turned back toward her trailer. "Alright, let's get this over with."

We passed a dozen people who congratulated me on my second-place finish.

"Funny, how I forgot all about that," I grinned at Ace. "That's about $1800 in the pot for the new truck."

"Slowly crawling away from that junk yard truck," he teased.

I laughed with a nod.

When we approached Sammie's trailer, there was no sign of her. I stood at the door and after a glance at Ace, I knocked.

There was no response.

"Sammie?" I called out and knocked a second time.

There was still no answer, so I slid her phone out of my pocket and knocked a third time. When she didn't answer, I opened the door.

A faint grating sound came from inside; with Ace right behind me, we stepped into the trailer and looked for the source. The odd noise was coming from Sammie who was lying across her bed, fully clothed and with boots on. She was sound asleep and snoring loudly.

"Well, then," I chuckled and looked back at Ace, "I guess getting furious and barrel racing tuckers a princess out."

He chuckled, "I'll get her journal and see where she had herself sleeping tonight."

I placed her phone on the shelf next to the bed and followed him to her truck.

"She has a stall in Waco for the rest of the week," Ace tossed her journal back on the truck seat. "What do you think?"

"It's only three hours away. Let's just load the horse and get on the road. I doubt she will get upset if we get her there early instead of the middle of the night."

A half hour later, we were pulling out of the fairgrounds.

"Is there a Costco around here?" I asked and looked it up on my phone.

"Probably, why?"

"She likes their already cooked roasted chicken, so I thought I'd buy her a couple as a peace offering," I grinned.

"Apology through food. You sure chocolate wouldn't be better?"

"Well, if it doesn't work on her, a big chocolate frosted, chocolate cake will help me."

She was still asleep when we stopped at the Costco in Katy. I bought three chickens and set them in the sink. The cake was secured in the oven. The smell of the chicken should have woken her, but she was curled up in the middle of the bed and breathing deeply. After admiring her freckles again, I threw a blanket over her before walking away.

Ace was on the phone when I stepped into the truck.

"…she's sleeping, and Granger and I are driving her to Waco." After a pause, he nodded as if the person he was talking to could see him. "Just tell them we'll have her call as soon as she wakes but let them know she is perfectly fine and safe." He tossed his phone on the seat, "Her parents couldn't get ahold of her and got worried. They knew I was here too, so they called Lauren."

He turned the truck onto the highway and the constant talking started. We never ran out of topics to discuss.

Ace turned into the large parking area in Waco, "We can park anywhere tonight. There is plenty of room to move it tomorrow."

"She usually parks close to the stalls."

Once we were parked, we met at the door of the trailer to enter together with apprehensive glances at each other. Sammie was sitting at the table stabbing one of the roasted chickens with a fork. She was now in sweatpants and a hooded sweatshirt with a large horse on the front. Her hair was pulled back letting her blue eyes stand out as she looked up at us. She didn't say anything; she just placed a large piece of chicken in her mouth.

We slid onto the bench seat across from her.

"I got a message to your parents that you were sleeping and would call when you woke," Ace told her.

"Must be why my phone is so noisy," She mumbled around the food.

The phone was still sitting where I had placed it.

"You haven't checked your messages?" I asked in surprise.

She shrugged in disinterest and took another bite.

"They are probably trying to congratulate you," Ace shook his head.

"For what?" She stabbed the chicken again.

Ace and I looked at each other then went back to her.

"Sammi, you won Rosenberg," I smiled.

Her fork stopped mid-air and she looked between the two of us as if I was lying to her.

"You won," Ace confirmed.

She still didn't seem to believe us, so I pulled out my phone and pulled up the results from the rodeo. The Facebook page already had a picture of her rounding the third barrel and announcing her as the winner. I turned the phone to her.

Her blue eyes widened when she saw the image.

"That's a fierce picture," Ace grinned. "Here's the video."

He turned his phone to her as the announcer called her name. Her fork slowly lowered to the ground, and chin dropped open.

"It really felt good," she whispered.

"It really looked good," I grinned. "You want to see the video I took from the chutes?"

"Of course," she nodded.

Since her hands were busy with the chicken, I started the video and held the phone for her. She stared at it. At the turn around the third barrel, the crowd cheered and as she crossed the timer my voice boomed, "Hell, yeah!"

Her eyes didn't leave the phone as the video replayed.

"Can you send those to me?" She finally leaned back and looked at us.

"Already done," Ace said.

"That's why my phone has been so noisy," She slid off the seat and retrieved her phone. "Well, heck, look at that."

"What?" Ace and I asked at the same time.

"Dozens of messages," Her eyes lit with delight.

As she typed, Ace retrieved us both a chicken and we demolished them, then he went for the cake. When he pulled it out of the oven, Sammie's phone was placed on the table. We didn't talk as three forks dove into the uncut cake. Sammie watched the videos again.

She set the phone and fork down with a slight smile, "I need to get that bad ass horse out of the trailer. Oh, and I call him Sergeant now because he is mine and we are a team." After sliding on her boots, she opened the door then stopped and looked back at me. "Last time I looked you were at 27."

Ace looked at me in confusion, but I smiled at Sammie, "I ended at 25."

Her grin widened, "You beat your goal. Congratulations."

While she took care of her horse, Ace and I finished off the cake while I explained her comment. When we walked outside, she had the horse tied to the side of the trailer, a green Bemer blanket lay over him and she was sitting on the ramp typing on her phone. Two lawn chairs were sitting next to the door, so we slid onto them. Sammie glanced up at us then went back to typing as Ace and I began talking.

When Sammie stood and reached for the blanket on the horse, I turned to her, "You need any help?"

"No, I got it," she whispered and walked the horse towards the stalls.

"Think she is still pissed at me?" I glanced at Ace.

He shrugged, "What horse did you draw for tomorrow?"

"Hickock."

And we started talking again.

It was an hour before Sammie returned. The sun had gone down, but Ace and I remained in the chairs and tried talking but we were fighting staying awake. The truck was locked, and Sammie had the keys so we couldn't get in it to sleep.

She stopped in front of us and glanced between us, "I was thinking, there is no reason for you to sleep in the truck. There are two beds in the trailer, and you can just sleep on those.

My body sighed in relief, "You sure?"

Ace was already standing and folding his chair to tuck it under the trailer. I slowly rose, waiting for her answer.

"Yes," she nodded and opened the door of the trailer.

She hit the button and the slide-out with the sofa above it moved to create a wider floor space. From the storage under the cushions, she pulled out two pillows, sheets, and thick blankets then handed them to us. Ace was already converting the table into a bed. I had no doubt, he was as relieved as I was.

She locked the doors, then made her way to her bed, "I have a brother and a father; I've seen men's legs before," she chuckled. "So, I'd appreciate it if you didn't wear dirty jeans on the bedding." She smiled innocently then pulled the curtains closed that blocked her sleeping area from the rest of the trailer.

Within minutes, Ace and I had the beds made and I was sliding down onto the comfortable cushions. It was so much better than a truck seat.

Ace turned the light off and the trailer was so dark I couldn't see the ceiling above me.

"Dang, your black-out curtains work well," Ace said into the dark as he stumbled to his bed.

"Mom seems to think I get cranky if I don't get enough sleep," Sammie chuckled.

Neither Ace nor I said a word.

I started to relax after the very long weekend.

"Ace?" Sammie whispered.

"Yeah?" He exhaled.

"Thank you for getting us here, I'll never forget it and I owe you big time," Her voice was soft but earnest.

"It's been an adventure so far," he chuckled. "I look forward to the rest of the week."

Silence descended and I began to wonder why she had left me out of the apology. Maybe she was still furious with me. It was disappointing.

CHAPTER SEVENTEEN

GRANGER

"G-ranger?" Her voice was barely audible.

"Yeah?" I took in a breath in anticipation.

"This princess and her pretty pony will never forget what you did for us," she whispered. "I know it isn't in your nature to be such an…ass, but you confronting me like that…pushing me…there was no doubt my issue was mental, and I thought Lauren saying I wasn't taking control would fix the issue. When I was yelling at you, I realized it was because I didn't believe I deserved Sergeant Pepper and the belief my parents had in me."

"You more than deserve him," Ace said.

"And you proved it," I added.

"That run felt so good," Her voice was full of wonder. "I think it was the best run of my life…so freeing. I truly felt as one with Sergeant."

"I can't wait to see your run here in Waco," I said honestly.

"Agreed," Ace added.

She chuckled softly, "We're going to kick ass."

The trailer grew silent and the last thing I remembered was hearing a snore from Ace.

Ace's phone ringing interrupted the silence of the morning. We were all three awake but scrolling on our phones. Sammie had already been at the stalls taking care of Sergeant and had just crawled back into bed.

"What?" Ace answered. "You leave the horses and trailer at Greenfield's place? Ok...two trailers down from the stalls. Black and silver trailer, black dually truck."

"Plates say PPH 4," Sammie called out.

Ace repeated the comment then slowly sat up on the edge of his bed.

"My brother, Taylor, has arrived," Ace grumbled and slid on his jeans.

I was quickly up and doing the same, then stuffed all the bedding into the cubby hole.

"Did he bring coffee?" Sammie chuckled but hadn't moved from her bed.

Ace laughed, "As a matter of fact, he did."

"Awesome!" Sammie laughed. "I'll get out of bed for that."

Ace and I were standing just outside the trailer door when Taylor backed his large grey truck alongside Sammie's. Ace lowered the tail gate making a table for the three 4-cup drink carriers Taylor handed him.

"You can stop by anytime," I grinned at him as he handed me the fourth carrier.

"Not sure what everyone liked, so I got a couple different ones," Taylor chuckled and lifted one for himself.

He turned as the door to the trailer opened and Sammie stepped out in blue jeans and a white hooded sweatshirt. Her red hair held a slight curl down to her shoulders and the blue eyes seemed to beam along with her wide smile.

"Damn!" Taylor coughed with a grin causing her to laugh. "I call dibs."

"Fuck, Taylor," Ace shook his head. "Be a little more mature and respectful than that."

"Dibs?" Sammie chuckled.

"Yeah," Taylor teased. "I call dibs on you being my future wife."

I felt the inkling of irritation crawl up my spine but they both laughed, and she stepped out of the trailer and slid an arm around his.

"You bring me coffee on a day I'm recovering from a hangover, and I'll let you have dibs." She laughed as he handed her his coffee cup.

The chairs were set out and we spent the morning talking about the weekend so far and what to do with our time off between performances.

Taylor and Ace became our biggest fans during the performances and then our evening cooks.

"We get to celebrate two second place finishes for Waco tonight," Taylor grinned as he flipped steaks on the cook stove attached to Sammie's trailer.

"Out of the three races so far," Ace grinned, "Sammie has a first and second place, and Granger has managed three second place finishes in a row followed by interesting landings in the dirt."

They held up their assorted drinks and tipped them to me.

"Just trying to get a decent truck and maybe a brand-new pair of chaps. I've never had new ones," I laughed.

"What color?" Sammie shot up in her chair. "I'll help design them. I've designed for our family for years. Want me to show you?"

The rest of the evening was spent designing new chaps I didn't know I would even buy.

I stood on the back of the chutes and tried to get my mind to think of the horse and not what winning the rodeo would mean to the rest of the year. Just one horse at a time.

"What are you doing?"

I jolted out of my haze and turned to see the stock contractor glaring at me.

"What?"

"You're two riders out and you're just standing there."

"Fuck," I whispered and leaned down to the horse to adjust the saddle as he worked on the flank strap. "What's he do?"

"Buck," he grumbled with a smart-ass smirk.

"Good to know," I nodded as if he was serious. "I'll try to prepare myself for that."

After a ride that put me in second place again, I jogged back to the chutes and climbed up next to him to shake his hand. "Good thing you told me he bucks. That really helped a lot."

We both laughed as he moved down the line to help the next rider.

I was standing in the bleachers next to Ace and Taylor when Sammie's name was called.

"She's ready for this one," Ace exhaled in anticipation. "She had the third fastest time over all the brackets, so she has two after her."

"She'll get it," Taylor said confidently.

"She just has to..." I started but stopped when she flew into the arena.

All three of us leaned around the barrels with her and by the third we realized what we were doing and laughed as we yelled for her. She ran out in first-place but the next racer took it away from her. After the last rider flew out of the arena, Sammie took second place for the whole rodeo.

"Hell ya!" We yelled and jogged down the bleachers and out to find her.

She was standing next to Sergeant with her arms around his neck as he tucked his head over her shoulder. Her eyes were closed, and a happy smile graced her face. Three phones took the picture.

When she finally stepped away from the horse and saw us watching she grinned and said the three words every man wants to hear, "Let's have pizza."

Five large pizzas were ordered and delivered right to the trailer. Most of the parking area was empty and a few cowboys came to join us.

My phone alert rang out as I stuffed empty boxes into the rodeo grounds garbage cans.

Text from Aaron: I'll be there about 5 am to pick you up. Congrats on second

I glanced up at the group and sighed. Rodeo life changed day to day for me, but I sure wished moments like this would last longer.

"Mom was nagging on us to stay out of trouble," Taylor chuckled.

"We've pretty much stayed out of trouble," Ace grinned. "But we have a few more Texas rodeos to hit before we head home."

"What about you?" I asked Sammie and slid back onto my chair.

"I'm headed to Oklahoma to stay with my brother for a week then take a few horses back home," she answered and looked at me. "And you?"

"Aaron will be here at five in the morning, and we're headed to Redmond for the Circuit Finals."

"Well," Ace lifted his bottle in the air. "Here's to the fun of the last couple of weeks and making new friends and a lot of new memories."

"And to my heroes," Sammie tipped her bottle to both Ace then myself. "I will never forget what you guys did for Sergeant and me."

"Well, Princess, you and your pretty pony just keep kicking ass," I grinned at her.

"You, too," she chuckled.

"We may not have ridden here, but we put some money in the bank in Tulsa," Taylor huffed with a teasing grin.

"Keep at it then," I smirked. Our introduction may have been rough, but I liked him nearly as much as I liked his brother. They both had good hearts, enthusiasm for the rodeo life, and big futures ahead of them. And they were funny. I wished I would have had a brother to grow up with like they had each other.

At 4:50 in the morning, I slid to the side of the bed and tapped Taylor's leg since he was sleeping on the floor. His eyes barely opened until I waved my hand to the bed. He quickly scrambled and took my place.

His hand shot up to me, "Granger, it has been a pleasure meeting you and can't wait to run into you again down the road."

I shook his hand and grinned, "It's been an adventure."

"Good luck at the Circuit Finals."

I stepped out of the trailer just as Aaron pulled in.

For a week, I could think of nothing but Sammie and the Conner brothers' families. It made me miss mine that much more. I considered the Rawlins and Martin my family and I knew they thought of me that way too, but it just wasn't the same. I had no thoughts of seeing my father, but every day the need to see my mother grew.

After placing third at the Finals rodeo, I drove straight from Redmond to Walla Walla.

I pulled to the curb across from the house and turned off the engine. There wasn't a car in the driveway, so I leaned back in the seat and pulled out my phone. After twenty minutes of scrolling through Facebook and watching videos, a blue car turned down the driveway.

When it stopped, three doors opened, and a man stepped out of the driver's side door. Two kids around 6 and 7 years-old crawled out of the back seat.

I watched until they disappeared into the house. She must have moved. With a sigh, I set the phone in the holder then, just as my fingers touched the keys, an approaching white car turned on their blinker. I hesitated. When the car pulled to the curb directly in front of the house, I waited until the door opened; my head lifted as if I could see over the door.

When the driver stepped out, I took a deep breath and opened the truck door. I was halfway across the street when she shut the door then turned to look at me. When the tears glistened in her eyes, I knew I had made the right decision.

"Hi, Mom."

"Granger…" Her voice shook. "Son…I…"

I really didn't know what to say, but she hadn't aged in the two years since I had last seen her. Dark blonde hair cut to shoulder length and tucked behind her ears, and she was wearing a pink flowered shirt I had seen her wear a dozen times. There were just a few new wrinkles that appeared when her hesitant smile grew. "It's great to see you…you look great."

"I had no way of finding you." She whispered and took a step closer. "I didn't know where you went. I've been worried."

"I'm doing fine. Just traveling with friends."

Her eyes searched mine as if looking for the truth. "Granger, I wanted to find you and tell you that you weren't a shitty son."

I huffed and felt my throat constrict and tears rise. Out of all the things I thought she would say, that wasn't one of them.

"I was mad because Dad didn't want to be married to you and left me behind." I whispered, and her tears fell making my stomach constrict. "I wasn't mad at you; I was mad he left and there was nothing I could do about it. It took me a long time to realize that, then you moved us here and then disappeared."

"I tried my best to make sure to keep a roof over our heads and food in the cupboard," she cried. "It was so expensive in Bellevue and even here I had to get two jobs to cover the rent and the expenses your father left me with."

I was stunned, "What?"

"When he left, he just LEFT," she explained. "Me, you, the house, bills...everything."

"You had two jobs?" I gasped.

Her eyes narrowed in confusion, "Well, yes. Didn't you know that?"

"No, I just thought you were...or you didn't...that you didn't want to be around me because I'd been so...shitty to you."

"Oh, Son," she cried again. "The jobs were so close together that I would sleep in my car between ending one and starting the other."

"Mom, I had no idea."

"Now that I think about it, why would you?" She smiled hesitantly and leaned back against the car. "We didn't really talk even when we were in the same room together. I wasn't going to have you worrying about all the finances."

"I would have helped if I'd known," A deep sigh escaped. "I would have gotten a job to help."

"I have no doubt you would have, but it was not your responsibility to pay for your father's debts. I just thought you didn't want to see me, or I would have come home between jobs more often."

She smiled hesitantly and her fingers nervously played with her necklace. I couldn't believe it. She was wearing the turquoise necklace I had given her the first Christmas I left for the Rawlin's home. There was the truth.

I leaned against the car next to her and shook my head, "It tears me apart, Mom. I thought you were staying away on purpose because you didn't want to see me."

We stood quietly for a moment before her phone vibrated. She looked at the message and typed into the phone.

"It's Carl...I rent the basement to him and his two sons." She glanced back at the house and waved. "He was worried and wanted to know if he needed to come out."

"So, if you're renting to him, you don't have two jobs anymore?"

"No, the old bills are paid now, and I got a good raise in one job and his rent helps with the payment here, so I was able to quit the second job."

"So, what do you do with all your free time now?" I teased with a smile.

She laughed, "The first month, I slept a lot, then got into fixing up the house. Repainting and such. But I thought of you every day and wondered what you were doing, how you were..."

"I thought a lot about you, too."

I slid my arm across her shoulders and pulled her in close. She turned and held on to me, after a moment, she began to cry.

"I'm so relieved you're OK, and so disappointed we didn't talk all those years ago." She leaned away and wiped away the tears.

"Well, there isn't anything we can do to get them back, but we can make sure the next sixty or so we talk." I hugged her closer again as she nodded with a pleased smile. "And, if you want to know what I'm doing, just Google my name."

"Seriously?" She gasped and slid her phone from her pocket. After a moment, she gasped. "A cowboy? How in the hell did you end up riding bucking horses?"

We talked until the sun disappeared, and the stars were shining bright.

With a relenting sigh, she looked at her phone, at the house, then to me. "Can you stay?"

"My room the same?" I teased.

"It's painted," she chuckled. "Bedding changed and clothes boxed and in a closet downstairs."

I looked out at my truck then back to her, "Well, then, since it has clean sheets, I can stay the night, but I have a fencing job to get to tomorrow."

"I'll fix breakfast for you before you leave, and we can talk some more."

"That works for me but there is one thing you need to know."

"What's that?" She glanced at me with a bit of fear in her eyes.

"I hate pancakes." I grinned as she gasped.

"Seriously? You loved them when you were little."

We walked up the cement pathway to the house.

"I definitely outgrew them."

When her hand gripped the doorknob to the house, she turned and looked at me. Her blue eyes searching mine. "Granger," she whispered. "We are starting fresh; you're not going to disappear?"

"Mom, I won't disappear if you won't."

Her tears welled again as we wrapped each other in a strong hug.

I drove back to spend Thanksgiving with her and from the moment I drove into the driveway she was at my side. As hesitant the first trip to see her had been, this visit was full of humor, cooking, and doing nothing but watching football together.

My phone rang late in the afternoon, but I didn't recognize the number.

"Hello?"

"Granger Miller?" the woman's voice asked.

"Yeah," I said hesitantly.

"This is Lauren Conners, Ace's cousin."

CHAPTER EIGHTEEN

ACE

"What time is it?" Taylor yawned and stretched from the passenger seat.

I turned off the engine and looked out at the quiet ranch…home. It had been four weeks since we had driven away.

"Three-forty," I answered with a sigh. "Let's just sleep in the camper instead of waking them up."

"Yeah," he yawned again. "Monte and Liam would have us up for another hour with questions."

After releasing the horses in the pasture, we had three solid hours of sleep before the bangs started on the door and it unceremoniously opened.

"YOU'RE HERE!" Monte yelled and stomped up the few steps.

"Why didn't you come in?" Liam scrambled in behind him and crawled onto the lower bunk with Taylor.

"Didn't want to wake you up," I scooted to the edge of the bed so Monte could sit next to me.

Both were dressed and ready for school.

"How far away did you go this time?" Liam asked.

"Rosenberg and Waco then over to Arizona."

"I heard it was hot there," Monte said.

Taylor laughed, "Yeah, it was hot, but we stayed inside."

"With girls?" Liam grinned.

"There might have been girls involved now and then," Taylor chuckled.

"Did you win?" Liam asked.

"We sent videos to Mom to show you," Taylor yawned.

"She showed us, but it didn't say that you won or not. Quincy looked good, though," Liam shrugged. "When are you going to teach us how to tie calves, too?"

"When you..." Taylor started.

"On Quincy?" Monte asked quickly.

"You probably want to start with a slower horse at first," I chuckled.

"Old Jerry would work?" Monte twisted his neck to look at me. "Wasn't he one of your first?"

"Yeah, he'll work, he is over at Barry's with his horses," I nodded. "Have you been practicing with the hocks and steer head we left for you?"

"When we can," Liam sighed. "Dad has us pretty busy with motocross and every time we pick up a rope, he has something for us to do."

"I don't think he wants us roping," Monte exhaled.

I didn't say anything, if I did, it would just be confirming what he said.

"When you get home from school, we'll get some roping in then we'll get you on Old Jerry so you can start throwing off of him," I sat up and caught a glimpse of Rob before he disappeared around the open door of the camper.   No doubt he heard what Monte had said.

I glanced down at Taylor to see him staring out the door. He looked up at me and we shared a look of understanding.

"You two better head out to catch the bus," I said and pushed Monte off the bed to his giggles. "We'll be here for a week and can get some roping done."   I didn't care what Rob wanted. My little brothers wanted to learn, and I wanted to teach them.

Taylor and I followed the boys out the door then watched the pair run to the house for their school backpacks. We walked out to the barn to check on the horses.

"Man, I can't wait for a long hot shower," I called out to Taylor with a grin.

"It's only been two...no, three days since either of us took one," he laughed.

"And I'm ready for an all-day nap."

Taylor laughed and disappeared into one of the stalls. When he walked out, the door to the house burst open with Liam and Monte stomping out. As they neared, I could hear them swearing.

"What's up Lil Bros?" Taylor asked.

"Just a warning, Dad is in a really bad mood," Liam grumbled.

"He's getting ready to go ride and said after school we have to go to a club meeting and can't ride horses." Monte grumbled as they walked by us.

"They are boring," Liam huffed. "All we do is sit in a chair and fall asleep."

The school bus appeared, and they ran down the length of the driveway.

I looked at Taylor with a loud exhale of exasperation, "If it wasn't for that long hot shower and clean sheets on a big bed, I'd just get back in the camper."

"Me, too. But I also want to see Mom in person and not just over the phone."

I nodded and walked to the truck, "I'll move it down the driveway and out of the way."

"Put it in the shade, just in case." He smirked then walked back into the barn.

I backed the truck and trailer behind the tractors and hay trailer. It was the normal parking spot so it was out of the way and Rob couldn't complain. When I stepped out of the truck, Taylor was nearly at the house. The front door flew open allowing Rob's raised voice to echo across the ranch. I couldn't hear what he said but there was a lot of hostility in the words.

Just as I took a step, Rob walked out onto the deck with Mom right behind him. He turned and with both hands shoved her so hard she fell backward over the patio table with legs in the air. She disappeared behind the table and chairs.

Taylor and I took off running.

"You fucking son-of-a-bitch!" Taylor yelled.

Rob spun around and as Taylor ran up the first few steps, he kicked out and his heavy motocross boot hit Taylor in the chest sending him flying backward and sprawling out on the ground.

I couldn't run any faster and there was nothing I could do when Rob jumped from the second step, flew high in the air, and when he landed, one heavy boot was on the ground, and the other stomped onto Taylor's shoulder. Mom's scream filled the air as she scrambled from the tipped over table and chairs.

"Rob! You son-of-a-bitch! I'm going to kill you!" I yelled and tried to run faster.

Taylor was motionless.

Rob whirled around and ran down the side of the house to his motocross bike. I was twenty feet behind him when it roared to life, and he sped away with dirt flying out behind him. I ran for Monte's bike.

"Ace! Help me!" Mom's panic-stricken voice called out.

Rob, who was speeding away; he had been racing most of his life, there was no way I could catch him. I turned back with my hand already reaching into my pocket for the phone.

"Taylor?" Mom leaned over him with her left arm tucked to her side, but there was no movement from Taylor.

When I reached her, she looked up with tears streaming from fear filled eyes. Taylor was unconscious with blood streaming from a gash on the side of the head. I ran up the stairs and into the kitchen to grab towels. Mom took them and immediately pressed them against the gash as I hit the 911 on the phone.

"Are you hurt?" I asked with a voice high and shaking in panic and fury.

"I'll be ok." There were bleeding scrapes and scratches along one arm and her left wrist was already swelling.

"911, what is your emergency?"

In the distance, I could hear an engine roaring. I wasn't sure if it was Rob, but I wasn't taking any chances. I handed the phone to Mom, then ran into the house and to my room. A pistol and rifle were brought out to the patio.

"What are you doing with those?" Mom cried with wide eyes.

"That son-of-a-bitch is not getting near anyone in this family again," I growled. "He attempts to come back, and I'll let him know he's not welcome."

She didn't answer, instead she turned away with the phone in one hand and the other holding the towels to Taylor's head. His face had turned white, and his breathing was shallow with a slight wheeze with every breath. I knelt next to them and slid an arm around her and pulled her close while she talked on the phone.

Numbness, anger, disbelief, fear, and desperation raced through me until she lowered the phone. Sirens filled the air.

"Has he ever hit you before?" I asked through gritted teeth.

"Not really...no...he shoved me once a couple weeks ago, but never hitting or showed signs of aggression like that. Not to the boys...I just don't..."

Tears slid down her cheeks as she leaned into me and held Taylor's hand. My gaze moved to his shoulder that had taken the full force of Rob's weight. There was no doubt it was broken or worse.

We were silent as the sirens grew closer and my eyes watched in the distance for any sign of my stepfather returning.

CHAPTER NINETEEN

ACE

My hand shook as I pushed Barry's number as the ambulance with my mother and brother inside turned onto the main road. Three police cars had come, then they went on the search for Rob. One police car with two officers remained. They had introduced themselves as Officers Goldstrom and Sharp.

"Ace!" Barry answered. "You back yet?"

"Rob attacked Mom and Taylor."

"What?" He growled. "That's what those sirens were for?"

"Taylor is bad, still unconscious, Mom's banged up and bleeding a bit."

"Where are they?"

"Just left in the ambulance. I'm at the ranch with the police who are out looking for Rob."

"I'm on my way, then you can tell me what happened."

I lowered the phone but held it tightly in my hand, "Family friend, he's on his way."

"How far away is he?" Officer Goldstrom asked. She was tall with short black hair and her voice was low and full of pent-up emotions.

I pointed to the roof of his house that was visible across the horse pasture, "Just there. He'll be here in just a few minutes."

"How are you holding up?"

"I'm not," I answered with hands still trembling. "It happened so damn fast; I couldn't get to them."

"It's not your fault," she said firmly. "You did the best you could for your family."

"My family..." I exhaled and felt the knot in my stomach tighten. "My two younger brothers, thirteen and twelve, left for school minutes before it happened. Rob is my stepfather, but their natural father. I need to get to them before they find out from anyone else."

"I'll call the school and see if they can watch over the boys until someone gets there," she said and pulled out her phone.

"I have to ask about the guns on the porch rail," Officer Sharp said. He was shorter and older than Goldstrom but broad and muscular.

I nodded in understanding, "After he left, I went in and brought them out in case he returned."

"I would have done the same thing," he sighed. "But you need to know, until we find Rob, we have to take control of the guns."

"He attacked them, not the other way around," I growled then turned to look under the edge of the roof above the porch. "Mom has security cameras aimed at the door and porch for when she is alone out here. I don't know if they were on."

"Let's check it out," Officer Sharp said and turned toward the house.

"I can look on my phone." I was nauseous at the thought of watching the attack again, and internally hoped the cameras were off.

185

Much to my distress, and the officers' delight, the cameras were still on.

"The camera activates with motion and will stay on one minute or until the motion stops." There were over a dozen files saved. The video covered the top of the doors and out ten feet of patio in front of it including the table and chairs. The steps were also visible, and ten feet down the paved walkway.

"Is there audio, too?" Officer Goldstrom asked.

"No..." I exhaled in relief.

The first video of the day showed the doors open with Monte and Liam hands waving in the air and high fiving each other when they saw the truck and trailer. They had truly been overjoyed to see their big brothers come home. I took a deep breath at the thought of telling them what happened.

The video ended then the next began when Rob walked out of the house. He paced for two minutes while staring at the truck and trailer before disappearing down the stairs. A few minutes later, Rob walked into the house followed by Monte and Liam.

A short video of Monte and Liam carrying their backpacks flashed then stopped.

I knew what the next video was going to show and took a deep breath, my hands began to shake. Officer Goldstrom cupped her hands underneath mine.

The door opened with Rob stepping out then Mom. Their lips were moving when he turned to her, his hands hit her shoulders and I looked away as she fell back over the table. Moments later, the officer's hands cradling mine jerked, and both officers gasped.

"Son-of-a-bitch," Sharp growled.

Barry's truck turned down the driveway and sped toward the house.

"I need to send this to my phone and to the department," Goldstrom said softly and lifted the phone from my trembling fingers.

Barry slid to a halt with the door opening before the truck was at a stop. He nearly ran to me with eyes full of worry.

"Show him," I whispered to the officers.

They nodded and leaned the phone to Barry. I stepped down the stairs away from them and looked out to the pasture where Rob had disappeared. I had run as fast as I could, but the feeling of helplessness weighed on me. My eyes closed but the vision of Rob jumping on Taylor flashed and my eyes flew open.

"That fucking bastard," Barry growled. "Holy shit! Fuck!"

Then he was silent, within moments, he was stepping in front of me. When our eyes met, my lungs hurt, veins tingled, and muscles ached. I felt so lost and confused. My mind still in disbelief, I fell into his open arms, and we held tight.

"What can I do?" He whispered.

"Go get the boys from school." My voice quivered as I stepped back and took a deep breath. I looked back at the officers who had walked to their car. Goldstrom was on her phone and glanced at me then away. Officer Sharp was close to her, listening to the call when he looked at me. "Can I put away the guns now?"

He nodded.

Barry followed me into the house. I placed the guns in the cabinet and turned to him, "I'm going to the hospital now. I need to be with them. As long as I know you have the boys, I'm good and Mom will agree."

"Alright, I'll take them to my place until you call."

We walked out the door of the house together and I locked the door.

"Ace?" Goldstrom called out. "I'll take you to the hospital."

"Did they find him?" I stopped and stared at her.

She shook her head.

As we drove to the hospital, my mind went to Mom. *"...he shoved me once a couple weeks ago, but never hitting or showed signs of aggression like that."*

I pulled out my phone.

"Hey, Ace." Lauren answered.

"Has Rob ever hit Mom?" If she had told anyone she would have told Lauren.

"Well...not hit. She said he shoved her out of the way a couple weeks ago when they were arguing. Why? Did something happen?"

"He attacked Mom and Taylor this morning. They are on their way to the hospital."

"Oh, Ace!"

"Mom has scrapes, bruises, maybe a broken wrist. He kicked Taylor off the stairs then..." I envisioned the jump from the steps and Taylor's body jerking to the boot smashing into him. I couldn't get the words out.

"Ace, is Taylor alright?"

I took in a breath, "I don't know. He took a hard blow to his chest and was breathing odd. He was unconscious when the ambulance left. I'm headed to the hospital now."

"We're just outside of Salt Lake City. I'll have Kade take me to the airport and will be there as soon as I can. Call me when you know."

"Lauren?"

"Yes?"

"What were they arguing about?"

"You and Taylor were expected home and Rob was making arrangements to take the boys down to the coast."

I took another breath and stared out the window. "I'll call when I know."

A nurse ushered me through the emergency room, then down the hall with Officer Goldstrom following. The nurse finally stopped and with an understanding smile, she opened the door. Mom's body jerked as she twisted to look at the door and stood from one of the chairs in the room. The bed was missing. I opened my arms and she fell into them. There were no tears from either of us as we held each other.

"The headwound stopped bleeding by the time we got here. They are scanning him for damage to his heart, chest, and shoulder." She squeezed tighter.

"Did he wake up?"

"No..." she whispered.

"Barry went to the school to pick up the boys and take them to his place."

She nodded so I gently pushed her back onto the chair. She looked up at the officer in surprise.

Goldstrom nodded, "I'm here with the two of you until Mr. Macklin is found."

She stood by the door as we sat and waited.

When the doctor walked in the door he went directly to the monitor on the wall. Mom and I stood to walk next to him as an x-ray appeared on the screen.

"I'm Dr. Graystone," he started. "Taking this one thing at a time. My biggest concern is the internal injuries from the blow to his chest. There are four broken ribs and one of those punctured his lung, but it didn't collapse."

"That was the wheezing?" I asked.

The doctor nodded then continued, "His heart did sustain bruising, but, right now, it is pumping normally. We'll watch for any change in rhythm or blood clots. As for the bone damage," He pointed at a long vertical bone in the middle of the x-ray. "This is his sternum, and what protects the heart and lungs. As you can see, there is a significant breakage here causing pressure and he will be in significant pain, so he is under heavy pain medication right now."

"Did he wake up?" Mom's voice trembled.

The doctor turned to her, "No, and he is sedated until we complete the surgery. We will be looking for bone chips that could further damage the heart or other organs as well as realigning the crack."

"Ok...that will heal?" I exhaled.

"With a hit that hard, there will be significant bruising. It will also hurt to move and breathe." He pointed to his own chest. "Imagine, everything you do with your upper body involves that bone and the ligaments and tendons attached in the area."

"But it will heal?" Mom asked.

"Yes, just takes time," Doctor Graystone nodded then touched the monitor and another x-ray appeared. "Now, the other blow. This is his clavicle." He pointed to two dark lines. One at the top and another at the bottom. "Obviously, these are breaks and here, higher, is another break at the scapular neck. He'll have surgery to realign and repair. Bones heal. The issue here is what is commonly referred to as a 'floating shoulder'. Other than the bones, all the ligaments; trapezoid, conoid, coracoid and coracoacromial, have stretched or torn. Those need repaired." He touched the screen again and a skeletal picture of muscle and bones appeared. "You can see here how they all attach to the bone."

"Will that damage heal?" Mom asked then held her breath as he answered.

"With surgery, physical therapy, time...they should," he nodded. "I have seen these heal to near normal."

Mom's jaw clenched and she exhaled in a huff, "Doctor Graystone." He turned and gave her his complete attention. "Taylor is the son of a world champion team roper along with Ace. His jealous, angry stepfather did this to him because he has always felt he took a backseat to their father's memory since he passed when they were very young. He, and everyone else, could see the two brothers were on the path to repeating the accomplishments of their father. That petty, envious man kicked Taylor to the ground, then stomped on his shoulder with all his weight so he wouldn't be able to rope again." Her voice was full of contempt and an obvious challenge.

The doctor's lips pursed then twisted as he touched the monitor again and the x-ray of Taylor's shoulder appeared. He stared for a moment then turned to stare at her then back at the x-ray. His eyes narrowed in concentration before turning and looking at us.

"I'll make a call to a friend of mine in Houston. He is a specialist and the best in the country for Taylor's shoulder. I need to perform surgery on his chest to make sure there is no further damage and look for any bone chips. When Dr. Marks arrives, we'll do everything we can to repair the damage to the shoulder with today's surgery and there may be a few more. If Taylor follows instructions, and if you follow instructions to help him, then there is a good chance that he can rope again. BUT there is no guarantee." His voice was firm and full of determination. "You must understand, the next week is going to be very painful for him. The shoulder and sternum are going to hurt every time he moves. The punctured lung will have taken in blood, and he will expel that with coughing, which will be painful. If pneumonia sets in, there will be even more coughing. Plain and simple, he is going to have a very rough couple of weeks ahead of him."

I didn't know what to say but slid my arm around Mom's shoulders and pulled her in tight.

"The important thing is," Officer Goldstrom said from behind us, "He is alive, and he will recover."

We exhaled.

Ten minutes after the doctor had left the room, a nurse walked in with a nod to the police officer and a sympathetic smile to us.

"When the surgery is complete, he will be in the ICU. We have a room waiting for him so I can take you up there now for when he arrives." She knelt behind a chair and lifted a brown paper bag. "These are the clothes he had on, and his boots which they cut off."

"Shit, those were his favorite boots," I exhaled and took the bag. "He's going to hate that."

She smiled in understanding, "In this job, I've seen a few pissed off cowboys when they heard that. I did make sure they cut along the seam so they could be repaired."

"We appreciate that," Mom whispered and rubbed her fingers around the swollen wrist.

The nurse reached out and cradled the injured wrist in her hands and smiled warmly at Mom, "Taylor is going to be in surgery for hours. This is the time you get everything done and ready, so after he wakes, your full focus is on him. Let's get this x-rayed and your cuts cleaned." The nurse turned to me. "There is a waiting room just outside of x-ray where you can wait for her, then I'll take you upstairs to Taylor's room."

When Mom disappeared down the hall and with Officer Goldstrom on the phone by the door, I stood in the middle of the waiting room and closed my eyes. The image of Rob kicking then stomping flashed again and my eyes flew open. I needed to keep my mind busy, so I called Barry.

"How are they?" He answered.

"Taylor has a bruised heart and is in surgery with a broken sternum and clavicle, and Mom is in x-ray for her wrist."

I proceeded to tell him what the doctor had said.

"Alright," Barry exhaled. "We need to think of the boys here. I waited in the school office until they broke for lunch then I took the boys to the steakhouse to eat. I made up an excuse to swing by my house, but they are starting to figure out something is wrong. What do you want me to tell them?"

I sighed, "Tell them there was an incident at the house, and Mom and Taylor were hurt and are at the hospital. I guess that's what Mom would want."

"You want my advice?" He grumbled.

I sighed in exhaustion, "Always, Barry, always."

"Your mother will want to hold her sons. She will need you all together. If I tell the boys they are hurt, and we don't tell them what happened...well, they are twelve and thirteen and they will imagine the worst. They need the truth and need to be there with you and their mother."

I sighed. In my heart I knew he was right, but everything in me wanted to protect them from what their father had done.

"Alright, we tell them that Mom and Taylor are here, and you can bring them over. But we leave it up to Mom on what we tell them about Rob." I glanced at Officer Goldstrom who was now off the phone. She rolled her lips in a tight line and frowned.

"Alright, do you need anything?"

"Yeah, but I don't know what is happening at the house so the boys shouldn't go there until we do."

"Alright, I'll bring them to you then come back."

When I lowered the phone and slid it into my pocket, I looked at Goldstrom, "Did they find him?"

She walked in with a nod then motioned for me to sit. Doom loomed over me as I lowered into the chair, and she sat next to me.

"I know you've been through a lot today but, it is about to get worse." Her voice was calm, firm, and full of the dread I felt. "They found his trail on the bike and followed it through trees and across a stream then it went uphill, where they lost it."

"The tire tracks disappeared?"

"Yes, and after searching on foot, they found the bike and Rob down in a ravine. He was hidden by a cluster of rocks which is why it seemed he disappeared."

"Did they arrest him?"

"No..."

"The video shows he clearly attacked both of them." Anger and frustration shook in my voice.

"Ace, he was deceased."

CHAPTER TWENTY

ACE

Shock, frustration, a bit of relief, and then the ramifications of the truth made my whole body shake. Liam and Monte were on their way to the hospital, and I was going to have to tell them their father had not only attacked their mother and brother, but he was dead, too.

With elbows on knees, my hands covered my face as a growl escaped me.

Goldstrom laid a comforting hand on my shoulder and continued, "Knowing the boys had not been notified yet, and not wanting them to hear it from a friend or teacher from a social media post, we have only communicated by phone, not the radio. That way, no one knows he was found and that he has been recovered."

"Recovered...." As much as I hated the man, this was going to devastate the boys.

"Ace?"

I looked up to see Mom standing in the doorway with her wrist wrapped in a brace and cradled in her other arm.

"Barry is bringing the boys to the hospital," I blurted. "He...we thought it was best for the boys."

"Alright, but..."

"They found Rob and his bike at the bottom of a rocky ravine. He died." It was easier just to say it quickly.

She stared at me in silence, so I stood and ushered her to the chair next to me. Officer Goldstrom walked to the door but turned back slightly with a sorrowful glance.

Mom turned to her, "Was it an accident or suicide?"

"They don't know yet."

My heart and brain went numb.

Before Monte and Liam arrived, and not knowing what the media would report, we had decided to tell them the truth. With Mom on one end of the small couch and I on the other, the boys were between us as she told them everything. They were in tears by the time she told them of Rob's stomping on Taylor, then sobbing when they learned Rob had died. While they cried, we held them close and waited. Barry sat in the chair across the room and glanced grimly at us then looked out the window.

When Monte took deep calming breaths and began wiping away the tears, he looked at our mother, "Is it because of what I said?"

"It is not anything that the two of you said or did," she said firmly. "I don't know why he did what he did, we may never know why, but you two are not at fault for what a grown man did to another person."

"What Dad did to our brother," Liam grumbled.

He was next to me, and I pulled him in close, "For now, we focus on Taylor," I said to him and tried to contain my anger, frustration, and feelings of failure in protecting my family. "He has a long road of healing ahead of him, so we'll all be there for him."

Neither responded and we sat quietly waiting.

My text alert rang out in the room.

Text from Lauren: I'm in the waiting room outside of ICU. They won't let me come back.

I tipped the phone to Mom so she could see. Tears welled in her eyes.

"I'll go talk to her," she said softly and stood.

"Don't go, Mom," Monte whispered and grabbed her arm.

She knelt next to him and smiled softly, "Lauren is in the waiting room and I'm going to talk with her. I'll be right back."

"Can I go with you?" His chin quivered as he tried to hold back the tears.

"You stay here with us men and let the ladies talk," Barry stood. "When Taylor is out of surgery, I'll run to the ranch and get some clothes for Ace." He smirked at me. "Your brother stinks." Both boys turned to look at me and Mom walked out of the room.

"You do," Liam gave me a sideways glance. "How long has it been since you took a shower?"

I huffed, "A few days."

Monte rose from the couch and walked to a door in the corner and opened it. "There is a shower in here you can use." He stepped into the restroom and closed the door. After a few minutes, we could hear his sobs. Without a word, Liam rose, walked to the door and stepped in with his brother.

I stood next to Barry, and we stared at the door.

"They are as close to each other as you and Taylor are," Barry whispered.

"And, no matter what we say, they will blame themselves for what their father did," I sighed.

"Do you know what Monte said?"

"No."

Two hours later, Barry had returned with a bag of clothes, and I had just finished a long hot shower when the doctor appeared at the door. Barry and Lauren were in the waiting room, so it was Mom, Monte, Liam and I standing to face him together. The doctor's gaze went to Monte and Liam then to Mom in a questioning look.

"These are Taylor's little brothers. We are all in this together, so they can hear whatever you say," she said firmly.

"Alright, everything went very well." He smiled and we all exhaled. "There was no further damage to the heart, no bone chips, or excessive blood. The punctured lung will cause him to cough up blood for a day or two; that is normal. There are pins and plates holding together the sternum and clavicle." He paused and looked at Mom. "We were able to successfully sew the tendons together. We'll have to contain any movement and give them time to heal, then there will be physical therapy. We'll watch for a buildup of scarring which may require a minor surgery in the future."

"So, he will be able to rope again?" She took a deep breath.

"What?" Monte gasped and looked at her with wide eyes. "He can't rope?"

"Oh," Liam exhaled. "I didn't even think..."

"He will throw again." Mom looked down at them then up to the doctor.

"As I said before," the doctor started. "As long as he does as he is told, you all follow directions on how to help him, then there is a good chance. His arm will be in a sling now so we can watch the surgical site. Somewhere down the road, we will put on a hard cast so we immobilize the shoulder so he can't injure it when it starts feeling better."

"He will rope?" Liam's voice shook with worry.

"Yes." Mom huffed.

The doctor nodded to him, "He will rope, we just won't know for another few months to what level."

A nurse appeared at the door and looked from us to the doctor. "They are ready to bring him in."

Doctor Graystone nodded to her then turned to us. "If you'll wait in the waiting room, we'll call you in once he is settled."

"Alright," Mom looked at the nurse. "THE moment that he is settled."

"Yes, ma'am," the nurse nodded and stepped aside.

When we walked out the swinging doors of the ICU hallway and into the main hallway, Lauren and Barry stood from their seats in the waiting room. Just down the hall, but in view of the doors were Officers Sharp and Goldstrom. I nodded to them but made sure Mom and the boys were in the waiting room before I walked down the hall.

"How is Taylor?" Goldstrom asked.

I told them what the doctor had said.

"Glad to hear it," Sharp looked behind me to the waiting room. "I'm sorry we had to interrupt, but we need to talk with your mother."

My spine straightened and I couldn't stop myself from glaring, "She doesn't need this right now. She just witnessed..."

"We know, Ace," Goldstrom placed her hand on my arm. "We truly understand what she is going through, but to put this to rest as quickly as possible, we need to ask her what happened."

"You have the video, you know exactly what happened," I growled.

She nodded, "But we need to hear it from her for our records, then we can close the case."

"Your brothers were already at school?" Sharp asked.

My head jerked to him, "They weren't there. Leave them out of this. They lost their dad today and have to come to grips with what he did."

"Ace, I have to ask the question," Sharp sighed.

I looked at Goldstrom, "You did what you could to protect them this morning. Do that now."

"We are, Ace," She nodded, and her hand squeezed my arm. "Since you have officially stated they were not home, we do not have to talk to them. We will do whatever we legally can to protect them."

I took a deep breath to calm my irritation. "Thank you."

"It's been a long day for you," Goldstrom sighed. "Give us five minutes with your mom then we can let you be with Taylor."

Another deep breath with a nod and I turned to the waiting room. Mom was standing at the door watching, so I lifted my chin to the officers so she would understand. She turned back to the room, said something, then walked down the hall.

I left her with the officers and walked back to the waiting room. Lauren met me just outside the door.

"How are you?" She asked softly.

"Monte asked Mom if Rob attacking Taylor was because of what he said." Her eyes changed just enough I knew she knew. "What did he say?"

Lauren looked back into the waiting room then back to me, "Just before the boys walked out the door to catch the bus, he told Rob if they didn't get to take roping lessons from you and Taylor after school, then he would never ride a bike again."

I shook my head, "Then it was what he said."

"No, Ace," Lauren huffed. "It might have been the straw that broke the camel's back, but the camel was already sick."

As much as I wanted to laugh at her analogy, I just shook my head, "I had no idea."

"I'm not sure anyone did," Lauren whispered.

"Mom never said anything to you?"

"She just said that once you and Taylor were on the road, Rob changed...he was jealous of you at first, but it escalated each time you came home. Evidently, he said something about going with you next time you had a brother's weekend and that was shot down. Then, he got possessive of the boys."

"Yeah, no kidding," My head hurt, muscles ached, and brain was just plain tired. "Thanks for telling me, Lauren, and for coming so quickly."

The nurse appeared at the door. Liam, Monte, Mom, and I held hands as we walked toward Taylor's door.

"Has he woken yet?" Mom whispered to the nurse.

"No, but there was just the superficial cut on his head. No major issue so it is the sedation that has been keeping him unconscious." The nurse stopped as her hand touched the door and she looked at Monte and Liam. "He is lying in bed, just looks like he is sleeping. His arm is in a sling and a bandage over the wound on his head plus there is an oxygen mask over his nose and mouth to help his breathing. But there is an IV attached to him for fluids and to administer medication to him. There is another machine that will be monitoring his heartbeat, oxygen levels, and blood pressure." She paused and gave them a reassuring smile. "Everything is there just to watch over him."

"Like what we see in the movies?" Liam whispered.

"Yes," she smiled then turned to the door.

Everything she described was accurate and much to my relief, he looked better lying in the bed than he had on the brick walkway. His hair had been washed and lay softly, his cheeks were tinted in color instead of the white when they had hoisted him into the ambulance, and there was no wheezing when he took a breath.

The nurse walked to the monitor as we gathered to the side of his bed. Mom took Taylor's hand in hers.

"When he wakes," the nurse said softly. "I will give you a few minutes with him, then I need to ask him a few questions so we can make sure he isn't in pain."

"Ok," Monte and Liam whispered.

The nurse smiled at me then walked out the door, closing it behind her.

An hour later, I stood at the window and stared at nothing as the morning's attack replayed in my mind. Both boys were sitting on the small sofa, heads tilted back and staring at the ceiling. Mom was sitting in the chair next to the bed holding Taylor's hand when it suddenly jerked. His head moved to the side then a groan escaped.

"Fuck…" Taylor whispered and groaned again while the boys and I hurried to the bedside.

"What have I told you about swearing, Young Man?" Mom whispered.

Taylor's eyes opened and he looked right at her, "But, I fucking hurt." He groaned.

"And there you go again," Her voice held a light-hearted tone, but her eyes were full of relief.

Taylor's gaze moved to each of us then around the room, "What the hell? Why am I here?"

"What was the last thing you remember?" I asked with gut burning in anger at Rob.

Taylor's eyes squinted at me, "I was walking to the house when Rob…" He stopped and looked at Monte and Liam.

"We know everything," Monte whispered.

"I'm not sure I do," Taylor grimaced and tried to move his arm then groaned.

Mom took a deep breath and squeezed his hand tightly, "Rob kicked you in the chest and you hit your head and injured your shoulder when you fell."

"Truth, Mom," Monte nudged her.

Taylor's eyes looked at Monte then back to Mom.

She nodded, "After Rob kicked you and broke your sternum, he then stomped on your shoulder and broke your clavicle."

Taylor stared at her for a moment then turned and looked at me.

"You'll be in here for a few weeks as they watch over you, then you'll go home and recover for a few months." I shrugged lightly as if it wasn't a big deal. He continued to stare at me when I realized what he wanted me to answer because he wasn't going to ask Mom or the brothers. I sighed, "I had just parked the truck down the driveway. Rob took off on his bike before I could reach you." The room was quiet, and Taylor's eyes narrowed. "When the police found Rob, he had wrecked the bike down a ravine. He died."

Taylor's eyes closed and he said nothing.

"The nurse said she needs to talk to you after you wake up," Mom's voice shook, and she started to rise but stopped when Taylor's hand squeezed hers. He didn't open his eyes.

"Monte, Liam," I stood back from the bed. "Let's go tell Barry and Lauren he's awake." Neither said a word as they walked down the hall in front of me.

The media coverage was almost nonexistent because of Officers Goldstrom and Sharp. Rob had been buried with Mom, the boys, and just a few of his friends at a short graveyard service. I stayed at the hospital with Taylor. Lauren went home to Idaho the day after the service.

An exhausting week later, Barry had taken Monte and Liam home for the night. Mom was asleep on the sofa, and I stood at the window and stared at the dark night sky.

"How bad is the break?"

I turned to Taylor's whispered voice.

"How bad?" He repeated.

I walked to his bedside and took a deep breath, "The doctor said that everything looked good after the surgery. They repaired all the torn ligaments and tendons. If you do everything he tells you, and we do everything to help you, then you should be able to rope again."

"You telling me the truth?"

"He just didn't know to what level you could get to."

"So, there is a chance we can't..." His words trailed off.

"But there is a chance we can."

He sighed and looked at the ceiling as his eyes began to glisten. "Rob was trying to ruin that for us."

"Yes, he was," I sighed. "Mom said he was jealous and always felt he took a back seat to Dad."

Taylor's eyes shifted to me, "Is it jealousy if it's the truth?"

"I don't know if it was always the truth, but I guess the older we got, the more we accomplished in roping, then the more we and everyone else brought up Dad. And it made the Lil Bros want to be with us more."

"Especially after this last summer when we got out on the road."

"That's what Mom said."

"You need to go find someone to rope with."

"No."

He turned back to me with a glare, "What the fuck do you mean 'no'?"

"I'm not roping without you."

"Then, what the hell are you going to do?"

"I have no idea, but I'm not roping without you."

The day before Thanksgiving, Taylor was released from the hospital. Barry and his wife, Clara, joined us for the large dinner.

After spending nearly all my time the last few weeks at the hospital, it was odd being in the house without Rob. Liam and Monte were emotional and moody and had hidden their motocross bikes in one of the barns. Everything in their rooms that had to do with motocross they had put in a box. Mom wouldn't let them throw the boxes away, so they were stuffed in the attic instead.

After dinner, Monte and Liam were in their room when Mom set up her laptop on a table in front of Taylor's recliner in the living room. Lauren and Jamie appeared on the monitor.

"Man, you look good," Jamie grinned at Taylor.

"Mom made me wash my hair," he chuckled.

They chatted for a few minutes then I heard Lauren ask.

"Where is Ace?"

"Right here," I stepped in next to the recliner.

"I have a request and we all expect you to say yes," She smiled slightly but I could see the determination in her eyes.

"He doesn't have a choice," Taylor huffed.

"For what?" I asked cautiously.

"We are leaving for the NFR on Saturday morning," Lauren said. "All of us are going to get Jess and Ryle's horses checked in and us settled in before it starts."

"I look forward to cheering them on," I nodded.

"I would like you to come to Idaho and take care of 3.3 while we're gone," she stated.

"Leave here?" I huffed in disbelief.

"Yes," Mom answered. "While you were helping bring Taylor home yesterday, Barry took your truck and trailer in to get serviced and have the tires checked."

I looked around the group then back to Mom. "Are you kidding me?"

"No," she stated. "You've been at the hospital for weeks and now that he is home, there is no reason you can't go up and help Lauren. They will have a better time and relax if they have you there."

I didn't know what to say even though I did agree with her and normally I wouldn't hesitate to help Lauren.

"Then we leave in an hour." Barry stood. "Let's go get the horses."

"What?" I gasped.

"You're taking the horses to keep them in shape and get some riding in." Barry walked to the door. "I'll keep you company on the way there, then fly back Saturday morning."

"Keeps Mom's focus on me," Taylor smirked.

I looked around at all of them, "You're all in on this?"

"Yes," Clara nodded. "Tell us what you're going to be doing in the next 15 days that you can't help out your cousin?"

I looked down at Taylor.

"I will video call with you every day so you can see I'm just fine," he promised. "Normally, you would jump at the chance to stay at the ranch for two weeks and we both know it. So just go."

An hour later, Barry was driving down the driveway with me still a bit stunned in the passenger seat.

"Ace, how long has it been since you've had more than four or five hours sleep at a time?"

"Arizona," I answered honestly.

"I've driven thousands of rodeo miles while entertaining myself," he grinned. "So, lean that seat back and go to sleep."

I slept for ten solid hours.

CHAPTER TWENTY-ONE

SAMMIE

I stopped the truck at the exit onto the main road and looked at the sky. A few raindrops hit the windshield. Maybe it wasn't a good idea to try and get home tonight. It may only be five hours, but I would be driving directly into the ice storm.

My phone was in the holder, so when I pushed the call button the ringing echoed in the cab.

"You headed back yet?" Mom answered.

"Just leaving the arena and it just started raining." I grimaced at the sky. "Clouds are dark and ugly."

"It's not just raining here, it is sleet and coming down hard," she huffed. "Once the sun goes down and the temperature drops, it will turn to a snowstorm."

"Yeah, the roads are going to be horrible. I can drive as far as I'm comfortable, but I don't want to sit in a snowstorm on the side of the road all night."

"And I don't want you too either. You just stay there."

"I can check on a stall here or call around…" The rain began to pelt the window.

"We'll start making phone calls and see if someone has room for you. A lot of our friends are down in Vegas for the NFR or on their way there to beat the storm."

"You make calls and I'll search my phone to see if there is someone close."

"Stay where you are until we find something. The arena is safer."

"I know," I whispered and ended the call.

My finger slid across the phone as I scrolled through the contacts. I didn't really have a lot of friends in Boise but there were a few club members I could call if I was desperate…which I was quickly becoming.

I turned up the heater and clicked the knob for the wipers to go faster, then I continued scrolling. I stopped at a name and looked up as if I could mentally gauge how far away her ranch was from the arena. It wasn't too far, and it was worth a shot, so I pushed the button with a hopeful breath.

"Sammie?" Her voice echoed in the cab as she yelled into the phone.

"Hi, Lauren, I must have caught you at a bad time."

"We're walking through the casino part of SouthPoint."

"Oh, I forgot you were going to Vegas."

"You need something?"

"I'm in Boise and there is a big snow and ice storm coming through, I was looking for a place Sergeant Pepper and I could ride it out."

"Go to the ranch!" She yelled. "Ace is there taking care of it while we're here, but I'll text and let him know you are on your way."

"I'd ask if you're sure, but I really would rather stay in your bunkhouse rather than the side of the road."

"I would rather you be there, too," she laughed. "So, get moving before the storm hits and text me when you arrive."

"Thanks, Lauren," I sighed in relief, ended the call, and sent a text to my mother.

It only took twenty minutes before I was pulling off the highway, but the rain was coming down with such force the wipers could barely keep the windshield clear enough to see. When I turned into her driveway, I drove straight to the barn, pulled to the side and began backing up to the stable doors. I wanted to park the closest possible to get Sergeant Pepper released.

A barely visible form waved their arms in the air to indicate for me to stop. I turned the engine off, wiggled into my coat, and flipped the hood up. The last thing was sliding my phone into my pocket before opening the door. I was pelted by freezing rain drops and a shiver ran down my back. By the time I reached the stable, the horse trailer gate was being closed and Sergeant Pepper was being led down the middle of the stable. I love horse people that moved into action without needing to be told.

I jogged to catch up with him, "Thanks, Ace."

He turned and smiled as he walked into the stall, "Welcome back."

I laughed with a relieved sigh, "It's such a great place I just couldn't stay away." I flipped back the hood of my coat.

"Sammie?"

I turned to the voice and gasped in surprise.

"G-Ranger? What are you doing here?"

"Building fence," He answered with a grin.

"I hope not in the rain," I laughed.

He shook his head with a smirk, "We barely had the equipment stashed in the truck before it hit."

Ace walked out of the stall and closed the door. Sergeant Pepper's head was already in a pile of hay.

"Well," Ace said and stepped to the barn door to look out at the bunkhouse that was at least thirty yards from us. "We still need to get over there before we can settle in."

"We can rush to the truck, and I can drive us closer," I offered.

"Sammie," Granger huffed. "That's what coats and hoods are for."

We laughed and flipped the hoods up and with a tipping of the head into the rain, we ran as fast as we could across the graveled driveway, up the cement walkway, across the porch, and into the welcoming door.

I was assaulted by warmth and the aroma of the wood that blazed in the fireplace.

"Nothing says welcome like that," I chuckled and slid off the coat.

"Nice to see you dressed for the occasion," Ace chuckled as he hung up his coat.

My hair was up in a messy knot on top of my head, I wore old grey sweatpants, mud boots, and a dark green hoodie. "I was settled in for a five-hour drive home."

"Well, at least you're comfortable, because none of us want to run back out for your bag," Granger teased and flopped onto one of four recliners.

Ace chuckled, "Hungry? We were just going to figure out what to have for dinner."

"Starving," I laughed. "In fact, I'm starving for the pizza that's in my horse trailer."

"You have pizza?" They both huffed.

"Three-meat, thick crust; a large because Dad likes the leftovers when I get home and two servings of garlic sticks," I grinned at Granger. "Does that make you want to run back out in the rain?"

"Oh, yeah," He stood and slid his coat back on. "You want me to grab anything for you while I'm out there?"

"There is a gallon jug of chocolate milk," I answered with a giggle.

"Pizza and chocolate milk?" Ace shook his head in disbelief. "You are the perfect woman."

We all laughed.

"And you missed out with your brother putting dibs on me," I teased.

His smile faded and he turned away.

The reaction surprised and worried me, so I turned to Granger with questioning eyes. He shook his head, then ducked out the door and into the rain.

"I best send a couple texts to let Lauren and my mom know I arrived," I said light heartedly and slid onto a seat at the kitchen table.

"I sent Lauren a text when you pulled in," Ace said and tossed a roll of paper towels on the table and opened the refrigerator door.

"Thanks."

Text to Mom: Safe at Lauren Conners' ranch, Sergeant Pepper tucked in barn and happy.

Text to Lauren: Thanks again. Ace and Granger have us safe and warm.

Ace had opened a can of marinara sauce and placed a large bottle of parmesan cheese on the table. He finished with three large glasses.

"How long have you been here?" I relaxed back in the chair.

"I came in yesterday morning as the crew took off for Vegas."

"All of them?"

"With Jess and Ryle competing and the rest of them having helped them get there, yes. They are all down there for the next two weeks. I'm here until they get back."

There was something about him that made me worry…there was no energy in his movements and no light in his eyes like the last time I had seen him.

"It has to help Lauren relax and enjoy herself knowing she has someone trustworthy here taking care of the place."

He nodded as the door opened and we both looked to see Granger enter. He hovered over the pizza box with the milk jug dangling from his hand.

I chuckled and hurried over to take them from him.

"I hope it's worth it," He grinned as he slid out of his coat. Unlike Ace, his eyes were bright and filled with life.

I turned to hand the pizza to Ace who was still distant. He opened the top of the box and smiled, "Damn, I can hardly wait." He slid the box into the oven.

"So, Sammie," Granger slid onto one of the chairs next to me. "Why were you out on the streets alone this time of night?"

I chuckled, "Barrel race in Boise and I was headed home."

"By yourself, on a five-hour trip just for a race?" Ace asked as he opened the jug of milk and began filling glasses.

"Not the first time I've traveled alone," I shrugged.

"Five hours this time of year?" Granger huffed.

"Still not the first time," I smiled.

"So, you've had a great six weeks since Waco, and you're sitting at the top of the world standings, and you go to a local race?" Ace's eyes narrowed.

"It's still sanctioned," I chuckled.

"Ah," Granger nodded with a knowing grin. "It was local, so it was against some of those racers you ran against over the summer."

"…the ones that made fun of you." Ace nodded with a smirk.

"Wow, nothing gets past you two," I laughed.

"And how did it go?" Granger asked.

I shrugged again and pulled out my phone to scroll to the Facebook page of the group that hosted the race.

"Well," A satisfied smile appeared. "It looks like Sergeant Pepper won the whole damn thing."

Both men roared in laughter.

"Good for you, Sammie," Ace nodded. "Making a statement."

"That horse is just outstanding," I sighed. "Since we clicked and began working together, I just can't get enough of him."

We chatted about horses and the Texas trip through dinner then moved to the living room and each stretched out on a recliner. My chair sat between the two of them.

"It's been a long day," I yawned.

"The third door on the left is a free room," Ace sighed and turned the television on. "It's the bunk room so you have eight beds to choose from."

"If I fall asleep right here, just throw a blanket over me," I yawned again.

"Do they have any NFR things going on tonight?" Granger asked.

"Nah, first thing will be the welcome ceremony and back number night on Tuesday," Ace answered and stopped scrolling when a western appeared.

"Big Valley," I relaxed even more. "I love that show."

I'm not sure I even made it through one episode before I fell asleep, but the television turning off had my eyes opening to the sudden silence.

Ace was still in his recliner and staring at the embers of the fire. A clanging of dishes behind me indicated Granger was there. I sat up and Ace turned to me. His brows were together in a deep frown and his eyes were glistening. He looked so sad.

"What is it?" I whispered to him.

He shook his head and turned back to the fire. The light behind us turned off leaving only the light from the dwindling fire illuminating the room giving it a warm glow. Granger returned to sit on the edge of his recliner with his elbows on his knees and a concerned expression.

"Talk to us, Ace," Granger whispered.

Ace took in a shaking breath and wiped away a tear.

"Please, Ace," I turned in the chair toward him. "What's wrong?"

"Taylor…" He stammered and wiped away another tear.

"Is he alright?" I gasped with heart racing in sudden dread.

"He's alive," he said softly.

"Talk to us, Ace," Granger's voice was low and encouraging.

"Last month," Ace exhaled and looked into the fire. "Our stepfather attacked Mom and Taylor." He took in another deep breath. "I was walking down the driveway at home, Taylor was almost at the house when Rob and Mom walked out onto the deck. Before we knew it, Rob started yelling at Mom and pushed her...making her tumble back over the patio furniture. Taylor and I took off running to them, but he was closer and got there before me. When Rob saw him come up the stairs, he kicked Taylor in the chest making him fly back down and he hit his head, and it knocked him out."

"Oh, Ace…" I gasped with tears rising.

He turned to me with anguished eyes, "That's not the worst part. Rob screamed at him, then…he jumped in the air and when he came down, he stomped on Taylor's right shoulder…with all his weight. I ran as fast as I could, but I couldn't get there in time."

"Oh, my God," I gasped.

"Son-of-a-bitch," Granger moaned.

"When he saw me running at him, he took off and got to his dirt bike before I could reach him. I was going to chase after him, but Mom needed help. She wasn't hurt bad, but she was scared."

"And Taylor?" I cried. "Did he wake up?"

He took in another quivering breath and exhaled heavily, "Not until after he had surgery."

Granger and I remained quiet and waited for him to continue. My stomach ached as I envisioned the carefree smiling cowboy that put dibs on me being attacked by his own stepfather.

"When he woke up, we had to tell him about his shoulder," He turned to us and the light from the fire reflected in his glistening eyes.

"His sternum was broken, and his heart bruised...a lung punctured. The clavicle was broken and the top of his humerus where the ligaments come together. They call it a 'floating shoulder'."

"How bad is that?" Granger asked.

"The bones will heal but it's the damage to the ligaments and tendons that worry the doctors. There are two ligaments with names longer than I can pronounce and they stayed together. If they had separated..." He shook his head with a deep sigh. "He had surgery and is in a brace and cast for months until the ligaments and tendons heal. Then months of therapy."

"Will he be able to rope again?" I whispered and dreaded the answer.

He sighed again with a shake of the head, "They don't know."

"Ah, damn, Ace," Granger huffed. "You two just started roping for the year."

"We filled our permits and just bought our cards. We roped that first month...and that's it," He leaned back into the recliner and stared at the fire. "I don't know what to do. Taylor wants me to find another partner, but I just don't have the heart for it. We have been dreaming of this year of traveling almost our whole lives. Mom told me to come up here for the two weeks and try and clear my head to think."

"How is she?" Granger asked.

"What happened to your stepfather?" I asked.

"Physically she is fine; nothing was broken," he started. "Mentally...well, she's pretty messed up. She's focusing on taking care of my little brothers." He turned and looked at me. "He was on his motocross bike when he ran away, and they found him a few hours later down in a ravine. He hit a bunch of rocks...he died."

"What?" I exhaled in disbelief.

"Damn," Granger muttered.

"He was my stepfather since I was five; fifteen years. I don't remember my real dad, so he was the only father I knew, and the first fourteen years were good."

"Do they know why he…did what he did?" I asked.

Ace shook his head with a slight shrug of the shoulders, "Not really, but we believe he was jealous and tried to stop us from achieving our goals. Just…none of us ever saw a violent side of him."

"Did I miss this in the news?" I asked.

"I don't remember hearing anything about it or I would have called," Granger added.

"No, we've kept it quiet," Ace said. "With the NFR and the World Series of Team Roping going on right now, everyone is focused on those."

"Can I call Taylor?" I hoped.

"He has his mood swings," Ace answered. "Sometimes he's good and others…well, not so much."

"You two had lots of big dreams together," I sighed. "But, when you think I can, please let me know."

"He promised to call each morning to check-in, and he'd only call when he was in a good mood so next time you can answer," he smiled. "That will get his mood up."

Granger opened his mouth to say something then chuckled and stood to look out the door. "The rain has stopped, so I might get more fencing in tomorrow."

"I have no plans for the next couple of days," I said and stood. "So, I can stay and help."

"I remember hearing that you've put in a mile or two," Granger smirked.

I laughed at his referring to my infamous rant in Texas. I turned to Ace who stood from his chair, "You said third door?"

He nodded and we walked down the hall; each of us disappearing into our rooms. There were four bunk beds, an end table, long bench along the wall, and a bathroom with just a shower, sink, and toilet. It was decorated in blue; comfy and cozy.

I crawled under the thick quilt and looked at my phone.

Text from Mom: Good to hear, love you and congrats on the win. I bought the picture and video and will send to you.

Text from Lauren: Glad you're there, stay as long as you like, Ace will need the company.

I agreed with her.

I watched the video of the day's run. Sergeant Pepper looked fierce. I closed my eyes and dreamt of our next year together.

I was the first person to wake the next morning and moved the curtains to the front door to look outside. Footsteps echoed behind me, and I turned to see Granger.

"Well?" He asked.

"It's all white," The fresh layer of snow looked beautiful. I couldn't wait to see all the horses in it.

"How much?" He leaned over my shoulder and looked out. "Well, so much for fencing."

A shrill of a ring echoed in the building.

"What the hell is that?" I looked around for the source.

"Sammie! You awake?" Ace appeared.

"Yeah," I answered. "What is that?"

"An incoming video chat from Taylor," Ace smiled. "Let's give him a morning surprise."

I laughed as he handed me the phone and I pushed the button.

Taylor was looking down when he appeared, so I kept quiet and quickly took in his appearance. His dark brown hair was a matted mess with the left side sticking straight up, face pale through the whiskers, and his chest was bare except for the white brace and sling over his shoulder. It made my heart hurt. When he looked up, he jerked backwards with wide brown eyes that had dark circles underneath.

"What the hell?" He gasped.

I laughed, "Good morning."

The call was disconnected.

CHAPTER TWENTY-TWO

SAMMIE

I looked at Ace in surprise and slowly handed him the phone, "I think he hung up on me."

The message alert rang out. Ace read the message and started laughing, "It says, 'what the fuck? You could have warned me. I'll call back.'"

We laughed.

"How did he look?" Granger asked and walked to the coffee maker.

"Rough," I said honestly.

"Was he at least wearing a shirt?" Ace asked.

"No shirt, hair a mess, and he looked pale with dark circles under his eyes," I answered.

"He only showers when he stinks," Ace sighed. "Only a couple times since the whole thing happened."

"He'll be showering every day now that Sammie might answer the phone," Granger chuckled and hit the on button of the coffee maker.

"Well, it will take him a while to clean-up," Ace grinned. "So, I'm headed out to do chores."

"I can help," Granger and I said at the same time.

"Let's get it done," Ace said and turned back to his room.

I ran through the snow to my trailer and dressed in two layers of clothes under my knee-length winter ranch coat. I didn't worry about showering; I had all day to do that. I pulled my thickest beanie hat out of the dresser, pulled it over all my hair, then added a thick wild rag around my neck to keep warm. Last thing was my lined work gloves.

Granger and Ace were walking to the tractors when I stepped out of the trailer.

The first tractor roared to life as I approached. Both men turned and looked at me, then right into my eyes. It was a bit unnerving. "What?"

"Your eyes," Granger squinted as he looked at them.

"What about them?" I asked warily.

"It's like the blue is beaming," Ace smirked.

"Like neon," Granger added.

I shook my head in disbelief, "It's just the white of the hat and the blue of the scarf makes them standout."

"And hiding that distracting red," Granger chuckled.

"My hair is distracting?" I gasped with a laugh.

"To your blue eyes? Yes," Ace agreed then walked to the second tractor with the enclosed cab. "Who wants to drive?" He asked and looked between us.

"I can," I answered.

"No clue how," Granger shook his head.

The second engine roared to life.

When Ace stepped in next to us, he looked at Granger, "No time like the present to learn then. Sammie can feed with this one and I'll show you how with the bigger one."

"I'm all in for learning something new," Granger grinned.

Ace nodded in appreciation then turned to me, "Take a round bale and drop in the feeders over the fence alongside the road. There are two of them. Then feed the horses in the stable. Only my four and yours are in there with Maggie. The instructions for her are written outside her stall. We'll handle the tractor work for the rest of the herd since we're not in a hurry and he can learn."

"Sounds good," I nodded to him, grinned at the anxious Granger, then climbed up into the smaller tractor. The enclosed cab was heated, which was a great surprise.

I had the first bale speared and was headed down the driveway before Granger made it to the bales. I took out my phone to take a picture of the two men then one of the horses running in the pasture as I approached. Most were quarter horses but there were a few draft horses breaking through the five inches of new snow. I loved mornings like these even if they weren't my horses.

Once my portions of the chores were complete, I moved my truck and horse trailer away from the barn and parked alongside the fence. I also stuffed clothes in a bag and took them to my room.

Text from Ace: Last bale placed, going to waste fuel out in the pasture and let him play to get used to it.

Text to Ace: I will make breakfast. Has Taylor called back?

Text from Ace: thanks, and no he hasn't

I glanced out the back window of the bunkhouse and could see the tractor moving out onto the pasture. It went left then right then in a large circle. The front tine that speared the hay was maneuvered up and down.

While I cooked bacon and French toast, I thought of Taylor and the injury. My curiosity got the best of me, and I had to look up the injury on my phone. The more I read, the worse I felt. With roping the center of the brothers' lives, the chance of Taylor being a high-level competitor again was slim. Their dreams of going to the NFR together in team roping may have been lost.

I wiped away tears and searched the internet for any story concerning the attack but found nothing. It didn't help that I had no idea what their stepfather's last name was. The hum of the tractor approached, so I set the table and placed the food in the middle.

The shrill of Ace's phone ringing announced their arrival into the house. Ace smiled at me then answered the video call himself with a big grin.

"What the hell?" Taylor grumbled. "I didn't go through all the trouble of washing my hair just to look at your ugly face."

We all chuckled as I took the phone from him. I looked at Taylor and gave him a big smile, "Good morning, again."

His hair was combed to perfection and there was a little more color in his clean-shaven face. But it was his happy smile that warmed my heart.

"Hello, future-bride," he answered. "How in the heck did you end up with Ace?"

Granger tucked his head over my shoulder, "You going to care about me being here, too?"

Taylor laughed, "Hell, no. Damn, Sammie, you keep some rough company."

I wrinkled my nose playfully, "They were my heroes last night and took in a wayward cowgirl."

We settled around the table and the two men filled their plates.

"Hold on a second," I said to Taylor, then propped the phone up on the table against the salt and pepper shakers so I could see him as we talked. Ace and Granger moved their chairs closer. "Can you see all of us?"

"Yeah," Taylor nodded. "Breakfast time?"

"Sammie made breakfast while we did chores," Ace answered with a teasing grin to me.

"Hey, I did chores, too," I slapped him playfully.

The four of us talked while we ate breakfast.

Taylor looked off camera then back, "I have to go to the doctor, so I gotta go."

"Call us when you get back and we'll all have lunch together while you update us," I told him eagerly.

He smiled with a nod, "I'll do that."

When the call ended, we sat quietly for a few minutes before Ace turned to me with eyes full of tears. "Thank you, Sammie," he whispered. "You are the ray of sunshine that is going to get him through this."

Words failed me so I just nodded.

"Sunshine and alien blue eyes," Granger chuckled and stood away from the table.

"Now I'm an alien?" I laughed and the dark mood was instantly broken…just like I knew he had intended.

Ace chuckled and picked up my dish from the table, "You cooked, we'll clean."

"Then what?" Granger asked. "You need help with anything else around here?"

"Not much to do outside until it warms up," Ace answered. "No doubt there is a layer of ice under the snow."

"Anything inside?" I asked.

"The indoor arena is basically finished," Ace answered. "I guess we can exercise the horses."

"Yeah, can't help with that," Granger shook his head.

Ace and I both looked at him.

He chuckled and shrugged, "I've never ridden a horse before."

"Seriously, Dude?" Ace asked.

"You're kidding, right?" I looked at him like he was crazy. "Isn't that what you do for a living?"

"Broncs, yeah," Granger grinned. "But I've never ridden a horse that didn't bust out of a chute."

"Never?" Ace and I gasped.

"Never," Granger shook his head again. "I didn't grow up with animals and until Leo and Spence invited me to the clinic, I had never even had a chance."

"What are you going to do if you have to at a rodeo?" Ace asked.

"Why would I?" Granger huffed.

"Victory laps," I grinned. "Can you imagine winning at Pendleton and they throw you on top a horse that you have to jump two fences then do a victory lap around a racetrack?"

"That," Granger laughed. "Would scare the hell out of me, and I would just have to lead the horse."

"Ah, hell no," Ace shook his head.

"And the NFR?" I laughed. "You going to walk your victory lap there, too?"

"Go get your boots," Ace growled. "No friend of mine is going to be walking a damn victory lap."

"I would be ashamed to be associated with you," I laughed.

Granger chuckled and looked at Ace, "You serious?"

"Yes, go get your damn boots. We have all day and five horses plus a dozen of Lauren's we can ride," Ace said and walked to the door.

A half hour later, I was putting a boot in the stirrup and rising above Sergeant Pepper. Ace's four horses were saddled and tied to the hitching post inside the arena.

"You can ride whichever one you want," Ace told an anxious Granger. "Left to right, you have Bear, Quincy, One Spot, and the buckskin is Stomping Dog."

We both turned to him, "Stomping Dog?"

Ace smirked, "Because we can't keep him from trying to stomp dogs, but he is my tie-down horse; real smart."

"I like that name, so I'll choose him," Granger answered and followed Ace to the horse's side. "Is he gentle?"

"Why?" I chuckled. "You afraid he'll buck?"

Ace laughed and Granger shook his head.

"My suggestion would be; don't pull his rein up and back too high," I teased, and they both laughed.

"Don't lift the rein high, don't lean all the way back, and most definitely don't spur him down the shoulder." Ace stepped aside with a grin and waved Granger on the horse.

Granger stepped up to the horse and mounted it like he had done it a thousand times.

Ace gave him a questioning look.

"I've watched a thousand westerns, been around hundreds of cowboys, and if that wasn't enough, I just watched Sammie get on her horse." Granger grinned down at him.

We chuckled and Ace adjusted the stirrups then moved to the next horse in line and mounted.

"Hold your reins like this," Ace demonstrated. "He doesn't need much; you can use one rein on him."

"Some need more than one?" Granger asked.

"It depends on the discipline and training." I answered.

"Squeeze your legs and he'll move forward," Ace instructed.

The horse began to move, and Granger grinned, "I really do have the inclination to prepare to get tossed."

We chuckled.

"Just relax in the saddle and we'll just walk around the perimeter of the building," Ace told him.

We rode for hours in the arena and out in the fields. One pasture full of horses at a time, we herded them into the arena so they would have time on dry dirt. By the time we were done, Granger was relaxed, comfortable, and moving freely. I took at least a dozen pictures.

We were sitting at the table with bowls full of soup and grilled cheese sandwiches when Taylor called. Ace had set up a 'podium' for the phone so it was at eye level. He hit the accept button and Taylor and a brunette woman who looked just like her sons were on the screen.

"Hi, Mom," Ace smiled but there was worry in his eyes.

"Hi, Son," Charlene said as her eyes moved between the three of us.

"Is everything okay?" Ace asked and, since we were so close together, I could feel his whole body tense.

"It was a good visit," Her eyes were reassuring as she spoke. "All the test results were positive, and he is healing well. They put a cast on to make sure the shoulder is secure so it will still be a couple of months before we really know anything." She looked at me. "I just wanted to meet the person that finally got my stinky son to take a bath."

"Well, I can guarantee it wasn't for me," Granger grinned.

We all chuckled, and I leaned forward, "I'm Sammie Parkston."

"Ah, the barrel racer I heard so much about," Charlene's smile widened. "I've been told you had a couple great runs in Waco."

"Second in that one but first in Rosenberg," Taylor announced with a 'crushing' smile to me. "And placed in every run the rest of the month."

"Money in the world standings," Charlene's eyes twinkled with a knowing smile. Who couldn't tell that Taylor had a crush on me?

"She was number one after the second weekend," Taylor continued.

Granger chuckled, "She's about third or fourth now."

"Plenty of year left to get back to that top spot," Charlene smiled. "Well, I'll let you four have lunch." She turned to Ace with a concerned look. "He is healing well. It's all good."

"I'm fine now," Taylor smiled at me. "Now I have something to look forward to at every meal."

I returned his smile, "I'm glad I can help."

"I'll talk to you later," Charlene said and disappeared from the camera.

"What did you guys do today?" Taylor asked just before he took a bite of a burrito.

After the meal was done, the phone call ended, and the dishes cleaned, Granger stood in the middle of the room and looked at Ace.

"I hate just sitting around. Does anything need done?" He asked.

"We can always take the ATVs down the road and make sure the fence is still up and the stock tanks aren't frozen over," Ace answered.

We spent the rest of the day checking the fence and playing on the ATVs.

I was the first person awake on Tuesday morning and, as silent as possible, bundled into my coat, slid on my boots, and stepped into the cold morning. Enough snow had fallen overnight to cover our tracks from the previous day. The horses in the pastures were still eating on the round bales we had placed the day before, so I fed the horses in the barn.

I leaned against Sergeant Pepper's stall door and watched him eat. He was a beautiful horse and filled my soul with love, pride, and the belief in my dreams.

"You should be serenaded," I whispered to the horse. He turned and looked at me as if he understood what I said.

With a chuckle, I trudged through the snow to my trailer and retrieved a guitar. After finding a chair to place at the horse's stall door, I slid off my gloves, and made myself comfortable.

The first chords strummed had Sergeant Pepper's head lifting and swinging to me as he chomped a mouth full of hay. I turned sideways so I could look down the aisle and into his stall then gingerly picked the first chords of a song. The music echoed into the building.

"Great acoustics in here," I smiled at my horse as he ate and watched me.

My favorite warm-up song echoed into the building and had my whole-body relaxing.

The solitude of the silent building and the serene snow-covered pastures, led to the choice of my next song; *The Sound of Silence.* My eyes closed in peace as I played. By the end of the song, I felt the horse's warmth at my side and his breath slide down my back. The softness of his muzzle swept across my cheek, and I smiled. This simple thing…the music…connected us and my heart warmed.

My fingers moved across the strings in a soulful song filled with love for the mighty steed that was my partner in my dreams. He remained at my side as I played the next song. With eyes still closed, I envisioned him running across green pastures and the song became stronger and faster as I matched the cadence of his strides. When he came to a stop, the music eased to the soulful, body swaying rhythm. His muzzle brushed my cheek again and I felt as one with him and I turned into his warmth. One more song was completed before I felt his head rise and I knew he was looking at something.

My eyes opened to see Ace and Granger leaning against the barn wall watching me; Taylor was on the screen of Ace's phone.

"Don't stop," Granger whispered.

I smiled and continued with a song I knew they would know. Two more and I stopped and crossed my arms over the top of the guitar. Sergeant Pepper walked back to his feeder.

"Damn, Sammie," Granger exhaled. "That was beautiful."

"I'm damned impressed," Ace grinned.

I looked at Taylor on the phone, he was smiling, and the adoration was shining in his eyes.

"Just the best Sammie," He nodded. "I hope you don't mind, I recorded it."

"I don't mind if you just keep it to yourself," I smiled.

"Why?" Granger huffed. "Sammie, that was beautiful…seriously just…"

"Yeah, what he said," Ace nodded to him. "Why?"

"Long story which involves a nightmare of a solo at a recital," I stood and stretched. "I play for me and now Sergeant Pepper."

"How long have you been playing?" Taylor asked.

"Since I was four," I answered and was not surprised by their shocked expressions. "My Wyoming uncle taught me. He would let me sit with him and pick at the strings while he played. That moved into him teaching me the chords and how to read sheet music by the time I was six."

"All by heart?" Ace asked.

I nodded, "Something in my brain just clicks with music and once I hear the song or read it, then I can usually play it after that."

"How many songs do you know?" Taylor asked.

I chuckled, "One cold snow stormy day at home a couple years ago, I played as many as I could and Mason, my brother, wrote them down."

"How many?" Granger asked.

"Last count was 87 because we got tired of it and moved on to putting puzzles together, but I would guess another thirty or forty," I answered.

"Damn," They huffed.

"That's sixteen years of learning, playing in recitals, and in a few competitions," I shrugged. "Once I learn a song, it just doesn't go away." I slid the guitar back in the case. "I'm starving, have you eaten?"

"Not yet, we came out to do chores first," Ace answered.

"I got those done already, so you guys get to fix breakfast," I grinned and walked out of the barn with them following me. I walked toward my trailer.

"Where are you going?" Granger asked.

"Put the guitar away," I answered.

"No," Ace reached out and pulled on my coat to turn me away from the trailer and pushed me toward the house. "That goes in the house. We're not done listening to you yet."

I chuckled.

"Do you sing, too?" Taylor asked. I had almost forgotten he was on the phone with us.

I laughed, "Unfortunately, no. My voice is terrible, so I am instrumental only." I looked at Granger and Ace. "You three sing?"

"Ace can," Taylor said. "He has a great voice."

"I have a 'in the car, road trip' voice," Granger grinned. "I can sing, but no one will want to record it."

We laughed as we walked into the house.

"Well, let's give you all a chance to prove yourselves," I grinned. "I'll play a couple songs you know while you're cooking breakfast."

"Like what?" Ace asked.

I smiled, "Something tells me, you'll all know '*Amarillo By Morning*'."

They did and it was a fun morning of food and music.

Granger's head was down reading his phone, "It's supposed to stop snowing today then just be gusting wind tomorrow and nice the rest of the week; up into the 50's."

"That will melt the snow," Ace leaned back in the kitchen chair and sighed. "Then we have a muddy mess."

"But I can fence in a muddy mess," Granger shrugged. "If you don't need any help outside, then I'll kill some time in the gym."

My head shot around, "There's a gym here?"

"Yeah," Granger nodded. "The last door on the end."

I stood and walked out of the room. By the time I had changed into gym clothes and tied back my hair, both men were in the room running on the two treadmills. The music was blaring the full two hours we worked out.

Ace was making smoothies when Taylor called for lunch, "So, what did you do this morning?"

"We introduced the blue-eyed alien to the gym," Granger chuckled.

"G-Ranger," I huffed.

"Blue alien, I like that," Taylor laughed. The color was back in his face and the dark circles under his eyes were beginning to fade. He was wearing a baseball cap with the 3.3 ranch logo on the front and had a t-shirt pulled over the top of his casted shoulder. He looked better; healthier. I glanced at Ace and could see his eyes relaxed and enjoying the visit with his brother. They teased me through lunch about being a blue-eyed alien. I thought it was funny, but still gave them a bad time.

"Can we say hi?" A younger version of Taylor peeked over his shoulder and looked right at me. "You're Sammie?" He asked and when I nodded a wide smile appeared. "I'm Monte, the best looking of us four brothers."

I chuckled as another head appeared and grinned at me, "That's only in his mind, I'm Liam and you sure are pretty."

We all chuckled.

"So, you're the charming one of the four brothers?" I teased.

Liam nodded, "Of course."

Monte glared at him, "You don't even know what that means."

"Sure I do," Liam grinned at me. "It's like George Clooney in Ocean's Eleven when he talks to Julia Roberts; always low and with a big smile."

We laughed and the phone call lasted just a little longer than normal.

Just before dark, we were outside checking water troughs and horses. I stood behind the arena and looked at the dozen horses that were around the hay bale. A few were laying in the hay, a few eating, and others wandering around and pawing at the snow. The draft horses and younger horses were in the field that ran along the edge of the road to my right. The pasture to my left held the older horses.

But it was the herd in front of me, the 'in-training' horses that drew my attention. I didn't know what the men were doing so I walked out to the herd. All their heads turned to look at me with ears up and eyes alert. A palomino and a sorrel with a wide white blaze walked to greet me. I smiled and ran a hand down their necks and backs. Damn, they were nice horses.

The moon was full and lit the snow, so the night was nearly as light as day.   My breath was a mist as I walked around each horse; not one walked away from me. That says something about their owner. It was a goal I strived for with each of my family's horses.

"I know I have dozens of horses at home," I said to them all. "But I sure would love to take all of you home with me."

A large dark red bay walked up to me and sniffed at my hands as she looked for a treat. Her mane was braided high up on her neck starting behind the ears and ending in one long braid down her shoulder.

"That must look spectacular when let loose," I whispered to her and ran a hand down her nose. Sergeant Pepper was a brown bay, and this one was a red bay. I had no doubt when she was in her summer coat it was more of a blood bay. I was going to have to look her up on Lauren's website. A black horse appeared from around the bale of hay. In the dark eerie night, the horse looked like a black ghost. I slid a hand down its long nose and sighed.

A loud whistle echoed into the silent night and a dozen horse's heads lifted and looked. I turned to see the two men waving at me.

"Well, I'm coming back in the daylight to look you guys over." The horses turned back to the hay.

"They are outside at the grill," I propped the phone on the table podium and smiled at Taylor.

"But it's cold and snowy," he huffed.

"I know!" I laughed. "But they were just determined to have grilled steak since a gusting windstorm is coming in tonight."

"Can't say that I blame them."

"Me, either; plus, I get to eat the rewards of their cold cooking adventure."

We nodded and smiled then grew quiet. I glanced out the window at the two men bundled in hats and coats and huddled over the grill.

"Taylor," I nearly whispered and leaned forward.

"What?" He copied my move.

"Are you alone?"

CHAPTER TWENTY-THREE

SAMMIE

"Yeah, Mom and Lil Bros are outside."

I paused and considered if I should say anything but then just blurted it out, "I'm terribly sorry for what happened to you, and for the death of your stepfather. Ace said you had a good life with him when you were growing up."

He leaned back with a deep sigh, "Thanks, but I really don't know what to say."

"I know, and I don't mean to pry or upset you, but if you need anyone to talk to, I'm here for you."

"You're doing a great job helping Ace. Each time I call I can see he is more relaxed or calm or…I don't really know how to say it."

"I understand, and I see it, too. The acceptance of what happened and the 'moving forward' will come in time. Each day will be better."

"The problem is," His whole body slumped in the chair. "Move forward to what?"

The distraught look in his eyes made my heart ache, "You cannot live on the 'what ifs' of your future until you know how the shoulder heals."

"Yeah, Mom says that too. She tells me to just focus on this week and not worry about next week until it gets here."

"It sounds like you have a great mom."

"We do, but my injuries are only physical because I don't really remember everything. I didn't see him attack me, but Mom and Ace did.   I know Ace is holding in a lot of guilt because he couldn't get to me in time."

"I'm not sure that will ever go away," I said honestly. "But it will ease once you're throwing again."

He exhaled, "But, Ace needs to move forward and not wait for something that may or may not happen in a year."

I nodded, "Have you talked to him about it?"

"Not since he left."

I glanced out at the two men still standing on the back porch, "What do you want him to do?"

"He needs to be roping," Taylor sat up. "Once this story is out, he'll have offers from half-dozen if not more ropers to ride with."

"I know how hard it is when your dreams start to unravel," I leaned against the table and thought of the summer before. "He may have a partner, but the heart to leave you behind this year isn't going to be there."

"I don't know how to help, Sammie," He shook his head, and I could see his eyes start to glisten with tears. "I call every meal because I love seeing you, but mainly because I know it helps him to see me getting better."

I heard the back door begin to open.

"I'll try to think of something," I whispered.

"Thanks."

"Is Taylor already on the phone?" Ace asked as he walked into the room. His hood and coat were covered with a light layer of snow.

"Just keeping Sammie company while you two idiots barbeque on a freezing night," Taylor called out.

"You're just jealous you don't get any steak," Granger set the large platter of sizzling steak on the table so Taylor could see it.

"I can have steak and barbeque in 50-degree weather," Taylor smirked.

"But you can't spend four hours playing on the ATV in the snow," Ace grinned.

The relaxed teasing continued between the brothers through dinner with me and Granger sharing pleased glances. We spent the evening watching the NFR highlights, predictions and the back number ceremony.

Wednesday morning, I woke to the window in the room shaking against the blowing wind. After bundling in warm sweatpants and shirt I made my way to the kitchen to find both men already awake and cooking breakfast.

"They weren't kidding when they said wind gusts," I slid onto one of the kitchen chairs.

"And it's supposed to be like this all-damn day." Granger sighed. He was leaning against the kitchen counter and typing on his phone.

"I've been out to check the animals a couple times," Ace added. "Maggie is the only one I worry about, but she is tucked in the barn; warm and eating."

Granger looked up at me, "Do you know Delaney's brother Logan?"

"I met him briefly in Pendleton," I answered.

"He and Lacie Jae got engaged yesterday," Granger said.

"She does the *Coffee With Cowboys* podcast?" Ace asked.

"Yeah, she announced it on yesterday's podcast," Granger nodded.

"When my parents bought Sergeant Pepper, I met Camille, Lacie Jae's sister," I shrugged.

"She is a nice lady," Granger slid onto one of the chairs. "So, what are we doing today? I hate sitting around doing nothing."

"Gym work, I guess," Ace typed on his phone. Within seconds the phone rang, and Taylor was on the screen. "So, brother, since you've been sitting around doing nothing, we're stuck inside today."

"Lonesome Dove," Taylor smirked.

"Enough said," Ace chuckled and set the phone on its podium. Monte and Liam soon appeared to join the morning breakfast chat.

When the call came to an end, Ace pointed to a wooden cabinet next to the large television, "Hundreds of DVDs in there but my guess it will be right on top."

I opened the cabinet and gasped, "Puzzles!" I cried out in delight making both men laugh at me. I chose a 1500 piece puzzle with five horses running through the snow with snowcapped mountains and a blue sky behind them.

"Damn, Sammie," Granger shook his head.

"I have put puzzles together all my life," I chuckled and dumped the pieces out onto the kitchen table and began turning them over. "You just look at the big picture then start a bit at a time, and it just connects."

"So, you're not just a music savant," he chuckled. "You're a puzzle savant, too."

I laughed and my mind wandered over the pieces, and I could already see pieces that need to be brought together.

Our windblown day was spent with me at the table putting puzzles together and the two men in recliners watching Lonesome Dove. I made chocolate chip cookies, Ace made super nachos, and Granger promised to make steak fajitas for dinner. An hour before the saddle presentation was to start, we paused the movie and adjourned to the gym to work off all the food.

I was on the floor doing pushups when I glanced over to the men. Granger was working with the strength training bands, but Ace was sitting on the end of a bench, dumbbell in hand but staring at the wall. His eyes were glazed as if he were somewhere else.

I stopped and rolled back to sit with knees captured in my arms and took a deep sigh. My heart hurt for him.

"Where you at?" Granger tossed one of the bands at Ace whose body startled as his head jerked over. "Where you at?"

"I was thinking about Dad, what he was thinking all those times he went to the NFR." Ace dropped the dumbbell onto the ground but didn't move to stand.

"How many times did he go?" I asked.

"He went seven times, had qualified for the eighth right before he died in the accident. He was the returning world champion" His voice was low.

We sat quietly, not moving, just waiting for him to talk. After a moment, his eyes cleared, and he looked right at me. "Want to see something pretty cool?"

"Absolutely," I internally smiled at the softness in his eyes.

He turned to Granger who nodded.

"Follow me," Ace replaced the dumbbell into the stand then walked out of the room.

Granger and I followed him down the hallway and out the front door. The sudden blast of cold air had us chuckling and turning back for our coats. We followed Ace to the main house and down the long hallway.

His hand rested on the door handle of the last door, he turned and looked at us with a grin. "This is the inspiration we have had all our lives."

He opened the door and when we walked in, Granger and I gasped.

"Holy cow," Granger whispered. "This was all your dad's?"

The walls were covered in framed buckles, posters of magazine covers in dark leather frames, and pictures of Austin Conners with dozens of other athletes and celebrities set on the end tables. At least two dozen saddles were on display around the entire room.

A large rug with the Texas star was on the hardwood floor between two large leather sofas and in front of a rock fireplace. On the wall to the left of the door, centered and framed in leather, was the world champion gold belt buckle.

"On each side of the Championship buckle are the buckles he won throughout the year that led to the Thomas & Mack," Ace smiled proudly. "Just under the champion buckle are the three go-round buckles he won the nights of the finals…and, of course, the saddles he brought home that week."

To each side of the collection of buckles was a large, framed picture. The first picture was his dad standing in the NFR finals jacket on and he was holding up his #23 back number. The second picture he had his left arm around Charlene and his right arm around Lauren. All three were beaming proudly.

"Wow, Ace, just wow," I whispered as my eyes moved from buckle to buckle then print to print.

Granger's hand was moving from one saddle horn to the next as he inspected each one. "This is a hell of an inspiration room."

"Once Mom and Rob were married, she had all this sent up here for Lauren. The minute we get on this ranch, Taylor and I come here to feel a little closer to him." He sighed deeply. "To see what fate took away from us. One man, in some unknown hurry passed him on the highway just before a corner. When the semi hit him, his car was pushed into Dad's door then everything flipped." He walked to the picture of his father riding a running bay horse with rope twirling over his head and eyes focused on a brown calf running in front of them. "That's Maggie." He pointed to the horse. "This was the last picture of Dad."

Tears welled as I looked at the man. He was so young, younger than my own father. Such a tragedy to be taken from his wife and two little boys. So much was lost; memories, dreams, laughter, and family.

"I see this and just can't help but think..." Granger whispered then stopped.

"What?" Ace and I asked.

"You had your father taken from you at such a young age, and my father decided to just walk out on me, then Sammie has..." He hesitated with a glance to me.

"The perfect dad," I admitted with a bit of pride, love, and guilt. "Always there when I need him, supportive, and loving."

"We have definitely had different journeys getting here," Ace nodded.

"Ace? Can I ask you something personal?" I asked with a bit of apprehension.

"One thing about the three of us, we can ask anything of each other," He answered with a nod to Granger then to me.

"You were so young when your mother remarried, Austin was gone, but why didn't you ever call your stepfather 'dad'?"

"Dad may have been gone, but he was still a large presence in our lives." He answered and walked to the picture of his father and another man standing next to each other and holding their NFR back numbers. "Dad's championship partner was Barry Wylder. He helped Mom for years after Dad died and taught Taylor and I how to rope and has coached us all our lives. Plus, we have pictures in our rooms, and then this room. He was such a presence that Rob just never could overtake that. I guess Mom introduced him to us as Rob, and Barry always talked to us about Dad, that we just never saw him as dad. We believe, that was the beginning to what happened with Taylor."

Silence took over as we wandered the room. I stood in front of the NFR go-round buckles, and my finger rested on the edge of the frame. "As much as I want that championship buckle, this...this buckle would let me get on that stage and let me thank my parents and brother for everything they have done for me. In front of all those people that would understand."

"You have passion, ability, and the horse that will get you there," Granger encouraged.

Ace nodded, "Lauren told me that Dad's biggest thing to tell everyone trying to succeed was, *If you're a roper or a racer, you'll get nowhere unless you have a horse that matches your dreams. Doesn't mean how much the horse cost you, because a horse doesn't know how much you spent. It's the heart, willingness, and athletic ability the horse has for what you're doing.*"

"You have that horse, and YOU have that heart, willingness, and ability to partner with him to get that go-round buckle," Granger added with a believing smile.

My heart grew for both men. They believed in me and Sergeant Pepper, "Well, you two will be on that stage with me so I can tell everyone how much your belief in me helped build the belief in myself."

"You have to believe…you just got to believe you can do it before you can do it." Granger whispered.

"That's what Martin told Craig, then Craig told Brodie when they met?" Ace asked.

"Yeah," Granger exhaled.

I looked at the two men and sighed, they had both lost someone important to them: a father and a mentor. The mood in the room was heavy.

"Well," I walked toward the door. "I think this deserves cookies and ice cream."

A half hour later, I was pulling a fresh sheet of chocolate chip cookies out of the oven while Granger was filling three bowls with ice cream and Ace was pouring the chocolate syrup over the top. Then it was back in front of the TV.

"They are going to live-feed the saddles presentation to Brodie on Facebook," Granger said. "I want to watch."

"Me, too," I nodded. "I can get my laptop from my trailer."

"We can just use the big screen," Ace picked up the remote. "It connects to a computer, too."

"Really?" Granger huffed.

"They watch a lot of rodeos and their own videos," Ace added.

Within moments, his Facebook page was on the large screen, and he was scrolling through to find the live feed.

"I'll put together the nachos," I offered as both men kicked out the footrests of the recliners. "What do you want to drink?"

"A beer," Granger huffed.

"You're not twenty-one," Ace grinned.

"Neither are you," I teased.

"Neither are you," Both men smirked.

"So, beer for all of us?" I laughed.

"Yeah," They chuckled.

The presentation began and silence took over the bunkhouse. A tall man stepped to the podium and began the introduction. When Brodie stood, everyone stood with him for a standing ovation.

"That's great," Ace whispered.

When Brodie began his acceptance speech, I stepped next to Granger and placed a hand on his shoulder. His back was tense.

Toward the end of the speech, Brodie took a deep breath; "*My Pops says you have to believe…you just got to believe you can do it before you can do it.*" He wiped away tears and so did Granger. "*Those were some of the first words Craig said to me when we were five-years-old.*"

I knelt next to Granger's chair and took his hand.   Other than his hand tightening around mine, he made no indication I was there.

Brodie spoke of developing a bareback and saddle bronc clinic in Craig's honor. Granger nodded and his eyes narrowed. When the speech ended and the live feed stopped, Granger took a deep breath and turned to me with a squeeze of the hand.

His smile was warm, "Thank you."

"Always here for you," I whispered then stood. "I'll get the nachos."

"And another beer, Wench," Ace called out with a chuckle.

I laughed but pulled another beer out of the refrigerator. When I returned, he was scrolling through his Facebook feed on the monitor. Granger was texting on his phone.

"A clinic for Craig is pretty cool," Ace mumbled.

"Yeah, I'm texting Brodie to let him know I'll be there and help any way I can," Granger nodded.

I handed him a beer, "Tell him I will be there, too."

"I'll be there, too," Ace said. "I'll do whatever they need."

"Thanks," Granger sighed and sent the text.

"On top of all the rodeos they will be going to, they are adding a wedding and a clinic," I grinned. "They are going to have a busy summer."

Thursday morning the wind had stopped, most of the snow had been blown away, and we were piling metal fence posts and cattle panels on the tractor. It was a full day of fencing. We worked well together with Granger as the boss. It was impressive to see how precise he was with the posts and panel installation. We were back in the recliners for the opening ceremony of the rodeo.

We sat quietly and watched the introductions and the grand entry. Delaney, Brodie, and Logan rode in together and the camera focused on them just as they smiled up into the stands and waved.

"Do you know the Rawlins?" Granger asked Ace.

"No, never met any of them," he answered.

"I know Delaney and have met their dad a few times and spoke with Logan at Pendleton." I mused as the riders rode out of the arena and the camera went to the first bareback rider.

We watched silently until the team roping started and I heard a sigh from Ace before he tipped up the beer and emptied the bottle.

"Weird, isn't it?" Ace mumbled as Ryle Jaspers and Jess Corday rode into the arena.

"What?" Granger asked.

"That those two men, in that arena at the National Finals Rodeo, live in this house we're in," Ace answered.

"Sit in these chairs," I smiled.

"And probably bought the beer we're drinking," Granger chuckled.

Ace and I laughed and the solemn mood that had descended dissolved.

When the pair of team ropers made their way out of the arena after a successful run that placed them fourth. I lifted my beer in the air.

"A salute to them," I grinned. "…with their beer."

Ace and Granger chuckled, leaned forward and tipped their beers against mine.

"And here's to being in that arena with them next year," I added, and we tipped beers again.

Friday morning, I stepped out of my room to the sound of giggles in the main living area. Before I reached the room, Ace's chuckles joined Granger's giggles.

"What?" I asked

They both looked up from Granger's phone and their humored eyes turned to disbelief.

"Seriously, Sammie, did you even look in the mirror?" Ace asked.

My hands went to my head as my face flushed in embarrassment. It must be bad if he actually said something.

"I'm going to put on my hat to build fence," I huffed and tried to finger comb my hair. "Why would I spend time styling it?"

They both chuckled.

"What's so funny?" I smirked.

"Leo sent me a video of all my buck-offs the last couple years," Granger answered with another giggle.

"He the one that abandoned you in Pendleton?" I stepped in next to him so I could look at his phone.

"Yeah, but he's still a good enough friend to spend his time to put this together for me," There was a bit of defensiveness in his voice.

"Sorry," I muttered. "Can I see it?"

"Put it on the big screen," Ace grinned. "That way we can watch it in all its glory."

"That good?" I asked and slid onto my recliner and anxiously waited. My fingers were still trying to comb my hair.

"Oh, yeah," Granger huffed. "It starts with my first rodeo, and I came off at 2.6 seconds and landed on my head."

He started the video on the large monitor. The horse burst out of the chute, took two long strides then bucked twice sending Granger flying with feet high above his head. I gasped when he landed, then laughed as he jumped right up and turned to the camera with a grin. Video after video of different flying dismounts had all three of us laughing.

"Damn, Dude," Ace shook his head with a grimace at the last video had him landing flat on his back and visibly gasping for air. "Did you ever ride one?"

"Yeah, took a while," Granger grinned and closed the video then started another.

He burst out of the chute and the horse bucked from the first jump. A rhythmic motion with the spurring matching the kicks; it looked great, until the end. When the pickup man swooped in to help him off the horse, Granger jumped at him and missed. He landed on the other side of the horse…on his head.

"Oh, hell," I laughed.

"I'd never had to get off the horse's back like that," Granger chuckled. "And it didn't get better until this last spring. I finally managed not to try and push them off, pull them off, scratch the hell out of them, or wrap my arms around their necks and strangle them."

In the next video, the pickup man pushed Granger's arm down to his waist and wrapped his own arm around Granger before stopping the horse and letting him drop.

"I tried just jumping off once and nearly broke my leg," Granger shrugged.

"You need practice," Ace huffed as his phone alert rang. "It's Taylor for breakfast."

With breakfast with Taylor and morning chores completed we walked out to the barn to ride. I was thinking of Granger's video when an idea popped in my head, "Granger, do you have your saddle with you?"

"Of course," He huffed and swung his arm to a truck with a canopy parked by the barn. "Everything I have is in that rig."

The comment caught me by surprise. Everything he owned? Where did he live?

"That your new one?" Ace asked.

"Naw, just had the old one repaired," Granger answered with a sigh. "It holds lots of memories."

254

"Can you go get your saddle?" I grinned. "I have an idea."

"For what?" he asked warily.

"Trust me," I giggled. "Saddle and bronc rein."

He paused with narrowed eyes then shrugged and walked to the SUV.

I turned to Ace, "Saddle up your most bomb-proof horse and I need to borrow Stomping Dog."

"Alright, I think I know what you're up to," he nodded.

When Granger strode into the barn with the saddle slung casually over his shoulder, Sergeant Pepper was tied to a hitching post, and I was throwing my saddle on the buckskin. Ace had his horse saddled and had disappeared into the arena.

"What are you up to?" Granger stopped.

"Put your saddle on Sergeant Pepper," I grinned. "He will play your bucking horse. Ace will be the pickup man."

"What?" Granger chuckled.

"You obviously need practice going from the bucking horse to the pickup man," I teased. "So, I will lead Sergeant Pepper while you pretend he is a bucking horse."

We could hear the tractor start in the arena.

Granger shook his head with a grin, "You want to subject your prized barrel horse to that?"

I shrugged, "Lauren said to keep him anticipating and not expecting so…there is that, but you need to take your spurs off."

With a shake of the head, he unstrapped his saddle and tossed it on Sergeant Pepper. The horse turned and looked at him as if to ask what the hell he was doing.

"It sounds like Ace is grooming the arena, so you have soft dirt to land on," I chuckled. "So, while he does that, you ride his horse, and I will lead Sergeant Pepper to warm them up."

Ace had already made a pass along the outside edge of the dirt, so we lapped the arena until he stopped.

"Let's do it at a walk to start," I suggested as they switched horses. "It will give Sergeant Pepper an idea of what is going to happen."

Ace was sitting on his horse, but Granger was still just standing next to Sergeant Pepper.

"What's taking you so long?" I asked.

Granger looked up at me with a grin, "You don't get on a bronc saddle from the ground, you slide down onto it…it's just unnatural to do it this way."

Ace and I chuckled.

"Go climb the fence and I'll bring him alongside of you," I nudged the horses forward.

At a walk, trot, and eventually a gallop, he slid from Sergeant Pepper and with Ace's help perfected his dismount.

"I can't wait to try that from an actual bucking horse," Granger laughed when we finally stopped the practice and walked the horses toward the stalls.

"Maybe save your head a bit," I teased.

"When do you ride next?" Ace asked.

"Chase Hawk Memorial in a couple weeks," Granger answered. "Down to Odessa, then to the San Antonio qualifiers."

Ace looked at me.

"Odessa, Midland then to Arizona; I don't have to hit the Qualifier, I qualified already." I answered.

He nodded then disappeared into the horse's stall without a word.

I glanced at Granger and whispered, "You want to stay with me in Odessa? We can travel together when possible."

He nodded and disappeared into the next stall.

Somehow, we needed to get Ace with us.

CHAPTER TWENTY-FOUR

SAMMIE

Text from Mom: It's Saturday, you plan on coming home soon?

Text to Mom with pictures and videos attached: Having fun with the guys and playing with horses, building fence, watching the rodeo. Unless they get tired of me, I will be home Sunday after the NFR is over.

Text from Mom: Another week? Love the video of them riding behind the horses in the snow. They are quite handsome, so I don't blame you.

I chuckled and glanced at the two men saddling their horses for a trail ride.

Text to Mom: Personalities are better than their looks.

I stepped up into the saddle of Sergeant and waited.

Text from Mom: I look forward to meeting them. I'll let your father know. Have fun.

Text to Mom: Thanks, love ya

It was 50 degrees with beautiful blue sky as we walked out of the driveway, across the road from the ranch house, and into the farmer's fields. Granger was riding the buckskin, Stomping Dog, and Ace rode his roan horse, Bear.   After an hour of playing in the field, Ace removed his lariat from his saddle and started twirling it above him.

He glanced at Sergeant, "He doesn't mind ropes?"

"His previous owner is a breakaway roper, so I'd guess he has been around them before." I answered.

"You rope?" He asked me.

"No, I went from cutting to barrels. I can hold it and toss it and if I'm lucky I might get close," I chuckled.

We both turned to Granger.

"Why would you even bother asking?" He smirked.

Ace grinned, "Well, you can now feed with a tractor and ride a horse pretty decent, you might as well learn to rope."

"Why?" Granger huffed.

"Continuing your cowboy transformation," I chuckled.

"Going from just a bronc rider to a true cowboy," Ace added. "You just never know when you might need it."

Granger shrugged, "Wouldn't hurt; just something new to try."

After the trail ride was finished and horses tucked away in their stalls, the roping lessons commenced. When darkness descended and we walked to the house, Ace exhaled a heavy sigh, "Let's go out tonight for the rodeo."

Grinning, I threw my hands in the air, "I'm in!"

"That means you actually have to do something with your hair," Granger laughed.

"Oh, bite me, G-ranger," I laughed. "Give me 45 minutes to get showered and dressed." With that, I went out to my trailer to retrieve 'going out' clothes. I chose black stockings, ankle boots and a sapphire blue sweater dress that stopped just above my knees and had long sleeves and a full cowl neck. It would be fun but warm.

When I walked to the main house, Ace was walking into the barn.

Forty minutes later my text alert beeped.

Text from Ace: You about ready?

Text to Ace: 30 seconds!

My makeup was done to perfection with the browns and dark blues highlighting the blue of my eyes, and my hair was left down but curled in soft tendrils. The red of the hair and blue of the dress, and black of the tights were a perfect combination.

There was a light tap on the door of the room, so I twirled around one more time to look at the dress then nearly skipped to the door. Both men were on the other side with bright grins and white dress shirts and blue jeans. Granger's blonde hair was still a bit damp, but both had shaved, Granger leaving his mustache and goatee, and I caught a faint hint of cologne.

"Well, you two clean up nice," I teased.

"And your hair is actually styled," Granger huffed.

"I was almost expecting a messy ponytail on top," Ace laughed and swung an arm out into the hall inviting me to walk in front of him.

Granger held my coat for me to put on while Ace threw a few logs on the fire before we walked out the front door.

"Which vehicle do you want to take?" Granger asked.

Ace grinned and took my arm, "Take her other arm so her boots don't get dirty."

I laughed as the two men lifted me inches off the ground as we walked toward the barn. My feet moved as if I was touching the ground, and we were chuckling as we approached the barn.

"Didn't we already do chores?" I asked as they set me on the bricks of the barn floor.

"Yeah," Ace walked to a side door that had a keypad.

When the door slid open, the light was on as Granger, and I stepped in the door.

"What the hell?" Granger huffed.

"A saloon?" I gasped.

An elaborate western bar ran down the left side of the room. A large mirror graced the wall behind it and sitting underneath the mirror were rows of drinking glasses and bottles of alcohol. Old-time photos of Lauren and her Uncle Austin were framed and placed on the wall to each side of the elaborate mirror. The whole wall looked like it could have been in an old western movie.

The other three walls were covered in action photographs of Lauren, her daughter Jamie and a woman I didn't recognize. Gold buckles, trophies, leather engraved rope cans and bags, framed prints, ribbons, and other awards. Trophy saddles were in each corner.

A dozen tables with chairs and barstools that looked like western movie props were set around the room.

"I can't believe you're just showing us this," I huffed to Ace.

"We've been here all damn week," Granger added.

In the center of the large wall was a long canvas of Lauren riding her blue roan horse at the Pendleton Roundup. The horse's legs were stretched out in front and in back of him giving the illusion he was flying. With black cowboy hat, black hair flying loose behind her and over a black long-sleeved western shirt she looked fierce. It was a powerful image but adding to it was the intense stare she had to the finish line.

"Absolutely powerful," I exhaled in disbelief. "I want an image just like that."

"You can do it," Ace nodded.

He walked to the side of the room and plugged his phone into a speaker system. Dwight Yochum's voice filled the room as we wandered to take in all the photographs and awards.

Ace stepped behind the bar, "What do you want to drink?"

"Wine," I grinned and continued my inspection of the room.

"Beer," Granger answered and slid on the bar stool in front of him.

"Whiskey for me," Ace grinned and filled the glasses.

"Little Big Town!" I laughed and Ace picked up his phone and within moments their song *Wine, Beer, Whiskey* boomed into the saloon.

"It's our theme song!" I laughed and two-stepped across the floor and sipped the wine. When the song came to an end, Ace started it again and both men stood to two-step with me around the room. We laughed and drank all the way through it.

Next to the door was a wooden cabinet with a dart board attached. Ace opened the double doors to reveal a large monitor. Within minutes the pre-show for the NFR was playing. The sound was off as the music continued until the grand entry of horses and riders began.

Ace set nacho ingredients on the bar and we ate, drank, and laughed through the whole rodeo.

"I'm so glad you finally decided to share this secret room with us," I teased Ace.

"Yeah," Granger nodded and tipped his beer toward us.

We clinked the glasses together.

I was swinging in circles on the bar stool when the buckle ceremony began, and Granger's phone alert dinged.

"Kind of late, isn't it?" I came to a halt and grinned at him.

"It's Brodie," Granger read the message. "Zeke drew Destiny's Ignatius tomorrow night."

"Ah, your nemesis horse…we'll see if the champion can conquer the un-ridden stallion. That should be a great battle," Ace said. "Who did Brodie draw?"

"Ricky Bobby…good horse. He should get a good score on him." Granger answered.

When the lights were turned off and the door closed behind us, the two men each took an arm and lifted me in the air again as we walked back to the bunkhouse. I was relaxed from the alcohol and atmosphere, so I crossed my ankles and let my legs swing.

"We need to do that again," I grinned.

"Let's save it for next Saturday night," Granger suggested.

"Championship night," Ace nodded.

I woke late on Sunday morning, but there was no sound from the house, so I slid on my over-sized hooded sweatshirt, over-the-knee slippers and brushed my hair loose from its curls. I was pleased it still looked decent, so I didn't pull it into a ponytail.

The men's doors were closed, and it was still dark outside, so I made coffee, threw a log on the fire then pulled out my phone.

Text from Mom: Would love a morning song before church.

Text to Mom: Two minutes

I pulled the guitar from the case and set the ottoman next to the fire and made myself comfortable. With the phone positioned so they could see me, I called my parents. I was already a few chords into *The Sweet By and By* when their smiling faces appeared on the video call. They were sitting at the kitchen table with cups of coffee held in their hands and both started singing softly as I played. Two more of their favorite hymns were played before I began Dad's favorite, *Amazing Grace*. They both sang as they looked into the heavens.

When the last chord fell silent, they looked at me with proud love-filled smiles.

"No better way to start this glorious Sunday," Mom sighed.

"And now we will share at church this morning," Dad grinned.

"I love you both," I blew them a kiss and the screen went dark.

Granger and Ace's doors were now open but they had not left their rooms so I continued my morning concert with songs I knew they would like.

With a grin, I searched the internet for the sheet music for Little Big Town's *Wine, Beer, Whiskey* song. I played their song and strummed along with it.

Chuckles from both men filtered down the hallway just before they appeared and two-stepped toward me. They were so fun and had me laughing as I played the song twice.

"Choir songs to drinking songs," Granger laughed.

"Sounds like a good Sunday morning," Ace grinned.

I leaned down into my guitar case and pulled out the drumsticks that Mason used when we traveled together and handed them to Granger.

"Keep the beat and keep your key lower than Ace's," I instructed. "I got one for you two. Pull up the lyrics for Blake Shelton's *The More I Drink* on your phone. Take turns on the lines then combine on the chorus."

The first time was rough, but we laughed and sang it over and over until they did it perfectly. Then we went back to our theme song.

The guitar and drumsticks made it out to the barn with us as we completed chores. The day was filled with roping practice, the two songs, and looking for more.

The guitar was finally put away when the rodeo began.

Back in our recliners with beer in hands, we watched as Logan Rawlins won a tough, fast round of steer wrestling. When the saddle bronc started Granger stood and paced behind his recliner. The tension in the air was thick. Brodie's ride was outside the money and when Destiny's Ignatius was loaded into the chute, Granger shook his head.

"Look at the size of that stallion," he exhaled.

"Fills up the whole damn chute," Ace nodded.

"With everything in me, I want to be in Zeke's boots right now," Granger whispered.

"You think you can ride him now?" Ace asked.

The gate swung open, the horse launched into the air, and seconds later the rein was yanked from the cowboy's hand with a wild toss of a huge head. Zeke hit the ground at 6.9 seconds.

Granger exhaled and fell back into the chair, "I don't know, but I at least want another chance. I'm going to ride every bronc I can get on before I draw him again."

"That's a good plan," I nodded. "You can ride with me anytime you need a place to sleep. You need to hit all the big rodeos, too."

Granger nodded, "Denver, Houston, San Antonio, and the American and every damn rodeo in between. I have a few fencing jobs lined up down south to get entry fees saved."

Silence descended as we watched the rest of the rodeo.

I cheered when Delaney ran to second place, "She's on top of the ground tomorrow night. They are going to get a buckle, I just know it."

When the buckle ceremony began, I sat cross-legged in the recliner and leaned forward. The entire Rawlins family and Martin took the stage. Logan introduced each family member.

"That's what I want," I whispered into the silence. "I want my family and you two on that stage with me. I want to thank my parents on that stage."

"You'll get there," Ace said softly.

"Just stay focused," Granger added.

Monday night ended just as I predicted, Delaney and Gaston won first place and celebrated on stage. My gut was churning in wishes and dreams of being there with my parents at my side.

Tuesday morning, I woke with a shiver and curled under the covers. My phone alert dinged into the quiet room.

Text from Ace: Temp dropped to 17 degrees last night. Turning furnace up. Stay inside, I'll handle the chores.

Text to Ace: Let me know if you need me.

I sat up long enough to pull on the hooded sweatshirt and yank the comforter off the top bunk to add to the blankets covering me. Rolling into a ball, I stared at the wall and thought of the nights before; of Logan and Delaney introducing their family at the buckle ceremony. My stomach ached and spine tingled from the desire for that moment.

Trying to shake the feeling and build confidence, I played every video from the races since Rosenberg. It was noon before I rolled out of bed and took a quick hot shower then dressed in blue jeans, oversized sweater and thick socks.

Neither man was in sight when I walked into the main room of the house, so I opened all the cupboards and looked for ingredients. An hour later the house smelled of warm chocolate chip cookies, a chocolate Bundt cake, and I was pulling out the last sheet of oatmeal chocolate chip cookies when the door opened. They were bundled in coats, hats, gloves, scarves, snow boots, and had very red faces.

"Oh, damn that smells good," Granger huffed as he peeled off the extra layers of clothing.

"Don't tell me you were practicing roping in this weather," I teased and placed the hot cookies on the table.

"Nah, just had to thaw a couple frozen water lines," Ace answered.

"We moved the foals and yearlings into the arena so they could get out of the snow." Granger added.

We sat around the kitchen table all afternoon eating, putting together puzzles, and sharing stories of growing up. I proudly showed them cutting videos of me in different stages of my life. They were both impressed.

Our lives had been so different, but I was so glad that we had all come together in this bunkhouse.

I sat cross-legged on the recliner with a large bowl of popcorn in my lap and a mug of hot chocolate at my lips. My eyes stared at the television as the first barrel racer ran into the arena.

"Aren't you focused," Granger slid back on his chair with a bag of chips and a Coors.

"I want to be there," I whispered.

"You'll be there next year," Granger smiled.

Ace fell into his chair and flipped the footrest out. He also had a Coors and a bag of chips.

"After all this junk food today," Granger smirked. "I need to spend a lot of time in the gym or I'm going to be too fat to fit in my saddle."

I chuckled, "Delaney is fourteenth rider tonight and I read she is riding her backup horse. We saw him in Othello when they won that rodeo."

She flew into the arena on the dark brown horse named Maestro. Her cowboy hat, jeans, and long coat matched him perfectly.

"She has some really cool outfits this week," Ace mused.

"Look at that horse!" I bounced in my seat. "He is stunning…that turn…damn that stride… he's in the deepest dirt and look at him fly around that third barrel."

"Look how tight that turn was," Ace grinned.

"He could win this thing," Granger added.

The horse flew across the line stopping the clock in first place.

"Yee...haw!" I laughed. "One more rider! She could win two buckles in a row on two different horses!"

Delaney won and I was cheering and giving the two men high-fives as if I had won it myself.

"That brown horse is just phenomenal," I leaned forward and watched the replay.

Ace chuckled, "You know, that is the horse she bought from Lauren."

"Yeah," I nodded and leaned back in the chair. "He is powerful."

"So," Granger said loudly. "Delaney bought the brown horse from Lauren."

I turned to Granger with a confused raise of the brow, "That's what he just said."

Granger grinned at me with an expectant look. Ace chuckled and I looked at him.

"What?" I asked the pair.

Ace shook his head with a wide grin, "We are on Lauren's property, and she only raises Maggie foals."

"AHHH," I screeched with a laugh. "That brown horse was born, raised, and trained HERE!"

"He is half-brother to Quincy, Bear, Stomping Dog, and all the rest," Ace confirmed. "She just sold him in August."

"Funny how things play out," I grinned. "If I hadn't bought Sergeant from Delaney last January, she would not have bought Maestro as Gaston's backup."

"It was all meant to be," Granger nodded.

I pulled out my phone.

Text to Delaney: Congratulations again, LOVE that brown horse!

Just as the gate for the first bull rider was opened, my video alert rang out.

"It's Delaney!" I gasped.

CHAPTER TWENTY-FIVE

SAMMIE

When I accepted the call, it was Delaney and Lauren on the screen. Ace and Granger leaned in to see them.

"Oh my, you called me!" I gasped with an unbelieving laugh. "You should be out celebrating!"

Both women were beaming with wide eyes and flushed faces.

"Can you believe it?" Lauren gushed.

"Yes!" Ace and I shouted.

"What an awesome horse," I grinned.

"That's what we're calling about," Delaney said. "We were just talking about you and Pepper…"

"…and how Delaney bought Maestro as a backup for Gaston because you bought Sergeant Pepper." Lauren finished.

I laughed, "We were just saying the same thing."

"But you need a backup for Pepper for this coming year," Delaney said.

"You going to sell me Maestro? I don't think I can afford him now," I laughed.

"No, but you don't want to overrun Pepper, so you need a second horse," Delaney answered.

"I'm going to make you the same offer I made Delaney when she bought Maestro," Lauren grinned.

"What!?" I gasped.

"I have as much confidence in you making it to the NFR this coming year as I had with Delaney having success with Maestro," Lauren continued. "And I love seeing Maggie horses in this damn arena. So, I'll send you a list of horses that I think will work for you, and you ride them while you're there. If you find one that clicks, I'll make you a damn good deal on him."

I stared at them with jaw dropped and my back beginning to tighten.

"Do not turn her down on this offer," Delaney grinned then looked past the phone and nodded. "We have to go."

"I can't believe it…" I exhaled.

"I'll send the list in the morning," Lauren said just seconds before the video ended.

I stared at the phone as it slowly lowered onto my lap.

"That's awesome," Ace said as he relaxed back in his chair. "Then, next year, you'll both have Maggie horses in the Thomas and Mack."

"All three of us, because I'm taking Stomping Dog so I can ride him in the grand entry," Granger told Ace.

"And if Jamie makes it, that will be four," Ace nodded.

I leaned my head back, both hands covering my eyes, and tried to relax my heart.   Stress…I could feel the stress and the pressure begin to make my temples ache.

"Sammie? You, OK?" I heard Granger through the fog.

"Take deep breaths and just relax," Ace said softly.

"Remember, no one has more expectations from you than you do yourself," Granger added. "All you have to do is your best and they will be happy."

My heart rate eased, "Why is it, I can take the encouragement and belief from you two but if anyone else says it, I begin to stress-panic?"

Granger shrugged, "Maybe we don't mean as much to you as everyone else."

I sighed with a nod and leaned forward, "That's true."

They both chuckled.

"You have an idea which one you're interested in?" Ace asked.

"No," I laid a hand over my trembling stomach. "I don't even want to contemplate until I see the ones she is offering."

The list was sent at 5:25 in the morning and I was curled under my pile of blankets in bed looking at the blood-line paperwork at 5:26. The problem was, I didn't know the five horses by name. She also sent me instructions of how to get on her computer and look at their records.

I slid on a hooded too-large sweatshirt over my t-shirt and shorts and pulled on my over-the-knee slipper socks. With phone clutched in my hands, I quietly made my way to the monitor. As the computer turned on, I put wood on the fire and made a pot of coffee then curled into a blanket on the recliner.

The first horse was a dark palomino, with a white mane that reached below its shoulder. Large quarter horse rump, powerful slope of the shoulder, well-defined muscles and an intelligent eye…everything I loved in a horse. My heart clenched and stomach ached. I leaned forward and buried my face in the blanket. If I accepted the offer, I would have the added expectations from Lauren and her whole group of family and friends. By using my savings to buy the horse, it would add financial pressure because I would not accept more money from my parents for the cost of traveling and entry fees.

"Coffee smells good," Granger said but I didn't rise from the blanket. "That is a great looking horse. One Lauren is offering?"

"Yes," I mumbled into the blanket.

"If Delaney and Maestro would have come in second or third last night, would you have thought any less of them?"

"No."

"When you lost the first race of the year, did anyone think any less of you?"

"Yeah, I did."

He chuckled, "Anyone else?"

"No," I sighed into the blanket.

"When you won Rosenberg, was anyone happy?"

"Of course."

"Was there a difference between the support family and friends gave from the lost race to the winning race?"

"No."

"Then stop stressing and just enjoy the opportunity to own one of those horses."

I leaned up and glared at him. He smiled and handed me a cup of coffee.

"Stop fucking stressing," he repeated. "It does you absolutely no good at all, in fact, it makes things worse. If you just relax and have fun, everyone, no matter what happens, will still support you and care about you."

I took the cup and turned to the palomino. He was right. No one was making it harder on me than me.

"Lauren wouldn't sell one of those horses to just anyone," Ace said from behind me. I turned in surprise since I hadn't heard or seen him walk in. "Pick one out and enjoy the hell out of it. JUST HAVE FUN."

I turned back to the palomino on the screen.

"What do you think of that one?" Ace sat in his recliner and relaxed.

"Perfectly balanced," I smiled. "And a direct son of Frenchman's Guy."

"I don't know barrel horses," Granger huffed. "But even I have heard of that stud."

"Which one is next?" Ace asked.

The next horse was a bay horse, Corona Cartel, racing stock. The solid black ghost horse that had appeared around the bale of hay was followed by a sorrel with a slim blaze. With lip caught anxiously between my teeth I clicked on the next picture and my heart sighed in relief. It was the blood-bay horse with the long braid I had played with in the pasture. In this picture the mane was brushed to shine and flowed down to its shoulder, just stunning to look at.

"Mare or gelding?" Granger asked.

"Mare," Ace answered. "She's one I was looking at. I was hoping Lauren didn't add her to this list."

"And I am so happy she did," I sighed.

"Those blood-bays are real sharp," Ace added.

"Blood-bay because it looks so…deep red?" Granger asked.

"Yeah," I sighed.

I aligned all five pictures next to each other; palomino, brown-bay, black, sorrel, and the blood-bay.

"You going to ride all five?" Granger asked.

"Yes," I nodded. "I wouldn't judge a horse by beauty alone…which, seriously, all of them are beautiful but, I need to feel their movement and gauge their heart."

"Well, temperature outside is back up, so it sounds like chores, breakfast, then a full day of riding," Ace leaned back in the chair. "Go back to that bay mare so I can see her again."

"No, I don't think so," I smirked.

Placing the five halters and lead ropes on the hitching post in the inside arena, I glanced out the door to see the horses running through the snow-covered pasture. Granger and Ace were on horseback behind the herd of fifteen horses running toward the arena doors. I quickly took out my phone and recorded as the horses approached then trotted into the dry dirt. Ace and Granger were grinning as they stopped at the door. I took a picture of the ruggedly handsome pair. Their eyes were shining in laughter, grins surrounded by their days' old whiskers; and I felt lucky to be part of their friendship.

"Chasing horses is seriously fun," Granger laughed. "Can we run them out and back in again?"

"No!" I laughed. "I want to be the one that wears them out."

"After Sammie is done riding, we can bring each of the herds in here, so they have time on dry dirt," Ace said.

"Good plan," I nodded.

Ace rode forward to the herd and called out to Granger, "We'll let the ones we don't need back out into the field. Take it one or two horses at a time until we get down enough Sammie can safely walk into them."

I sent the videos to Taylor then watched as the pair slowly rode into the loose horses. The brown-bay I was searching for trotted away from the herd and toward me. Knowing Lauren had trained the horses so they were approachable, I took one of the halters and caught the horse. He pranced next to me but didn't push me or fight the lead rope. The sorrel horse was the next to be caught. He was so tall the tip of my head barely reached the top of his back. He had to be at least 16 hands tall.

Half the herd had been let out of the arena when I caught the palomino. Granger and Ace stopped the horses at the arena doors and waited for me to catch the black and then the blood-bay.

Two hours later, the sorrel and brown-bay were released out into the pastures. Granger and Ace had disappeared, so it was just me with the three remaining horses. Ed Sheeran's music echoed into the arena while I took my time with each horse; but I could not decide. All three were striking to look at and were a dream to ride.

Lauren had designed the arena to hold a standard pattern for barrels, so I set the pattern then retrieved my training video camera from my trailer and recorded myself with each horse. Slow practice patterns first, then a fast competitive run as if I was at a race. With a frustrated sigh, I shut the gates of the arena and let the three horses run in the dry dirt while I prepared stalls for them. I still had days at the ranch, so I didn't have to make a rash decision.

When I walked out of the building, there was no sign of the men. The bunkhouse was empty, too.

Text to Granger & Ace: Done riding, horses stalled, what are you doing?

While I waited for an answer, I started the computer in the bunkhouse and put up the pictures and videos I had taken of the three horses. I watched them over and over until the roar of the ATV's came down the driveway. When the machines were turned off, I could hear the laughter of the two men. It made me smile.

The door burst open, and they were grinning with red cold-bitten faces.

"We were racing around the conditioning track down the road," Ace answered.

"Oh," I huffed. "I rode that with Sergeant Pepper last time I was here. I should take the three horses down there tomorrow."

"You're down to three?" Granger asked and looked at the three horses on the monitor. "A blonde, brunette, and a red head."

I looked at Ace then to Granger and laughed, "Sounds like you're talking about us."

They both chuckled.

"I'm not too blonde," Granger took off his hat and messed his hair.

"Dirty blonde on top, maybe," Ace teased. "But the fuzz on your face is a true blonde."

I laughed as Granger rubbed the whiskers on his jaw, "By the time it grows out, you'll look like Paul Newman as Buffalo Bill."

"In what, another ten years?" Ace laughed.

Granger shrugged with a smart-ass grin, "Probably."

He did have pretty blue eyes like Paul Newman, I conceded; "He had a goatee and mustache…and really long hair."

"Well, now I have a goal," Granger laughed.

"What made you decide on those three?" Ace tipped his chin to the monitor.

"The feel of riding them," I answered. "Watch these…"

I played all three videos.

"The pali is Frenchman's Guy, the black is Slick By Design, and the bay is Dash to Fame," I shook my head in amazement. "The top stallions in the barrel racing world."

"Well, Lauren isn't going to breed Maggie to just any stud," Ace chuckled.

"I'm still a bit shocked I get to choose one," I sent the three videos to Lauren and Delaney to get their opinions. Then I sent it to my parents.

Ace disappeared to his room, Granger started the grilled cheese sandwiches, and I curled into a kitchen chair at the table to keep him company and put together another puzzle.

"Who won the race?" I asked.

"There was no race, we just chased each other and experimented with how fast we could go around the corners."

I chuckled, "One of those moments mothers cringe over?"

I watched the black mare run and when she was done, I realized he didn't answer me. His back was to me when I set the phone down.

"G-ranger?"

"Hmm?"

"Tell me if I'm crossing a line and I'll stop, but is your mother in heaven?" I hated asking that question, so I tried to ask with a warm vision.

"No," His voice was low. "I visited her last month after I left Texas then spent Thanksgiving with her."

"So, you have a good relationship with her?"

"Not like you and your mother or Charlene and the brothers, but we are…working on it."

"Charlene reminds me a lot of my mother," I agreed. "Was it hard after your father left?"

"He told me before he left that it didn't have anything to do with me, that he just didn't want a life with my mother, and I needed to stay and be with her." He didn't turn and talked more to the stove and the grilling sandwich. "I was mad at him and resented her for it and stayed in my room a lot reading and watching movies. When I started coming out, she never seemed to be there. I didn't know, until last month, that she was working two jobs."

"So, you were alone all the time?"

"Until I was fifteen and two scrawny teenagers asked me if I would go help them build fence."

"Leo and Spence…"

"Yeah, and Dale, Leo's dad. They were really all I had for friends until we started going to clinics where I met more people like Craig and Brodie and then rodeos."

"And, lucky you, you got to add us," Ace appeared with a smirk.

"Someday I may consider it lucky," Granger finally turned with a grin and placed the grilled cheese sandwiches on the table.

"Don't you know how to cook anything else for lunch?" Ace huffed as he reached for the first sandwich.

He chuckled, "Yeah, Martin was a single dad for a number of years and taught himself how to cook. When I stayed at their place when I was doing fencing jobs for him, he taught me. But I like these."

"Well, after this, I'm going to the gym to work off the last couple days," I chuckled.

Granger was the first to finish his dinner then disappeared down the hall.

Once I heard his door click closed, I whirled around to Ace so fast that he took a step back in surprise, "What?"

"His father abandoned him."

"I know that," he whispered.

"And his mother basically did, too," I huffed in a low voice. "Then Leo and Spence did in Pendleton."

"Not the same…"

"They LITERALLY left him on the side of the road, that's how we met."

He nodded in agreement.

"Well, I can tell you right now," I growled. "I will NEVER abandon him."

"I won't either, Sammie," Ace glanced down the hall. "I've only known him for a couple months but feel like he is a brother already."

I exhaled, "He has a good heart, and I just can't imagine…"

Granger's door opened.

"We have an hour before the rodeo starts," Granger shouted down the hall. "I'm headed to the gym!"

Ace and I shared a look of agreement then walked down the hall.

Thursday morning, chores were done, and I pulled the cinch tight around Sergeant as Granger stepped into the saddle on Stomping Dog. I glanced out at the pasture and saw Ace sitting on the horse named One Spot and staring out into the trees. He wasn't moving, so I looked to the trees to see what had captured his attention. I couldn't see anything. When his head lowered so he was looking at the ground, I waited. Minutes went by without a movement.

"He's lost," Granger whispered from behind me.

"Yes, that he is," I sighed and stepped up into the saddle. "Let's go see if we can help."

I rode alongside Ace so when I stopped, we were knee to knee and facing each other. Granger rode in on the other side.

Ace's eyes slowly rose and looked at Granger then over to me. They were distant, and the dark circles under them were more prevalent against pale skin.

"How can we help?" I whispered to him.

"I couldn't sleep," Ace sighed, and his body slumped. "The vision of Taylor lying unconscious and his head bleeding...breathes wheezing…it wouldn't stop."

"You know it wasn't your fault," Granger said.

Ace turned to him, "That doesn't stop the visions."

"You need something else to focus on," I told him, and he turned blank eyes to me. "Ace, you need to focus on you for the next year and make sure you're…"

"I had a long talk this morning with Taylor and he is pretty insistent that I find a partner and rope for the NFR like we had planned," Ace shook his head. "I just don't think my mind-set would be fair to anyone I roped with."

"You're also calf roper," Granger said.

"Ace," I reached out and took his wrist to squeeze tightly. "I know your dream was with Taylor…"

"There is no guarantee he will be able to rope competitively again," His body slumped in the saddle. "We have lived under Dad's shadow all our lives and if we couldn't match what he did, at least we wanted to get our names, together, in the NFR records to honor him."

My heart hurt for them and the loss of their dreams, but maybe not.

"Ace," I implored. "Imagine this…"

"What?" He sighed.

"Ladies and Gentlemen," I announced. "You have just witnessed Ace Conners make his first run as a tie down roper in his first NFR. He is following in the footsteps of his world champion father, Austin Conners. Ace also won enough money in team roping to qualify for a run at the All-Around Champion title. The entire qualifying amount of $4,000 was won with Austin's youngest son, and Ace's brother, Taylor Conners."

There was silence as both men looked at me until Ace's body began to rise.

"That gets all three of you in the conversation together," Granger nodded with a hopeful smile to Ace. "If Taylor isn't able to rope in the future, this year would be the only chance to have his name as part of a qualifying event at the NFR."

Ace looked at Granger then to me before nudging his horse forward to the barn at a trot.

"Ace?" I followed with Granger at my side.

"I'm on the wrong horse," he called out. "Quincy is Taylor's calf-roping horse, he trained him, won the high school nationals on him, plus he was horse of the year. I will use him."

"Ace Conners also qualified for the NFR using Taylor's home-trained horse," I finished the announcement.

"Perfect, Sammie," Granger grinned at me.

When Ace dismounted from his horse, he was already different; shoulders high, stride wide, and determination in his eyes.

Ace Conners was now a man on a mission.

CHAPTER TWENTY-SIX

SAMMIE

With Ace on the horse, and Granger driving the ATV to pull the sled, I videoed the first practice. In my mind, it was going to be a historic moment.

We rode until it was time for lunch with Taylor.

Ace turned to us as we walked to the bunkhouse, "Don't mention this to Taylor."

"Ok," I murmured but didn't understand why until after lunch.

"Can you send me the videos you took this morning?" Ace asked.

"Sure," I nodded and did as he asked.

"OK, now I need you to record the introduction you did in the pasture and send it to me," Ace walked to the monitor and turned on the computer.

I recorded the intro, then Granger and I watched as he put together a compilation of the videos then added the introduction.

He played it three times before he sent it to his mother and brother.

"I didn't want to blindside them with the decision," He muttered with a voice cracking in emotion. "This will give them time to process it and they can call when they are ready."

"That is so thoughtful," I sighed with a smile to him. "You're a great son and brother."

"THIS time," He smirked and took in a deep breath. "I need something to do."

"I was going to take the three horses down to the conditioning track," I offered.

A half hour later, I was riding the blood-bay mare down the center of the road with the two men on each side of me riding their horses and ponying the palomino and black horse.

They stopped at the opening of the large field, and I loped the horse around the track. Sometimes when I ride, I feel as one with a horse, but as much as I loved this mare's looks, there was something that didn't click. After loping the first lap, I stretched her out for a run on the second. Halfway through, I pulled her back to a trot then a walk by the time I reached the two men.

Through the cutting industry, I had been around men all my life, but never had I seen two men that could talk as much as these two. They barely stopped as I switched my saddle from the bay to the palomino. I took off at a slow lope as their chatter continued. The horse was comfortable to ride with a longer stride than the bay. Three laps around and I was switching to the black mare.

I patted her on the neck as we started the first lap at a long trot then to a rocking lope. At the start of the third lap, I imagined us on the green mile in Pendleton and leaned forward and gave the horse the cue to run. She stretched out and completed a full lap with a stride that ate up the dirt. My heart was racing by the time we slowed to a trot. We were both huffing when we stopped next to the two men.

They both grinned, turned the horses, and we walked down the road back toward the house.

"So, you going to give her a barn name?" Ace asked.

I laughed, "You know who I decided on?"

"You were concentrating with the other two and smiling the whole ride with this mare," Granger added. "It's pretty obvious."

"Gives me a chance with this bay," Ace grinned. "You have a barn name already?"

I looked from Granger to Ace and grinned, "It's quite obvious the only thing I can name her is Grace."

Text to Mom: Chose the beautiful black mare. She is a dream to ride and so fast.

Text from Mom: What did you name her

Text to Mom: Grace

Text from Mom: Ah, I see what you did there, send me pictures, wear black hat and Pendleton coat.

Text to Lauren: The beautiful black mare please

Text from Lauren: Perfect! I love her. Very smart, loving personality, and athletic. When do you leave? Cade and I are flying in Sunday morning. Should be there by noon.

Text to Lauren: I'll wait.

"Thanks G-ranger," I smiled as he took my hand while I stepped out of my trailer.

"Anything for you, Princess," he chuckled and waved a hand toward the barn. "Your pretty ponies are all brushed, cleaned, and wearing flashy halters for their pictures."

I laughed and wrapped my arm through his. For the spur-of-the-moment photo shoot, I wore knee-high black leather boots, and the brown, navy, and dark green Pendleton jacket my parents had bought me for Christmas the year before. The black hat gave me the opportunity to not do my hair. I loved hats for that reason. I had also taken a few extra minutes to apply a little extra eye makeup so I looked better for the pictures I knew my mother would share on social media.

Ace was holding a digital camera when we approached, and he took our picture.

"I want one of all three of us, too," I told him.

"Well, let's get yours done first," he nodded.

Dozens of pictures were taken of me and my beautiful pair of horses before the two men caught, brushed, and haltered Quincy and Stomping Dog so they could join in the group picture. After both men changed into black coats and hats, we set up the timer on the camera. It took dozens of pictures to get all four horses and three humans posed correctly.

"One last setup," I declared. "In this order, Quincy, Ace, Stomping Dog, G-ranger, Grace, me, then Sergeant."

After releasing the horses back to the pasture, Ace positioned the four-wheeler in front of the bunkhouse so he could set the camera on it with the timer activated. We sat at the top of the bunkhouse porch with our feet resting on the steps and smiled at the camera.

When the camera clicked, we didn't move. Instead, we sat quietly looking out at the serene scene around us; the horses in the pasture, birds flying in the bright blue sky, and a few barn cats making their way from the barn and to the fields. It was peaceful and a moment to remember forever.

I thought of the moment I met each man and would never have dreamed we would end up on a remote ranch, secluded from the world for two weeks. They were my heroes.

"I know we still have a couple of days left, but right now, in this moment, I want to thank you both for coming to my rescue...twice," I smiled. "Thank you Ace for getting me to the race in Rosenburg and to you G-ranger for pushing me past my mental block. To both of you for the time here. You two have truly changed my life."

"It goes without saying..." Ace sighed. "How much I appreciate the two of you being here. Sammie, for your giving something to Taylor to look forward to, and helping him...and me, through this aftermath of the attack. And, Granger, thank you for giving me something to do by teaching you how to go beyond your bronc rider status to being a cowboy, too."

Granger and I chuckled.

"Well, I do love learning and maybe, someday, I might have a reason to ride a horse or rope something." He looked up to the sky then over to Ace and me. "After listening to you two talk about your families while we were in Texas, it made me miss my mom. So, because of you two, I went and saw her for the first time in two years. I cannot tell you how much...," he paused and took a deep breath. "She and I missed out on a lot of life together, but we're in a good place now. You've changed my life, too."

The sun set behind the trees causing a pink sunset sky and the temperature dropped ten degrees.

The call for Ace came while we were completing the evening chores. He disappeared to the back of the barn to take the call while Granger and I walked to the bunkhouse.

Granger was straining the spaghetti noodles while I was pulling the garlic bread from the oven when my phone rang.

I glanced at it but didn't recognize the number, "Hello?"

"Sammie?" The woman's voice was low.

"Yes?"

"This is Charlene, Ace and Taylor's mother."

I looked at Granger with wide surprised eyes.

"Hello, Charlene," I replied softly.

"I just want you to know..." Her voice was tight with emotion and trailed off. After a moment she continued. "Anytime you are traveling through Texas, you have a home here with us."

Tears rose and my lungs constricted, "Thank you."

"No, young lady, thank you for what you have done for my sons," I could hear the tears in her voice. "You have a HOME here when you need one." After a breath she sighed. "I need to call Granger."

"He is right here, I'll give him the phone," I whispered and handed him the phone.

He looked at me with furrowed brow and jaw clenched but took the phone.

"Hello, Charlene," he said it as if guarding himself. "Yes…thank you…I will…take care."

He lowered the phone and ended the call.

"Makes my heart hurt," I whispered and took the phone.

"Yeah, that woman has been through a lot," he whispered.

It was interesting that he had thought of what Charlene had gone through and I had thought only of the brothers. When Ace entered the house, we did not mention the phone calls; we filled our plates and watched the rodeo.

Granger was in the kitchen loading the dishwasher when he received a text. He looked over his shoulder to me as I sat at the table. "Would you see who that is?"

I read the message then nearly gasped.

"It's a text from Brodie," I looked up at Granger. He turned and looked at me expectantly. "He drew Destiny's Ignatius tomorrow night."

Granger's chest rose then fell as he exhaled the breath, "That's going to be epic."

Friday morning, while I was driving the tractor and placing a round bale in the front pasture, a truck pulling an enclosed trailer drove down the driveway. I was a bit shocked since I had been at the ranch for over a week, and no one had come or gone. It was as if we were in our own world and the visitor was an intruder.

Ace greeted the driver as Granger parked his tractor and I drove toward them. Ace's head began to nod, and the driver stepped out of the truck and the two men stepped to the back. A large item was removed from the back of the trailer. By the time I had the tractor parked, the man was driving away, and Ace was talking on his phone as he stood next to the delivered item.

"What is it?" Granger asked as he fell into step next to me and toward Ace.

"I don't know."

As we neared, Ace was grinning as he spoke. I got a good look at the delivered item and smiled.

"It's a sled and tie-down calf, I believe it is called a Tuf Kaf," I explained. "You pull the sled with the ATV and when he ropes the calf dummy, it comes off the sled. It has moveable legs so he can jump off the horse and tie it."

"That's cool," Granger nodded. "No doubt what we're doing today."

I chuckled in agreement.

Ace slid his phone into his pocket and shook his head, "It's from Mom and Lauren."

"They believe in you, too," I grinned at him.

"Well," he huffed with a nod. "Let's get to work."

He and Granger pulled the sled toward the barn as I took another 'historic moment' picture.

For the first time in 10 days, Taylor did not call to join us for breakfast. Ace tried to call but there was no answer. It was a somber morning of practice.

We all felt anxiety when we stepped into the bunkhouse for lunch. Ace's phone did not ring, but Granger's did.

"It's Martin," he said before accepting the call. "Good morning…yeah…just came in for lunch…yeah…is everything ok? Alright…"

For the first time since I had arrived, Granger lowered himself to sit on the long sofa instead of his recliner. Ace and I shared a nervous glance.

"Yeah…" Granger whispered into the phone. His hand went to his forehead and eyes began to glisten. "Absolutely for sure?"

I sat next to him and placed a hand on his arm in silent support. I didn't know why, but whatever Martin was saying, Granger was having a deep emotional reaction. Ace stood next to us with his hands in fists at his side.

"That is so unbelievable," Granger's voice shook. "How are you and the family handling it?"

I glanced at Ace and squeezed Granger's arm.

Granger nodded, "Yeah…I understand…I'm leaving here on Sunday…take care…and I am so stunned but over the top happy for you…yeah, I can imagine…OK…see you Monday morning."

He lowered the phone, ended the call, then just stared at the ground. A silent tear fell, then another before he wiped them away.

"Granger?" I whispered.

"You know Martin's son Craig died last summer in a car accident?" His voice shook and he wiped away more tears.

"Yeah, Craig was your friend and mentor," Ace answered.

"Of course, heartbreaking..." I whispered.

Granger nodded, "Last winter in San Antonio, he hooked up with a girl in a bar, and Martin found out this morning that she got pregnant."

"What?" I gasped.

"They are sure the baby is Craig's?" Ace huffed with wide eyes.

"A DNA test was done before they even told Martin," Granger nodded and looked from Ace to me. "And she had twins. Craig has a son and daughter."

My body tingled in shock, heart constricted, and the tears quickly rose.

"I can't even imagine what Martin is going through right now," Ace exhaled. "Does she live close so he can see them?"

"The girl signed over complete custody of the twins to Martin," Granger's voice was low and full of disbelief. His phone alert beeped, and he lifted the phone again. "Martin was sending pictures."

The first image was of a man I guessed in his mid-forties holding two very tiny babies in his arms. He was smiling down at them. The next photo was a close-up of the twins next to each other.

"Oh, my..." I whispered and the tears fell. "They are so tiny...they can't be a week or two old."

"He asked me not to share until they have a chance to come to grips with it and Brodie is riding Destiny's Ignatius tonight...all three have to try and focus on the rodeo," Granger's voice shook. "It's all so…overwhelming." He stood and walked down the hall to close himself into his room.

I wiped the tears away and looked up at Ace, "I am so overwhelmed by this. I can't imagine what the family is going through."

Ace nodded and silently turned to the kitchen, "I'll just warm up last night's spaghetti."

I stepped out into the afternoon sunshine and let the chilly air help clear my mind. "Just too much emotion," I whispered to myself as I walked toward my trailer. The image of the two babies in their grandfather's arms brought tears again but I took deep breaths to contain the emotions.

A movement to my right stopped me in my tracks. It was by the main house where no horse or cow would be wandering, and the chickens were all tucked safely in their coop. Maybe one of the many cats.... A flicker between the trees had me turning with my back straightening in concern.

CHAPTER TWENTY-SEVEN

SAMMIE

A man was walking down the driveway and I instinctively turned and took a step back toward the bunkhouse. I hesitated just long enough to see a wide smile under a black cowboy hat.

"Yeee!" My feet pranced and I nearly danced down the driveway to him.

We were both giggling when I wrapped my arms around his neck and carefully tucked myself under his good arm as he squeezed tight.

"I can't believe you're here," I whispered.

"I can't believe it took me this long to decide to come up here," He chuckled, and his good arm squeezed tighter.

I leaned back and placed a hand along his jaw, "Taylor, it is so good to see you. Ace is going to be so surprised."

"Well, before we let him know I'm here, let me very sincerely thank you for helping him."

"He is driven to make this happen for you two."

"I'll be pushing him to make it happen," His voice was low and earnest. "This is…"

"What the hell?"

The voice was behind us, and we turned to see Ace striding toward us with a wide grin. Granger walked out of the bunkhouse right behind him.

"Your coach arrived," I chuckled at Ace and stepped away from Taylor.

"You rode on a fucking airplane?" Ace gasped.

"Mom wasn't going to let me do that, so after getting the OK from Dr. Greystone, Barry called in a favor, and I flew up on a private jet instead of commercial." Taylor grinned.

The four of us stood in the chilly air as greetings of surprise were shared.

"No luggage?" Granger asked.

"I had the Uber driver drop me off at the gate so I could walk down and take in the beauty of this place," Taylor answered. "I couldn't carry it, so luggage is still up there."

"I'll run up and get them," Granger offered.

"It's just a small bag," Taylor smiled. "I came up to get the training started correctly and be the co-pilot on the drive home Monday."

The brothers began walking and I was surprised that they didn't go to the bunkhouse, they walked right to the back of the main house. Ace typed in the security code then held the door open for us to walk through.

He looked at us with a smile, "Always the first place we go."

Granger and I leaned against the sofa that sat in the middle of the room and watched the brothers look at their father's trophies and pictures. I took a quick picture of the two as they looked at the world champion trophy buckle. Taylor glanced at the portrait of his late father with his mother tucked into one arm and Lauren tucked into the other.

"Mom is going to Vegas," he announced.

"Really?" Ace huffed. "She hasn't been there since the NFR after Dad died."

"Lauren asked her to come because she and Cade are getting married tomorrow," Taylor nodded.

"Ah, that's awesome," Ace huffed.

As the brothers continued around the room, Granger had his phone out with the picture of the twin babies on the screen. He sat quietly and just looked at the image.

"It's a bit the same," I whispered, and Granger nodded.

"What's that?" Taylor asked.

Granger told him of Craig and the miracle of the babies.

"They will know him in the stories you and his family tell," Ace said. "Just like we know Dad through stories and videos."

"Even though we don't remember him, we are lucky enough to have pictures of him holding us when we were little," Taylor added.

"And Barry who has always kept Dad alive in memories for us." Ace nodded.

They looked around the room again.

"Life isn't fair," Taylor sighed. "But the babies found their way to his family so they will get to know him."

"And cherish every story," Ace added.

A melancholy took over the room and I felt the tears rise again. "I need to walk." I stood and walked to the door. "I'll go get your bag."

"I'll go with you," Granger nearly ran me over to get out of the room.

We were silent and lost in our own thoughts as we walked up the driveway to the gate.

Granger picked up the bag and slung it over his shoulder. On our way down the drive, I stopped and looked over the estate Ace and Taylor's father had built to raise his children and help cowboys and cowgirls reach their dreams. It was a great legacy for the brothers and Lauren.

"What would you want your children to know about you?" I asked Granger.

He hesitated then answered, "That I was never afraid to try something new and give it my best effort no matter how foolish I might feel. You never know when something you have never done before becomes your driving passion in life." He glanced down at me. "And you?"

"That I didn't give up. I faced challenges with perseverance and heart and tried to be a good person through it all."

The brothers were stepping into the bunkhouse when we turned into the drive.

"Well, so far," Granger smirked. "I think we've done a pretty good job."

"Me, too."

"Where are all the cookies?" Taylor called out as we entered the bunkhouse.

"We ate them," Granger laughed. "You think we would leave any cookie leftovers?"

"I'll make more," I assured them.

"While she bakes, we'll pull up the PRCA Business Journal and see what we have time to get you entered into." Taylor told Ace and a laptop was set on the table.

"The Denver qualifier should be up first," Ace said as he slid onto a chair and read the online journal. "Damn…it's the same weekend as your Chase Hawk rodeo." He glanced at Granger.

"We'll have plenty more, plus the internet to watch each other," Granger nodded.

A half hour later, all our journals were sitting on the table next to the plate of warm cookies and Ace was entered into the qualifier. Odessa was highlighted in all our journals; it would be the first rodeo that we would compete in together.

"Ace? You have a notebook or extra journal around here?" Granger asked.

"Probably a dozen in the drawer under the monitor," Ace answered.

Granger chose a thick leather-three-ring journal and set it on the table next to his rodeo journal but didn't open it.

We spent the afternoon planning the first six months of the year.

"Let's rodeo as much as possible together," Granger said. "I can't always because of the X-treme Broncs."

"And we'll have timed-only events," Ace nodded with a glance to me.

"And I'll have barrel races, too," I nodded. "We need to try for the same brackets at the tournament rodeos, but anytime we are together, like Odessa, I expect you three to be staying in my trailer."

Taylor leaned back with a glance to Ace.

"You're not getting out of this," Ace huffed to his brother. "I will need you at my side, whether for support or coaching. You may not be able to rope this year, but that doesn't mean you're not part of the team."

"We're in this together," Granger said to Taylor.

"I would be terribly disappointed if you weren't with us," I smiled an innocent smile.

Taylor sighed, "I will be there when I can, but I need to be with Mom. It wasn't just seeing me get hurt, she lost a husband, too, and the Lil Bros lost their dad. I need to be there for them."

We all nodded as his words and reality sunk in. We didn't say anything, but each reached for another cookie.

The brothers were talking about a friend that was taking calves to their ranch for practice. Granger was sitting at the end of the table writing in the journal he had retrieved from the drawer. I sat quietly watching videos of my races and Grace until the rodeo began.

"Here we go," Granger stood as the saddle bronc riding started. "He's second to last."

He paced behind us through each rider until Brodie slid into the chute and on the stallion's back.

"And this horse?" Taylor asked.

"I turned out of Kennewick last summer when I drew him," Granger huffed and started bouncing as if he was getting ready to ride.

"He was and is unridden. I wasn't ready for him, but Spence tried in Pendleton and hit the ground on the first jump."

"It broke his clavicle," I added with a glance to Taylor's cast.

"He didn't want to ride anymore after that," Ace sighed. "So, now Iggy, the horse, is Granger's nemesis."

"I'm gonna ride him," Granger growled. "But right now, Brodie…"

The chute gate swung open, and the horse launched into the air.

Granger's body rose and fell with Brodie as if he was riding alongside him. When the horn blared, Brodie flew out of the saddle and Granger jumped in the air with arm pumping. "Yeah, yeah, yeah!" he yelled. "He fucking did it!"

"That was a hell of a ride," Taylor nodded as the ride was shown again.

The camera focused on Brodie walking through the arena, fingers to the sky and yelling; "That's for you, Craig!"

The 93-point score was announced.

"Hell yeah, hell yeah, hell yeah," Granger grinned and bounced around the room.

Just as the bull riding finished, his phone rang.

"Damn, it's Brodie," Granger jumped from this chair and paced in the kitchen as he spoke, and we listened to the one-sided conversation.

"Yeah, Man, you fucking did it…he would be so happy for you right now. I am… I'm ready to burst….yeah…hell of a day for you all. Yeah, Martin called this morning and told me….sent me a few pictures, Uncle Brodie…ha…Uncle Granger. Never thought I'd be called that…I don't even know what to say…yeah….yeah…I told Martin I'd be there first thing Monday morning…can't wait….so happy for you and the whole family...yeah, you got a buckle ceremony to get to...so damn proud and happy for you...yeah, next year I'll be there...have fun."

The call ended and his loud exhale echoed in the room. He didn't reappear so I looked back over the top of the recliner and saw him back at the table writing feverishly in the journal. He was there until the buckle ceremony started then back writing after it was done.

At one-thirty in the morning, Ace and I switched rooms so the brothers could bunk together. When I closed my door, Granger was still at the table writing in the journal.

Saturday morning, we were in the recliners to eat breakfast. Monte and Liam were on the big screen for a video chat telling us about their mother leaving for Las Vegas and refusing to take them with her. They were staying at Barry's house. Ace and Taylor were grinning ear to ear as they talked to their little brothers. After breakfast, I called my own brother.

"You're lifting your leg too high."

"Get the slack!"

"Push him over, don't let him crowd ya."

"Nice wrap"

One of the barstools from the saloon was placed in the middle of the indoor arena. Taylor was sitting and slowly spinning in a circle as he yelled at his brother who was riding Quincy while Granger drove the 4-wheeler. Taylor was bundled in a heavy coat, scarf, gloves, and with a blanket around him to keep him warm. Catching a cold and coughing would still be painful for him.

I rode Sergeant and ponied Grace next to us as we walked around the arena and out of the way of the training. The two horses were now traveling partners and I wanted to make sure they got along well before getting them into hectic rodeo grounds and arenas.

Taylor stood and stretched his body, and the training was immediately moved into the bunkhouse. The furniture was moved to the side as a roping dummy was placed in the middle of the room. Granger, Ace, and I took turns roping. With a chuckle, Taylor sent a video of us to Lauren. She responded with a "not the first time". Our training was interrupted long enough to watch a live feed of her and Kade's wedding. It was short, sweet, simple, and yet, romantic.

We were all surprised when the 'live feed' continued, with Delaney Rawlins and Ryle Jaspers exchanging marriage vows to a song by Toby Keith. When the video ended, Granger was looking down at his phone with lips twisted as if in thought.

"What's up G-ranger?" I asked and looked over his shoulder at a picture of a woman, a huge horse, and Brodie Rawlins.

"That's Brodie wearing the buckle from the win last night, Destiny's Ignatius, and River Westmoreland, who owns the horse, is holding the buckle they won." Granger answered. "They were dating for a couple of weeks. Hopefully, this means they are back together."

"Who did he draw for tonight?" Ace asked.

"Major Huckleberry, bad ass red roan," Granger answered. "We're setting up in the saloon still?"

"Awesome," Taylor grinned. "Let's order pizza. Mom wouldn't let me order any at home."

"We're dressing up again?" I asked with a grin.

"Why the hell not?" Granger chuckled.

Four large pizzas, three orders of garlic twists, a jug of milk for Taylor, then our drinks were set up on the bar: wine, beer, whiskey. The song was played, and Taylor and I slow-danced around the room together. My knee-length gold dress shimmered in the lights, my hair was loose down to my shoulders, and I wore comfortable knee-high leather boots.

The moment I could see he was beginning to strain, I put his butt in a chair at a table instead of the bar stools, and wouldn't let him move again.

"This sucks," Granger pulled a chair over so he could put his feet up and leaned back in his chair.

"What sucks?" Taylor asked.

"Tonight is our last night here," he answered with a smile at me and Ace. "It's like we've been living on our own planet."

"Reality hits tomorrow," Ace nodded. "Lauren and Cade are flying in and will be home around noon, then we head out Monday morning."

"I'm out as soon as Lauren and I do the paperwork for Grace," I sighed.

"I'm out tomorrow night, too," Granger took a swig of whisky. "I have to go face those two itty-bitty babies and the loss of their dad again."

"Ah, man," Taylor exhaled. "Let's just forget all that shit and concentrate on the rodeo."

We laughed and cheered for Brodie when he won the saddle bronc average, then I screamed and jumped around when Delaney won the Barrel Racing World Championship. I couldn't have been happier.

When the rodeo was over, we closed the saloon and with Granger and Ace each taking an arm, they lifted me in the air so my boots were just inches off the ground. The four of us very slowly made our way to the bunkhouse.

Not quite ready to end the last day together, we sat in the recliners with the last of the ice cream and toppings in our bowls. The pictures from the impromptu photo shoot were on the screen and we laughed as we went through them. We each chose our favorites and Ace sent them to us. Taylor had a sketch book balanced on his lap and tucked into the cast as he was drawing. He started chuckling then turned the image to Ace who laughed.

When he turned the image to me, I couldn't help but laugh. A large black cowboy hat had red hair sticking out the bottom across the forehead and down one side. Large blue eyes with exaggerated black eyelashes looked back at me. There was no nose or mouth and the side without the hair was undefined.

Ace and Granger had thoroughly inspected my truck and trailer before I walked out the door with my bag over my shoulder. Taylor was carrying my guitar case as he walked along side of me to the trailer. Grace and Sergeant were tied to the side with traveling boots in place and ready for the seven-hour trip. Mom and Dad were both anxious for me to be home, but I think it was more meeting Grace, although I knew they would deny it.

I could hear the clock ticking to the end of our two weeks of isolation since Lauren and Cade were due at any moment.

"I'll watch both of you online next weekend," I told Ace and Granger.

"Two rounds," Ace nodded. "Friday night, then Saturday morning. The top ten for each round automatically qualify, then the averages of the two fill the rest of the spots."

"Then we'll all be together in Odessa after the New Year," Granger added and took the bag for me and set it into the trailer.

My phone alert rang out as the sound of a car coming down the driveway reached us.

Text from Dad: Roads are clear, will have dinner ready for you. Drive safe.

Text to Dad: Will do Dad, thanks, love ya much!

An hour later, I set the newly signed paperwork for Grace on the seat of my truck then turned to the three men waiting next to me to say goodbye. Mixed emotions ran through me as I looked at each of them. I was anxious to be home but also anxious for the future.

"This has been the most life changing two weeks for me," I said honestly. "I could get mushy, but I'm just going to give you each a quick hug then we'll see you in January."

Ace was first, then Granger, and when I stepped to Taylor, he shook his head with a wide grin. Surprisingly, he slid a hand behind my head and his lips were suddenly on mine. It wasn't a short kiss.

"Damn, Taylor!" Ace huffed.

"Come on, man," Granger grumbled.

When Taylor broke the kiss, he leaned down and whispered, "You'll never look at me the way you look at him, so I knew I only had the chance for one."

I chuckled in amused confusion as he stepped back. With a glance at Granger and Ace, I stepped into the truck and quickly shut the door. After a final wave to them, then a wave to Lauren and Cade who were standing on the porch of the bunkhouse, I drove away.

Following the drive, was an hour of settling Grace into her new stall next to Sergeant 's, then an hour of telling my parents about the week while devouring the lasagna and French bread.

When I finally crawled into bed, I sat crisscross in the middle and looked through all the pictures on my phone. For the first time in months, I signed onto Facebook and attached the image of Ace, Granger, and me standing with the four horses.

"Three roads brought us to this point in our lives and careers. Our family and friends are our rock, our foundation; but these two men at my side are my iron and I am theirs. I have heard many variations of Proverb 27:17, but my favorite is:

*'Just as iron sharpens iron, a person sharpens
the character of his friend'*

Granger Miller, Ace Conners; our three roads are now combined, and we have become each other's iron to obtain our mutual goals to qualify for the NFR and beyond.

This next year will be memorable, fun, and most of all, challenging. Best of luck to all my true friends and competitors. May we all have the year we have dreamed of our entire lives."

CHAPTER TWENTY-EIGHT

GRANGER

At seven o'clock Monday morning, I pulled over to the turnoff of the highway five miles from the Rawlins' Ranch. Thoughts of Craig had filled the drive from the 3.3 Ranch to the hotel in Bend. The night he died had invaded my dreams and I woke early with a headache and empty feeling in my chest for the loss of him again, not just for me, but for the two babies I was headed to meet. Two cups of coffee later, I had finally left the room and driven toward the ranch, but now, I sat in the truck and stared at the traffic passing by with dread hanging over me.

Hoping to change my mood before reaching the ranch and Martin, I opened Facebook on my phone and was surprised to see dozens of notifications from a post Sammie had added the night before. It was my favorite picture of our photo session and her statement hit me in the heart.

*'Just as iron sharpens iron, a person sharpens
the character of his friend'*

Text to Sammie: Proverb 27:17

Nothing else needed to be said. I felt the strength of her and Ace as if they were in the truck next to me, so I pulled back onto the road and five minutes later turned down the Rawlins' driveway.

When I parked next to the arena, there were four riders at the far end of the pasture and disappearing into the trees. I looked back at the house to see Martin standing at the door. He flipped a hand in the air indicating me to join him, so I grabbed my bag and with long strides made my way into the house. He had already walked through the kitchen and was turning down the hall to the bedrooms. Without letting myself think of where we were going, I followed him to just outside of Craig's bedroom.

"It's best to just do it instead of thinking about it," Martin nodded with a compassionate smile.

"Just rip the band aid off," I exhaled and walked into the room.

Two cribs replaced the bed; one decorated in blue with bucking horses and the other in white with pink ponies. The dresser had been replaced with a diaper changing table and the closet was open showing a tall bookcase. Stacks of diapers and baby clothes on the shelves had replaced Craig's clothes. Two low-back cushioned rocking chairs set next to the cribs. But, every picture, poster, buckle, and the light blue chaps the Rawlins' late mother had given him were hanging on the walls just as Craig had left them.

I lowered my bag to the floor next to the chairs then stepped to the cribs. The tiny babies were nestled into cradling cushions, both sound asleep, pink, healthy, and just beautiful.

"Martin..." My body and mind were numb in disbelief and wonder. Tears rose and my breath shook.

"I know," He stepped in next to me. "We've been like that for the last three days, then, walking into this room." He paused and took a breath. "Until we arrived home last night, I had not been in this room since the accident. It was...hard."

I leaned against the crib to steady myself and Martin took my arm and pushed me over into one of the chairs. Then he turned, and much to my horror, he lifted the little girl from the crib and lowered her into my arms.

"I've never held a baby," My voice shook, and arms trembled as I cradled her.

"And yet, you're holding her like you're a natural."

Our eyes met at the words. "A natural", it was what Craig called me the time I rode that first bucking horse at the clinic and every time I rode a rank bronc.

"Grab my bag," I whispered. "There is a journal setting on top."

He pulled out the journal then took a seat in the other chair, "And what do we have here?"

"I just spent time with Ace and Taylor Conners. They lost their father when they were two and three. When they heard of Craig's babies, they told me they would know their father by stories we tell." I nodded to the wall full of pictures. "And by those pictures and videos." I looked down at the little baby girl in my arms. "I spent the last couple of days writing to them. Telling them all the stories I have of their father. All those little things they need to know about him."

Martin was quiet and didn't open the journal, he just held it to his chest. When I glanced at him, tears slowly made their way down his cheeks.

I turned away and looked at the wall of pictures. To the side, in a large 11 x 14 frame, was the picture taken in Union Oregon of Spence, Leo, Brodie, me, and Craig. It captured the laughter, comradery, teasing, and dreams being chased. Those were the moments I wrote to the babies.

My gaze moved to the little boy in the crib then down to the baby in my arms. The moment I met their father played in my mind, and my lungs tightened; tears welled again. Then, the last time I saw him, he was talking about the future with Camille. In his eyes, I could see him as a husband to her and a father to these twins. He would have been a fun father; a loving, protective father to his babies. As I took in the little girl's pink cheeks, long eye lashes, and fuzz of blonde hair, I swore to Craig's memory that I would be there for him. I would do whatever I could to make sure they were loved, protected, and raised with the spirit of life that he lived and so eagerly shared with me.

When we walked out the door, Martin pushed a small white square device that sat on a shelf by the door.

"What is that?" I whispered.

"Mrs. Anderson, from down the road, set this up while we were still in Vegas. She decided we needed a baby monitor so that is the camera, and we have a screen in the living room that we can carry and place wherever we are and still check on them."

We walked into the living room, and he pointed to the monitor sitting on the long kitchen table. The two cribs were visible.

"That's cool," I nodded then looked out the large front window to the horse pasture. Delaney's barrel horses that were in Vegas and teamed with her to win the championship were pawing at a fine layer of snow. "Where is everybody?"

"Evan, Logan, Brodie, and River just went for a ride to check the herd. Camille and Lacie Jae are in town shopping for more stuff for the babies and groceries. Delaney and Ryle are on their honeymoon in Key West."

He set the unopened journal on the table and slid onto one of the chairs, "You listen to the Blazing Trails podcast last night Devan dropped? It's the family interview."

"No, not yet. I was going to on the way home." I sat across the table from him.

"You're coming back for Christmas?"

"Yeah, and I need to talk to you about that. You know about my dad...that he left?"

"Yeah."

"But I've never told you about my mother." I told him everything from the point my father had left, time I'd spent in my room, signing the approval to go to the bares and broncs clinics, and everything else up until I left at Thanksgiving just a few weeks before.

Martin was quiet and just nodded a few times as I spoke. When I was done, he turned and smiled, "I have always wondered...not what I was expecting, but I'm glad you two are back on track. Are you bringing her for Christmas?"

I exhaled the last bit of anxiety I had in telling him the truth and shrugged, "I didn't know what you would say."

"I'll expect you Christmas Eve morning."

I smiled in relief. It would be Martin's first Christmas without Craig and I couldn't imagine being anywhere else.

I glanced at the monitor showing the two cribs, "What are their names?"

"Caleb; after the young man that unraveled the mystery and brought them to us. Her name is Lillian Eloise after Craig's mother and the Rawlins' mother who he thought of as his own. We started calling her Lilly, but it just didn't seem right. Logan, Brodie, or Delaney's daughter should have that name. So, we call her Ellie."

"Caleb and Ellie, I like that." I sighed. "How did he find them?"

We were still talking an hour later when the back door opened, and we could hear voices coming down the hall. The hum of Evan's wheelchair announced his arrival and the father, and two sons appeared around the corner.

I bounced from my chair to greet the trio and give Brodie a celebratory embrace before stepping back, "I thought River was with you."

"She got a call from her dad. She's out in the barn talking business," Brodie answered just as a cry from the baby monitor rang out.

Brodie and Logan both disappeared down the hallway and reappeared on the monitor. I chuckled as the two cowboys each turned to the door with a tiny baby nearly hidden in their arms.

"Boy, never thought I would see that," I turned to look down the hallway where the two men reappeared. Logan carefully lowered the baby into my arms.

"What do we have here?" Evan said and reached for the journal on the table.

Martin slowly reached out and placed his hand over Evan's and stopped him from opening it. Evan looked at him in surprise, but Martin turned to me to explain. As I told them of the stories, Evan tapped the top of the book then rested a hand over it. Silence lay over the room until Brodie exhaled.

"That is the just…" He turned and looked at me. "It's a binder so you can add more pages?" I nodded. "Is it alright with you if I write stories and add to it?"

"Of course," I huffed.

"That's a damn fine idea," Evan grinned. "I've got some stories to add."

"Me, too," Logan chuckled. "Maybe some that will have to be a PG13 version for when the twins are older."

The back door opened, and River walked into the kitchen. Her shoulder length dark hair was straight and held back by a black cowboy hat. I knew she had never been to the Rawlins' Ranch before, but she looked comfortable and at home. She quickly lifted her phone and took a picture of the five of us men and the two babies. I needed to remember to ask her for a print of the picture to add to Craig's journal.

I had only met her once at the NILE rodeo in Billings the month before, but when her eyes fell on the little boy in my arms, I immediately turned my back to her, "Not happening."

She laughed and carefully lifted the little girl out of Brodie's arms.

"Everything good with your dad?" Brodie asked as he relented.

"Yes, and no," River slid on the seat next to him and smiled at the baby. "He got a call from one of the stock contractors he used to work with, and the guy has decided to retire and has offered us his herd."

"Really? That's good, right?" Brodie huffed.

"You have room for more stock?" Evan asked.

"Yes, and yes," River exhaled. "Out of all the stock contractors out there, they gave our business first chance at the herd, and yes, we have room for them."

"Good stock?" Martin asked from the kitchen as he prepared bottles for the babies. "How many?"

"Just horses or bulls, too?" I asked.

"He's keeping the older retired horses. Good stock, a little over a hundred horses, no bulls," she answered.

"And the bad?" Logan asked.

"We have the land but will need to run more fencing to manage the pastures." She took the bottle Martin handed her, "Depending on weather, they want us to move the horses within the next month, which means a lot of fence needs to go up between now and then."

"Well, here's your man," Martin told her with a nod to me as he tilted up my arms to position the baby properly, then showed me how to hold the bottle.

River glanced at him then over to me.

"He's been fencing for years," Evan said. "Does a damn good job."

"Precise and honest," Logan added.

"Plus, since he's a bronc rider, he can help testing the new herd," Brodie grinned.

She turned and looked at me, "Can you ride a ranch horse?"

I kept my eyes on the baby nursing on the bottle and didn't have time to answer.

"He just told me he spent the last two weeks learning to ride and rope from one of the best ropers in Texas," Martin informed her.

I glanced from him to River.

"Alright, you're hired," she nodded.

"Just like that?" I chuckled, since I hadn't said a word.

"Look at the four men that just recommended you," she smiled. "Would you hire you with their glowing recommendations?"

We all chuckled, and I nodded. "I would and I will, but I have the Chase Hawk rodeo next weekend, and have to be here for Christmas."

"Brodie is going to that rodeo, too, then coming to the ranch. No problem with Christmas," She looked at Brodie. "Text Dad and let him know I've hired his extra hand before he does."

Ace and Sammie were going to love how fast my knowing how to ride and rope came in handy.

Saturday morning, Brodie and I were sitting in the meeting room at the arena in Billings, Montana waiting for the stock draw for the evening rodeo. The Denver Qualifier roping was on my phone, and we watched as Ace's name was called. The man at the podium in the room announced the process in which we would draw.

"How does the qualifying go again?" Brodie whispered.

"Top 10 from yesterday's round instantly qualify, Ace was 15th. Top 10 from today also automatically qualify, then they fill the rest of the 40 spots with the average leaders from the two runs." I glanced up at the podium as the first cowboy and horse were drawn.

Three other cowboys leaned over our shoulders to watch as Ace walked into the box.

"I hear his brother got hurt and can't rope?" One of the cowboys asked.

"Yeah," I mumbled just as Ace nodded.

"Brodie Rawlins," The man at the podium called out.

"Well, shit," Brodie slowly stood but hesitated just long enough to see Ace throw the rope.

"Brodie?" The man huffed.

Brodie starting walking backward toward the man as he kept his eyes on me.

I chuckled and called out, "He got him."

"Time?" Brodie asked.

"Eight flat...that won second place last night," I answered with a grin.

"Hell, yeah," Brodie grinned then turned to the podium to choose the horse I wanted to draw: THE Black Tie.

"Granger Miller." My name was announced next.

"Bastard," I muttered to Brodie when we passed each other as I made my way to the front.

He just laughed.

Text from Granger to Sammie and Ace: P27:17 WAY TO GO ACE

Text from Sammie to Granger and Ace: P27:17 I am so excited! I was screaming!

Text from Ace to Grander and Sammie: P27:17 Odessa bound! See you in a couple of weeks!

We sat on the long bench behind the chutes as the bareback riders took the platform.

"First time I came here was with you and Craig and I won enough to buy that little truck," I said to Brodie as he leaned against the wall and stretched out his legs and casually crossed them at the ankle. He looked so relaxed, but I could feel the energy for the ride beginning to build. I had drawn 'Outclassed' who was a powerful horse and couldn't wait to get on him.

"What's going on with Leo and Spence?"

I sighed, "Leo's girlfriend talked him into quitting and Spence decided to concentrate on circuit rodeos. He doesn't want to go full time. I'll ride with Sammie and Ace when we can."

"I need to ride with Logan at some rodeos because we're adding team roping this year," He leaned forward and unzipped his bag. "You want to ride together to the Extremes and other rodeos?"

I couldn't have been happier, "Sounds like a hell of a year."

We started with his winning the buckle on Black Tie and my ride only a half-point behind him for second.

Text from Mom to Granger: I just watched the rodeo on the internet. How exciting! Congratulations!

Text to Mom from Granger: Thanks, Mom. I'm OK placing 2nd behind Brodie but I'll get him on the next one. You'll meet him at Christmas.

Text to Granger from Mom: You sure about me going there?

Text to Mom from Granger: Yes, and at this point, if you don't show up, they will be disappointed and upset with me.

Text from Mom to Granger: OK, I will do it.

Text from Granger to Mom: Can you take some time off and come to the rodeo in Denver, Houston, or San Antonio? They are tournament style and will last three days each just to get to the finals.

Text from Mom to Granger: I have always wanted to go to Texas! Just tell me the dates and I will be there!

Text from Granger to Mom: I will be fencing in Nebraska for the next couple of days. I'll be there on the 23rd and we can go over my schedule. You are welcome to any you can go to.

Text from Mom to Granger: I am so excited to spend time with you.

CHAPTER TWENTY-NINE

GRANGER

"His name is The Buckskin," Nolan pointed into the corral to the horse looking back at us. "River has a real knack for naming bucking horses, but not much in the saddle horses." He chuckled and took the halter he held and slid it over a bay's nose. "This is Xavier, my horse. The Westmoreland's sent him to me while they were in Vegas." He turned and grinned at me. "River thought he was hers, but I took a bit of a liking to him."

"He's a damn good-looking horse," I haltered the buckskin.

"An even better ranch horse," Nolan walked to the barn. "Only a couple times in my life have I connected with a horse like I have with him."

I turned and followed him to the barn and tack room. It was my first morning at Nolan's ranch after Brodie and I had driven down after the rough stock rodeo. Brodie was driving to the Westmoreland ranch while Nolan and I were riding the two miles. A long duster borrowed from Nolan protected me from the brisk morning air. A thick frost covered everything.

"We'll go in the back gate and push the broodmares to the ranch so we can check them over," Nolan said as we mounted the horses.

"Do you know where he wants the fencing?" I asked as we walked away from the ranch and down a long frosted over dirt road.

"Put a *they*, not just a *he*, on there," Nolan smirked. "River is a 50/50 owner of this business and has as much say into everything as her father does."

"Point taken, and will do," I nodded my appreciation. "Do you know where THEY want the fencing?"

"We did some discussing on it yesterday while you two were at the rodeo, but they mainly focused on the horses and were waiting for you to go over the fence."

"How much acreage do they have?"

We talked about the property and history of the Westmoreland Stock Contracting Company as we found the brood mares and slowly walked them toward the ranch. I was honest with him concerning my lack of riding experience, and he respected the honesty and began teaching me how to ride in the mountains and the difference when pushing horses compared to pushing cows.

"You ride up to the house and let them know we are here. I'll go back to that stubborn mare that's lagging and keep her company."

He turned back and I rode toward the large barn with multiple pens on the outside with doors that led to indoor stalls. I didn't see any horses in the pens until the last door that opened into the largest corral.

The first time I had seen the horse was in Kennewick when I decided to withdraw from the rodeo. The last time I had seen him in person was in Pendleton as I helped carry Spence from the arena as the horse completed a victory lap.

Destiny's Ignatius stood in the corral and watched as I neared. He was massive with a muscular body, dark brown hide, and a white blaze down his face. The long forelock and thick mane made him look even bigger. I stopped the horse I was riding and stared at the stallion. Not once, since I had accepted the job from River, did I even think about the stallion or connect that he would be on the ranch. I was used to seeing him in pens and chutes at rodeos, not here on their ranch standing calmly in the corral.

He slowly walked toward the fence and the gelding I was riding turned to look at him but didn't move. When the stallion lifted his nose over the tall fence next to me, I slid off a glove and stretched my hand to him. He bumped it a few times before holding still and letting me scratch the softness of his muzzle then up his nose. I brushed the long black hair away from his large brown eyes and we just stared at each other.

I was lost in time as my hand stroked his face down one side then the other. He seemed to enjoy the quiet moment as much as I did.

It was surreal.

A noise down the fence broke the moment as we both turned to see a woman walking towards us. She tucked something inside the front of her coat before zipping it up and sliding on a glove. Iggy turned and walked towards her but when she stretched out a hand to him, he sidestepped away from her then looked over his shoulder at her as he walked back to the feeder full of hay.

"That's a look of 'how dare you try to touch me'," the woman chuckled. "I don't believe I have ever seen anyone besides River be able to pet him like that. I'm Gloria Westmoreland."

"Granger Miller," I returned her smile then looked out at the horse. "We had a long, silent conversation in Kennewick last year."

"Ah, that's where I've heard your name before, you turned out on him."

"Yes, ma'am, I did. At that point, I wasn't mentally ready for him."

"And now?"

I grinned and looked back at her, "I won't turn out any horse again."

"From what I've heard so far, you'll be getting plenty of practice in the next month as they go through the new herd."

I laughed, "No better way to spend a winter."

"You tell me that again at the end of those months." She laughed and looked behind me as Nolan rode in. "Coffee and doughnuts in the barn. You best hurry before those three finish them off."

Just inside the barn door was a wide-open space where we found River, Brodie, and a man I had last seen on the platform in Pendleton when we shared a look concerning Spence and Iggy; Adam Westmoreland, River's father. They were sitting around a table and each biting into a sugar-coated doughnut. They looked at us with humor dancing in their eyes.

"And what did I just say?" Gloria chuckled as she walked by us.

Nolan slid the door closed to block out the cold then tapped on a door to our right, "This will be your room. It's heated, bathroom, bed, dresser, and they were even kind enough to put a television in there."

I grinned at him then stopped before reaching the table. On the wall to my right was a large mural of a stallion rearing on his back legs. I recognized him as Iggy's sire. It was beautiful. To the side of it was a large map of what I assumed was their ranch. To the left, starting halfway down, were four doors about 20 feet apart; barn doors with the top separated from the bottom. I looked to my left at the wall. On the other side was the corral. I looked back at the door Nolan had tapped on, then to the group at the table.

"So, you're telling me, I'm going to be stalled in the barn with Iggy?"

The laughter echoed throughout the barn. It set the tone for the next five days of planning, staking, and the beginning of miles and miles of new fence.

"Who are they?" Mom whispered as we approached the Rawlins' home.

"In the wheelchair is Evan, the father and owner of the place. Next to him is his daughter Delaney, then Camille, and Lacie Jae. Someone from the family always comes out on the porch to greet people coming in for Christmas."

"That's a wonderful tradition."

"I met Lacie Jae here last year then her sister Camille in San Antonio."

"How did he end up in the chair?"

"A round bale of hay fell off their trailer and pinned him against the tractor. He can walk for a couple of minutes then his spine begins to hurt."

When I pulled in next to the barn, her gaze wandered to the corrals, pastures, cows, and horses. "You've been coming here?"

"Yeah, I help them fence and work cows...branding and doctoring when I'm not on the road."

When we approached the house, we were welcomed with wide smiles and a quick wave from Lacie Jae.

"Merry Christmas!" They called out.

Mom went straight to Evan and reached out a hand. He took it with a pleased smile.

"Thank you," she whispered as tears filled her eyes. "Thank you for taking in my son."

Evan smiled in understanding and placed his other hand over hers. "He's a good kid."

I chuckled since I was twenty and not even a teenager anymore, but I guess, in their eyes, I would always be a kid.

"Here comes two more cars!" Lacie Jae cheered with a quick hug to Mom then she pushed us to the house door.

When I entered the kitchen, Logan was already cooking, four cowboys and two cowgirls were scattered between the kitchen table and sofas, but I didn't see Martin.

"Where...?" I started.

"Nursery," Logan grinned and nodded to my mom. "Shayla...nice to meet you, you have an interesting son."

We both chuckled as I led her down the hall. She turned the corner and stopped with a gasp at the mass of saddles, trophies, buckles, and pictures on the wall. Then there was the exercise equipment that filled the rest of the wide space.

"They've been at it a few years," I smiled and nodded to the door of the nursery.

The baby boy was lying in his crib and staring at the colorful pony mobile twirling above him. Martin was just lifting the little girl from the changing table.

"Mine," I quickly stepped to him and reached for the baby. "Martin, this is my mother, Shayla Miller. Mom, this is Martin Houston."

I cuddled the baby close as they shook hands.

"Thank you, for taking in my son." She whispered to him. "He has told me a lot about you and your son."

He nodded with a warm smile, "He is a nice, hardworking young man and was a good friend to Craig."

Martin waved a hand to the pictures and buckles on the wall.

As I sat in the chair and rocked Little Ellie to sleep, Martin introduced Mom to Craig. When they came to the picture taken in Union of Leo, Spence, Craig, me and Brodie she stopped and stared. Her hand trembled as her fingers reached out to touch the frame. Silently, Martin stepped back and lifted Little Caleb from the crib.

Minutes passed as she stared at the picture before she spoke.

"I am so confused," she whispered and wiped away tears.

"About what?" I asked in concern.

She turned to me and looked at Martin, the babies, then to me. "If our past hadn't happened...if we had talked and you wouldn't have left...you wouldn't have had this..." She turned back to the picture then pointed to a few more images of me with Craig, Brodie, and the family.

"You wouldn't have had these friends, these moments, met Craig and..."

Martin sighed. "We can second-guess ourselves and everything we have done...maybe if I had raised a son that would have said 'no' to someone that needed help and just did what was best for him and his rodeo career, then maybe he would still be with us today. He wouldn't have been on that road the moment that car ran the stop light. Would I have wanted that? Yes, but would I have wanted to raise a son that said 'no' to a friend, no. Life has a way of turning out the way it wants, not the way we want." He took a deep breath. "Your son stepping away from your home, brought him into mine, which has helped heal the wound from me losing my son."

Tears streamed down her face as she took his hand.

"Now," he cleared his voice. "Have a seat next to your son and hold his 'nephew' as he holds his 'niece'."

In that moment, the wounds inside me from my father leaving and Craig's loss began to heal.

Christmas morning, everyone received a Christmas stocking with oranges, nuts, candy, and gas gift cards to help them to the next rodeo. And, much to her surprise and delight, Mom's stocking also included a small photo album of pictures they had taken of me throughout the years.

We were the last to leave on Christmas day with Evan and Martin walking us to my truck.

"Granger," Evan reached out a hand. "We have one more thing for you."

"You guys have already given me more than enough," I shook my head. "And, you know that."

"This is different," Martin smiled.

"Here," Evan shoved an envelope in my hand. "You'll be riding with Brodie part of the year, so we have decided, whether you like it or not, we are sponsoring you."

"There is a check in there to help with entry fees, gas, hotels...whatever you need," Martin grinned.

"That includes a few patches and stickers of the Rawlins' brand," Evan added.

"And don't hesitate coming to us if you need anything else," Martin smiled proudly. "We have to keep Ellie and Caleb's Uncle Granger on the road."

I was a bit stunned and gripped the envelope as if it was going to fly out of my hand. I looked between the two men and wondered how lucky I was to meet them.

As we drove away from the ranch, Mom turned and looked at me.

"I wish the last few years of not talking and not knowing where you were hadn't happened, but I will never wish away those memories you have meeting and traveling with your friends and this family." She turned and smiled at me with love glowing in her eyes. "I cannot wait to join you in this adventure."

I smiled at her as my heart warmed. "I cannot wait to share it with you."

CHAPTER THIRTY

ACE

Mom to Ace: Are you there yet?

Mom to Ace: Son, why haven't you responded?

Mom to Ace: If you don't answer me....

Mom to Ace: ARE YOU THERE?

Ace to Mom: I was driving. My mother told me not to text and drive at the same time

Mom to Ace: And NOW you listen to your mother?

Ace to Mom: I have on occasion. I just pulled into grounds. Getting ready to unload horses.

Mom to Ace: Are Granger and Sammie there?

Ace to Mom: Sammie is here, horses stalled, trailer setup and she blocked a spot for me to park the truck and trailer next to her. She's a pro at this. Granger and Brodie will be here in an hour. We head from here to Denver, we are all in the second bracket.

Mom to Ace: OK, we'll head to Denver in the morning. Lil Bros are pretty excited.

Ace to Mom: Taylor?

Mom to Ace: Apprehensive in seeing all the people after news on his injury got out.

Ace to Mom: Make sure he doesn't back out. He just needs this one then he'll be good. He has a big support team here and I need him here.

Mom to Ace: I know, I told him the same thing.

Our first night in Odessa, had Brodie laying in a sleeping bag on a padded mat on the floor between my converted bed and the kitchen counter. Granger was on the converted sofa while Sammie was tucked away in the front in her secluded room. Her last words before the trailer had gone silent were: "I'm so glad you three are here with me; iron sharpens iron."

When Taylor arrived, his hard cast had been replaced by an almost hidden black sling against a black coat. When the story of his injury and not being able to compete had been broken to the industry, Rob's attack and death had not been mentioned nor linked to him. We would try everything we could to make it easier for the Lil Bro's and protect them.

Within minutes of Taylor stepping out of the truck, a dozen ropers surrounded us. Monte and Liam relaxed as they had half a dozen champion ropers watching them rope the dummies next to the trailer.

An hour later, Taylor turned to me with a wide true smile, "All is good, go get it done."

"Iron sharpens Iron."

I thought of those words as I stood behind the roping chutes next to Quincy and watched Brodie and Granger preparing their broncs for the ride. Brodie was the first out and took the lead with an 85-point ride. At this point, it was almost expected that Brodie would keep the lead from Granger. But, this time, riding a horse named Red Wings, Granger took the clear lead. The cheering, yelling, and energy of the two men and the family in the crowd fueled my own energy.

While we waited in the area next to the roping chute in the arena, I had pure focus and determination. As I rode into the box and backed into the corner, I could hear Taylor's voice yelling at me to "Trust Quincy". I did and ran the near perfect run. With an 8.2 second run, I was sitting in second place with only one more rodeo performance to wait through.

I was back behind the panel again when Sammie's name was called, and she raced into the arena on Sergeant. Tight turns and quick kicks had them flying out of the arena with a 15.35 second run. She took the lead and I yelled with fist pumping the air.

The celebration at the trailer with my family and the Rawlins was flat out fun. That was what we had wanted. Not just to win or place, but to have fun doing it.

The next night, as we sat in the trailers in Denver, Granger and Sammie were announced as the Odessa winners, and I held my place in second.

Three nights later, the celebration continued as we all qualified for the Denver semi-finals. The next morning, Sammie emerged from her room and grinned at me and Granger as we were still lying in bed.

"What?" Granger yawned.

She sat on the top step where she could easily see both of us, "You guys know the company, Quanstils?" We nodded. "My dad went to high school with the owner of the company and since my dad started competing, they have been his sponsors. Actually, they sponsor the whole family as part of their western family value theme."

"That's cool," Granger muttered.

"Well," Sammie grinned. "They contacted Dad this morning and wanted to know if we, the three of us, would consider their sponsorship with the 'iron sharpens iron' concept behind it. They believe in it as much as they believe in family values. Friendships are as important as family. That is what they want to express with our help."

"I'm in," Granger grinned.

I nodded, "I have a few sponsors, but not a clothing company so that should be OK."

"They are an outerwear company…coats, hats, gloves, and such," she explained.

"What do we do?" Granger asked. "Just wear patches and talk about them?"

"They'll want a photoshoot with us in their coats." Sammie said as she typed into her phone. "I'm texting Dad and letting him know."

"Think they'll make me shave?" Granger ran his fingers down his overgrown, shaggy beard.

"Hopefully make you clean it up a bit," I chuckled.

"You don't like my beard?" He huffed with humor.

Sammie scrunched her face at him then her hand shot out and waved in the air toward him, "All that...I wouldn't change a thing. It makes you who you are."

"That isn't necessarily a good thing," I grimaced.

Laughter rang out. That was the best thing about the three of us.

Text Taylor to Ace: Where are you?

Text Ace to Taylor: Denver

Text Taylor to Ace: No shit, narrow that down

Text Ace to Taylor: On Quincy

Text Taylor to Ace: Good to know since tie down is next.   What am I going to tell you?

Text Ace to Taylor: To congratulate Granger for making the finals

Text Taylor to Ace: You are such a pain in the ass

Text Ace to Taylor: Trust Quincy

Text Taylor to Ace: He knows what he is doing and so do you.

Text Ace to Taylor: Gotta go, I'm at a rodeo getting ready to compete

Text Taylor to Ace: TRUST QUINCY

I handed the phone down to Granger as he strode in next to me, "Good ride."

"I'm hungry," he huffed. "Go get it done so we can go eat before Sammie runs."

"On it," I nudged Quincy to the arena as I flipped the piggin' string over my head.

I worked on keeping my mind focused and as 'matter-of-fact' as possible as I rode into the arena. Over the years, I realized it was easier to break it down step by step rather than focusing on the run and the money behind it. I needed the money for the standings, but I wasn't going to get it if I didn't focus on the process first. Barry had drilled that into us over the years.

I adjusted my hat, the piggin' string between my teeth, then the rope. Then, I did it again just before backing into the box.

"Trust Quincy," I told myself. Trusting him was nothing more than letting him do his job and focusing on my own. I could do that. The calf turned in the chute and looked down the arena. I nodded.

Two swings and the rope was flying to settle down over the calf's neck. I stepped off the horse who was sliding to a stop then forgot about him as I ran to the calf. Flank, turn, string, wrap, one...two...tighten...step back and jog to the horse who was patiently waiting. He kept the rope just tight enough to keep the calf from standing but not tight enough to drag him. I stepped back on him and he immediately took two steps forward to loosen the rope.

"Ladies and gentlemen! That was an 8.6 second run and should easily get this young roper into the finals on Saturday."

I let out a deep breath.

Granger and I stood behind the arena fence with unbitten hamburgers in our hands as Sammie's name was called out. Breaths held until she raced into the arena, and we leaned into each barrel with her.

The announcer's voice rang out, "Ladies and gentlemen, that was a 14.88, the second fastest time of the entire rodeo. Only Delaney Rawlins had a faster time at 14.84. That is how close this race to the end is going to be. Sammie Parkston is on fire in Denver!"

The hamburgers were devoured before we reached the stalls. Her feet did an excited jig as we approached.

"Can you believe it!" Her blue eyes shone with pure happiness. "We all three made the finals!"

Saturday night, I stood behind the fence and watched Brodie and Granger again preparing their horses. This was definitely going to become a habit throughout the year. Granger was the first to ride and nearly fell off the horse at the 7 second mark but rode it to the buzzer. He placed third in the rodeo with Brodie second, and Brody Cress taking the Denver championship.

When I backed into the box for the run, I broke it down again. I didn't have to hear Taylor tell me to trust Quincy. I just did. With a 7.5 second run, I placed third overall behind Riley Webb and Kincade Henry. Three young-guns, as the announcer pointed out had taken the top three spots. My mind went to the money...it should get me somewhere in the forties in the standings. It was a good start.

Granger and I stood next to each other on the bucking chutes as the barrel racing began.

"Lauren's daughter, Jamie, raced here, didn't she?" Granger turned to me.

"She was third in her bracket and didn't make the semi-finals," I answered.

"Well, I'd bet your horse trailer that either Sammie or Delaney takes the win here," Granger grinned.

I huffed a laugh, "Glad you said the trailer and not Stomping Dog."

"Ah, he's mine. You just haven't realized that yet."

I laughed as Sammie's name was called.

Breath held...each barrel leaned...and she raced out with the lead with a 14.83 second run.

"Girl is on fire," the announcer yelled. "Next is World Champion Delaney Rawlins..."

The red roan and blonde ran into the arena for a near perfect run of 14.88 seconds.

"Sammie won the whole damn thing," I fist-pumped the air.

"DAMN SAMMIE!" Granger hollered.

She ran out into the arena and to a group of people holding her new buckle and awards. Pictures were taken then she climbed into the back of a truck for the victory lap.

The picture that ran online showed the truck passing in front of the bucking chutes. Sammie was pointing at Granger and I as our arms were in the air, big grins on our faces, and mouths wide open as we yelled at her. The energy and elation radiated from all three of us.

It didn't take two days before it was printed and hung in the trailer as the start of our memory wall.

All three of us qualified for the Fort Worth semi-finals and had four days off before the rodeo. For the first time, we traveled back to Sammie's hometown of Madres, Oregon for our first official sponsor photoshoot with Quanstils Outer Wear. Modeling was something new for Granger and me, but Sammie had completed a few sessions for the company as she grew up. It was a rough start with strained smiles and tense bodies but once the horses joined us, we relaxed and felt at home.

Then, they dressed us in dark oil-skin leather cowboy hats, gloves, knee high dark winter snow boots, and matching high-collared calf-length duster coats. On each article of clothing and the boots were embroidered swords with tips together and the words Iron Sharpens Iron.

We walked out of the dressing tents together to a slight rise to the ground. The sky was silver, white, and dark grey, and the trees dark green with just a hint of snow on their limbs. It was an ominous vision.

"This is so cool," Granger adjusted his hat and looked down at his boots then over to us. "I feel like a musketeer."

"Me, too!" I laughed.

Sammie's hair had been curled and fluffed down her shoulders and back and with the dark coat and hat, her alien blue eyes shown with humor. "I love these coats."

Jared Marx, the designer of the coats and director of the photo shoot walked toward us with a pleased smile, and a wide deep case. It looked like an exceptionally long briefcase. "They look as fantastic on you as I knew they would."

"We love them," Sammie chimed as she lifted the tall collar a bit higher.

"Let's get you positioned for this next session," Jared said and directed us to stand at the rise of the hill, Sammie in the middle facing him, and Granger and I just turned a bit toward her. "Now, for the fun part." Jared grinned and knelt to open the long case.

He opened it toward us, and we gasped, laughed, and shouted to the sky. Three long intricately engraved and gem adorned swords shown from the red velvet lined case.

Very carefully, Jared pulled the first sword from the case and handed it to Sammie, her hand trembled with excitement. It was adorned with gold swirls and red and green gems.

"Be very careful with them," he handed an embellished sword to Granger then to me. I could hardly contain my excitement. "They aren't extremely sharp, but they will still injure you."

"I can hardly breathe," Sammie laughed. "I feel like Arya Stark from Game of Thrones."

"I have gone from musketeer to The Vikings', Bjorn Ironside," Granger's voice growled as he lifted the sword to the sky. They had trimmed his beard and dark blonde hair, but he looked like he was born to be a Viking. "And you, sir," he said to me and tipped the sword. "Shall be, Aragorn of Lord of the Rings."

"Perfect!" Jared whooped and turned to the photographer who was already taking pictures. "Lift them so the tips are together just forward and above Sammie. Stand strong..."

For an hour we posed and played with the swords. Just as we were having to relinquish the weapons back to the case, the snow began to fall against the silver and grey clouds. We got to play and shoot for another hour.

"Wait until Leo and Spence see these," Granger laughed. "Now I can tell them I know how to fence and fence."

Sammie's parents joined us as we drove to the Rawlins' home for dinner, Granger's mother was already there waiting for us. It was my first-time meeting Craig's three-month-old twins.

In the morning, we were back on the road to Fort Worth with Shayla joining us for a fun filled experience. Between the rodeo performances, we took Shayla to every tourist attraction in the area, and she spent time at our family ranch. The smile rarely left her face.

There was no doubt in my mind, when Granger won the semi-finals and was paired with one of his favorite horses, The Black Tie, to win the whole damn rodeo, he won it for her. The image that made the cover on the next rodeo magazine was the mother and son in an embrace just after he left the arena. They were grinning at each other with the trophy buckle between them. It was special and within minutes of seeing it, Sammie had the image printed and pinned to our memory wall.

Text from **S to G/A**: I really miss you guys!

Text from A to S/G: It's only been three days

Text from G to S/A: These weekends we all go different directions are weird. There won't be many this summer.

Text from **S to G/A**: I got bored last night and finally started that Facebook page for us.

Text from G to S/A: I barely use my personal one

Text from **S to G/A**: I made personal one private and only use the new

Text from A to S/G: What did you call it?

Text from S to A/G: IRON SHARPENS IRON WITH CONNERS-MILLER-PARKSTON

Text from G to S/A: That's great, about time

Text from **S to G/A**: I sent you the link, we 3 and Camille are admins on it. She said she would help only when we ask.

Text from G to S/A: Nice, I like that

Text from A to S/G: I like the header picture of us and the horses from 3.3 ranch

Text from **S to G/A**: Post positive and keep it clean!

Good Evening Everyone, this is Lori Ann Marker with *On The Road Rodeo News*;

In the middle of December, Sammie Parkston, who currently sits 3rd in the world standings, wrote a post on Facebook concerning Proverb 27:17, *'Just as iron sharpens iron, a person sharpens the character of his friend.'* She went on to state that she would be traveling with saddle bronc rider, Granger Miller, and tie-down roper Ace Conners. Their three roads had come together and with the unlikely grouping of roper, racer, and rider, the three have been on fire the last three months starting at the Sandhills Stock Show and Rodeo in Odessa Texas, they have won or taken home a check from every rodeo they have attended together; which includes Denver, Fort Worth, Houston, Austin, and the San Antonio tournament style rodeos.

I have known Ace Conners since his high school rodeo days and I know it has been hard on him not having his brother at his side after his accident last fall, but there is no doubt that Sammie and Granger have helped fill that void.

As I said, Sammie is currently third in the world, with Granger sitting in fourth. They both had money earnings since the beginning of the rodeo calendar in October, but Ace started his climb in December. He had the longest of the roads so far, but within these last few months, he has climbed to 31st in the world standings for tie-down.

With the winter tournament rodeos now over, the traveling begins, and it will be interesting to watch their journey.

Iron sharpens iron has been a theme in rodeo forever. We all know you have to have the right people in your corner to help with your animals, travel, and at home. These three prove with every ride that they are now a force to be reckoned with and we can't wait to see how the year unfolds for them.

We wish them the best this year.

CHAPTER THIRTY-ONE

SAMMIE

Text from S to G/A: G-Ranger, where in the H did you get that shirt last night?

Text G to S/A: Bought it at secondhand store. Cool isn't it!

Text S to G/A: That has got to be the ugliest shirt I have ever seen! Looks like ketchup and mustard swirled together to make paisleys.

Text A to S/G: I agree with her.

Text G to S/A: What? It's cool.

Text A to S/G: No, it is just plain ugly

Text S to G/A: Ugliest I have EVER seen. Relieved you didn't wear that at a rodeo.

Text G to S/A: Well, I like it

Text Sammie to Camille: Hi, can you do me a favor?

Text Camille to Sammie: I'll give it my best try

Text Sammie to Camille: Did you see Granger's shirt last night?

Text Camille to Sammie: Unfortunately

Text Sammie to Camille: If I send you money, can you buy him a good one and switch with the ugly? Covertly

Text Camille to Sammie: LOL, love to. My pleasure to pay

Text Sammie to Camille: OK, thanks, but please send me the ugly shirt, I have plans for it.

Text Camille to Sammie: Can't wait to see what that is.

Text from G to S/A: I haven't seen either of you since I wore the paisley shirt. But it's missing and replaced by a brown one. Either of you have anything to do with it?

Text from A to S/G: I have other things to worry about than your shirts

Text from S to G/A: What? By magic? But I will do a hallelujah dance

I set the plate containing the large hamburger and pile of French fries on the table and slid onto the chair. I couldn't eat before the run and by the time Sergeant was stalled next to Grace, my stomach was growling. The first bite of the tall burger was juicy, sweet, and very satisfying; worth the wait.

"Excuse me."

I looked up across the table to see a young girl, maybe thirteen, looking at me with wide, anxious eyes.

"Yes?" I squeezed around the food.

"You're Sammie Parkston?"

I chewed quickly and swallowed before answering with a smile, "Yes, I am."

Her cheeks turned pink, "I've been following you on the Facebook page and I think you, Grace, and Sergeant are just wonderful."

"Thank you," My stomach always swirled in these moments. "They are such dynamic horses."

"I love seeing their pictures on Facebook," The girl giggled. "I've been watching your page for pictures of them."

"Well, I'll make sure to post a couple special for you tonight. What's your name?"

"Nellie," She took off the straw cowboy hat she was wearing. "Can you sign my hat for me?"

"I'd love to, do you have a pen?"

As she dug into her large bag, Granger and Ace approached from behind her. They both held plates and large cups and took chairs on each side of me and gave Nellie a polite smile. Her eyes widened and hand froze with pen in hand. Her pink cheeks turned red.

"Would it be alright if Granger and Ace signed your hat, too?" I smiled innocently.

She glanced at both men who were smiling at her, but she didn't say a word.

"Please?" Granger asked.

"I would be honored to sign it," Ace reached for the hat and pen and took them from her trembling fingers.   "Is it OK?"

"Yes…." she whispered. "I would love all three."

Ace signed just his name, I signed "Enjoy the Ride" followed by just my first name, and Granger signed his name followed by P 27:17; the iron sharpens iron proverb.

When Nellie took her hat, she giggled, thanked us, and quickly strode away.

"I liked how you signed that," I said to Granger before taking another large bite.

"I have no imagination for coming up with phrases or little quotes like yours," he answered.

"Well, I might just have to steal it," Ace answered.

"I think we all should," I added. "Help strengthen our resolve every time we write it."

"So, how do we share it when they ask for a kiss or hug?" Granger chuckled.

"I just give out autographs," I huffed. "You two might as well be in Hawaii."

They looked at me with narrow confused eyes.

"What the hell does that mean?" Ace huffed.

"For as many leis as you give out," I teased.

They both snorted, then heads fell back in laughter.

The next morning, I was lying in bed scrolling through Facebook when I saw the picture of the three of us laughing so hard we had tears in our eyes. The caption under the picture asked: What do you think is so funny?

I shrieked so loud I woke up both men. Moments later, laughter filled the trailer.

Text from Sammie to Taylor and Granger: You have Stomping Dog warmed up?

Text from Granger to Taylor and Sammie: Warmed up, boots on, and ready to go.

Text from Sammie to Taylor and Granger: He still has no idea we are here?

Text from Taylor to Sammie and Granger: No clue

Text from Sammie to Taylor and Granger: We'll have to move quick. I'll get the saddle off while you bring Stomping Dog. Taylor, you stay on watch.

Text from Taylor to Granger and Sammie: I'm standing behind the roping chute and can see him. He's tying up Quincy to the hitching post now. Heading to the restroom. You'll have to go quick. He's sixth rider out.

I peeked around the back of the horse trailer in time to see Ace stride away from Quincy. He disappeared around the front.

Text from Taylor to Granger and Sammie: GO!

I ran for the roan horse and released the breast collar and cinches as Granger trotted the buckskin to me. We threw the saddle from one horse to the other and had Quincy hidden before Ace returned.

Hiding behind a truck, we watched as Ace checked the cinch on the horse then stepped up onto the saddle. He trotted toward the roping chutes.

"Well, that was anti-climactic," Granger chuckled.

"Let's get closer," I whispered, and we stealthily made our way to the group of tie-down ropers.

Taylor was standing behind the chute and just nodded to Ace when he rode to him. Granger and I made our way to hide two horses away but within ear shot of them.

Ace leaned down and patted the horse on the neck then began his ritual of adjusting the lariat. When he was called as the next rider, he took off his hat, set it back on and pressed it on tighter. Then, he adjusted the piggin' string between his teeth, swung the rope, then reached down and patted the horse again before nudging him to the back of the chute and the aisle where he would enter the box.

Once Ace walked into the box and positioned the horse's rump to the back, Granger and I made our way to stand by Taylor. Ace's full concentration was on the calf in the chute. He nodded and sprang out of the box. In 6.9 seconds he took the lead and jogged back to the buckskin horse. He stepped into the saddle and loosened the slack in the rope. When the judge nodded, Ace's shoulders lowered, and he grinned with a pat to the horse's neck.

As he neared the exit gate, another roper nodded to him, "Nice run, but why did you switch horses?"

Granger, Taylor, and I chuckled.

"What?" Ace looked at the roper with a raised brow.

"When we were warming up, you were on Quincy," The roper pointed out.

Ace's head dropped down to the horse, and he froze. With eyes narrowing, he looked out at his trailer then back down to the buckskin. "What the hell?" He muttered in clear confusion.

The look on his face was the last straw; we couldn't hold back any longer and bust out in laughter. Ace's head jerked to us, and he just stared a moment before the grin appeared then the laughter. It would go down in my journal as the jackpot he won on the wrong horse.

Text from Sammie to Ace and Granger: You two know that every picture the photographer took of the second barrel has you two behind it?

Text from Ace to Sammie and Granger: That's funny. Never even considered it.

Text from Granger to Sammie and Ace: That's just a bonus for all them ladies.

Text from Ace to Taylor: You still have that drawing you made of Sammie?

Text from Taylor to Ace: Yeah, why?

Text from Ace to Taylor: I need a high-resolution copy

Text from Taylor to Ace: Does she know about this?

Text from Ace to Taylor: No

Text from Taylor to Ace: Well then, I want in on it.

Grace pranced as we slowly made our way to the entry gate while waiting for the official to give the signal to run. Envisioning the pattern, I took calming breaths and stroked her shoulder. We were the 6th team out of 32 running in the morning slack. Unlike the rodeo performances, there were barely twenty people in the stands and most hovered in the shade covered corners.

The official turned and flipped the clipboard at me. The reins were loosened.

Grace was instantly in a full stretch run into the arena toward the first barrel. It was a smooth, whipping fast turn. As we lunged away from the barrel toward the second, I could hear deep voices yelling, "GO GRACE! RUN GRACE RUN!"

We slid around the second barrel in near perfection to the voices yelling, "GO GRACE GO!"

The horse propelled toward the third barrel. As we turned, I could hear, "RUN LIKE HELL GRACE!" As if she knew what they were commanding and recognized their voices, her strides widened, and she ran with hoof pounding speed. My heart was racing as my mind was laughing at the men.

We pulled to a stop and pranced in a circle before trotting to the exit gate.

"That's the funniest thing I've seen in a long time," The lady opening the gate laughed as we made our way out of the arena.

"What was?" I stopped and looked down at her.

She pulled the gate closed and laughed again, "Your cheering squad behind the second barrel. They setup during the rake."

I turned back to see Ace, Granger, and Taylor walking along the bleachers toward the steps. It was quite obvious they were carrying signs.

"Oh, Lordy," I shook my head. "What did the signs say?"

"Oh, Hun," The gate lady grinned. "You need to see for yourself."

I trotted down the lane to chuckles from the crowd. As I turned into the parking lot, the three men appeared and held up the signs for me to see. In the middle, was a large version of the cartoon drawing Taylor had drawn of me with a black hat, red hair and big blue eyes. The other two signs called out, "TEAM SAMMIE". And the best was Granger shaking pom poms in the air.

If that wasn't enough, all three were wearing white t-shirts with the same cartoon drawing imprinted on the front. Their grins were wide and mischievous. I laughed so hard, I nearly fell off the horse.

When the rodeo page announced that Grace had taken the lead, it was accompanied by a picture showing the horse and I in a perfect turn with both of us looking at the third barrel. Right behind us, and clearly visible, were the three men and their signs.

Text from Sammie to Ace and Granger: Guess what I'm wearing!

Text from Ace to Sammie and Granger: Aren't you at that charity function?

Text from Granger to Ace and Sammie: It was some kind of costume event. You a buckle bunny?

Text from Sammie to Ace and Granger with picture attached: Funny, maybe next time.

Sammie was standing next to Grace in the picture. She wore black leather lace-up knee-high boots, a dark red riding skirt that flowed to the top of the boots, black and gold corset that cinched her waist tight, a black shirt that was adorned with lace up her neck and down to her wrists. Her red hair was curled in tight ringlets, and on top, she wore a black leather steampunk top hat. The band of the 10-inch-tall hat was gold gears intwined with black lace that matched her shirt. A red rose the color of her skirt was attached to the band. With her nose tipped in the air to the side, she smirked at the camera giving her an air of sophisticated arrogance.

Text from Granger to Ace and Sammie: BEST COSTUME EVER.

Text from Ace to Sammie and Granger: That is awesome! Way better than a buckle bunny.

Text from Sammie to Granger and Ace: It's so fun! Mom's idea. I'll send more pics tonight.

Two weeks later:

Text from Granger to Ace and Sammie: Guess what I'm wearing.

Text from Sammie to Granger and Ace: You're helping the Rawlins branding? Probably wearing cow poop.

Text from Ace to Granger and Sammie: Sure as hell hope it's not that yellow and red horrible shirt.

Text from Granger to Ace and Sammie with picture attached: Nope, still can't find it.

In the picture, Granger and Brodie were standing in the Rawlins' arena next to a small herd of cows. Cowboy hat, boots, and jeans as usual, but strapped to each of their chests were baby carriers. The six-month-old Caleb was attached to Brodie's chest while Ellie was attached to Granger's. Hooded sweatshirts covered the twin's heads, and their little legs dangled from the bottom of the carriers with tiny cowboy boots covering their feet. All four were grinning at the camera.

Text from Sammie to Granger and Ace: The cutest ever!

Text from Ace to Granger and Sammie: Best uncles those two could ask for.

CHAPTER THIRTY-TWO

SAMMIE

Text to Granger: Taylor is having issues in physical therapy and needs minor surgery on shoulder. He had to cancel trip to AZ. Ace in bad shape for the jackpot so I'm headed there for support.

Text from Granger: Where are you?

Text to Granger: In Vegas at cutting show with family. I can catch a flight and be at the Phoenix airport at 4:00 this afternoon.

Text from Granger: Gives me time to drive there, I can be at airport to pick you up.

Text to Granger: It's a big event so hotels may be hard to come by, we may end up sleeping in your SUV.

Text from Granger: Just home to me, but Ace has their camper there.

Text to Granger: Perfect, I will text you when I arrive

I slid onto the seat of Granger's SUV and stuffed my bag over the console to the back.

"He is going to be so freaking surprised," I grinned.

"Yeah, I texted a few minutes ago to wish him good luck, told him I was still in California."

When we arrived at the equine center, Ace was standing next to his truck and trailer with rope in hand but staring blindly at the practice steer. Both horses were tied to the side of the trailer, heads down and nearly asleep. Neither had a saddle on.

We stepped in on each side of Ace.

"You even know how to throw that thing?" I asked.

"Need me to show you how to saddle a horse properly?" Granger added.

Ace's shoulders lowered and head tipped up to the sky, "You have no idea…," he whispered.

"Yeah, we do," I said softly.

"That's why we are here," Granger nodded. "So which horse you need saddled?"

Ace turned and looked at me with a relieved smile then turned to Granger, "Last time you decided I needed Stomping Dog, so let's go with Quincy this time."

We all chuckled at the memory.

"While you guys ride, I'll go get us something to eat. There has to be a good vendor here somewhere," I looked up at Ace. "You eaten anything today?"

He shook his head, so I tapped him on the arm for added comfort, then turned away.

Once he placed second in the roping, we sat in lawn chairs next to his truck.

"So, how is Taylor doing?" I asked.

"Last time I talked to him he had been working out at physical therapy and running," Granger said.

Ace shrugged, "They finally had him start swinging the rope a few weeks ago but it just kept getting tighter and the ache wouldn't go away."

"The surgery today supposed to fix that?" Granger asked.

"Yeah," Ace sighed. "They were doing something with the tendons...loosening them up or something, then he should be able to throw without an issue. And, if this works and eases the tightness, they'll have him swimming to help strengthen it," Ace leaned back and stretched his legs. "Mentally, I think he's improved and has a positive outlook."

"That is huge in recovery," I smiled and looked around the equine center parking lot. "So, we're staying here then?"

"You take Taylor's bed and I'll hit the floor," Granger nodded.

"And, what do we do until then?" I asked.

"I have something," Ace chuckled with a sly grin and stood to crawl into the camper. He returned with a bottle of Pendleton, a deck of cards, and a handful of shot glasses. When he sat them on a small table between the chairs, we both reached for a glass...I took the smaller one.

"What are we doing?" Granger grinned and opened the bottle.

Ace pulled the cards from their box, "I shuffle, one of you separates the cards in three piles, and the other chooses a pile for each of us. We draw one at a time; low card must take a shot."

"Oh, fun," I grinned. "Good thing my glass is smaller than yours."

"Normally," Ace set the pile of cards in the middle and Granger separated them. "The low card also has to give the high-card a five-dollar bill."

"That works," We both grinned.

Text from Sammie to Ace and Granger: When are your birthdays?

Text from Ace to Sammie and Granger: June 19

Text from Granger to Sammie and Ace: June 4

Text from Sammie to Ace and Granger: June 10 and we're all turning 21!

Text from Ace to Sammie and Granger: F'ing Party!

Text from Granger to Sammie and Ace: Right before Reno!

Text from Sammie to Ace and Granger: At my parent's ranch!

Text from Sammie to Ace and Granger: Delaney just texted and switched Reno perf nights with me so I ride Thursday night with both of you. So, Granger in Wed perf, Ace and me Thursday slack then all three in Thursday perf. Yaa Hoo!

Text from Granger to Ace and Sammie: We'll have Friday to run in Utah then back to Reno for the Championship Night Saturday. The first of our big summer run! Great way to start!

Text from Ace to Granger and Sammie: I was afraid that would happen! Good on Delaney! Way to be confident G!

Text from Granger to Ace and Sammie: Union then 2 rodeos in UT then Reno

Text from Sammie to Granger and Ace: I won't be in Union. That is Xtreme Race in Reno so you guys get a boy's weekend without me. DON'T forget our group birthday party Sunday before Reno Rodeo!

Text from Granger to Ace and Sammie: THAT WILL BE A BLAST, glad we have a couple days to recover.

Text from Ace to Sammie: Hell of a way to start the week.

Text from Sammie to Ace: I have a great idea for Granger's Bday present, but you will need to reach out to Leo and Spence.

Text from Ace to Sammie: Why don't you reach out to them?

Text from Sammie to Ace: Because, I have never met them and don't want to.

Text from Ace to Sammie: I haven't met them either, but we will be seeing them at the summer rodeos...especially the fall rodeos. Reach out now and get over it.

Text from Sammie to Ace: Aarg

Text from Ace to Sammie: Did you just growl at me? Like you did in Rosenburg at Granger?

Text from Sammie to Ace: Yes, but not as angry.

Text from Ace to Sammie: Good to know, but reach out to them. BTW for what?

Text from Sammie to Ace: A big photo album of his rodeo pictures he couldn't afford when he started. Just rodeo pictures showing his journey.

Text from Ace to Sammie: Love that idea, I'll go in cost with you but contact Leo and Spence. They were a big part of that. Besides, it will probably be just pictures of him flying through the air and landing on his head.

Text from Sammie to Ace: LOL true, Alright, I really want this for him so I'll do it.

Text from Ace to Granger: You find Sammie's gift yet?
Text from Granger to Ace: Yeah, made arrangements for delivery too
Text from Ace to Granger: Can't wait!

Text from Granger to Sammie: You think of anything for Ace yet?
Text from Sammie to Granger: No, I was hoping you thought of something
Text from Granger to Sammie: The guy has everything I can think of to get him
Text from Sammie to Granger: Yeah, I know. We need to think outside the box

CHAPTER THIRTY-THREE

SAMMIE

After a whirlwind successful two weeks prior to our birthday party, we had been really looking forward to three down days before we started at the rodeo. All three days at home in Madras.

I stood in front of the mirror and looked at my reflection. Mischievous eyes twinkled and a bright humored grin greeted me. The black tank dress fit perfectly, but I added red knee-length knit capri shorts underneath. Black and red stylish ankle boots did a bit of a jig as I turned away from the mirror and picked up the shirt from the bed. I slid it on and secured it with a red belt that matched the shorts.

With a giggle, I stepped out into the hallway and walked down the hall. Mom was standing at the door waiting for me. She chuckled with a grin when she saw me then glanced out the door.

"He is by the coolers and snack table. You said Camille and Delaney?"

"Yes, where are they?"

"Out by their truck."

I pulled out my phone from the shirt pocket.

Text from Sammie to Camille: You and Delaney go over to Ace and Granger.

I walked to the kitchen window where I knew no one could see me. The Rawlins family, Lacie Jae, and Martin were sitting around a large table. Leo's dad was there by the grill with Leo and Spence. I still hadn't talked to either of them; the arrangements for the images for the album were done completely by text and email.

Mason had flown in from Oklahoma and was standing with baby Ellie in his arms, while Shayla held baby Caleb. Granger and Ace were with them.

"Here come the girls," Mom whispered with a humored chuckle. "Let me get out there so I can record this."

I waited until she nonchalantly walked to the side of the yard and Delaney and Camille were next to the two men. Laughing to myself, I nearly danced to the back door.

When I walked out, a cry of laughter erupted from Camille making Ace and Granger look toward me.

"I KNEW IT!" Granger yelled. "I KNEW YOU TOOK IT!"

I twirled in circles to show off the ugly red and yellow swirled paisley shirt Camille had stolen from him.

"It is wonderfully ugly!" Camille laughed.

"It looks terrible with your red hair," Brodie grinned.

"I agree," I laughed at his honesty and turned to my mother. With a wicked grin, she handed me a pair of scissors. I turned to Brodie and held them up, "You want to make the first cut?"

"You are not cutting up my shirt!" Granger laughed and started walking toward me.

I spun to Brodie and handed him the scissors. "Hurry!"

Before Granger could reach us, Brodie had both sleeves cut off, and the scissors were aiming for the material around my waist.

Laughter rang out when Granger's arm wrapped around me, and he lifted me away from Brodie and the scissors.

"I can wear it without sleeves," Granger carried me back to the coolers.

But it was useless. By the time the birthday presents were set on the table to be opened, the shirt had been cut in strips and there were headbands, bow ties, arm bands, hat bands, or wristlets on every person at the party.

"Ace first on gifts!" I called out and slid the box to him.

Ace opened the box then lifted a piece of paper out of it. I looked behind him as the door to the back of the house opened.

"Read it out loud." Granger grinned.

"All it says is *turn around*," Ace chuckled then turned. "Son of a...." He gasped and stood to walk to his mother, Taylor, and the Lil Bros racing out the door to greet him.

"We rented an Airbnb for them to stay in the whole week with Shayla," I laughed. "You had everything you needed, but them at the beginning of our summer run."

Liam and Monty quickly made their way to me and gave me huge hugs.

"Thank you for talking Mom into this," Monty grinned.

"I couldn't believe it," Liam added. "This is going to be the best week."

"I am so happy she said yes," I hugged them again.

"Now, Granger's turn," Ace pushed the box toward him.

Granger leaned forward and lifted the tag, read it, and his brows rose in surprise.

"Who is it from?" His mother asked.

"Leo, Spence, Ace, and Sammie," Granger answered with a very pleased smile as he looked at the four of us.

"Oh, how nice!" Lacie Jae grinned at me.

Granger opened the box and lifted the album out. His grin was wide and laughter deep as he flipped through the pages of picture after picture of him flying through the air or landing on his head. Everyone leaned around him to look at the pictures and laugh with him.

When the last page was flipped, Granger turned and looked at me. "Thanks...it means a lot to me," he whispered. "It's your turn."

He stood to walk into the house with Ace. As I waited, I looked around at our families gathered together; talking and laughing. I couldn't think of anything more that I would need than this group.

When Ace and Granger returned, they both had a hand behind their backs.

"Oh, my!" I giggled in excitement.

They stood side by side in front of me and grinned.

"In the next few months, we will be together, but there are times when you'll be alone in that trailer missing us terribly." Ace grinned and I laughed with a nod.

"So, we want to make sure you don't get lonely," Granger added.

The trumpets from the song Wine, Beer, Whiskey echoed in the air. Camille was holding up her phone as the song began to play.

Ace's arm slowly came around to the front to reveal a black curly-haired puppy with gold highlights that barely filled his hand. I squealed in delight.

"This is Jack, he has your back," Ace laughed as he handed me the puppy.

Granger's arm came around him and he held a gold curly-haired puppy with black highlights. "This is Jose, he likes to play."

"They are so tiny!" I cried and nuzzled them and immediately fell in love.

"They are miniature Airedales," Granger stated. "You're not like anyone else, so we wanted to make sure you had puppies like no one else."

"I just love them," I snuggled them more and looked at my two best friends. "This is just the best."

"We talked to your parents and your Wyoming uncle, plus Charlene," Granger nodded to her. "They can puppysit when you need them to."

"Add us to that list," Evan wheeled in next to us. The seven-month-old Ellie was nestled on his lap; her hands clapping at the ride.

I knelt next to her and showed her the puppies. She squealed and a little hand patted the puppies.

"One more gift before we party!" Dad called out and set a box on the table.

"We said no presents but ours to each other," I stood and looked at him disapprovingly.

"Well," he smirked. "You can say what you want, but your parents are going to do whatever we want."

"It's from all of us," Shayla slid her arm through Granger's and grinned at her son. "Don't complain, you'll love it."

Charlene held up three strings that were attached to the top of the box, "This is one of the reasons I said yes to the trip." She grinned at her son. "Now, you each have to hold a string and when I tell you to lift it, the top will come off and the sides will drop to reveal the gift."

"Pretty damn fancy, Mom," Ace teased.

"Just want to make sure you all see at the same time," she chuckled. "And, watch your language."

"Yes, Mother," He whispered and took the string from her.

"Alright, everyone ready?" My mom asked and glanced around the group.

"Is it going to jump out and bite us?" Granger asked as he held the string up and turned sideways to the box.

"Probably," Dad drawled, and everyone laughed.

"Let me have those puppies," Martin quickly took them from me, and Camille and Lacie Jae immediately took them from him.

"Alright," I turned back to the table and stepped back as far as I could without pulling the string.

Dad laughed, "You are safe, Dear Daughter."

I wrinkled my nose at him and giggled.

"Here we go," Charlene said with an arm around her younger sons. "One, two, three..."

We pulled the strings and the top rose, the sides fell, and sitting on top a black velvet pillow were three sets of spurs. Shiny black heel bands and shanks with a stainless-steel rowel fit for each of our disciplines. Along the shank, was a P 27:17 inscription in silver and the heel bands had our names in script with the words 'iron sharpens iron' underneath. Three swords with tips together shone in stainless steel.

Gasps rang out. My hands went to my chest in surprise.

"Mom," Granger exhaled in disbelief as he turned to her. "You can't...they are too much..."

She patted his arm with her cheeks turning pink, "Well, they are from your parents…which includes your surrogate fathers." She nodded to the grinning Martin and Evan. "When I told them about the idea, they insisted."

Granger turned to them with wide eyes, "I don't know what to say. I've never had anything like these. Mine have always been from thrift stores or bought secondhand."

"And a bit rusty," Martin nodded. "And now you have new."

Ace held his mother in a tight hug, and I quickly turned to my parents and wrapped my arms around them. "Thank you, so much."

"We believe in you, Sweetheart," Dad whispered.

"And are so happy you found such great friends to share this journey with," Mom added.

"Hey, I designed them," Mason huffed from behind.

I laughed and threw my arms around him. "They are beautiful."

"I'm really supposed to wear those in the arena dirt?" Granger chuckled with the shining spurs held high for everyone to see.

"That is what they are for," Taylor laughed.

I took a dozen pictures of the spurs sitting on the black pillow then chose the best and posted it on our social media sites. When I looked up from my phone, I was met by Leo and Spence. They both looked at me with shoulders high and eyes concerned.

"Thank you for your help getting the images together for the album," I said quickly before they could speak. A knot of irritation grew in my stomach as I thought of them leaving Granger on the side of the road in Pendleton.

"I was surprised you asked us," Leo stated.

"We really wanted it for him," I looked between them.

"We wanted to say…" Spence exhaled then took a deep breath. "Granger has been a great friend…"

"Ever since we met him," Leo added.

Spence nodded, "We had a lot of fun together to start, but it was easy to see he was always going to be a better bronc rider than us and had bigger dreams than us. I don't know if he told you or not that he told me not to ride Iggy in Pendleton."

"He has never spoken to me about it," I said honestly.

"Oh, well," Spence mumbled. "He told me not to since he had turned out on him, but I was stupid and thought I could do what the best riders in the world couldn't. I paid the price for my stupidity."

I didn't say anything.

Leo exhaled with shoulders rising even more. "When we were at the hospital, I knew I was going home but didn't say anything to Granger. It was pretty selfish of me to leave him there, but he would have talked me into going…and I just couldn't do that." He shook his head, and his eyes were narrowed. "There are a lot of things in this life I will regret and leaving him there will be one that I'm not sure I will ever regret. It was the right thing for him…I didn't doubt he would find a ride."

"We're glad it was you, Sammie," Spence quickly added. "You and Ace have been the best thing for his dreams." He glanced at Leo then continued. "We were holding him back. You two, and we're sure of this, will help his dreams come true."

"The three of you…iron sharpens iron…," Leo smiled. "You three will make it together. You three were meant to make that journey together and push each other along."

"Without a doubt, Sammie," Spence nodded. "I believe, with all my heart, that in the end, you giving Granger a ride that day was meant to be."

Leo exhaled, "It was wrong of me to do it, and I've apologized a dozen times to Granger, and he accepted my apology with the first one."

I looked at him as if asking him what he wanted from me.

"We've talked to Ace," Leo sighed. "He seems to be OK with us, but even getting all the pictures for Granger's present, you didn't talk to us; just emails and text messages."

"We know you had to deal with the initial shock from Granger in Pendleton and know you may not be as forgiving as Ace. But we would like you to at least understand…"

"I do," I finally nodded, and their shoulders lowered. "I understand how important you are to G-ranger, and that he did, completely, forgive you. I have told myself a hundred times that him and Ace coming into my life was meant to be, so I agree with you there."

"But?" They both asked.

"I had just gone through having friends tear me down and I struggled to get back on track," I admitted. "Having gone through that, I suppose I took that animosity I have for them and placed it on you for what I perceived, at the time, as you doing the same to him."

"We have done nothing to tear him down," Leo's eyes widened. "We've always…."

"Supported him," I finished and the anxiety I had for the pair dissolved. "You got him into saddle bronc and have built him up. I understand that now."

"We're good then?" Spence's voice was high as he asked.

"We are," I nodded with a reassuring smile. "Between the four of us, we'll get G-ranger as far as we can get him.

"Starting Wednesday night," Leo grinned.

Wednesday night, I was able to sit with the families in the stands closest to the chutes in Reno and watch Granger. The Rawlins were at a rodeo in Utah with Camille and Lacie Jae. The rest of the families that had been at our birthday party were in the stands except Granger.

The saddle bronc riders appeared on the bucking platform and Liam and Monte stood, waved with both arms, and yelled until Granger turned with a grin and waved back.

"Now he knows where we are so he can wave at us when he dismounts," Monte declared.

"I love your logic," Charlene laughed.

Granger stood behind a large red roan.

Monte turned and looked at Evan, "Who is that horse?"

"Major Huckleberry," Evan answered. "Brodie rode him in the 10th round of the NFR last year."

"Did he do any good?" Liam asked with a smirk.

Evan chuckled, "Scored an 88 and placed third."

"Oh," Liam shrugged.

"But it helped him win the rodeo average title, which is pretty good." Ace shook his head.

"Well, that is good then," Monte turned and looked out at the chute just as Granger stepped over the panel. "Let's see if he can beat Brodie's score."

"Yes, let's do," Evan chuckled.

The gate swung open, and the red roan leaped into the arena. The strong high kicks and a sideways leap did not dislodge Granger who looked strong, fierce, and energized. The buzzer rang out and Granger turned to the pickup man to complete a picture-perfect dismount. He turned back to our screaming group and pointed a finger then waved at the two boys.

"Told ya!" Monte yelled at his mom then turned to Liam. "Pretty darn cool when we know one that waves at us."

"Yep!" Liam agreed.

"Riding a bucking horse is just cool," Monte turned to Ace. "I want to do that. It looks like fun. Do you think Granger can teach me?"

"90!" Shayla shot to her feet and clapped with the crowd. The happiness and pride radiated from her.

"Well...," Ace's eyes shot to their mother who didn't indicate she had heard the question.

"How about Brodie?" Monte turned to Evan. "Granger said he helped him learn. Can they teach me?"

"Me, too!" Liam stood.

Evan looked at Charlene then back to the two teenagers staring at him. "That is something you have to..."

"He went to clinics," Monte turned to Liam. "Granger said he went to clinics to learn. We can do that."

"There have to be lots in Texas," Liam nodded and looked back at Evan. "Are there?"

"Yeah...," Evan nodded with another glance to their mother who was now looking out at the crowd and not indicating she was listening to the conversation. "But you have to ask your mother."

Both boys turned to look at her, "Can we?" They asked in unison.

Charlene finally turned and looked right at them, "There is no reason you can't try, if that is what you want."

"YES!" They both shouted and grinned at each other as Granger approached.

Baby Caleb screeched when he saw his uncle approaching and began bouncing on Martin's lap. With an amused grin, he lifted the boy to Granger who tucked him safely into his arms. Ellie was grinning at him but was content on Ace's lap.

"Mom said we can try riding broncs," Monte grinned at Granger.

"Nice ride," Evan chuckled. "Took the lead."

"Lots of performances after this one," Granger nodded.

"Can you teach us how to ride bucking horses?" Liam asked him. "And Brodie, too?"

Granger looked at the two boys then at Charlene.

"Mom said yes," Monte repeated.

"If she said yes, then..." Granger started.

"We are hosting a clinic next month," Evan stated.

"Can we, Mom?" Both boys turned to her.

"When is it?" She turned to Evan.

"End of August," he answered.

She turned to the excited Lil Bros, "You have school, but there will be others."

"Ah, dang," Monte sighed.

"You have a week on the road with us pretty soon," Ace reminded them. "You'll get to see more bucking horses."

"Can we go back and look at the bucking horses?" Liam asked and bounced off the bleacher.

Monte quickly stood and looked at his mother, "Is it OK?"

"Well, I guess..." She looked at Granger.

"I'll go with you," Ace answered and stood with the baby in his arms. "Ellie will like seeing the horses, too."

The two men, with babies in their arms, hurried down the fence to keep up with the two teenagers.

"Hell of a combo," Martin chuckled.

"You're sure about this, Mom?" Taylor asked.

She released a long deep breath and looked at him, "They love to rope and ride with you, but they don't have the passion for it like you and Ace. I don't believe they will ever ride their bikes again, and they haven't been so excited about anything else until this." She smiled as she looked down the fence where the boys had disappeared. "I have always pushed you to try new things, and if this helps them through their father's loss and gives them something they are passionate about, then yes, we'll let them try."

Taylor took her hand and squeezed it.

Our attention was brought back to the arena when the first tie down roper ran out of the box.

CHAPTER THIRTY-FOUR

ACE:

Text from Ace to Sammie: Where did you go?

Text from Sammie to Ace: Checking on horses

Text from Ace to Sammie: Get your guitar and get back here

Text from Sammie to Ace: Why?

Text from Ace to Sammie: There is a jackass here thinking he is the best guitar player in the world. You can prove him wrong

Text from Sammie to Ace: I don't do that.

Text from Ace to Sammie: Come back over, listen for a few minutes, then nod when you're ready and I will go get your guitar.

Text from Sammie to Ace: I'm not going to nod.

Text from Ace to Granger: How far out are you?

Text from Granger to Ace: Riding with the Rawlins family. We just turned off the main road. Ten minutes maybe. Why?

Text from Ace to Granger: Come over to Sammie's trailer before unloading. You got to see this.

Text from Granger to Ace: What?

I didn't answer.

When Sammie returned, she glared at me then lowered into her chair amongst the large group of people gathered in a circle around the coolers filled with ice and drinks. But, after five minutes of listening to the arrogant cowboy strumming on the guitar and talking about all the jobs he turned down because he wanted to focus on rodeo, her lips rolled into a tight line. Another five minutes of cringing to each note he hit wrong, her head lowered, and she took a deep breath. When the guy turned and looked at the petite blond next to him and gave her a 'come hither' look as if she would be lucky to be with him, Sammie's head turned, and she looked right at me. I waited...she nodded. I nearly ran to her trailer.

When I returned, a few people had made their escape.

"You think you can do better than me?" The guy growled when he saw the guitar case.

I wanted to say yes even though I had no idea to play, but just shook my head, "Probably not, I just thought Sammie could play that song she promised me and give you a break."

Every person around the area looked at me with relief.

Sammie didn't say anything as she opened the case and lifted her red guitar. Anyone that knew anything about instruments knew it was a high-end guitar.

After a deep breath, she strummed her fingers across the strings a few times before looking up at me, "Which did you decide on?"

"Our theme song," I grinned.

She smiled and shook her head, "Not yet, when G-ranger gets here."

Instead, her eyes closed, and her fingers began moving. The Sound of Silence echoed over the campfire, and I watched the people around us begin to smile and relax. The guy that had been playing lowered his guitar to the side.

When her song came to an end, with her eyes still closed, she smiled slightly and strummed a few chords that everyone knew: *On the Road Again.*

Phones were held in the air recording as everyone began singing and halfway through the song, I looked up to see the crowd around us had doubled. Sammie's eyes opened and she looked right at me, "You have to sing it."

Take me Home, Country Roads began, and everyone joined me in singing.

Granger, Martin, and the Rawlins family walked in beside me as the song ended. Delaney had the baby girl in her arms while Martin was carrying his grandson. The twins were asleep.

"Do the first one again!" Someone called out.

Sammie started *The Sound of Silence* again, and a deep baritone, perfect-pitch male voice sang along.

When the song faded out, and she started *Ring of Fire,* Granger turned to me, "She doesn't like to play in public, how did this happen?"

Sammie turned to his voice and smiled, "G-Ranger, you finally made it. Next one, get ready."

I grinned and Granger whispered, "Get ready for what?"

"Theme song," I answered and pulled out my phone to queue for the trumpet sound for *Wine, Beer, Whiskey.*

"Hell yeah," Granger laughed, and Sammie grinned at him.

I turned to Martin, "It's going to wake them up."

He just smiled, "They have been asleep in the truck for a few hours, and they love music so it will be a good way for them to wake up."

The song faded, and Sammie nodded to me, I hit the button on my phone making the trumpets echo in the air as Granger and I stepped in behind her.

Laughter and clapping began as we sang the song. By the end, the whole crowd was singing, and Martin's grandbabies were awake with wide eyes roaming over the crowd.

"Do it again!" Was shouted from the crowd.

So, she did.

Granger took the little girl twin in his arms and danced with her. Then little Caleb stretched out his arms to me, so I bounced him to the tune, and he erupted in laughter.

The next song was for the babies, but everyone sang it to the smiles and giggles of the twins. Old MacDonald was sung by thirty people making pigs oink, cows moo, horses whinny, and more. Laughter erupted when the song came to an end.

Sammie looked out at the large crowd and took a deep breath. It seemed she had come out of her music bubble and realized how many people had just watched her play. Much to the distress of the crowd, her guitar was lowered into her case, and she stood while shaking her hands to the side.

"Freaking awesome, Blue-eyed Alien," Granger grinned at her, and the name made her eyes sparkle and shoulders relax.

"Thanks, G-Ranger," She laughed and took the baby Ellie from him.

"Sammie, Sammie, Sammie!" Lacie Jae, with wide excited eyes, rushed to her side and took her arm. "Please, please, please!"

"What?" Sammie laughed.

"Logan and I have been trying to find something for the wedding guests at the reception to do while we're taking wedding portraits. Can you please play?" Her eyes begged.

Sammie's eyes widened and jaw dropped, "I don't know."

"No pressure," Logan stepped in behind his future wife with a wide grin.

"It would only be for a half hour or so," Lacie Jae added quickly. "We have a DJ going to play after everyone is done roping."

"It's the week before the clinic," Evan reminded her. "And you have volunteered to help at that. You can stay at the ranch between rodeos if you need."

Knowing it was a big decision for Sammie, Granger and I stood quietly waiting for an answer.

"Well," Sammie exhaled. "As long as G-ranger and Ace are on stage with me."

"I'll be there with you," Granger smiled proudly at her.

"We'll do our 'road show'," I grinned.

"It's going to be a wedding to remember." Martin beamed.

CHAPTER THIRTY-FIVE

SAMMIE

Text from Taylor to Sammie/Granger: Ace said you had a 'guess what I'm wearing' thing going on. So, he said to ask you and then send this picture.

The image attached was Ace standing in front of a bar, his arms stretched out to his side with a stein of beer in one hand, and legs spread in a wide supporting stance. A woman had her arms around his neck, legs wrapped around his waist, and lips firmly planted on his. His right eye was visible; wide and staring at the phone for the image.

Text from Sammie to Taylor/Granger: OMG! She's like a second shirt!

Text from Granger to Taylor/Sammie: Aren't you in Spanish Fork and have the Lil Bros with you?

Text from Taylor to Sammie/Granger: YES, and they are shocked and loving it. Said Ace was their hero and are sure this happens to him all the time.

Text from Sammie to Taylor/Granger: And he left you three to make-out with some woman? Does he even know her?

Text from Taylor to Sammie/Granger: No, never seen her before. The four of us were at The Barbeque Pit eating after slack and he went to the bar to get a beer. She walked in, took one look at him, and was suddenly wrapped around him.

Text from Granger to Sammie/Taylor: What did he do?

Text from Taylor to Sammie /Granger: Set the beer on the counter, had to physically pull her arms and legs from around him, push her away, then politely explained he was with his three brothers and didn't have the time.

Text from Sammie to Granger/Taylor: What did she do?

Text from Taylor to Sammie/Granger: They whispered to each other then she took off.

Text from Granger to Taylor/Sammie: What did they whisper?

Text from Taylor to Granger/Sammie: He wouldn't tell me.

Text from Taylor Granger and Sammie to Ace: WHAT DID YOU WHISPER?

Text from Ace to Granger/Sammie/Taylor: Politely said she was too aggressive and wasn't interested. Now, would you like to know how slack went?

Text from Sammie to Ace/Granger/Taylor: First round was 8.1 and tied for third. Second round was 9.1 and out of the money but average put you 17.2 and second overall. Taylor kept us updated.

Text from Granger to Taylor/Sammie/Ace: Lil Bros having fun?

Text from Taylor to Sammie/Granger/Ace: Yeah, enjoying their taste of the rodeo road, they are excited about traveling with G and S, too. Ogden, Deadwood then Lewistown before Joseph.

Text from Granger to Sammie/Taylor/Ace: Then down to Rawlins's ranch so the Lil Bros can ride some steer before heading home.

Text from Sammie to Ace/Granger/Taylor: So much fun! Can't wait. See you tomorrow.

Text from Taylor to Sammie/Granger: Just to warn you. Ace is determined to help strengthen my arm and we rope every second he isn't competing.

Text from Sammie to Taylor/Granger: Good for him! I can't wait to see you two rope together.

CHAPTER THIRTY-SIX

GRANGER

With a hand to the small of her back, I guided Mom through the multitude of tables in the steakhouse in Joseph, Oregon. Each chair at the tables was taken, so we made our way to the bar.

"There are a lot of people in this little town." She leaned against the bar and glanced around the room.

"It's one of the favorite rodeos in the area." I motioned to the bartender for two beers.

"I read you drew Caballo Diablo and Kade Bruno got an 85 on him last year and placed second."

I leaned against the bar and grinned, "You're getting into this."

"I am loving it!" She chuckled with a nod to the bartender as he slid the glass of beer to her. "I've been researching all the stock contractors and their horses. It is the only way I can be a part of this side of your life."

"I can arrange for you to ride a bucking horse," I teased.

"I'll leave that up to you," She laughed with a firm shake of the head.

"If you change your mind, Evan and family will be here pretty soon, and he has a good lesson bucking horse named Popover."

She giggled, "Popping off his back?"

"If you're not careful, you'll "pop over" his shoulder."

"Still, I'll pass." She shook her head with another chuckle. "Since they have predicted you'll stay in the top 15, I took the first two weeks of December off from work so I can go with you."

"That's awesome," I grinned at the proud look she gave me. "I honestly love having you around."

"I am so proud of you," She smiled with her eyes dancing in happiness then glanced behind us at the customer-filled tables, then to the sides of the room. "Looks like we'll be waiting at the bar for a while, so I'm going to use the restroom now."

"I'll be right here guarding your spot."

I glanced at my phone for messages then up to the bartender whose eyes were looking behind me at the door. In the mirror behind the wall of bottles, I caught a glimpse of a woman he was watching. Long brown hair, tight blue tank top, and jeans that showed her every curve. Her gaze searched the room then stopped when she looked in my direction. If I had been by myself, maybe...more than likely, but I just glanced back at my phone.

"Hello, G-ranger." The voice purred, but it was not the right voice to be calling me that name.

I slowly turned to look at the brunette and smile politely, "Have we met? I'm sure I would have remembered you."

"Fate had not brought us together yet," Her voice was low and seductive, and a fingernail slowly slid down my arm. "But, now, here we are."

"And fate has not been too kind for it to happen on this day," I sighed.

"You're all alone here..." she pouted.

"No, I'm actually with my mother."

Her eyes widened slightly, and a flash of irritation was quickly hidden. "Maybe later..."

I could see Mom approaching with wide inquisitive eyes and with a polite smile to the woman. "No, we're traveling together the whole weekend and meeting with a group of friends here in just a few minutes."

"You could sneak out tonight and we..." The brunette started with her hand flattening against my stomach.

"Hello," Mom's voice chimed. "Granger, are you going to introduce me to your friend?"

The woman's hand dropped away from me. A slight smile appeared, "You're sure?" she asked and completely ignored my mother's presence.

"I'm sure," I nodded.

Without another word, the brunette turned and walked out of the restaurant.

"Did I just "cramp your style"?" Mom chuckled and reached for the beer.

"Sort of," I laughed.

She grinned, "I had to take a second glance when I saw her. She looked like a lady I used to work with; could have been twins."

"What about you? Am I cramping your style?"

"No," she chuckled. "I went out with a guy for a while but…it was not meant to be and at this point, I would rather spend time with my son."

A waitress walked toward us and stopped when I held up a hand, "We have a large crowd coming in, do you think there will be room for us, or should we try somewhere else?"

"How many?" She asked and glanced around the dozens of full tables.

"Around twenty and we'll need two highchairs for twin 8-month-olds," I answered.

"Alright," she nodded. "The tables in the corner will be clearing soon. When I get one cleared, I'll sit you two at it and start pushing them together as others clear."

"Sounds like a plan. Thank you, Ma'am," I smiled, and her eyes brightened.

"I'm Kellie," She flashed a flirty smile then walked away.

"Wow, I really am cramping your style," Mom laughed.

An hour later, six tables were pushed together and 22 people encircled them with non-stop chatter. The Lil Bros were staring at Evan as he told them stories of Craig and Brodie riding steers at their age. I took a quick picture and sent it to Charlene.

Text from Charlene to Granger: Warms my heart. They are having so much fun.

Text from Granger to Charlene: And what are you doing while you're home alone?

Text from Charlene to Granger: Not alone. Lauren, Andrea, and Jodi are here, and we've been to just about every spa in the area and tomorrow we're headed to San Antonio to shop and go to the Riverwalk.

I read the message twice then turned to Ace, "Who are Andrea and Jodi?"

"Andrea is Lauren's best friend; since they were 10 years old. Jodi is Andrea's brother's ex-wife but they get along like they are still sisters."

Text from Granger to Charlene: Sounds like you're having more fun than the 4 brothers.

Text from Charlene to Granger: Well, don't tell them that! I need a little "poor mother" leverage.

Text from Granger to Charlene: LOL, I won't.

"Who is that with Delaney and Camille?" Mom leaned toward me and whispered.

I glanced up to see the two women followed by a pretty, slender, red head. A blonde, brunette, and a red head; all beautiful. Much to my surprise, a chair was pushed in next to Evan and when he looked up at the red head his eyes shone with happiness. I nearly gasped out loud when she leaned down and kissed him.

"What the hell?" I whispered.

Brodie chuckled, "Pretty damn weird, isn't it?"

"Who is she?" Ace asked.

"Her name is Sawyer. She's been riding with Delaney and Camille the last few weeks. When we were in Calgary, she helped Dad take the horses to Wyoming. When we got there, THAT had happened." He waved his hand toward the happy couple and chuckled. "Shocking, but she is really a nice lady, great with horses, mainly because her mother is a champion…legend in the reining industry. Sawyer has an eleven-year-old son that is staying in northern Idaho with her mother for the summer."

"And she makes Dad very happy," Logan added. "And none of us are adjusted to that yet. I don't think they are either." We all chuckled.

"They are glowing," Mom whispered then turned to him. "You're three weeks away from becoming a husband?"

Logan chuckled, "Yes, and, luckily, my bride has kept everything somewhat simple."

Lacie Jae grinned and wrapped her arms around one of Logan's, "With traveling for rodeos, the wedding, and then the bronc clinic to honor Craig, it only made sense." She turned to Mom. "You're coming with Granger, aren't you?"

"Well…I…" Mom stuttered and looked up at me.

"She is my plus one," I nodded to Lacie Jae.

"I wouldn't miss it," Mom smiled at me.

Someday, I hoped she would understand just how much it meant to me for her to be back in my life.

CHAPTER THIRTY-SEVEN

GRANGER

"Go through that gate and it will lead you to the bleachers. He's sitting at the top." I watched her walk away.

"Isn't that River?" Sammie asked as she and Ace walked up next to me and stopped.

"Yeah, she flew in this morning," I answered.

"I thought she wasn't coming over until Kennewick in a couple weeks when they bring the horses?" Sammie huffed.

We watched River slowly climb the steps of the bleachers of the Hermiston Rodeo Grounds to make her way to Brodie.

"She came over to be with him," I sighed. "It was one year ago today…"

Both their heads jerked to me.

"Why didn't you say anything?" Sammie gasped.

I just shrugged as River sat in front of Brodie and his arms wrapped around her. She melted into him until she was barely visible.

"Oh, my heart hurts," Sammie cried. "For the loss of Craig again, but for what River has done by coming over to be with him." She turned to me with glistening eyes, "You, OK?"

"A bit melancholy," I admitted with a sigh. "I talked to Martin this morning and he is staying at the ranch and playing with the twins. They are both crawling now and barely stop. Their laughter and energy will help him."

"They are nine months now?" Ace asked and I nodded.

Sammie sighed, "They will help and yet, break his heart."

We were quiet a moment watching Brodie and River then turned and walked to the trailer.

Both Brodie and I were bucked off before the eight-second horn and Ace's throw was late, but he still managed to catch the calf. Sammie's turns were a bit wide and took her out of the money. When we drove out of the Hermiston rodeo grounds, Ace had placed fifth overall for the rodeo and added a bit more to the standings. With Ace driving, Sammie and I cuddled with the puppies. They were relaxing and fun; two of the best decisions Ace and I ever had.

Sammie was in the back seat with the guitar at her side. "Well, we put that behind us and just look forward. Let's practice for the wedding."

"How many songs?" Ace asked.

"She said about forty-five minutes worth, but I think we should be prepared for an hour, at least," Sammie answered and handed me the puppy. "We'll start with your duets; *Cowboys Like Us*, *What You Going to do with a Cowboy, then The More I Drink*...and have you guys heard of Mac Davis?"

"Yeah," We answered, and she laughed as she tapped her phone and one of his songs began to play. Our laughter joined hers.

Our stage was a flatbed trailer that was parked between the Rawlins house and their arena. Garlands of blue and white roses encircled the edges of the trailer, the arch where the vows would be shared, and along the rail of the porch behind the house. On top of the trailer was Sammie and her two puppies. She playfully pushed them away from the guitar case then leaned back on the stool and lifted her red guitar to her lap.

"Looks patriotic up there," I chuckled. Baby Caleb was strapped to my chest, and he was nodding off to sleep.

"The cowboy way of life is patriotic," She grinned and strummed a few chords then adjusted the microphone. "Go out to the edge of the driveway and let me know how this sounds." She turned and looked around the yard and spotted Ace with Ellie in the carrier strapped to his chest. "Ace! Go up on the porch and let me know how it sounds."

He obediently skipped down the walkway and bounced the baby. Ellie squealed in laughter. The pair had been inseparable all morning.

Sammie strummed a few chords then looked out at us, "Well?"

"Play a song," I called out.

The babies' favorite song played out of the speakers with Ace and I singing about the ants marching one by one and Caleb's eyes opened wide, and he began to bounce.

The caterers walked around the corner and began singing with the song. The voice of the bride, Lacie Jae, and the maid of honor, Camille, and the bridesmaid, Delaney, filtered out of the house windows as they joined the chorus. Sawyer and her son, Rafe, walked out of the house and their voices joined in. The deep voice of Logan and his best man, Brodie and groomsmen, two of his steer wrestling friends joined in the chorus as they posed for the photographer in the arena.

When the tenth little ant marched up the hill and yelled 'the end' everyone cheered and laughed.

"Thank you, Sammie!" Lacie Jae called out. "That was fun!"

Sammie grinned across the yard at me, "Sounds good?"

"Perfect," I nodded and turned to a truck driving down the long driveway.

"Grandma is here!" Rafe yelled and ran for the truck.

"Victoria Rafael Taylor," Sammie whispered.

"You know her?" I asked.

"Met her a few times when we sold each other horses. She is a remarkable horsewoman."

"Rafe was showing me her reining videos last night. That reining cow-horse is pretty fun to watch and you're right, she is remarkable."

The older woman slid out of the truck and wrapped her arms around her grandson. It was easy to see the pair adored each other. A man I had seen before stepped out of the truck.

"Harrison," I greeted him with a strong handshake. "Good to see you."

Introductions were made between the people in the yard.

"I hate to interrupt this," Sammie smiled politely. "But we need to do a practice song with your microphones to make sure everything is ready."

Sammie returned to the decorated flat-bed trailer, but, wanting to simulate our road trip drives we replaced the stool she had been using with the backseat of a SUV, so she looked like she was sitting in the truck. A steering wheel on a makeshift stand had Ace's microphone sticking up the middle of it. He was on her left and to her right, we had pulled a dashboard from a truck at the junk yard, and it became my drum. I bounced the drumsticks across it to check the sound and we laughed.

"Considering how many times you've hit mine and Sammie's dashboards, I'm surprised they aren't dented," Ace teased, and I grinned.

"Test the horns," Sammie instructed.

Ace keyed the Mexican horns on his phone and played it into the microphone.

"NOT UNTIL WE ARE BACK FROM TAKING PORTRAITS AFTER THE WEDDING!" Lacie Jae yelled from inside the house.

We chuckled.

"OK, how's this?" Ace called out to her then looked at Sammie. "George Strait."

Her fingers slid across the strings, and he began with '*I Cross My Heart*' and I joined with the chorus. Within a minute, Delaney appeared out the backdoor wrapped in a robe and waving her arms, "STOP!"

The song died mid-tune.

"What's wrong?" Sammie gasped.

"You ruined Lacie Jae's makeup," Delaney grinned. "You have her in tears. Evidently Logan sang that to her once and it brought up all those emotions.   She wants to know if you would play that when she walks down the aisle instead of the wedding march."

Two hours later, the song echoed across the ranch. Every chair was filled, the bridal party had finished their walk to the arch, and Evan was slowly standing from his wheelchair. With him on the bride's left and Martin on the right, a beaming Lacie Jae was slowly walked up the aisle. Her white lace dress flowed behind her and long lace sleeves looking like wings fell nearly to the ground. A halo of white and blue flowers graced her head. She looked like a fairy princess walking down the aisle. Logan wiped away tears as she approached.

It took all my control to keep my voice from shaking as the song came to an end. Ace and I stepped back to sit on the bench with Sammie. As the minister began, I looked between my two friends and whispered, "Out of all the rodeos, concerts, fairs...and everything else we've done, I think this is one of the best."

"Agreed," they whispered.

As Lacie Jae had requested, once the minister introduced them as husband and wife and they began their walk down the aisle, I started the sticks on the dash, Sammie started on the guitar, and Ace hummed the beginning of Pharrell Williams song, '*Happy*'. I began with the lyrics and within moments everyone began singing and clapping with the song until the bride and groom disappeared into the house. The bridal party made their way down the aisle with Delaney and Camille on each side of Evan until he reached his chair.

Sammie set her camera on Ace's makeshift microphone stand and positioned it so she could see the entire crowd. She wanted to gift the bride and groom the recording of what they missed while taking wedding portraits. When she nodded to me, she hit the record button.

"Alright everyone," I said into the microphone and the whole crowd, in what seemed a coordinated move, turned to look at us.

All three of us chuckled.

"We have been asked to entertain you while the portraits are being taken, so we decided to share with you a bit of our road trip entertainment. We have the phenomenal Sammie Parkston on the backseat guitar, Ace Conners behind the microphone steering wheel, and I'm Granger Miller on the dashboard drums. Since Ace is the lead vocalist and Sammie is our whole band, they elected me to speak. I apologize now for any 'bad' language that escapes me." The crowd clapped and laughed. "We're going to start with a favorite of mine...it is a bit of a theme for Ace and I and no doubt you all know it so please sing along; it helps cover my voice: George Strait's *Cowboys Like Us*." They laughed again and joined in singing every song. "And now the theme song Sammie has given the two of us...a little Mac Davis." The crowd roared in laughter as we sang *It's Hard to be Humble*.

For an hour, they sang and danced until the wedding party appeared. Ace reached for his phone, nodded to me and Sammie, then held the phone to the microphone as the trumpets played.

The wedding party joined the loud crowd with Lacie Jae's arms in the air and waving her bouquet as we sang our theme song. It was our last song. As everyone began preparing for the team roping jackpot, their reception DJ began to set up on the flat bed.

The jackpot, then wedding celebration lasted until sunrise.

The next afternoon, still in bed recovering, my phone chimed. It was the special tone that let me know when a draw was posted for a rodeo. I lifted the phone and barely got one lid to rise to look at the email with the draw for the Kennewick rodeo.

I read Destiny's Ignatius and shot straight up in the bed at the elation of drawing the horse at the same rodeo where I had turned out on him the year before. An ache swirled my brain and I rubbed my eyes. Just to confirm, I looked again. It was Destiny's Inferno next to my name. The elation dropped. It was Iggy's full brother; just as big, but Inferno did not have the dramatic bust-out that Iggy had. The sigh was deep until I realized Inferno was a horse that could help me get to the short round.

Text from Granger to Brodie: I was close.

Text from Brodie to Granger: I had to do a double take on yours. You'll draw Iggy someday. I'm with Scarlet Lady. She's a good one.

Text from Granger to Brodie: Wish you were traveling with us, but we'll meet up in Kennewick for the short round.

Text from Brodie to Granger: Me too…positive thinking.

With only one day to recover, Sammie, Ace, Leo, Spence, and I drove to and rode in Miles City, Montana, Bremerton Washington, then Kennewick Washington for the first round.

I stood on the platform behind the Kennewick bucking chutes. A year before, I had been there behind Brodie, protecting him from reporters as he rode in honor of Craig. His quest for the saddle was a feat to be remembered. My withdrawing from the rodeo was also the decision that I would remember for the rest of my life. I was setting my saddle on Inferno's back, but two chutes down was Iggy. *The day would come*, I thought to myself as Dawson Hay adjusted his saddle on the horse.

My mind switched back to Inferno.

"It's about time you got on one of my horses," Adam walked up to me with a grin. "Not the one you want, but he'll let you know you rode him."

"Let's make sure I do," I chuckled.

"Ladies and gentlemen," the announcer called out. "Our next rider has all but notched his belt to Vegas this coming December. He currently sits 7th in the world standings..."

The voice faded away as Adam tightened the flank strap, and I adjusted the rein. Rising above the panel, my heart beat a little faster. The horse was as big as his brother and filled the chute. I couldn't get the tip of my toe in the stirrup.

"He is impatient once you're on," Brodie said as he reached down and turned the stirrup for me. "Get yourself set and go. Toes out, get to the mane, fire your feet."

I leaned back, listened to his words and put fire into my veins, then nodded.

One lunge out, barely into the arena, and the horse's back hooves were high into the sky. I fired my feet down to take the impact of his front hooves hitting dirt, then fired them back to the saddle to prepare for the next buck. I fired them down again as fast and hard as I could. Body jolting kicks made it hard to keep myself in form. Each kick felt like it was dislodging me, and I was surprised I didn't get thrown off. The buzzer blared and I instantly reached down to grab the rein. Another buck, and there was no keeping in the saddle; I was flying through the air but managed to land on my feet and out of the way of the pick-up man. Slowly walking to the chutes as the pickup men tried to catch the horse, my eyes went to the replay on the big screen. The dismount looked like it was on purpose which made my grin wide when I looked up at Brodie.

"Hell yeah!" Brodie yelled.

"It sure looked a hell of a lot better than it felt." I nodded over to a grinning Adam who was now adjusting the strap around Iggy.

"That's a score of 88-points and takes the lead with three riders left to go...and all three are national finals qualifiers. It's a heck of a night to be at the rodeo! First, we have Jacobs Crawley on Calgary Stampede's Cracking The Till..." The announcer continued as I turned to help Brodie with his horse.

Jacobs' gate swung open, and I glanced up to watch, "Sweet ride." I turned back to Brodie as the 87-point ride was announced. "Toes out, get to the mane, fire your feet." I repeated his words to me.

He chuckled, leaned back, and nodded. He was Mr. Consistent when it came to his style. It was a beautiful ride but didn't have the body jolting power that Inferno gave me. I wasn't surprised at the 85-point score.

Only Iggy and Dawson Hay were left to ride, and I edged closer to Adam as Brodie climbed the chutes and stood next to me as he unbuckled his chaps. River appeared to stand next to him. Everyone on the platform was silent and stood patiently waiting for the chute to open for Dawson and Iggy. Every bronc rider on the platform wanted to be the cowboy on that horse.

"For the last ride of the night, needing an 89-point ride to take the lead, is champion rider Dawson Hay and the stallion from Westmoreland Stock Contractors, Destiny's Ignatius. There have been a half dozen rides in the seven seconds on this horse but only one rider has ridden past the eight. That was Brodie Rawlins in the ninth round of the National Finals Rodeo last December. This horse has...and there's the nod."

My body lifted as the gate swung open and I envisioned myself on the back of Iggy as he lifted into his signature rear-out then first lunge that ended with a near vertical kick back. Every rider on the platform was moving their bodies with each jump. It was a huge swing of the massive stallion's head that tipped Dawson to the left and the rein slid out of his fingers. He was halfway to the ground when the horn blared.

"It's rare a horse dislodges Dawson..." The announcer yelled.

"You can't get much closer than that," Brodie exhaled.

"I love watching him show off," River whispered with a wide smile.

Adam stepped in front of me, "Your stall mate did good. Forty-six points for him."

I laughed and the tension and anxiety of watching my nemesis horse buck without me melted away.

"I don't know what more they can ask for from a buck like that," River glanced at the officials then sighed with a smirk at her dad. "Don't talk about the scores…just move on." She turned, then looked back at us as she made her way down the steps. "I'm going to have a beer."

"No doubt we'll both be in the finals Saturday night," I said to Brodie as we followed her.

"Iggy will be back out, so maybe," Granger grinned.

"You think I can be that lucky to get both brothers at this one?"

He shrugged, "They'll be in Lewiston and the finals in Pendleton again, too."

"Since I have every intention of making it back to the finals in Pendleton, which gives me four more tries to get him this year."

Friday night as we drove back to Kennewick from Coeur d' Alene, my phone alerted me to the draw for Saturday's championship. My chances went to three when I drew Calgary Stampede's Cracking The Till.

Sammie parked next to Delaney's trailer with Brodie and Mom waiting for us.

I gave Mom a strong welcoming hug, "How did the setup for the clinic go?"

"Everything is ready," she chimed. "I am so glad they asked me to help."

Brodie grinned, "You're part of the family now so it's a bit expected of you."

"I have no problem with that," Mom beamed.

Ace handed me the lead rope for Stomping Dog, "We have the clinic tomorrow morning, then Monday," he said with a heavy tone. "Tuesday, we need to sit down and look at the rest of the year."

"Yeah, I agree," I nodded.

"I may have to send Stomping Dog down to Texas to have him ready if I need to go back and forth."

Sammie sighed, "Dad is headed to Texas on Monday and said he would haul him if you wanted. I'll miss Monday morning at the clinic since I have to take Sergeant and Grace into the farrier at the ranch. But, it's only an hour away so we should be back at lunch and can help with the jackpot."

"And group picture," I nodded and ran a hand down the horse's shoulder and grinned. "Which means clinic t-shirt on Monday." He wasn't fond of t-shirts. He only wore them to bed.

"If I have to," Ace huffed then nodded to Sammie. "Let's just figure on taking him there Monday morning of the clinic."

"First," Sammie grinned. "Let's go win this damn rodeo."

With the highest first-round ride of the week, I was the last bronc rider to bust out of the chute. I felt strong, invincible, and young riders that would be going to the clinic the next two days were in the stands watching. I wanted to show them, before teaching them.

With an 89-point ride, I took the lead for the night, and won the rodeo I had drawn out of the year before. A sense of pride rushed through me as I was greeted by Brodie, Leo, and Spence at the back of the chutes.

When the platform was clear, Brodie and I stood quietly and waited for Ace to make his run. After a few moments, Brodie spoke while looking out at the roping chutes.

"The next two days we will be surrounded by dozens of people in our tribute to Craig's legacy, but right now, when it's just the two of us, I want to say..." he hesitated. "Riding together this year has been a lot of fun, and if I couldn't ride with him, well...," I nodded as my chest grew tight. "He was always cheering for you, always looking to see how you did at a rodeo and called you a "fucking natural" dozens of times." He took a breath and exhaled as if letting loose the turmoil that had been riding with him since Craig's death. "He would be so unbelievably proud of you for coming back a year later and winning the rodeo you turned out on. Inferno and Cracking the Till would have gotten the best of you last year, but your hard work, determination to grow and improve...you deserved that win tonight."

"Thanks, means the world to me," I whispered.

"Just remember, when you finally get on Iggy, be prepared for that shake of his head."

We were quiet until Ace's name was called. His run placed him 3rd for the rodeo.

When the barrel racing started, Brodie, Adam, and I were sitting with River at a table on the overhead walkway. Ace's cousin, Jamie, was the first to run into the arena. Her 17.27 second run held for the win through eleven riders including Delaney and Sammie.

I placed a handful of orange fish crackers on Ellie's highchair tray. She grabbed them and turned to Caleb in his chair next to her. For a full two minutes the pair spoke to each other in their own twin language.

"Babbles," I finally laughed, and the twins looked up at me with grins. "You two just babble and babble like you know what you're saying to each other."

Ace stood next to me and laughed, "Sounds like a pair of drunks to me."

I couldn't help but agree. "Monte was a babbler when he was a baby, but Liam was really quiet. Mom said it was because we always anticipated what he needed so he never found a need to talk. I was eight and nine when they were born; only eleven months apart from each other. Mom let us help as much as we wanted, and we enjoyed them more every year as they grew."

"Which is why the four of you are so close," Granger nodded.

"Yeah," I grinned at him. "Sometime when you're around the Lil Bros, ask them what 'that what shall not be discussed' means."

Granger chuckled, "What's it mean?"

"The fact that Taylor and I helped change their diapers."

We both laughed.

"Alright, Uncles Granger and Ace," Lacie Jae giggled and lifted Ellie up in her arms. "We have to get them ready for their introductions at the clinic."

I grinned, lifted a giggling Caleb from his chair, and followed her down the hallway to deposit him into his crib.

"I'll leave it to you to get these little babblers dressed," I grinned and turned to make my way back to the arenas.

The backyard that held over two hundred wedding guests the week before was now taken over by thirty riders with their gear strung around them. The training equipment from the barn was set up in the driveway. Large buckets filled with ice and water bottles for the expected 90-degree day were placed along the fence.

"I know I was on the waiting list," A young cowboy was talking to Martin. He wasn't much older than I was when I had gone to my first clinic, but he did at least have boots and a cowboy hat. "But, I thought maybe I could come watch or if someone didn't show up, I'd be ready." His voice shook with nerves and eyes were hopeful.

Martin nodded and I could tell he was holding back a grin, "What's your name?"

"Frankie Struthers, Sir."

"We didn't have any no-shows," Martin said, and the teenager's shoulders lowered. "But you made the extra effort to show up, and one more rider isn't going to make a difference to our schedule, but it might to your future. Go get your saddle and get ready."

The cowboy gasped, grinned, and huffed, "Thank you, Mr. Houston." Then he turned and ran for the car that was the last in line down the driveway. His arm waved in the air. The driver's side door opened and a woman with a wide grin appeared.

"You are my hero," I grinned at Martin.

"Kids got initiative," Martin chuckled then glanced at me.

He didn't have to ask, I just nodded, "I got him."

Just as Craig had done for me six years before, I took the young cowboy under my wing and stayed with him all day.

Evan started the morning meeting with the welcomes then the introductions of Martin, Brodie, and the twins. Then a run through of the program of how the two days of clinics were planned. He introduced the nine professional saddle bronc and bareback riders that had taken time out of their rodeo schedule to honor Craig and help fulfill the dreams of the cowboys at the clinic.

Then, he turned to me, placed Caleb in my arms, and turned back to the crowd.

"Anyone here go to or see the rodeo in Kennewick last night?" He asked and they all raised their hands. "This young man came to one of these clinics and had never even been near a horse before. He became one of my son's best friends and one hell of a rider as you saw last night when he won the rodeo." He turned to me with a smart-ass grin. "Granger Miller, do you have any words of wisdom for these cowboys?"

We hadn't discussed me talking to the group, but I knew him well enough he might just throw it at me, so I had prepared myself.

"Listen to the old cowboys and prepare for the unexpected," I smirked at him then turned to the kids. "NEVER assume you know everything. I didn't get to this point by myself. As Martin and Brodie can confirm, I asked A LOT of questions when I first got started. You don't learn if you don't. Every cowboy you were just introduced to had questions about when they first started and even the years that followed. So, my words of wisdom are: ASK QUESTIONS AND MORE IMPORTANTLY, LISTEN TO THE ANSWERS."

"Let's get going," Martin called out and the crowd rose to begin checking their equipment.

Brodie and I took the twins to the large playpen in the yard where Lacie Jae could watch over them and still be able to see into the arena. A large umbrella was placed to the side to protect the babies from the sun.

The flatbed trailer was parked alongside the fence and Evan had rolled onto it to overlook the action and would be one of the judges at the jackpot at the end of the second day. Logan, Ace, and Martin were the pickup men, Delaney and Camille worked the gates, while River, Sammie, and Adam helped with the steers and horses the contractor had brought. Mom and Sawyer were preparing the meals and making sure everyone was fed. Dozens of family members were also ready to help as needed. The weather was a perfect 80-degrees which meant the babies got to stay outside the whole time.

At the end of the day, everyone was tired, happy, and sitting around the porch discussing how successful the day had been. A few parents had left, but all the riders stayed to camp out under the stars. Sammie and Ace were entertaining the group with sing-along songs. Craig would have loved it.

I stretched out on the outside lounger and listened to the horses and steers in the field, and the young cowboys talk, laugh, and some were already snoring. The lights to the ranch house had gone out and the light in Sammie's trailer where her and Mom were sleeping was turned off. Crickets could be heard, and a slight warm breeze swept by. It was perfect.

It had been hours since I checked my phone, so before closing my eyes for the night, I checked on the stock draw for Walla Walla and Ellensburg. Both were good draws. On a whim, I clicked on the Facebook icon and saw the Messenger was highlighted.

I read the message in disbelief.

CHAPTER THIRTY-EIGHT

GRANGER

Message to Granger: Son, a friend of mine copied me on a post from Shayla stating she was working at a rodeo clinic this weekend and that you had won a rodeo last night. I researched and saw you have been rodeoing for years. I'm surprised at the path you have taken but it seems like you are in with a good crowd. I am not a social media person, but here is my phone number so you can call me back.

After reading the message a dozen times, I slid the phone into my pocket and closed my eyes.

"Camille, can you help me?" Lacie Jae asked as she walked through the kitchen and down the hall. "It's supposed to get in the 90's today so the twins will take their naps in here where it is cool. They'll sleep better that way."

"And you want me to take the monitor out to the corral fence," Camille stated then dutifully followed.

"Granger, pay attention," Mom huffed.

I turned to see her holding a large platter of biscuits out to me. My mind had been replaying the message from my father. Should I tell her or not? Her bright teasing smile answered me. I was not going to say a word to her. Sammie and Ace had left to take Stomping Dog to her dad and have her horses shod. I'd wait until they returned and talk to them after the clinic. I set the phone on the counter and took the platter of biscuits from her.

With a smile and a kiss on her cheek I walked out to the large crowd of cowboys and cowgirls settling in for breakfast before the day of riding started.

"When do I get to ride a horse?" Frankie asked as I sat down next to him.

"You rode three steers yesterday and did a great job," I smiled. "We'll get you on Pop Over this morning and see how that goes."

"He a horse?"

"Yes, a great horse for beginners," I answered. "Delaney and Camille have both ridden him."

Frankie's eyes widened then turned to the two women. "I seen pretty bronc riders before, but I never would have thought THEY would have done it. Do you think they would ride him today?"

I chuckled, "As much as he loves to buck, Popover is getting a little older now, so they only buck him once or twice a day. Would you rather one of them rode him or you ride him?"

Frankie grinned, "Me."

"Good answer," I laughed. "We have video of them riding you can watch."

An hour later, I was helping him adjust his bronc rein then adjusting the position of his feet.

"Do you believe you can ride this horse?" I asked.

"Yes, I do," He looked at me with wide anticipating eyes. "Once I get in rhythm, like the ladies did, I can get all the way across the arena."

"Nod when you're ready and not a second before," Delaney said from outside the chute.

"Yes, ma'am," he nodded.

"Did you mean to nod as a yes to what I said, or for me to open the gate?" She grinned at him.

"Oh...just to say yes to what you said," he stammered.

"Lesson learned," I grinned at Delaney then looked back at Frankie. "You answer by talking here, not by nodding."

"Ok," Frankie huffed then lifted the rope high, I adjusted it, then he nodded.

Three jumps out and he was picking himself off the ground. "I can do better than that."

At lunch, the group gathered around the table and attacked the hamburgers, potato salad, chips, and brownies Mom and Sawyer had prepared. I had Caleb sitting on my lap as he devoured a chunk of watermelon, and his head would nod forward as he forced his eyes open. Ellie's mouth was wide open, and she fussed every time Brodie took the spoon away to stab another piece of watermelon.

"They are so tired," Lacie Jae grinned. "But they were so busy this morning playing and watching all the action they didn't nap."

"Once we get started, let's get them down for a nap," Martin said. "Inside..."

"Yes," Lacie Jae agreed. "We put the monitor on the fence next to the trailer this morning just in case."

"Granger?"

I turned to Frankie.

"You said that they would buck Popover sometimes twice a day? Do you think I can try him again?"

"I'll talk to Evan and if he says you can then we'll get him in the chute for you." I appreciated his eagerness. Iggy may be my nemesis horse, but Popover was now Frankie's.

An hour later, Frankie was sliding onto the back of the horse.

"You watched the video from your ride this morning," I said to him. "What did you do wrong?"

"I didn't hold my toes out and the stirrup came off and I couldn't stay in the saddle."

"Alright then, toes out."

"You ready?" Delaney asked from the other side.

Frankie smiled at her, "Almost." He answered without a nod.

Delaney grinned at him, "Lesson learned."

He leaned back, took a deep breath, then nodded.

Everyone cheered for him as he made it the length of the arena before Logan swooped in and lifted him from the saddle.

"Let go of the rope," Logan yelled, and the rope flew in the air as Frankie was dropped to the ground.

"I DID IT!" He jumped high and fist pumped in the air. He was nearly dancing as he made his way back to the chutes.

High fives were shared down the chutes and his grin couldn't have been wider. For the first time, I reached back to pull my phone from my pocket to take his picture, but it wasn't there. I had left it on the kitchen counter.

"Go get your saddle and we'll get you on another before we start the jackpot," I told him and climbed down the back of the chutes. A vehicle going down the driveway caught my attention. I glanced around the yard, but everyone was up at the fence watching the next rider including Mom and Sawyer. Lacie Jae was on the trailer next to Evan.

I stepped through the gate while watching the SUV as it turned out of the driveway and onto the main road. As I turned toward the house, I glanced at the monitor hanging from the fence. The two cribs with sleeping babies inside should have been on the monitor but it was the closet doors in the nursery that were on the screen.

Lacie Jae must have hit the monitor when she laid the babies down for their nap, so I walked to the back door.

"You need something?" She jumped from the trailer and walked toward me.

I was already on the top step of the porch, so I turned as she approached, "I left my phone on the counter in here and wanted to get a few pictures of the riders."

"They are having so much fun and doing really well. I've taken some pictures I'll share with you." She followed me into the house. "Everyone, even the instructors, are having fun."

"It's a good group for sure," I picked up the phone and slid it into my pocket.

"We could have filled this clinic three times," she mused. "Evan and Martin were thinking about having a spring and fall clinic."

"I would have gone to both when I was younger," I chuckled.

She opened the doors to the refrigerator and pulled out a large tray of brownies and cookies.

"I'll carry them," I quickly took the tray from her and started to turn to the back door. "But, first...." I slid the tray onto the kitchen counter and turned down the hall. "I saw the baby monitor is pointed to the closet, so I was going to move it."

"What?" She gasped and followed me down the hallway. "I double checked it after laying the babies down."

"I don't know what happened, but..." When I turned down the hallway, I could see the front door leading out of the house was cracked open. "Why is that...?" I turned the corner into the nursery and looked at the camera that was clearly aimed at the closet.

Lacie Jae walked in to look in the cribs.

She turned to me with wide eyes, "They aren't here."

"What? I didn't see them outside."

"I JUST put them in here then walked outside," her voice shook. "No one has been near the house since lunch."

"Let's go look...the front door was open...," I walked out of the nursery and glanced at the door. "Why would that door be open?"

Lacie Jae was right behind me. "It was closed when I laid them down. Nobody should have been out that door." Her voice held the confusion and fear that was creeping into my heart.

I flung the door wider and stepped out onto the porch. Dozens of trucks, cars and the stock contractor's semis were in the pasture. Everything was normal...except that SUV that had left when I was at the corral gate.

"Go tell Martin someone took the babies." I ran down the steps and around the corner.

"NO! WHAT?"

I always left the keys in my truck when I was at the ranch and ran for it with wide strides. Brodie was walking out of the barn and startled when I ran toward him.

"GET IN MY TRUCK!" I yelled.

Without hesitation, he dropped whatever was in his hands and ran to my truck.

"What the hell?" he asked as I slid behind the wheel.

"Someone took the twins, I'm sure I saw the car leave."

"No fucking way? Why would anyone...how...?" He gasped and reached for his phone.

I flew down the driveway and turned in the direction the car had gone. "If they get to the highway and turn towards Bend, they'll be gone."

I pulled out my phone and pushed Sammie's number then hit the accelerator.

Her voice echoed into the cab of the truck.

"Hey, how's it going?" She answered.

"Where are you?" I yelled.

"Just about through Redmond."

"Pull over as soon as you can so you can see traffic go by."

"Why?"

"Because someone took the twins."

CHAPTER THIRTY-NINE

ACE:

"Someone took the twins." Echoed in the cab.

I turned to Sammie as we both gasped.

"Like stole them? Kidnapped them?" She cried.

"Yes," Granger's voice answered in controlled panic. "Ace?"

"Yeah," I nodded.

"Do you remember the SUV that Aaron just bought?"

"Yeah..." I pointed at a pullover on the side of the road for Sammie to drive to.

"It looks like that except it is a gray color and had something on top..." Granger said.

"Like ski racks?" Brodie's voice asked.

"Exactly," Granger answered. "Grey SUV like Aarons but with ski racks."

Sammie slowed down and pulled to a stop. "I have the trailer and horses in it. I can't pull out very fast...especially with this traffic."

"We're turning towards Redmond...," Brodie's voice was faint.

"What?" I asked.

Granger answered, "I'm on the phone with you, Brodie is on the phone with Martin. Everyone at the clinic is running for their vehicles to help in the search. Logan and Delaney are headed towards Bend."

"Anyone call the police?" Sammie asked.

"Yeah," Brodie huffed. "Evan is on the line with them now. They are getting every law enforcement agency on it, especially at the entrance to Bend."

I pulled my phone from my pocket, "I'm going to aim my phone down the highway and video every car that goes by just in case."

"If they come this way...," Sammie stuttered, "I need on the other side of the road so I can just pull out instead of doing a U-turn through traffic."

The blinker turned on and she stared at the approaching vehicles. My phone aimed at every car coming toward us.

"There!" She pointed but as the SUV grew closer, it was easy to tell it was too big. "No..." She sighed and drove the truck and trailer across the highway to another pull-out and parked so I could still see the traffic.

"This is surreal," Granger's voice could barely be heard.

"I'm going to kill whoever fucking did this," Brodie growled.

"What about their mother?" I asked the question I was sure everyone else was thinking.

"Evan is on the phone to the police department in Denver to see if they can find her." Granger answered.

Sammie leaned forward, "Ace? Is that...?"

"What?" Brodie and Granger yelled.

I leaned forward and lifted the phone to aim at the approaching vehicle. Without confirmation, Sammie turned on the blinker and started to pull forward. The grey SUV with ski racks drove past us.

"That's got to be the car," I muttered.

The roar of the engine drowned out Brodie and Granger's voices on the speaker system. Sammie's eyes darted to the monitor on the dash that displayed the horses in the trailer. The engine roared again. The back end of the grey SUV was still visible but pulling away. The engine roared again.

"WHAT THE HELL IS GOING ON?" Granger yelled.

"We spotted a grey SUV with ski racks going by," I answered. "Sammie is going as fast as she can."

"Where are you?" Brodie asked.

"We just passed the 124 exit that takes you to the Expo Center," Sammie answered.

The turn signal on the SUV began blinking and I looked at Sammie while still holding the phone to video every turn.

"Where are you?" I asked.

"Flying down the road with three state troopers next to me as they are flying to Redmond," Granger answered. "Brodie is talking to Martin, Martin to Evan, and Evan to the police to let them know you spotted them."

"I hope it's them," Sammie began to slow down and turned on her blinker. "They are turning off the highway..."

"Don't lose them!" Brodie yelled.

"I'm doing the best I can," her voice shook. The light turned green, and the grey SUV turned, when the truck approached the stop light, it turned yellow. "Heaven help us, I'm going through."

"What?" Granger asked.

"Through a yellow light that just turned red...they turned on...." I cranked my head to see the street sign. "Something like Odem Med...at Burger King...going west."

A horn honked behind us, and Sammie glanced at the horses on the monitor then let out a long exhale. Her eyes searched for the grey SUV. "There..." She whispered and the engine roared again. "They are turning to the right on Southwest Canal Boulevard toward the farm store."

"The sheriff wants to know if there is any clear evidence that this is the car that took the twins," Brodie grumbled.

"Other than Granger giving us a description of a car that just happened to drive by us in about the same time-frame that the car would be going from the Rawlins' Ranch to Redmond?" I asked. "No."

"I'm following this car until it stops, and we know for sure," Sammie growled. "Even if it's...damn..."

"WHAT?" Brodie and Granger yelled.

"Traffic circle ahead and some idiot is slowing down and there are cars backed up. The grey car already went through it, but I can't see them." I lowered the phone and looked at the buildings around us. "Why would they go off the main road? Why not get the hell out of town as fast as possible?"

"Why Redmond and not Bend where they can disappear faster?" Brodie asked.

"I can't see them..." Sammie's sigh was filled with the anxiety and fear I felt.

"Me either," I opened the door to the barely moving truck. "I'm going to run ahead and see if I can see anything...the car or where they may be going."

"What's happening?" Echoed from the truck as I stepped out and ran down the side of the road.

The water-filled canal ran parallel to the road to my right, but when I reached the traffic circle there was no grey vehicle in sight down the road. To my left was a huge apartment complex and a neighborhood full of suburban homes. I would never find the car that direction. To my right was a Safeway grocery store with a parking lot full of vehicles. It was my only choice to search. I turned around and looked for Sammie. After waving my arms toward the store I turned and ran down the road and into the parking lot.

I ran as fast as I could with visions of the last few months of spending time with the twins flashing through my mind. The joy they brought everyone that met them. Their giggles, babbles, and even when they were sleeping peacefully in my arms. We had to find them; just had to. If the SUV wasn't in this parking lot, then we would have lost them; lost the chance of rescuing the twins. That couldn't happen. The thought had my heart racing, hands trembling, but legs running as fast as they could. My lungs began to burn.

The parking lot just in front of the store had trees scattered throughout. I weaved back and forth through cars and trees until I spotted ski racks...but they were on a white car...another set of ski racks...on a red car. My heart was racing as I darted through the cars until, parked down the aisle in front of the main doors, was a grey SUV with ski racks on top. I ran to it while pushing Sammie's button on the phone. My heart was pounding and breaths coming in gasps.

"Well?" She answered.

"The car is here, parked in front of the store."

"I'll be right back; I need to let them know."

Pushing the speaker phone, I came to a stop next to the vehicle and peered inside. No baby car seats were on the back seat, "Son-of-a-bitch." My heart sank. Had they already dropped them off somewhere or transferred them to another car? Was this even the one Granger had seen?

Just to be sure, I pulled the handle on the door and much to my surprise it popped open. But the only thing on the backseat was a rolling bag. The top was unzipped, and blue familiar material was visible. I leaned in and yanked the bag out. When it hit the ground, the baby blanket decorated with the Rawlins' steer head brand fell out.

"Sammie!" I yelled into the phone and looked toward the store. "Sammie!"

I ran for the door and prayed the babies had not been dropped off somewhere else. Sammie's truck was just pulling into the parking lot.

"Ace..."

"The steer head baby blankets were in the back seat. It is the car! I'm going inside."

The double doors to the store whooshed open and I collided with a woman's cart as she made her way out. It nearly toppled over, and we both reached to set it up straight.

"What the hell? Slow down," she grumbled.

"I'm sorry…" I muttered as my eyes searched every face I could see.

A few people glanced at me but didn't say anything.

Why would the kidnapper have come to a grocery store? The only reason they would have stopped was if they needed something for the twins. I looked down the front aisle and sighed. There were too many people in front of the registers for me to see through.

"What does she think she is doing parking right in front? Someone go out and tell her she can't park there!" A woman arranging produce on the display island called out.

I looked back to see Sammie rolling to a stop directly in front of the store doors, then I continued down the front of the store.

"Where is the baby aisle?" I shouted at a woman behind the counter.

She pointed to the far end of the store then looked to the woman complaining about Sammie. "Someone go tell her to move! She can't park a horse trailer there."

I ran down the length of the store, glancing down each aisle but saw no one holding babies. Coming to a stop at the baby aisle my heart sank again. There was no one in the aisle. There was just a grocery cart sitting in the middle. I started to turn away when I heard it. The very familiar sound of babies babbling. I squatted down to get a better look in the cart. There, trying to stand in the cart was Ellie with Caleb tugging at her clothes.

"Oh, son-of-a-bitch," My heart soared as I ran to them. When I looked down, both twins grinned up at me and squealed. They were happy and so innocent of the situation.

Tears sprung to my eyes and my stomach quivered in relief with lungs so tight I could barely breathe. I swooped the babies up into my arms and held them so tight they both groaned.

"ACE!" Sammie's voice echoed in the store.

I hit Granger's number on my phone.

"ACE!" Sammie screamed again then appeared at the end of the aisle.

"Sammie said you found the car," Granger answered.

"I found them," I barely got the words out.

"What?" Brodie and Granger called out.

"I have the babies in my arms," Tears of relief rose, and Sammie approached with the tears sliding down her cheeks and her hands over her heart.

"You have them?" Brodie gasped.

"Yes, I have them. Sammie and I are here in the baby section of Safeway, but they were alone." She took Ellie from me and hugged her tightly.

"YOU HAVE MY GRANDBABIES?" Martin's voice echoed from Brodie's speaker phone and into mine.

"Yes, I have them," I held out the phone to the twins who both tried to grab it. "Say 'hi' to Poppa."

"Poppa..." Ellie chimed.

"Poppa?" Caleb looked around us as if searching for him.

"Oh, Lord..." Martin's voice trailed off.

Sirens filled the air.

"Sounds like the Cavalry is here," I smiled at Sammie.

"I'll stay here with the cart in case they need to try for fingerprints," she whispered. "You keep them...."

Three police officers, Granger, and Brodie appeared at the end of the aisle.

"What's going on?" A man yelled from behind them.

As Brodie and Granger each took a baby from us, a tall police officer spoke to the man. "Are you the manager?"

"Yes," the man's eyes widened.

"I am Lieutenant Stacey, and this building is locked down. No one enters or leaves until it is thoroughly searched." The officer growled then turned to the other two officers. "We have two cars at the back of the building. Check everywhere." He turned back to the manager. "We need security footage from outside and inside the store...now."

"But..." The manager stuttered.

"These babies were kidnapped from their home, and who ever did it was in this store with them," the officer glared.

"We'll go get the videos," the manager hurried away.

"This is the cart," I told the officer. "The SUV is out front."

"I didn't see it when we came in," Brodie shook his head.

We walked to the front but were blocked from exiting the building by two large police officers.

"Let them through," Lieutenant Stacey instructed. "They led us here." He turned back to us. "I'll be out in a minute to talk with you."

When we walked out the doors, Evan's van was pulling into the parking lot. Sammie waved at them.

I walked to the grey SUV, which was no longer there, "Well, damn." I grumbled and looked at the group. "This is where it was parked." I pointed to the space and noticed just under the car that had been parked next to the SUV was the bag I had pulled from the back seat. I walked over and carefully used the tip of my boot to pull the strap and drag it into the open.

"Don't touch it!" One of the large officers from the front door yelled and quickly jogged to our side.

Martin's door was opening before Evan came to a stop. When his gaze landed on his grandchildren, his eyes closed, then his shoulders lowered. He stepped out to 9-month-old voices yelling, "Poppa!" Tears welled in his eyes as he wrapped them in his arms. Lacie Jae jumped out of the van while Evan rolled straight to me with a glance to the bag at my feet.

"Tell me everything," he ordered.

By the time I was done, a dozen vehicles arrived around us and the cowboys and families that had been at the clinic stepped out. The large officer held them back as the tall officer walked out of the store.

"We have cleared everyone inside the store, and no one has been found. There is no clear shot of the person going into the store, but once the truck and trailer were coming to a stop on the west entrance, the person ran out of the doors on the East side and took off; just seconds before we pulled into the parking lot." Lieutenant Stacey shook his head. "Unfortunately, no one paid attention when the babies were brought into the store, but the videos have been sent in to be evaluated."

"How long will that take?" Evan asked.

"We should have something within the next 10 –15 minutes. We have to move fast. Our guess is the kidnapper is leaving town as fast as possible, but thanks to the tall cowboy there, we can positively give them the vehicle they are driving, which means we have a chance of finding them."

I nodded to the bag at my feet, "I pulled this from the back seat and saw the blankets."

"They were specially made with our family brand," Evan added.

"We'll have to keep them for a bit." The officer knelt next to the bag and with a pen he pulled from his pocket, he opened the top of the bag to reveal both blankets and a very small black bag. With the tip of the pen, he lifted the black bag and set it on the ground, then wiggled the zipper down to open it. A dozen heads leaned forward to see what was in it.

"Is that what I think they are?" I asked and looked at the officer.

"What?" Came a chorus of voices from the cowboys and families.

"Yep," The officer nodded and rose leaving the bag and its contents on the ground. "Cameras."

"That's how they knew," Lacie Jae gasped. "It was the only time, all weekend, those two were in their room alone." Tears welled in her eyes. "I should have..."

"Nothing," Martin huffed at her. "You did what we have done for 9 months, let them sleep in their rooms. I told you at lunch they should sleep there."

"This is no one's fault, LJ," Brodie's arm slid around her.

"Just the son-of-a-bitch that placed those cameras there," Evan grumbled.

"How and when...where?" Granger asked.

"Where? Would be the front door," Evan huffed. "We don't use that door very often so none of us would have noticed them...and they are tiny."

Ellie wiggled in Martin's arms and reached into his front pocket where he normally kept treats.

"They need to eat," Martin announced.

"And probably a diaper change," Lacie Jae nodded then walked toward the store with determined strides.

The very large officer looked down at her when she neared. She was just over 5 foot tall, he had to be at least six feet tall and twice as wide as her. She spoke, and after a moment they both entered the store. She returned in less than 5 minutes with the officer carrying two large shopping bags for her.

"The manager is very upset and filled the bags with whatever the babies might need," she announced and reached for Ellie. Brodie took Caleb and they went to the back of the van where a changing station had been set up.

"What now?" Martin grumbled and looked at the officer.

"We'll need to go to the house where it happened," he answered.

"My son and daughter had driven towards Bend but when we got the call they were found, they went back to the ranch and are there with the sheriff's officers," Evan informed him.

"I'll contact them, the security video here is already in analysis. I'll call you when we find something." The officer nodded and with the help of his baton, carried the kidnapper's bag to his car.

Martin turned to the group of cowboys and family, "Let's get back to the ranch and see what we can do."

CHAPTER FORTY

ACE

Sammie parked the trailer by the barn then we removed her horses and thoroughly inspected each one.

"They look fine." She sighed with a relieved smile to me then her gaze went to the house where Martin, Camile, and Lacie Jae had taken the twins. "It's so unreal."

"Already feels like it was a bad dream."

We let the horses loose in the front corral with plenty of hay and water. Sammie looked them over one last time before we walked to the arena.

River, Adam, Shayla, and Granger were standing next to Brodie as he spoke to the group. "There is nothing we can do but stand around and wait for information. If you want or need to go, I understand, but right now, I have GOT to have something to burn this energy in my gut. I say we buck em'." Everyone nodded.

"Let's buck em'." Granger yelled and swung an arm to the corrals.

For the next two hours, I worked the gates for the riders as the professionals assisted them. Each person, whether rider or family member, was pulled off to the side and interviewed by the sheriff's officers.

Granger was helping a young cowboy named Frankie when I walked up to the gate and slung the rope around the handle.

"He's going to buck more than Popover, so make sure you have those toes out, and lift on that rein like your life depends on it." Granger adjusted his feet then lifted the rein higher. "You believe you can ride this horse?"

"I believe I may fall off, but I'll get back on and try again." Frankie's eyes shot to me then up to Granger, "Where did the pretty lady go?"

Granger chuckled with a glance to me, "Delaney is definitely better looking than that."

I laughed, "No argument from me."

"I guess gate men aren't all pretty ladies," Frankie shrugged then leaned back, lifted the rein, and nodded.

I flung the gate open, and the horse surged out, two long leaps, a hop, then finally a few bucks before Frankie rolled off the side. He jumped up with a grin and ran back to the chutes.

"How did it look?" He yelled.

"How did it feel?" Granger countered.

"It was fun, but I don't really remember anything," he laughed.

Granger leaned down and helped him climb the chute. His gaze moved to the house where Martin, Camille, and Lacie Jae were staying with the twins. He looked down at me then turned away.

When the last truck left the ranch for the night, Sammie, Granger and I walked into the house. Logan, Lacie Jae, Camille, Delaney, Brodie, Shayla, River, Adam, Martin, Sawyer, and Evan were looking at an image on the large monitor. The twins were back in their highchairs eating more watermelon.

"That is the best shot the Safeway cameras got of the person," Evan nodded to the screen. "Not even a good shot of the car."

"It was behind the trees on almost all of them," Camille huffed.

Denim jeans, a short-sleeved western shirt that was untucked, and a large hat that looked like a mix between a cowboy hat and a sombrero. The face was not visible.

"That doesn't help much," Sammie sighed. "It could be a man or woman."

"Well, hell," I huffed and pulled out my phone. "Maybe I got a better shot with my phone." They stood quietly as I scrolled through the phone to the last video I had taken.

"Can you link it to the monitor?" Camille asked.

"I'll try...should be able to," I clicked the Bluetooth and connected the phone to the monitor and the video appeared.

The car approached and I slowed the video down then stopped it when the license plate became visible. Martin lifted his phone and took a picture then I continued the video at a slow pace. The only thing we could see was that hat, dark sunglasses, and a slim chin.

"Could still be a man or woman," Delaney sighed.

"But we have a license plate," Martin smirked at me with a nod and called the sheriff.

"Anything on their mother?" Granger asked.

Evan nodded, "She's still in Denver; was at the college library when they found her and her brother. They are convinced, by her actions, that she didn't have anything to do with it. She's pretty distraught and angry."

"Like the rest of us," Delaney huffed.

Lacie Jae turned without a word and with a stoic look walked down the hall. Moments later, she returned carrying a suitcase that she placed on the table. She gave Martin a bland look then turned back down the hall.

"What's that for?" Granger asked.

Martin turned to him with a deep frown and a sigh, "I'm taking the twins away for a few weeks."

"What?" Granger gasped.

Tears filled Delaney and Camille's eyes. It was hard to keep my own feelings down.

"Just for a few weeks, until we know and understand what happened," Evan explained.

"At this point, there is no way of knowing if there were more people involved than that driver. We do whatever we need to keep them safe right now, until we...well, know something more," Martin shook his head. "I would just..."

"It is the right thing to do," Granger exhaled. "Where are you going?"

"One place that is safe, secure, and I know there is no way to connect us to them," Martin said and nodded to Sawyer. "Going to her mother's ranch in northern Idaho."

"Bijou Bay Ranch," Sawyer clarified. "It's remote with a lot of security and a stranger would be noticed right away. Rafe is there with Mom, and he loved spending time with the twins at the wedding."

A loud bang rang out and we turned to see Lacie Jae walking back down the hall after unceremoniously dropping another suitcase on the table. Logan sighed and followed her.

"Harrison is there," Granger looked at a frowning Brodie who just nodded.

"It is a wonderful place," Camille attempted a smile. "I spent a few days there in June."

"When are you leaving?" River asked.

Martin sighed again, "As soon as we get the suitcases loaded and the watermelon fiends cleaned."

Granger's gaze lowered to look at the ground, and I laid a hand on his shoulder for support. Sammie wrapped an arm through his.

With a solemn cloud over our heads, everyone but Lacie Jae and Logan walked out of the house and to Sawyer's truck. The babies were hugged and kissed by everyone, then settled into the car seats.

Martin turned to the group of family and friends, "Just so you know, I fucking hate this, but I have to do this for now."

Delaney threw her arms around him, "We all understand...hate it, but we understand."

"It ain't forever," Evan rolled his wheelchair next to the driver's side door and slowly stood so he could see Sawyer through the window. She smiled softly as he took her hand. "They'll be back as soon as there are a few answers."

Sawyer looked at the group, "I promise, we will keep them safe."

"We're just a phone call or video chat away." Martin said and looked at the house then to Camille. "She ain't happy, go help Logan calm her down."

Camille gave him a strong embrace then turned to the house with tears sliding down her cheeks.

We watched the truck disappear down the driveway before turning back to the house.

Logan and Camille were sitting at the table on each of Lacie Jae who looked at the group with a blank expression. We took seats at the long table.

Once everyone was down, Lacie Jae took a deep breath; her hands were laced together and sitting on the table in front of her. Her jaw muscles twitched as she looked at each person.

"I believe it is clear with everyone..." she started with a voice taught in controlled emotions. "...that the only time the person that did this could have put those cameras at the front of the house, was during our wedding."

Evan nodded and leaned back in his chair, "The wedding and this clinic were the only times our own security system was shut down in the last few months."

Lacie Jae exhaled, "I called the photographer and asked her to upload the crowd pictures somewhere we can see them."

"When is she...?" Delaney started.

"She texted a few moments ago to let me know she is starting the upload right now," Lacie Jae answered. Her head turned toward the front window, and we all turned. A plain white car and a sheriff's car were pulling down the driveway. "I called them to let them know, and they are here to review the images with us," Lacie Jae said flatly.

The sun had lowered but no one in the room looked at their watch. I glanced at the time in the corner of the monitor. It was 8:47. Brodie stood and walked to the back door. The monitor had been black but flashed with the photographer's website appearing. Lacie Jae moved the wireless computer mouse and the first image appeared.

Brodie walked into the house with two uniformed officers and one female in denim jeans, white shirt and blue blazer following him. She looked like a detective right out of a television show. With nods of greetings, the officers looked at the screen then quickly took a seat.

Hundreds of images were viewed before Sammie jumped up and pointed on the screen of the hat the kidnapper had worn. "There, you see it? They are way in the back…the back row by the corner of the house."

Lacie Jae's eyes closed, she took a deep breath, then saved the image to the computer and clicked to the next one.

"Nothing but hat, though," Delaney sighed.

"Can you back it up a few images?" the lady detective asked.

Without looking at her, Lacie Jae slid the mouse down the table.

"Thanks, I am Detective Monroe," She whispered and clicked the button. "These images right before the hat appears are of the same area, and the hat is not there. It comes in after the wedding starts." She began clicking through the images that jumped from the wedding to the reception.

"The photographer was shooting the wedding portraits in between those," Camille explained.

The photographer had taken pictures of Sammie, Granger, and I on stage then of the wedding party dancing into the crowd. The hat did not appear in another picture.

"May I have the mouse back please?" Lacie Jae asked flatly.

It was handed back down to her. She clicked out of the group of pictures and went to her Facebook page then to the Wedding Page which had kept everyone informed of the day's events.

Message from Lacie Jae: Please look at the attached image, the white hat. Look through any videos or pictures you took at the wedding and send us an image if you see someone wearing it. For now, please do not share this picture or request with anyone outside of this group. Thank you.

She pushed the mouse away from her, clasped her hands together, and rested them on the table. Her normal pale complexion was a deep pink.

"Now what?" Logan asked.

"We wait and see," Evan sighed.

The officers and detective rose and nodded their goodbyes.

"Like we said before," Evan turned to the family and friends in the house. "There is nothing we can do but wait until more information comes in. We know the twins are safe and so we carry on."

"Like nothing happened?" Delaney growled.

"No, that won't be possible," he assured her. "But we will go about our time as normal as possible. You all have rodeos to get to."

"I don't want…," Brodie started.

"I know we don't," Logan huffed. "But there is nothing to do but stare at each other. We continue on and let the son-of-a-bitch that did this know they didn't change our lives."

"They don't even know the twins aren't here," Adam stated.

"While you're on the road," Evan nodded. "I'll call and upgrade the security around the ranch."

Granger, Sammie, and I walked to her trailer. Without speaking, Sammie crawled up onto her bed while we converted our beds and pulled out the bedding.

When the lights were turned off, I sighed into the night and replayed the whole day in my head. My decision to send Stomping Dog to Texas with Sammie's father was the only reason we weren't at the clinic and were coming through Redmond at the time. It was the reason the twins were safe with their grandfather.

"Unbelievable day," Granger whispered into the dark. "Man, the damn clinic was just perfect. If it wasn't for seeing that car leave…"

"And us coming through Redmond," Sammie whispered.

"It's hard to believe that not one shot of the person at Safeway had a clear view," I added.

"I have a gut feeling that no one at that party will have pictures of the person since they were at the back," Granger sighed. "All their cameras were on the wedding and then us."

The trailer grew quiet, and my mind finally stopped racing with memories enough to begin to shut down.

There was a bang.

"Shit!" Sammie huffed.

"Hit your head again?" I chuckled.

"I have it," Sammie exclaimed and the light from her room turned on.

"Have what?" Granger asked.

"I…it…," Sammie scrambled from the bed, down the steps, and still in her shorts and tank top pajamas disappeared out the door.

CHAPTER FORTY-ONE

ACE

By the time Granger and I stood, pulled our jeans back on, and stepped outside, she was shutting her truck door and running for the house. We ran after her.

She banged on the door then disappeared inside.

"Evan!" She yelled and turned down the hall to the kitchen.

Granger hit the light switch in the kitchen as Sammie turned on the monitor.

"What is going on?" Logan stomped down the hall with Lacie Jae right behind him.

"I have it," Sammie muttered and focused on the monitor.

"Have what?" Delaney and Camille appeared with Brodie and River right behind them.

"What's all the yelling?" Evan rolled down the hallway.

"I have it," Sammie muttered with rising excitement.

"What?" Everyone in the room asked.

"While the crowd was watching the wedding, then us…while we were playing, I videoed the crowd for Lacie Jae so she could see it. I forgot…" Sammie glanced at Lacie Jae then back to her camera. "It was on my camera, not on my phone."

Granger's voice echoed into the room, "Alright everyone," then the whole crowd turned at once to look at him. Everyone in the room walked closer to the monitor as the first song echoed into the room.

Halfway through it, Sammie jumped forward and pointed on the monitor. "HERE!"

The white kidnapper's hat moved from the back of the crowd and slowly to the driveway.

"Where are they…?" Brodie whispered and stopped when it became clear where the person was going.

"The barn?" Delaney huffed. "What the hell?"

Silence filled the room as we waited to see what the kidnapper was doing. They walked into the barn and just a few minutes later walked back out, toward the back of the singing and dancing crowd, then disappeared down the side of the house.

"And that would be the last of them until today," Camille whispered.

"But what the hell were they doing in the barn?" River mused.

Sammie reversed the video to the beginning then played it again. The third time through, River gasped.

"Look at the barn window, up at the top," she walked around the table and pointed.

Sammie reversed the video again and played from the moment the person walked into the barn. A flash of an arm appeared in the window.

"What the fuck are they doing?" Brodie growled.

I turned and looked at the group. To me, it was clear what the person was doing, "They needed to see the back of the house, the arena, to know that no one was approaching the house as they went in the front door."

"There's another camera?" Camille gasped.

Brodie, Granger, and Logan shot out of the room and down the hallway to the back door.

"Do you think it's still active?" Delaney looked at me. "Would they have seen Martin leave with Sawyer?"

"There would be a signal, or something from the camera," Camille muttered and pulled out her phone. "They would need a network or link to connect to it. I'm looking to see if there is another signal transmitting around here besides the ranch network."

"Sawyer?" Evan said and we all turned to see him on the phone. He told her about the cameras. "That's true, OK, we'll get back to you as soon as we know anything…talk to you tomorrow."

He lowered the phone and looked at the paused screen showing the arm in the window.

"She lived in Arizona until last June when she had flown up to be with her mother when she was hurt. Last week, she flew back down and drove the truck up here and hasn't changed the license. If anyone saw the plate and can track the number, they will think they are in Arizona."

"Oh, thank heavens," Delaney whispered.

"There is no network in range for connection besides the ranch," Camille stated.

"But that doesn't mean they didn't hack into this network," River stated. "If they are smart enough to pull this off so far…"

"I'll call the sheriff," Evan nodded.

"Was there audio with the cameras out front?" Sammie asked.

"No, just video," Evan answered.

The back door opened, and the three men strode in with glares.

"There were two," Brodie threw them on the table. "One in each window."

"My guess is they knew they couldn't retrieve those after the kidnapping, so they would be careful not to leave prints or a network connected to them once they had the twins," Camille glowered.

"Leave them where they are," Brodie grumbled and walked into the kitchen to retrieve a bowl that he placed over the cameras. "Just in case."

"Play the video of the person walking out of the barn," I said and leaned a little closer as the video began. "That is the best shot of the person that we know of."

"Can you enlarge it?" Camille asked.

Sammie zoomed in on the video and we watched the person walk into then out of the barn and back to the crowd. The hat still covered most of the face, but the hips swung out just slightly and each step was placed in front of the other as if on a fashion runway. Slim calves appeared under a light blue, figure hugging dress.

"That's a woman," Sammie declared, and everyone nodded.

"Well, we narrowed it down that far," Evan exhales. "We know the twin's mother was in Denver when it happened…"

"Doesn't mean she didn't hire someone," River said.

"She doesn't have the money for that," Evan shook his head. "She was pretty desperate at the time she had the babies. Martin agreed to pay her college tuition so she could get on her feet again and be part of the twins' life in the future. He pays it directly to the university and not to her."

"When I met and talked to her when we were doing the DNA tests, she was just sweet and overwhelmed, but I didn't see anything in her that would cause alarm," Camille sighed.

"So, you're convinced it wasn't her?" Granger asked Evan.

"I'm not convinced of anything," he sighed. "We need to get this video to the sheriff to see if they see anything we don't."

"What about the other way around?" I asked. "We should be able to see all the videos at the store in case we see something that the sheriff doesn't."

"You're right, Ace." Evan nodded.

He reached out and took Sammie's hand with a sweet smile, "Thank you, between finding those cameras and now knowing we're looking for a woman, this video will hopefully lead us to more answers."

"Thank goodness," Sammie smiled.

"It's three in the morning," Delaney sighed.

"We should just head out," I turned to Sammie and Granger.

"Where?" Evan asked.

"Ace has slack in Walla Walla in the morning, then we head down to southern Idaho, then to Ellensburg." Granger answered.

As the group separated and walked back down the hall, I glanced at Lacie Jae who had not said a word through the whole revelation. Her head was down as she walked, and face flushed a deep red.

"We've made it to 29th place with about 4 weeks to go," I said to Quincy and backed the horse away from the trailer. "We're supposed to just do the work and not worry about the numbers." I told him as if the horse had looked at the standings. "You get the rodeos up here, and then you can rest when I head to Texas to finish the year with your buckskin buddy."

After I slid a hand down his shoulder, I stepped up into the saddle and began a slow walk to the warmup arena. I tried to clear my mind of what I needed to do and focus on how I needed to do it, but my mind kept going back to the moment I heard the twins babbling in the store. What if? It was a question we had all asked ourselves the last week. We had no answers to that question, as the police had no answers to who the person was. As far as we knew, there were no more answers than what we had seen the first 12 hours after the kidnapping.

I forced myself to stop thinking about the twins and focus on the ride in front of me. At a previous rodeo, the calf I had drawn had run in a straight line down the arena, but he was fast. To stay up with him, I was going to have to push the barrier. Stomping Dog was faster in these situations, but he was now at home in Texas with Taylor riding him daily to keep him in shape.

"Ace?"

My mind jolted back to reality, and I turned to see Sammie smiling at me from on top of Sergeant. "What?"

"You may want to head to the arena now with the rest of the ropers." She nodded to the group of men riding toward the gate.

I smiled at her and huffed, "Probably a good idea."

"Sometimes I come up with them." She chuckled and trotted away. "Kick butt!"

I was the second roper and as Quincy and I walked into the arena to back into the box, I could see Granger along the fence standing in front of Sammie who was watching from her horse. They helped relax my muscles and brain for a solid run of 8.8 seconds. When I rode out of the arena, I was in third.

"Nice," Granger nodded to me.

I stepped down from the horse and stood next to him, "You hear anything yet?"

"Yeah," he nodded. "They want us to call as soon as the horses are put away and we can log onto Sammie's computer in the trailer."

"He didn't say why?" Sammie asked and turned her horse away from the arena.

"Nope," Granger answered, and we followed her.

We anxiously put the horses away then stepped into the trailer as Granger made the call.

Evan answered the phone. "I'll get right to it. The car was stolen out of Spokane and was found at the bottom of a boat ramp in the Columbia River...completely submerged. It's a dead end. The police finally shared all the video footage they had at the store. Camille has edited it to include only the important parts and put it in a bit of a timeline of events."

Sammie brought the video up on the screen and we stood and stared as the grey SUV drove across the parking lot then disappeared behind trees. Moments later, the kidnapper was carrying the twins into the store. The image switched to inside the store as she placed them into the shopping cart then walked down the aisle. No one spoke to her as she walked along the front of the aisles.

"She's been there before," Sammie muttered.

"That's what we thought," Evan agreed. "But watch…"

The video switched to the outside with a figure appearing running across the parking lot. It was me darting between cars and trees until I disappeared behind the tree which hid the car. Within moments, I was running into the store. The video switched to catch me running into the shopping cart with the shopper and I catching it from turning over.

"Camille did her magic with editing videos and did a side by side from two different angles from the moment you came into the store." Evan said. The video of me was on the right and the kidnapper wandering down the aisle was on the left. "She matched the time on the video, so it is happening at the same time. While this is going on Sammie is pulling to a stop in front of the store."

The kidnapper was at the end of an aisle at the front of the store and turning when I hit the cart. There was a hesitation, then as I began walking, the kidnapper stopped at the end of the baby aisle and stared down the front of the store in my direction. When I turned to the clerk, the kidnapper hurried down the aisle. Then, suddenly, she ran around the cart and down the aisle leaving the babies behind. She turned at the far end of the aisle seconds before I turned down the same aisle. She was running up the next aisle as I stopped then knelt to look into the shopping cart.

The video turned to outside the store with the kidnapper stopping as the doors to the exit opened and she hesitantly stepped through as she looked down at Sammie's trailer parked at the other exit. When Sammie disappeared inside, the kidnapper ran for her car. As she turned out of the parking lot, Granger's truck and the police cars were racing in from the other side.

"So, fucking close," Granger huffed.

"In each scenario," Sammie groaned.

My gut ached. "No audio?"

"No," Evan answered.

"Go back to the moment I walked into the store on the split screen," I instructed.

"You see something?" Granger turned to me.

"Yeah," I whispered as the video began again. "Watch the kidnapper. When I came in and ran into the cart, no one said anything except the lady I hit. The clerk at the produce yelled about Sammie pulling in out front and stopping at the doors. Now, see the kidnapper turn…she's looking at me, not the store clerk…and she hurries around the corner before the clerk yelled for someone to go out and tell Sammie she can't park a horse trailer in front of the doors. I ask the clerk where the baby aisle is, then the kidnapper leaves the babies behind and runs down the aisle."

"She didn't mention the horse trailer the first time she said something?" Evan asked.

"No, just complained that she was parking right in front of the doors," I answered with the ache increasing.

"So, she is ducking out of sight before the clerk…" Sammie started.

"It didn't have anything to do with you and the clerk," I exhaled. "She saw me first, then hurried…"

"You had a baseball cap on…not a cowboy hat. How would she have known?" Granger frowned.

Sammie reversed the video and played it again.

"The kidnapper knew who you were after you entered…before anything else was said…" Evan whispered in disbelief.

"She knew me…knows me…why else would she hide so fast and when I asked about the baby aisle, she took off running and left the babies behind?" I shook my head. "I can understand why she would know Granger since he hangs with Brodie and the Rawlins…"

"…and Martin." Sammie nodded. "But why you?"

"She would have known you from the wedding," Granger stated.

"But, like you said, I was in a baseball cap in that store. People look different…sometimes I get second looks from people I've known for years when I'm not wearing a cowboy hat and in a t-shirt. I very rarely wear a t-shirt. The only reason I had one on yesterday is because of the group picture and you wanted everyone wearing the clinic shirt."

"It was also from a bit of a distance, she couldn't have seen the clinic information." Evan pointed out. "She knows you…personally. Not just from hanging around with Granger or our family."

We watched the video again.

"Not one good look of her face," Sammie sighed. "That damn hat."

"Which is why she was wearing it," Granger nodded. "And she has worn gloves the whole time."

"But she had stopped. She must have been thinking she had gotten away with it and felt comfortable enough to stop in Redmond instead of racing out of town." I stepped back and shook my head. "I don't know anyone that would do such a thing. I BARELY know anyone in this area besides you guys and not one woman I know would kidnap babies."

"I still wonder why, if she needed something for the babies, why she didn't go to Walmart down the road," Granger shook his head. "It's only another 5 or 10 minutes."

"There were no car seats in her SUV," I pointed out. "If the twins woke and were crawling around the back, maybe she stopped at the first store that would have supplies."

"Well," Evan sighed. "I'm glad we got the videos from the police because they never would have figured that out. We have one more clue."

"Which is so confusing," I shook my head.

"I'll let you guys get down the road," Evan stated. "You drive safe."

"Will do," Granger nodded and ended the call.

We were quiet as we prepared for the drive to Montana. My mind would not stop replaying the video and trying to think of any woman I would know that would be so cold-hearted as to kidnap twin babies.

When I pulled into the rodeo grounds, my mind and body were exhausted. Sammie and Granger took charge of the horses as I escaped into the trailer and slept.

I woke to the aroma of bacon. My eyes barely opened to see Sammie standing at the small kitchen counter slicing tomatoes. She glanced back at me and smiled.

"I was wondering how long it would take for you to wake to bacon."

"Not long; that's how Mom used to wake us up when we were younger." I closed my eyes and the store video played in my mind.

"Just so you know…"

I opened an eye and looked at her.

"Detective Monroe was not pleased you aren't answering your phone. She wanted to discuss the video and who you think it might be."

"I have no fucking clue." I rolled off the bed. The bedding was stuffed in the cupboard and the kitchen table replaced when Granger stepped into the trailer.

"They want your permission to get on your social media sites to look at who has been following you." Sammie slid a plate full of sandwiches on the table and a bowl of grapes.

"I don't post on anything besides our "iron vs iron" site." Half the sandwich disappeared with the first bite.

"We told them that and gave them full permission and the password to look at that page." Sammie retrieved a bottle of water and set it on the table.

"They also want you to walk them through the video that Camille created," Granger shrugged. "Evan already told them everything and told them to leave you alone until after you run today."

"I don't want to talk to them. We'll deal with it later." I sighed and reached for a second sandwich.

Granger sat on the steps that led to Sammie's bed. He looked at both of us as if trying to decide something.

"What?" I asked him.

Sammie turned and looked at him.

"I've been wanting to tell you something, get your opinion on something," he sighed and pulled out his phone. After a moment of tapping on it, he handed it to Sammie. She walked the phone to me as she read the screen.

I read the message and looked up at him in surprise, "When?"

"After the first night of the clinic," he sighed. "I was going to talk to you after you got back...after the clinic, but we all know how that went."

"Your first thought?" Sammie whispered.

"Shock," Granger shrugged. "I haven't heard from him since the day he left."

I read the message again then looked at Sammie. Her face was flushed. "Your first thought?"

She took a deep breath and looked at Granger, "As you have both pointed out, I have the perfect father so I just...I..."

"Just say it," Granger sighed.

She answered him by walking to the memory wall and pointing to the picture of him and his mother on the cover of the magazine. "That is happy. You have both been through a lot because of his leaving, but you're both happy now."

Granger smiled slightly and nodded, then looked at me.

"You obviously don't have an elation of joy that he contacted you," I leaned back on the bench. "My opinion is, it was his choice to leave. It's not his choice to come back."

"If it doesn't make you AND Shayla happy to have him back in your life, then wait until it does...if it does," Sammie added.

Granger exhaled as if releasing weight off his back. "You're both right."

Friday night in Ellensburg, we walked away from the rodeo before the bull riding was over. Sammie and Granger were in second, while my slack run earlier in the day then the performance run placed me third in the average. Two more performances would be completed before we would know if we would be coming back for the championship round on Monday afternoon.

When we arrived at the trailer, Detective Monroe and an older man were waiting for us. There was no doubt he was a detective, too.

CHAPTER FORTY-TWO

ACE

"Persistent, aren't they?" Granger mumbled and held out a hand. "Give me Quincy and I'll take care of him while you tell them, again, that you don't know who the lady is." I dropped the reins into his hand.

"Ace," Detective Monroe smiled.

"Ma'am," I nodded and glanced at the male officer.

"This is Detective Fortune; he is local and requested to accompany me to meet with you," she said

The man held out his hand, "I was on the rodeo trail in my twenties; team roping. I suggested she come meet with you after you rode."

"I appreciate it." After shaking his hand, I turned back to her. "Evan said he told you everything I said about the video."

"Yes, he did, but we've hit a dead-end," she nodded. "The car was a complete loss and the only thing we were able to get from the black bag you pulled from it were blonde synthetic hairs. Which means the kidnapper was wearing a wig. I would like you to walk me through the day from the time you left the Rawlins ranch that morning."

Detective Fortune glanced at her with narrowed eyes then back to me.

"Why?" I huffed in surprise. "Why in the hell would I need to go back that far?"

"We need to...," Her back stiffened.

"I had NOTHING to do with the kidnapping," My voice was deep and loud enough Granger and Sammie left the horse's sides and walked in next to me.

"I'm not saying you did," Monroe held out a hand in an effort to calm me down. "If it wasn't for you, they might have been lost. But, as you pointed out, the kidnapper knew who you were when you walked into the store."

"I'm from Texas," I growled. "I don't know more than a handful of people around here. I've spent the last few days trying to think of anyone that I know who would do such a thing." I glared at her in frustration and felt Sammie wrap her hand around my arm which helped bring the rising anger under control. "I do not know how she knows me. I do not know who she is."

"Please calm down, Ace," Monroe urged. "It is clear you are just as frustrated and confused as we all are at the attempted kidnapping."

Detective Fortune's shoulders rose, and he glanced between me and Monroe. "From everything I have read on this case, this was not an *attempted* kidnapping. This WAS a kidnapping and you three rescued those twins. You are not being accused of having anything to do with it. We have to do everything by the letter of the law, so we make sure when we get the kidnapper, they don't get released due to a technicality. We need to hear directly from you instead of second hand through Mr. Rawlins."

I took a deep breath and repeated everything that happened from the moment I entered the store and compared it to what the kidnapper had done in the video. When I was done, I looked at Monroe then to Fortune. "Is that enough? Can we leave now?"

Monroe nodded and glanced to Fortune.

"Where's your next stop?" Fortune asked with a slight smile. "I do miss life on the rodeo trail."

The tension in my body eased enough Sammie's hand dropped from my arm.

"Walla Walla perf then up to Dillon. Hopefully, we'll be back here on Monday for the championship round then on to Lewiston, Spokane, Puyallup, Colfax, and Cashmere," I smiled as the light of memories rose in his eyes.

"Then Pendleton," he nodded.

"After getting to hang there for a day or two we're down to Utah, Othello, and fingers crossed back to Pendleton for the Championship Round." Sammie said with a grin.

"Then we go to Texas to finish out the year," Granger added.

"Damn, I miss that," Fortune shook his head with a deep exhale. "I'll have to bring the grandkids out to watch you ride on Monday."

"Bring them by to say 'hi'," Sammie nodded then walked back to the horses with Granger following.

"If you think of anything, please let me know," Detective Monroe said and held out a hand to shake.

"I will," I shook it firmly then reached for Fortune's hand.

He shook my hand and after Monroe turned away, he slid a card from his pocket and held it out. Without a word, I slid it into my pocket.

I missed the calf in Walla Walla and in Dillon. As hard as Granger and Sammie tried to get my mind off the video my mind wouldn't stop. What if I had done something to someone that caused them to kidnap those babies? What could I have possibly done? The pressure of everyone looking at me for answers was tearing away at me.

"You got to get your shit together," Granger huffed as we drove away from the Dillon rodeo. "I called and talked to Martin, and we agreed it might help if you go play with the twins before we go to Ellensburg."

"Really?" Sammie asked from the back seat as she pulled her guitar from the case.

"We'll get there by ten tonight so he said he'll put them down for a late nap so we can visit a bit then sleep there before going to Ellensburg. It's only four hours and on the highway." Granger said and typed in the ranch address into the GPS on the screen.

To keep our minds busy, we sang our way to the ranch, and I was surprised to see we were not the only visitors. Logan and Delaney's trailers were in the parking area with a light from Logan's door revealing a small table sitting between the trailers. Lacie Jae was alone at the table watching us approach. With just the light from their trailer, I could see her smile was hesitant, and her normal pale complexion was a deep pink.

"You guys go ahead," I told Granger and Sammie. "I'll be there in a few minutes."

They nodded, waved to her, then jogged to the building where everyone was gathered.

I sat down next to Lacie Jae.

"Do you have the puppies?" She whispered.

I sighed and shook my head, "Wish we did. They really help relax your brain. But Sammie was worried about the heat this week and left them with her parents." I hesitated; her eyes stared out into the dark night. She looked a bit lost, so I leaned toward her. "You, OK?"

"No," she whispered. "I'm sitting out here preparing to record a podcast for *Coffee With Cowboys* and I just can't focus enough to say what I want to say." After a deep breath, she finally looked at me. Her blue eyes glistened with tears. "Would you help me?"

"Of course, how?"

"Normally, I can just start talking by myself and everything falls into place. This time, maybe, if I had someone to talk to, I could focus and get the words out."

"Alright, I'll sit here quietly, and you talk to me."

"Okay," she nodded and stood. "I'll get the equipment and send a text to Logan to keep everyone inside until we're done."

Five minutes later, we faced each other across the small table, and she pressed the record button. I sat quietly and watched her eyes go from soft, hard, angry, confused, determined, and resolvent. Her complexion turned white, then red, and multiple shades of pink. Her voice started low, rose, growled, softened, and ended with a huff. She was flushed with hand over her heart and fingers trembling when she pushed the end button.

We sat quietly for a moment before she smiled hesitantly, "Maybe, I got carried away," she whispered. "Maybe I should edit…"

"DO NOT CHANGE A WORD," I demanded. "You said everything that everyone is thinking and are too afraid to say because it makes it 'real'. Just listening to you makes me feel better. I've been so frustrated and angry and listening to you…well, I am more relaxed now than I have been since before Granger called last week to tell me the twins were kidnapped." I shook my head and exhaled. "You said what we all needed to hear. Do NOT change a word."

CHAPTER FORTY-THREE

Welcome to Coffee with Cowboys with me, Lacie Jae.

Hello everyone. You know why I'm here and what I am going to talk about so there will be no happy cheerful greeting of who I am. If you're here, you already know, and the normal cheerfulness would feel insincere.

This is an open declaration to the person responsible for the deplorable act last week. The rest of you, please listen carefully.

The best things that ever happened to me in my twenty-two years, are my friendship with my sister, becoming part of the Rawlins' family, and coming to know and love them all as well as Craig and Martin Houston. I had thought the worst thing that had ever happened to me, outside of the loss of my mother, was the physical abuse from an alcoholic father. But it wasn't. The worst thing that has ever happened was the loss of a wonderful, life-loving, beloved friend and son last year in a car accident. Craig's loss was devastating to everyone who knew him, who knew OF him, and to the family that loved him; including myself...I adored the man.

365 days ago, I was in Lewiston and recorded the first podcast since Craig had died and declared to continue on since life wasn't always about the good in life, it was also about the bad. That is why I am recording now about the unbelievable, the unfathomable, the...*dark, evil* side of life. No matter how we try to keep it out of our lives, some people do not give us a choice. That is what happened these last few weeks.

We know that the most wonderful day in my life, my wedding, was the day you put your plan into action. You used that day, which was enjoyed by hundreds of people, to infiltrate our happiness and place cameras around the ranch to watch over us. By doing this, you destroyed that beautiful day for everyone involved. It is no longer just the day that Logan and Lacie Jae were wed and officially started their life together. It is now the day you began your evil plan to kidnap Caleb and Ellie, the twin babies. The babies...the miracles that came into our lives months after their father had died in that accident. He didn't even know they existed, yet when they came into his father's life, they gave Martin hope, love, and his happiness back. He had part of his son...two healthy, happy little cherubs that brought joy into our lives.

Using that day, using the people...our friends and family...to hide yourself in their midst to camouflage your placing of the cameras...you used everyone there that day and it will NOT be forgotten.

I have had a very hard time this last week controlling my emotions. Logan has tried to help. Camille has tried to help...everyone in the family has tried to help. The problem is, they are all having the same lack of emotional control as I am. They are just as angry as I am.

None of us can comprehend the evil that must be in your heart and soul to set up your plan...to use the day you did...to take away...

Last Monday was a day to celebrate and honor the life of a young cowboy lost too soon. To honor Caleb and Ellie's father WHO THEY WILL NEVER HAVE THE PRIVILEDGE OF KNOWING. They will love him through our stories and videos, but they will never be held close by him, feel his unwavering love...truly know what a wonderful force of life he was. YOU WERE TAKING THEM AWAY FROM THEIR FAMILY WHO COULD GIVE THEM SOME IDEA OF WHO THEIR FATHER...THEIR DADDY WAS.

You used the day that was planned to honor him as a day to take away his children...these little miracles. I CANNOT comprehend that much evil in a person. I have tried so hard this week to contain the anger, the wrath, the fire that burns in my gut for how much I despise...hate you. I have never hated anyone in my life...not even my alcoholic father who would nearly knock me out with a punch or nearly break my neck by throwing me into a wall. With the help of friends, my new family, and the words of God, I have forgiven him. I WILL NEVER FORGIVE YOU.

And, I promise you now. You will be found, and you will pay for what you did. You have unleashed a power that will hunt you down. I'm not talking about just me, Martin, the Rawlins, Sammie, Granger, and Ace, the trio that, by the Grace of God and no doubt a helping hand from Craig above, were able to find you and those babies so quickly. We found you once, we will find you again and you will not get away this time.

Every person you used to hide behind at the wedding, every person that was at the clinic and had to endure the disbelief and horror when you took those sleeping babies from their cribs, and had to see their beloved grandfather realize his dead son's babies were taken from him. Every person that knew Craig, or heard of him, and every person that read of his loss and cried a tear...every one of them is looking for you. This...Cowboy Nation you have unleashed is coast to coast...millions of people will be looking for you. Somewhere, somehow, you said something to someone and that is going to lead this Cowboy Nation to you.

I will tell the listeners one thing that will help narrow down the search for you. We know a woman drove them from the house, carried them into the store, and ran for her life when Ace and Sammie arrived. We know more...but I will leave that up to the authorities to share when it is time.

Be warned, that this Cowboy Nation is diverse, and we cannot promise you anything when you are found. Your best recourse is to find a police station and turn yourself in...they will protect you. Take that as a warning or veiled threat...you decide.

Until then, we will continue to love and cherish those babies, and we will be watching, listening, and waiting for you to be found.

CHAPTER FORTY-FOUR

SAMMIE

We listened to the podcast twice on the way to Ellensburg. Ace stared out the side window at the passing scenery. Granger was quiet in the back seat; awake and listening but curled into a pillow.

Both Rawlins' trailers were ahead of us since Logan made the finals in steer wrestling and Delaney in breakaway. Normally, I loved driving in convoys but watching Logan's trailer, knowing Lacie Jae was with him, and listening to her words from the podcast brought a hollow feeling in my gut.

"She talked directly to you when she recorded it?" Granger asked.

"Yeah," Ace nodded. "Eye to eye, but I never felt like she was actually talking to me...almost like she was talking FOR me."

"I feel that," Granger said. "She said everything I've been feeling."

Ace exhaled, "The last few days, since we realized the kidnapper knew me, and everyone had run into a dead end trying to find her? I felt like the entire burden of finding her was on me. Like it was my fault it happened."

My eyes widened, "Ace, no one thought that."

"Maybe not you guys, but I just had this..." he sighed.

"Detective Monroe did that," Granger growled from the backseat. "Her questioning you the other day. I felt that she was focusing on you too much."

"And now? After Lacie Jae's podcast?" I asked.

"I realized I'm not the only one responsible for knowing who the woman is. I don't know why or how she recognized me from across the store, but I know there are thousands of people that are going to be looking for her. It's not just up to me."

"That's good," I nodded with relief.

"But I feel like we're missing something," Ace grumbled. "Every lead they had didn't work out...that they are telling us anyway. I know we can't do anything until something else comes up, but I just have this gut feeling that we're missing something."

"I agree," Granger said. "I just wish Martin would take them home."

"Maybe he will now that Lacie Jae has unleashed Cowboy Nation on the kidnapper, and she'll go into hiding. I can't imagine she would try again." I grinned. "Either way, there is nothing we can do until someone comes up with something."

"We focus on rodeo until that happens," Granger added.

"Get money in the bank," Ace nodded. "There aren't very many big paying rodeos...I need to focus on them to get to Vegas with you two."

"And you start with the win today," I smirked at him. "Get that buckle."

"After Lacie Jae posting that this morning," Ace sighed. "It's going to be the talk of the whole damn day."

Three hours later, Granger and I were standing on the back of the bucking chutes watching Ace enter the arena. I was so glad that at this rodeo tie-down was run before saddle bronc and barrel racing so my stomach could ease before I rode. I wasn't sure if Ace had looked at the standings, but the announcer let us know that his two previous runs here and the runs in Montana and Walla Walla had jumped him to 24th place. Only a few thousand dollars kept him from breaking under 20th. And that depended on how much the other tie-down ropers were earning at the same time.

Quincy burst out of the box with Ace already swinging...one, two, and the throw. The crowd roared as he stepped from the horse's side and catapulted toward the red calf. Seconds...8.3 and he was trotting back to the horse and stepping back up into the saddle. The six second waiting time seemed more like twenty.

The announcer reported Ace was leading the average for the win with two more riders to take their turn.

"Please, please, please," I whispered to myself, and fingers reached out to grip Granger's sleeve. "It's been a rough few weeks, please give him this...please, please, please." My silent chant continued as we waited through the last two ropers.

"Ladies and gentlemen, with that final run, the tie-down champion of the rodeo with 25 seconds on three calves is Ace Conners." The announcer yelled and the crowd roared.

"YES!" I screamed to the heavens then hugged Granger's arm. "Good luck!" I dodged around the bronc riders to make my way off the platform then ran around to find Ace.

His interview was completed by the time I arrived at the gate, and he took off on a horse for his victory ride. When he ran back out of the arena his grin was wide as he looked at me.

"Glad to have that over," he said to me as he passed by and received his buckle, spurs, cooler, and more then we hurried to watch Delaney take third in breakaway and get positioned to watch Granger slide onto the large bay, Tokyo Bubbles. I gripped Ace's sleeve as the gate swung open. The powerful kicks from the horse had me holding my breath the whole eight seconds and it exhaled in relief when he slid from the pickup man to the grounds.

"Go get ready," Ace said to me and pushed me away.

Stepping into Sergeant 's saddle, it dawned on me that, even though a few people had mentioned the kidnapping and podcast, the announcer had not. When I rode out of the arena, second in the rodeo, that changed.

"Ladies and Gentleman," the announcer began. "You would have had to be living under a rock if you have not read or seen on television the story of the Houston twin babies being kidnapped out of the Rawlins ranch home during a clinic to honor their father. I spoke briefly with Logan and Delaney Rawlins about the incident last night and they asked me to not mention it until after the three heroes that rescued the babies had taken their turns in the arena. Granger Miller, Ace Conners, and the young lady you just watched take second in the barrel racing, Sammie Parkston, were those three heroes. I'll say this, listen to the *Coffee With Cowboys* podcast by Lacie Jae Rawlins. She posted it this morning. It will tell you what to do. I agree with her. This Cowboy Nation will find that kidnapper and bring them to justice. For now, we thank Granger, Ace, and Sammie for their heroic efforts in bringing those 9-month-old babies back home to their grandfather." The crowd stood in ovation and began yelling.

I rode in next to Granger and Ace then stepped out of the saddle. It took an hour of shaking hands before we made it back to the trailer. Both the Rawlins' trailers were gone but Detective Fortune was there with his three grandchildren.

We let the young kids pet and sit on the horses while we talked about everything but the kidnapping. With the complaints of the kids, he finally motioned to tell them they were leaving.

"Where are you going next?" He asked.

"Sammie and I are in slack at Lewiston in the morning then we actually have Wednesday off then we're headed to Colfax, Spokane, Puyallup, and Granger has Friday night back in Lewiston," Ace answered.

"That's just me and Ace," I corrected. "Tomorrow, Granger and Brodie will be taking off for the week together. They don't have horses so they can get to more rodeos if they go by themselves."

"Good," the detective nodded. "You need a day." He escorted the kids into his car. When he shut the door, he turned back to us. "Find something to do out of your normal activities."

"We're going up the Snake River in a jet boat after slack in Lewiston," Granger grinned. "I've never done anything like that."

"Good," Fortune nodded. "Get relaxed, have a beer or ten, whatever suits you." He walked to the driver's side of his car but hesitated to open the door. "Once your mind is clear...or too relaxed or fuzzy to focus too hard, talk about what happened, you'll be surprised what little details you'll remember."

"I'll have to use that as an excuse next time," Granger chuckled.

The detective smirked, "But, don't look at it from what you went through. Look at it from the kidnapper's perspective; how they accomplished what they did."

"She," I grumbled with a nod.

"Don't take for granted it was only one person," Fortune opened the door and looked at Ace. "You have my card. Call me if you have questions or come up with something."

"Will do," Ace nodded.

"That was awesome," Granger grinned when we stepped out of the truck. We spent hours in the boat racing up the river and taking in the scenery and wildlife.

"We'll have to make that an annual trip when we come to Lewiston," I agreed.

"I'm good with that," Ace agreed and looked across the rodeo grounds to the hospitality shack. "They are still there. Let's continue with our 'out of the normal' and play cards over there."

"I'll get the cards," Granger said.

"I'll get the Pendleton," I chuckled.

We ate as if we hadn't been eating all day. The woman running the hospitality shack cleared the empty plates from our picnic table.

"Thank you, ma'am," Ace nodded.

"I'm Tracy; just holler at me if you need anything and thanks for coming to our rodeo," she smiled and walked away.

Granger set the bottle of Pendleton on the table as I placed the three shot glasses out. Ace poured the first round.

"Here is to Sammie's leading run this morning," Granger toasted with raised glass; the first round went down smoothly.

"Last year was a disaster," I chuckled as the second round was poured. "That was redemption."

"Then here is to redemption," Ace grinned and the second round was tossed back, and the third round was poured.

"Here is to Ace and Quincy's second place run," I lifted the glass to Ace then it was quickly tossed back. I took a deep breath as the warmth flooded through me and Ace poured another round. "Time to break out the cards."

"Light weight," Granger pulled out the deck of cards and shuffled them. Ace separated them in three piles, and I pushed a pile to each of them and slid one to myself.

"Low card takes a shot, high card earns a bill," I nodded and pulled the stack of ten $5 bills out of my pocket.

The first cards were flipped over; Granger took the shot, and they both threw a $5 bill at me. The second card was flipped, and Granger took another shot, and the bills were thrown at me again.

"Whoop, whoop!" I chuckled.

"You probably need that pain killer for that sunburn," Ace teased Granger.

Granger laughed, "That ride was worth the burn. Looking up those rock walls that shot up from the water...damn, I couldn't even imagine what the pioneers thought when they came to those canyons."

"Oh, hell," Ace laughed. "Could be how it got its name; Hell's Canyon."

"We need to float it next year." I flipped the next card over. "Those rafters looked like they were having fun."

"I agree," Ace poured the next round then flipped his card.

My card was a jack, Ace had flipped a queen, and we both grinned at Granger.

"Son of a bitch," Granger huffed then flipped his card and smacked it against the table. It was a king. "Ha!"

I laughed then shot the whiskey back before thinking about it. The warmth ran down my whole body and made my toes tingle. I tossed a $5 bill at him then quickly flipped the next card. It was a five.

"Oh, hell," My hands cupped my warmed cheeks.

"Excuse me."

We turned to the lady that had cleared our plates. She was holding a large platter of brightly decorated cookies.

"Evening, ma'am," Ace nodded.

"We have the most delicious cookies," she smiled at us. "Would you be interested?"

"Yes."

Three hands reached out for the cookies.

"Thank you so much," I barely got out before the first cookie was shoved into my mouth.

"My pleasure," she chuckled and walked away with a half empty tray.

Granger shoved a cookie in his mouth and flipped his card; a four. Relief rushed through me to the point I started giggling. I shoved another cookie in my mouth as Ace flipped his card then wiped away the mass of cookie crumbles on his lips and chin. It was a two and he managed to get the whiskey around the cookies.

My stomach gurgled. "I'm out."

"Can you make it to the trailer, or do you need me to carry you?" Ace teased with a wide grin.

"I don't know," I giggled and slowly stood. It took a few attempts to get my foot out from the picnic table. I swayed into the table as they cleared the cards and glasses.

"Your head fuzzy?" I asked as we slowly walked away from the hospitality tent and to my trailer.

"Yeah," they both answered and walked on each side of me.

"So, why, as a kidnapper, would I go after the twins of a dead man?" I asked and tipped into Ace then Granger.

"The grandfather is not rich, so it had to be to either sell or raise them myself," Granger mused.

"But, why them?" I asked. "With their history, all hell would break lose...like it did."

"The media coverage would be too great to sell the babies," Ace huffed. "So, it had to be to raise the twins themselves."

"But, again, why the twins?" I asked. "There is family around them all the time."

Granger nodded and turned toward the stalls where our horses were standing peacefully eating their hay. We stopped and stared at them. "She put a lot of effort and planning in the way she did it, and, I hate to say it, but there would be easier ways to kidnap a baby."

"That sounds so...evil," I could feel the anger rise in me again.

"Yeah, it does," Granger nodded. "But you have to be evil to even think of doing something like kidnap babies."

"Any babies," Ace nodded. "And this woman...evil woman...Evilina...."

"Good name for her," I huffed.

"But the question remains, why would Evilina choose to kidnap two babies that are surrounded by family instead of going after one?" Granger asked.

"It's personal," Ace concluded. "They knew Craig and wanted his babies?"

"The wedding and clinic were known months in advance," I sighed and turned away from the horses and toward the trailer.

"The wedding first to set their plan in motion," Granger said.

"That's blending into a crowd," I nodded. "But, coming during the clinic where there are forty rough stock cowboys? What kind of guts does that take?"

"Or stupidity," Granger said and opened the door of the trailer.

"With the wedding," Ace stepped into the trailer. "There were people spread out everywhere. With the clinic, everyone was at the arena. They were smart enough to know that."

I followed him in, and Granger stepped in behind us and shut the door. "If I hadn't left my phone in the kitchen, I wouldn't have seen Evilina leave, and her plan would have been perfect."

By the time I stepped into the restroom and changed into my shorts and t-shirt, both men had converted their beds and were lying on them staring at the ceiling.

"Evilina wants Craig's twins, knows her only opportunity is the wedding and clinic...."

"Wears the big hat to cover her face..." I curled onto my bed and sighed.

"Did Lacie Jae get any pictures back from people at the wedding?" Ace asked.

"A couple, but it was the same as all the others," Granger answered.

"How does Evilina know Craig and why does she want his twins?" I mused and could feel the whiskey begin to silence my mind.

"Other than the Rawlins and Granger, I had no connection to Craig. Absolutely none when he was alive so how in the hell does Evilina know me?"

"And going to the wedding alone...?" I whispered.

There were no answers to the questions as my mind went black.

I woke to the trailer rocking and glanced at my phone. It was eight o'clock in the morning which meant Brodie had picked up Granger and left. Pulling back the curtain, I could see Ace was driving the trailer to the horse stalls. All three horses had heads raised high and were watching us approach.

I scurried off the bed and slid on my boots so once he stopped, I could help load the horse. Ace glanced at me as we approached the trailer tack room.

"Nice hair," He chuckled and pulled out the halters.

My hands shot up to my hair that had been in a high ponytail for the boat ride. Most of the hair was out of the hair tie. I giggled and captured the hair again.

"Taylor texted this morning and wants to come up for Pendleton." Ace said as we stepped into the truck.

"That's awesome," I grinned and pulled out my phone to check for messages.

"Last year, we promised each other that we'd be in Pendleton this year and he figured that even if he wasn't roping, he should be here to tell me how to rope."

I laughed and my stomach rumbled. "Let's find a place we can pull this rig into and get a doughnut or two to soak up that whisky from last night."

"And coffee," Ace nodded as he pulled out of the Lewiston Roundup Grounds. "It's a 9-hour drive to Blackfoot."

"Let me know when you're ready for a break," I kicked off my shoes and sat crisscross in the passenger seat of my own truck and pulled out my phone.

"You've already calculated, so how do I stand?"

I scrolled to the standing on the PRCA website, "You're currently sitting second in Lewiston. Your 7.8 run equals the second place run by Riley Webb last year. If that holds, it's around $4k. With the win in Ellensburg, you'll be in the teens."

"Thank goodness," Ace sighed. "Who is in 15th now?"

"Who are you chasing? Well...Brett Landon, Tom Brock, and Wayne Danner are 14, 15, 16th, and within $4200 of each other."

"Wins are best, but placing and adding to the standings is what's important."

"Focus" I grinned at him.

"110%."

CHAPTER FORTY-FIVE

SAMMIE

Text from Granger to Sammie: We're a half hour from Puyallup.

Text from Sammie to Granger: I just parked. It's been a hell of a week!

Text from Granger to Sammie: They updated online, he is sitting 17th!

Text from Sammie to Granger: With a good run in Puyallup, he should get there!

Text from Granger to Sammie: You two sick of each other yet?

Text from Sammie to Granger: LOL, sometimes. We'll look forward to our third-wheel coming in.

Text from Granger to Sammie: So, I'm a third-wheel now?

Text from Sammie to Granger: Seriously? At some point or another, we're all a third-wheel to the other two.

Text from Granger to Sammie: That would be true

"Well, that was unexpected," I huffed as I started the engine on the truck and pulled away from the Puyallup rodeo grounds.

"You would have thought one of us would have made it into the finals," Ace sighed.

"Look at it this way," Granger smirked. "We'll get to Pendleton sooner and have better parking."

"And actually, be able to stay in the same place for a whole three days," I chuckled.

Ace turned to Granger, "Any word at all on Evilina?"

"No," Granger shook his head.

We spent the drive from Puyallup to Pendleton talking over every theory we had.

Monday morning in Pendleton, I stood just outside of the stalls of Sergeant and Grace. I had changed my mind a hundred times about which horse to run on this long pattern. Sergeant and I had run it before, and he was good with the turns. I knew we could improve on the year before, but Grace would be faster on the home stretch.

I heard someone approach from behind but didn't turn.

"Going to flip a coin?" Granger asked.

I chuckled, "I've considered it, but I think Sergeant can run in Utah and Othello, and I'll give this one to Grace." I turned to him and squealed in delight.

Little Caleb was strapped to his chest, and Ellie was next to them on Brodie's chest. Both babies were grinning and looking at the horses.

"Osy," Caleb kicked his feet and hands reached for Grace.

"Martin decided that no place could be safer than here in the middle of Cowboy Nation," Brodie grinned. "Logan and I roped this morning, so I get my turn with them."

"I couldn't even imagine Evilina would try anything here surrounded by all these cowboys," I agreed.

"Evilina..." Brodie smirked. "I forgot you were calling her that. But it is fitting."

"Have they heard anything?" I asked.

"No, every lead has died down and they are at a complete standstill," Brodie shook his head.

"Probably in hiding," Granger nodded.

"I am so excited to see them," I kissed each baby on the cheek.

"He's taking them home from here," Brodie grinned. "We'll get a bit of life back to normal."

I stepped into the stall and haltered Grace, "I'm so relieved."

Even though I normally didn't see the babies very often, just to know they were going back home to their normal lives filled me with energy. Grace felt it and we pranced our way into the arena. My mind wandered to the wedding; to Evilina. She had to have arrived by herself. Anyone that knew Logan and Lacie Jae knew that the only person in attendance in Lacie Jae's family was Camille. Which meant the two hundred plus guests were the Rawlins family and friends. Since none of them had identified the woman in the big hat, it was clear she had come alone. That seemed risky. But, how else could she have gotten to the wedding?

Then...I knew...I figured it out... My mind came out of the musing and shot around to the stands where I knew the men were waiting to watch Grace and I run.

"Next up is Lisa Lockhart followed by Sammie Parkston," the announcer said.

I looked over at Lisa as she took off to the first barrel then to the stands where I could see Ace, Granger, and Brodie. The babies were no longer strapped to them. All three waved.

My heart pounded as the answer rose in my heart and I wanted to go to them, but I needed to focus on the prancing Grace and the race. I turned back to the line and focused on the first barrel while bringing the black mare to a stop. She shuffled left then right...she was ready to go but Lisa was just turning the 3rd barrel. Deep breaths...focus on the first barrel. My fingers were gripping the reins too tightly, so I relaxed and took deeper breaths.

"That's a 29.15 for Lisa. Next, we have Sammi Parkston..."

I took a deep breath with heart and pulse racing. Clearing my mind, I nudged Grace to walk closer to the first barrel, as we neared the timer I gripped the reins, leaned forward and she was off. Hooves pounding, black mane flying, huffs of energy from both of us, we turned the barrel so close it bumped my leg. Too close, adjust, switch hands, change leads...we flew to the second. I prayed she could see the barrel in front of the brightly colored bucking chutes. Her head turned as the barrel became clear. We turned without hesitation between the barrel and chutes, and she dug in to fly to the third. My fingers gripped the saddle horn tighter as we neared the third barrel. My mind was focused...heart calm...and fingers relaxing on the reins as we turned the last barrel.

I leaned forward, hands tapping on both sides of her neck to let her know it was time to go fast. "Go Grace Go!" We flew...faster than she had ever run before. Riding a horse that was running with all her might down a long field would never get old…I loved it and reveled in the feeling of the wind hitting my face. My eyes went to the timer, and we were well past it by the time I leaned back to pull her into a trot.

The announcer's voice rang out as I turned to look at the clock and leaned down to stroke Grace's neck.

"After 38 riders, that run took the lead at 28.57. Great run, Sammie."

Deep breaths to contain the elation for the time and exhilaration from the heart pounding run. That was always so much fun…I loved it and loved the "Hell, yeah!" "Way to go Grace!", cheers from the sidelines.

I grinned over toward the three men that had been joined by Camille, Lacie Jae, and Delaney who was riding in the Wednesday performance. They all had hands clapping above their heads which made me laugh as we trotted in circles to cool down. This was the fun I had tried to keep into Ace the last week.

We had to remain in the arena until the next rake, but when we finally walked out of the tunnel, we were greeted by just the three men.

"Nice ride!" Brodie grinned.

"How did that feel?" Ace asked as his hand slid down the horse's neck.

"Outstanding," I huffed and stepped down. "But I have an idea."

"About what?" Granger chuckled.

Horses and people were walking by us, so I guided them all to the side.

"I got to thinking about Evilina," I huffed with hand over stomach to quell the nerves.

"Seriously? Evilina? After that run?" Granger shook his head.

"Before, but I didn't have time to go talk to you," I nodded and waved to a rider that yelled congratulations to me. "I was thinking, since she couldn't have been pretending to be there for Lacie Jae, she would have to be there for Logan."

"Yeah," they nodded.

"Ok, follow my train of thought here," I huffed. "If I was Evilina, and no one would know me as a friend of the Rawlins family and I couldn't say I was there for Lacie Jae, I could pretend I was a 'plus one' with one of the friends."

"Makes sense," Brodie shrugged. "But..."

"I know, I know..." I held up my hand. "Again, if I were Evilina, I would have tried to find someone going and try to get them to take me, so it didn't look suspicious. AND, if I went with someone that was busy part of the time, then I could have openly wandered around and into the barn by myself without anyone questioning it."

"But, who...?" Granger frowned.

"One of us," Ace looked at him. "During the time she went in the barn, we were busy singing, so no one noticed her."

"I'm not dating anyone," Granger huffed.

"Me, either," Ace added and looked back at me.

"But, if I was going to try for one of you," I began with a smile. "I would have studied both of you to the point I knew where you would be AND what you looked like."

"That's why she recognized me across the store and in a ball cap and t-shirt," Ace nodded.

Brodie turned and looked at him, "She could have followed you...stalked you for a while to find out how to 'meet' you."

"That's fucking creepy," Ace grimaced.

"But it makes sense, doesn't it?" I looked at each of them.

"It does to me," Brodie nodded.

"But I wasn't going to the wedding…" Ace started then hesitated. "Until the night of the sing-along and Lacie Jae invited us."

"That was posted on Facebook and Instagram," Granger nodded. "And the twins were there, too."

"Yeah, we were dancing with them in a couple of the posted videos," Ace agreed.

"So, she could have been following you two since that night," I grinned. "That will narrow down the timeline on the websites for trying to track her."

"Either of you connect with anyone that talked about the wedding?" Brodie asked.

"Not me," Granger shook his head. "None that talked about the wedding or future at all."

"Same" Ace nodded. "We've been traveling and not really staying in one town very long."

"There were other single guys at the wedding," Brodie pointed out.

"But how would Evilina know who was going?" I countered.

"Most of the people that are single, and she could have approached are here in Pendleton this week," Brodie nodded. "We can look at the guest list and spend the next couple days asking them."

"Good idea," I sighed.

"No, that was a good idea of yours," Granger huffed. "Damn puzzle wizard."

"I'm going to call Detective Fortune," Ace pulled out his phone.

"Now," Brodie said to me. "You go take care of your horse, take time to take in that ride, and take a breath. We'll go talk to Logan and Lacie Jae and make a list of people to talk to."

Tuesday morning, I rode Sergeant into the arena with Granger on Grace, and Ace on Quincy ahead of me. We rode to the far side and stood next to the wall to the bleachers and watched the end of the steer wrestling slack. Logan was backing into the box for his first-round run. His second would be Wednesday night.

Logan's run tied him for the fourth fastest in the morning's slack. He disappeared out of the tunnel then returned riding another horse and Brodie riding in behind him.

"When does Taylor get here?" Brodie asked.

"He flew into Portland last night and riding in with a friend of ours," Ace answered as he stared at the video on his phone. "They should be here before tie-down starts."

I glanced at the video he was watching. "Is that another Brazile run?"

Ace grinned, "Last year we watched this rodeo from a hotel in Arizona. A friend of mine had ridden here before and told me to study everything Trevor does; he won several times."

"You watched the whole rodeo?" Brodie turned to him. "Every day of the rodeo?"

"No, Thursdays perf. It was 115 degrees in Arizona that day,' Ace answered without looking up.

"So, you watched Spence break his shoulder," Granger smirked.

Ace's head finally turned, "I guess I did."

"I rode right before him," Granger added.

"I saw that," Ace chuckled. "You hit the ground and jumped up like it was nothing. I thought you were fucking nuts for wanting to ride a bucking horse. Then you ran out to Spence when he went down."

"Yeah," Granger nodded.

I didn't say anything. Those moments were what led to me picking up Granger off the side of the road.

"Funny how life turns out," Ace's head went back to his phone.

We were quiet until the team roping slack began. Logan and Brodie were the 11th team to run and took the lead. When slack was over, they had dropped to fifteenth.

Ace moved forward and began warming up Quincy as the rest of the tie down ropers entered the arena. Granger and I rode down toward the chute so we were closer for Ace.

"He's too nervous," I whispered. "He knows he needs this one...he needs to get to the short-round or all chances of the NFR are lost."

As the first roper backed into the box, Ace backed in next to Granger.

"Talk to me," Granger whispered to him and nodded to the rider running next to the chute and out into the arena. "Walk me through the process."

"Instead of the calf being in the chute next to you, they are about 30 feet back," Ace started. "When you're setup and ready for the calf, you nod to the guy sitting on the stool with the headset on. He tells the people in the back to release the calf then a rider helps push the calf down the long chute. The spotter on the stool will let you know when the calf is halfway and then 'here'."

"So, how do you handle it?" Granger prodded.

"Depends on how fast the calf is," Ace pointed to the next rider backing into the box. "We still have a barrier and have to gauge the run down the chute to how fast the calf is."

"And you have to run and stop on grass," Granger nodded. "Is that difficult?"

"Depends on the horse and how he stops," Ace continued. "Quincy is good at tucking under and not sliding sideways."

I sat quietly and listened to Granger keep Ace's mind busy with the technical aspects of the runs until Ace's name was called out. He moved forward and I glanced at Granger.

"Talk me through it in your head," Granger called out.

Ace didn't turn but he did nod.

"What's a good run here?" Granger looked at me.

"From the rest of the runs this morning, he needs to be under 10 seconds."

Ace shoved his hat down tighter as he approached the box, then adjusted the string between his teeth. The final tick of his routine was to swing his rope out then back under his arm. His chest rose and lowered quickly as he turned to the man on the stool.

He nodded, my breath stopped, and hand reached out to grab Granger's shirt sleeve.

"Come on..." Granger huffed as he stared.

The calf appeared at a run and Ace was right behind him. As he neared the end of the long chute, he had to pull Quincy up to keep from hitting the barrier too soon. He leaned forward with rope swinging. One...two...three...it was flying in the air and as Ace rose in the stirrup the rope settled around the calf's neck. Quincy slid to a stop as Ace stepped off and was suddenly propelled down the line. The calf turned and jumped toward Ace who caught him in his arms and quickly had him flipped and on the ground.

"Come on...." Granger growled and my fingers tightened.

Ace's arms flew to the side, and he immediately jogged back to the roan horse who was standing patiently...perfectly, like he always did.

My eyes shot to the score board as the announcer's voice rang out; "That was a 9.1 second run, and now we have..."

My scream and Granger's shout drowned out the announcer. Just behind us, was another familiar yell and we turned to see Taylor with his arm held out pointing his phone at his brother trotting down the long field.

"Hell, yeah!" Taylor grinned at us then turned the phone to himself. "You see that?" He laughed, nodded, then lowered the phone to look at us. "Mom, and Barry wanted to watch."

"No, Lil Bros?" I smiled.

"They are in school and hating every minute of it," Taylor chuckled. "Mom promised they could go to the Texas rodeos the last week."

"I can't wait," I huffed in delight. "And I'm so glad you got here in time to go walk the vendors."

For hours we walked the vendors, had a laughter-filled lunch, then finally made it back to my trailer which was parked in the same spot I had parked the year before but had been alone. Now, I had the three men joking, drinking, and eating spaghetti for dinner Mom had sent with me. Life had changed so much in the last year. To celebrate, we took a group picture, and I immediately printed it in the trailer and pinned it to the memory wall.

We spent the evening roping the dummy next to the trailer.

"How is your shoulder?" Granger asked Taylor.

"Feeling stronger every day," Taylor grinned. "Not sure I'll be calf roping and flanking a calf anytime soon, but it sure feels good to throw hard again."

"Confident in it?" I asked.

"Yeah," Taylor threw again and wrapped the plastic horns. "The doctors were pleased at the last checkup; both were there."

Ace's phone rang and Granger's dinged with an alert as I returned to the table. Ace walked away as he spoke, and Granger began typing.

Taylor set his rope onto the table as I settled into my chair and grinned at him, "It's so fun to have you here."

He grinned, "I was coming to coach him, but after that run, I think I'll just keep my mouth shut."

"You being here will just help with tomorrow's run, and another run like today's, he will be in Saturday's championship round."

"We head to Utah as soon as he runs?"

"No, Granger is in the perf then we'll leave when he is done. A wonderful 11-and-a-half-hour drive down, then thirteen hours back up to Othello for the Friday perf, then back to Pendleton for Championship round Saturday." I rolled my eyes and exhaled in exaggeration. "THEN, we drive to Marysville, California for an afternoon perf on Sunday."

Taylor grinned, "Maybe I'll just fly back Sunday morning."

"No way; we head for Texas Monday morning for Amarillo slack on Wednesday morning."

"All Texas for the final weeks?"

"All except for a quick flight for Ace to California to run in San Bernardino where he is borrowing a horse. The last rodeo will be in Mona, Utah."

"That was Brodie," Granger interrupted and glanced at Ace who was walking back to the table. "They contacted everyone at the wedding who would have brought a date and none of them had been approached by anyone."

"About what?" Taylor asked.

I told him about my theory, and he nodded and looked at Ace and Granger, "You can't think of anyone?" They both shook their heads. "You look at your journal and go through each rodeo?"

"Nope," Ace said and rose. "But that is a good idea."

Granger shrugged but also stood, "We've been on the road so much or staying with Sammie that it has been a bit of a 'dry' summer."

We all chuckled.

"I cramp their style." I laughed.

"Funny, Mom said she did in Joseph," Granger tossed his journal on the table and flipped it open.

"What about Union?" Ace asked as he slid onto his chair.

"What's in Union?" Taylor and I asked.

"Not even a consideration," Granger shook his head without looking from the journal.

"You're sure?" Ace asked. "She knew him."

"Who?" Taylor and I asked.

"Sort of," Granger answered, again without looking up. "They were near each other one night."

"But..." Ace prodded, and Taylor and I just looked between them.

"No, buts," Granger finally looked at him. "She is not a consideration."

"Don't just say it," Ace shook his head. "Convince me."

Granger sat back in the chair and glared at him, "Two years ago and last year at the rodeo. She contacted me after his death was announced then not again until this year's rodeo."

"Did she know about the wedding or clinic?" Ace continued.

"We talked about the clinic, nothing on the wedding, and she would not have considered going to the wedding with me as a couple." Granger leaned forward and turned his attention back to the journal.

It was obvious that Granger was protective of the woman they were discussing, so I kept my mouth closed but Taylor spoke.

"Who are you talking about?" He asked.

Granger looked at Ace and sighed in irritation then turned to Taylor. "A friend I see in the spring, in Union. She has absolutely nothing to do with this."

"She married?" Taylor asked.

"What the fuck does that have to do with anything?" Granger growled. "SHE has NOTHING to do with this."

It was obviously to all three of us that he just 'closed the door' on the discussion so I looked at Ace, "What about your Hawaiian adventures this summer?"

The tension dissolved and we chuckled.

"Just a couple friends," Ace shook his head. "Nothing out of the normal or anyone knew to hand a lei to."

We chuckled again and Taylor began to rise then stopped and lowered back into the chair as his brows came together and he looked at his brother. "What about The Shirt? You ever see her again?"

CHAPTER FORTY-SIX

SAMMIE

Ace tipped his head in thought, "Huh, she was unusual."

"Was that after the sing-along night?" Taylor asked.

"Now, who and the hell are you talking about?" Granger leaned back in his chair.

Taylor picked up his phone as Ace answered. "That's what Sammie called her when she saw the picture."

"Guess what I'm wearing picture?" I asked in surprise and reached for my phone to look at the picture Taylor had sent.

"Yeah," Ace nodded as he and Granger picked up their phones. "I've been approached in many different ways, but that one was a bit over the top and she was a bit pissy when I turned her down."

"After the sing-a-long?" Granger asked.

"I'm pretty sure it was just a week or two after," Ace nodded.

All four of us scrolled to search for the picture.

The woman's back was to the camera with arms and legs wrapped around him. I chuckled again at the one surprised eye of Ace's that was looking at the camera.

"Seriously funny pic," Granger chuckled.

"Not much to recognize of her," Ace smiled. "Brown hair, nice ass...I don't really remember much about her except she had blue eyes that matched her shirt."

"Funny detail," I teased.

"Did you take any other pictures of her?" Granger asked Taylor.

"Yeah, a couple. I'll send them to you," Taylor nodded.

"Did she say anything before attaching herself to you," I chuckled.

Ace shrugged, "Yeah, a bit. Something about being lucky to run into me."

"Did she say your name?" Granger asked. "Like she knew you or was just generalizing?"

"She said my name, and not asked it," he answered and slid his phone back on the table. "There isn't anything in there to identify her."

I looked at the three pictures Taylor had just sent. The first image was nearly identical as the first but Ace's eye wasn't visible. The next had the woman's hands wrapped around the back of his neck as if she was holding him still so she could kiss him. She had leaned back slightly looking up at him; her legs already wrapped tightly around his waist. Ace was right, there wasn't anything there to identify her and nothing to indicate she was Evilina. But, why would she attack him like she did?

"Was she pretty?" I asked Ace.

"Yeah," he nodded.

"So, she has a nice body and she's pretty," I looked around the three of them. "What makes her do something like that to a guy she hasn't even met?"

"Girls just like to have fun," Ace shrugged with a smirk.

"No...." I shook my head. "It's in the middle of the damn day and it's not like she was at a bar after the rodeo."

"He's cute," Granger chuckled with a teasing glance. "Maybe she was taking the opportunity while no competition was around."

"But WHY?" I huffed. "Insecurity?"

"Could be," Taylor nodded. "I had a friend's wife that cheated on him, and she said she just mentally needed attention. It wasn't the sex; it was the attention."

"That's sucky," I grimaced.

"What's your reason?" Ace smirked.

"For what?" I huffed.

"For going after a cowboy, you haven't met before," he answered.

"Have you EVER seen me go after anyone?" I countered with a glare. "No, because I never have."

"Never have?" Granger's brow lifted.

"No," I said curtly. "I have NEVER chased a cowboy or any other guy. Mom said, and I agree, there is plenty of time for THAT. Right now, I chase my dreams instead." All three just stared at me like I was that blue-eyed alien. "I'm also not insecure, have daddy issues, want or need THAT kind of attention, or just want to have sex." I continued. "I try not to judge people, everyone can do life the way they want, but seriously, I just don't understand that." I swung my hand at the phone.

"Well, as far as I know," Granger huffed. "After the rodeo and in the bar, I've seen a lot. But I've not seen anyone do that..." he swung his hand to the phones. "...in the middle of the day."

"I haven't either," Taylor shook his head.

"With someone I just met? I've had some pretty good flirting during the day, but that wasn't flirting, that was way more," Ace nodded.

"Flirting, yeah," Granger and Taylor both nodded.

I sighed and relaxed back in the chair, "So, Pendleton and cards?"

"No," Ace huffed. "Early to bed for me. I need a clear head in the morning."

"I've been up forever," Taylor shook his head. "It would put me out."

I looked at Granger and he shook his head, "Don't need the cards. I'll just take a glass."

"Me, too," After retrieving the bottle, I set two shot glasses down for the brothers and glasses for Granger and I. "We need a toast for tomorrow. It's going to be a great day and where better to toast with Pendleton than Pendleton?"

We stood, lifted glasses over the table, clinked them together, then tossed them back. The warmth and burn made my body shiver.

"Ah," Granger growled. "I LOVE whisky."

"Who did you draw?" Taylor asked Granger Wednesday morning.

I stood between the pair at the low wall next to the arena with Ace on Quincy on the other side. He leaned forward resting on the saddle horn as we watched the beginning of the tie down slack.

"Fizzling Dud," Granger grinned. "Another Westmoreland horse, just not the one I'm waiting for."

"The whole damn year and you didn't get him," Ace chuckled.

"Next year, I'll go to every damn rodeo they go to and better my chances," Granger grinned.

"What number are you?" I leaned forward and stroked down Quincy's long nose causing him to tuck his head toward me.

"You've asked me that twice," Ace chuckled. "Would you like me to write it down for you?"

I smiled but didn't look at him. "No, smart-ass."

"Did you hear anything on the calf you drew?" Taylor asked.

"It's red," Ace smirked.

"OK," Granger turned to Ace. "I'm curious on my question because I actually want to know. What did you learn from watching Brazile's videos that helped you yesterday?"

"Patience," Ace answered. "Don't try to rush and 'make it happen' instead of letting it play out."

"And, I have to make it happen," Granger nodded. "If I get a horse that doesn't have the energy or kick I need, I have to ride more aggressive and get it out of him."

"Makes sense," Ace huffed.

"You also make it look good with your style," I added.

Granger nodded, "I've worked on that."

Ace's name was called, and Taylor quickly phoned his mother while Ace walked to the box.

"Talk me through it!" Granger called out.

My fingers curled around the fence rail, and I took a deep breath. He needed this to get into the finals on Saturday and have a true chance of making the top 15.

Ace adjusted his hat, the string in his teeth, and swung the rope. This time, he rolled his shoulders and they rose as he took a deep breath. His head was down as he backed against the pads and positioned Quincy down the rail. Another deep breath and without looking at the man watching him for the call, he nodded.

"Here we go," Taylor said to the phone and lifted the camera higher.

"Come on, Son," Charlene's voice whispered from the phone.

Granger's hand rose and gripped the rail, my free hand went to his shirt sleeve and gripped the material.

There was silence from us as shouts of encouragement to Ace rang out from the other competitors when Quincy took off down the rail. He was behind...too far behind...my fingers gripped tighter. With a mighty heave, Ace threw the rope, and it sailed through the air with just an inch clearing the calf's nose and lowering. Quincy slid to a stop with Ace stepping out of the saddle and catapulting down the rope to the calf. The flank and tie were picture perfect. He jogged back to the horse and our eyes shot to the timer.

"What is it?" Barry's voice called out.

"9.9," Taylor exhaled.

"Is the calf staying down?" Charlene's voice was tight in anticipation.

"So far..." Taylor answered and repositioned the phone so she could see.

The judge nodded and Ace's shoulders lowered as he grinned at him.

"He did it," Taylor grinned.

I turned to Granger and shook his arm that I was holding, "Now it's your turn. We all got skunked in Puyallup, so we HAVE to make it to Saturday together."

"With Fizzling Dud, I have a damn good shot."

Hours later and after the first performance, I walked Sergeant and Grace toward my horse trailer. Granger walked in beside me carrying his bag and saddle over his shoulder. His hand shot out to take the lead rope for Grace.

"I'd have kicked your ass if you didn't ride that horse like that," I teased with a wide grin. "You two looked fantastic."

"It felt good," he chuckled. "So, we all three get to ride on Saturday."

"You still have a chance for Iggy?"

"He's only up for the championship round. I'll know Friday night after the perf when they do the draw."

Ace and Taylor already had the truck and trailer ready to go before we arrived with the horses.

Announcer:

The stage is set for the championship round of the Pendleton Roundup. There are many stories playing out right now in the chase for the top fifteen. One of those is from our "Iron Sharpens Iron" team of barrel racer, Sammie Parkston, saddle bronc rider, Granger Miller, who have both qualified for the NFR, and their third partner, tie down roper Ace Conners, is fighting for his qualification. After a successful run in Utah yesterday, Ace comes within $10,000 from the fifteenth position. With Brett Landon taking a nasty spill on his horse Thursday and breaking his wrist, only Tom Brock and Wayne Danner are now battling it out with Ace for the final two spots. All three men are in the championship round making it that much tougher to pull ahead of each other. Ace is on his way to Othello for tonight then, after tomorrow's champion round, they will be traveling to Texas for the final two weeks. Texas born and raised, makes it a homecoming of sorts for Ace. Stay tuned as the tie down race is going to be a good one; right down to the final rodeo of the season."

"Sammie?"

I turned to Granger standing at Sergeant's pen door next to the Othello Rodeo grounds. "Shouldn't you be getting ready?"

"I am," he held out his arm to me. There was a small box in his hand.

"What's that?" I turned away from the horse and stepped toward him.

"A gift for you," he smiled. "It's been a year since you gave me a ride to this rodeo."

My face warmed with a blush, "You got me an anniversary gift?"

"It's not much, but it is a thank you for picking me up last year and changing my road."

"Ah, G-ranger," I took the box and happily slid the lid off. There was a small hat pin inside of two horses standing side by side.

"It's not much."

I wrapped my arms around his neck and hugged him close, "It's everything," I whispered. "That day changed both our roads."

When I stepped away from him, we smiled at each other at just how much we had both changed over the last year.

"I take it she liked it?" Ace appeared at our side with Quincy in tow while Taylor was holding both puppies.

I laughed and attached the pin to my hat, "SHE loves it."

"We'll have to have a party to celebrate the anniversary of the three of our roads coming together," Ace started to turn. "Tulsa?"

"No," I huffed with my eyes rolling. "I don't even remember that, so it has to be in Rosenburg."

"Or Waco when I joined the group," Taylor appeared.

"Or both," we all said in unison and laughed.

When we drove away in the line of horse trailers departing the Othello arena, Granger was sitting in second place, Ace was in third, and Sergeant had us sitting in first.

I was driving with Ace in the passenger seat scrolling through his phone. Taylor and Granger were already leaning against the doors with eye lids falling and puppies curled into their arms.

Ace's phone rang in the quiet cab.

"It's Detective Monroe, seems a bit late," he lifted the phone. "Hello?" After a brief moment of silence Ace nodded, "Yeah, we're on our way back now. Won't get there until 1:00 or 2:00 in the morning...yeah, OK. Before the rodeo?"

I glanced at him then into the rearview mirror at Granger and Taylor both sitting alertly now.

"Alright, we'll see you around nine," Ace lowered the phone. "They have a couple leads on Evilina."

CHAPTER FORTY-SEVEN

GRANGER

"I didn't get to sleep all night," Sammie huffed as she slid out of her bedroom and down to the main floor. "Why couldn't they wait until after the Roundup?"

"Probably, because we're leaving right after," Ace opened the door for her, and we stepped out to see Detectives Monroe and Fortune talking with Sammie's parents and my mother.

"Morning," I stretched out my hand to Detective Monroe then to Fortune.

"Morning, Granger," Fortune shook my hand with a grumble then turned to Ace. "Thanks for meeting with us so early and I apologize for having to do it before the rodeo."

"I'm guessing you think we know the person," Ace stated.

"After you called about your hunch on the timing of you and Granger being targets as a date to the wedding, I've been focused on that," Detective Monroe said. "Unfortunately, after the sing-along video went viral, hundreds of people started following your group page and sent friend requests to your private ones."

"You narrowed it down?" Sammie asked.

Monroe shook her head, "We have a list of people that requested from both of you and liked the page." She handed Ace and I a piece of paper.

I glanced down the list and shook my head, "There's hundreds here."

"Just need to know if you recognize any names," Fortune said and handed me a yellow highlighter.

"Outside of friends?" Ace asked and took a highlighter from Fortune.

"We need you to just highlight those you recognize," Monroe answered. "We'll do the investigation and removal of the friends."

I highlighted a dozen names until I came across one that made me glance at Ace.

"Which name?" Fortune asked and looked at Ace.

"She doesn't have anything to do with it," Ace shook his head.

"You need to let us investigate and determine that," Detective Monroe said.

"I haven't been on my personal page in months." Ace shook his head and continued to highlight names on the paper. "I didn't even know she sent the friend request."

"Which one?" Monroe looked between us.

"I haven't seen her since last year," Ace handed her the sheet of paper. "In Arizona. At the time, I didn't have anything to do with anyone over here. And we certainly didn't have anything to do with the twins since they weren't born yet."

"You have to let us investigate," Monroe said again.

"Just tell them," Sammie whispered.

Ace sighed and looked from her to Detective Fortune, "Sunni Shoshanna."

"What a pretty name," Sammie huffed.

Ace nodded, "I called her Sunshine and she's from Georgia."

"Thank you, we'll go through these as quickly as possible and let you know," Monroe nodded.

"Again," Fortune huffed. "I'm sorry it was before the rodeo. Just focus, and good luck."

"Thanks," Ace and I muttered as they walked away.

Ace turned to me when they were too far away to hear, "I didn't see Union on there, but I also don't know her full name."

"She wasn't on there." I shrugged and turned to step back into the trailer. "And I didn't draw that damn horse again."

"Who did you get?" Sammie asked as they followed me.

My body ached; muscles tired from lack of sleep. I looked down at the dark brown horse in the chute in front of me and sighed. Marquee, she was strong, stout, and a consistent bucker. It was going to take all my strength to make the eight. Deep breaths and a look out to the roping chutes and watched for Ace. He was off to the side next to the fence with Taylor and Sammie standing next to him. Somewhere in the stands behind them were Sammie's parents and my mother. No doubt, Taylor had his family on the phone.

Ace was the second to last to run, and I needed food. I normally didn't eat before riding but this time, with the lack of sleep and not eating breakfast, I needed energy. I needed food. As the first tie down roper backed into the box, I turned and hurried down the platform and down the stairs. The hospitality room was right across the alleyway, and I made my way around the bareback riders that had already rode, and the bull riders that were waiting for their turn.

"Hey, Granger."

I turned to bareback rider Tony McGee. He had been one of the professionals helping at the clinic when the twins were kidnapped.

"Tony, how did you do?"

He shrugged with a grin, "Rode all three but not enough to get more than 9th."

"That's great, though," I shoved half a banana into my mouth. Turkey cold-cut sliders, cookies, grapes, and two protein bars were devoured. I downed a bottle of Pepsi for the caffeine.

"Hey," Tony called out as I walked toward the door. "Did they ever find who kidnapped the babies?"

"No." The word held the irritation I felt from the interview with the detectives.

"Scary fucking day," Tony shook his head.

I nodded and rushed back to the chutes. The tenth tie down roper was trotting down the arena following his calf and I looked down as I passed the chute with Adam Westmoreland standing next to it. He had been at the ranch when the babies were kidnapped, too.

"Granger," Adam nodded.

"How's it going?" I stopped next to him and looked down at Destiny's Ignatius in the chute.

"I look forward to the day I'm standing back here with you and your stable mate," Adam chuckled with a smart-ass grin.

"Me, too," I huffed and walked by him. Damn, horse.

While waiting for Ace's turn to ride, I settled the saddle on Marquee. My energy had risen, but mood had fallen. I tried to focus on the ride by envisioning the horse's previous trips out of the chutes until Ace's name was called.

"Talk me through it," I whispered to him as he backed the roan horse into the box.

He nodded and raced down the chute. 10.1 seconds later, he was running back to the horse. It was announced he was currently in second. He needed that damn win. Now, it was going to be a rush to the very end.

My focus turned to the horse in front of me. I needed to focus. As I set the saddle on her back, my mind flashed to the name of Ace's fall fling; Sunni Shoshanna. Terrific name and the picture he had shared of her in a little bikini showed exactly why he called her Sunshine. Golden blonde, blue eyes, tan, and her smile was bright and happy. She looked like sunshine. Just the opposite of Angelina who was tall, long black hair, dark brown eyes, and dark olive skin. She was sexy, fun, and since she worked out nearly every day, she had a well-defined muscular body. She wasn't sunshine, she was mystery. Angelina would have looked great with the tall dark, Ace, and Sunshine would have looked better on my arm. The thought was amusing.

I slipped the cinch under the mare and through the ring. I had no doubt that neither woman had anything to do with the kidnapping. And the only reason I was thinking of them now was because of the meeting with the two detectives.

The applause from the crowd brought me out of the haze and I stood and looked out as the champion tie down roper started his victory lap. Damn, that should have been Ace.

Once the breakaway roping began, I waited for Delaney and watched her place second on the buckskin and white paint she had traded for Sergeant . The trade had worked out well for both of them.

"You're third out," the chute boss pointed up at me.

My focus returned to the horse and the ride as the first chute was opened. A palomino bucked out...she was the same color as Sunshine's hair. A distraction...cramping my style... I rose above the chute and flipped my chaps back, why did I think of that? I needed to focus. Brodie appeared above me and popped my vest with his hand.

"What the hell?" Brodie grumbled.

"What?"

"Zip up your damn vest," He shook his head in disbelief.

I grumbled and zipped it up. That was always the first thing I did...way before climbing over the chute. My mind was distracted.

"I love riding this mare; she's good and solid," he said. "Get in rhythm, show off that style you're working on, and fire your feet. She'll help you get the points, just don't get too far ahead of her."

I nodded and looked down at the mare; her mane was long and full like Angelina's hair.

"Damn," I growled and shoved my hat down tightly on my head...a distraction, cramping my style. I looked up at Brodie with a bit of desperation. "I can't focus."

His eyes went out to the horse that busted out of the chute next to us then back to me, "Dude, maybe you don't remember how hard the ground is here. You want to end up like Spence with a broken shoulder and end your year?"

The memory of the pain in Spence's eyes, hours in the hospital, and months of recovery brought me out of my haze, and I returned to full focus on Marquee. The gate man appeared with a hand on the latch.

"You ready?" The chute boss asked.

"Toes out," Brodie grinned at me. "Remember, you're a natural, you can do this blind folded."

"Damn, that would suck," I huffed and tightened my fingers around the buck rein, shoved my hat down low, and nodded.

The gate was flung open.

Heels above shoulders, toes out, arm back, watch her ears, kick down, stretch back, heels to ass, back down...stretch...muscle memory...the adrenaline rush swept through me. The power of the horse mixed with the adrenaline. My heart raced and I didn't want to stop, but the pickup men appeared on each side of us. Reluctantly, I slid off the horse and gripped the arm that was held out for me then my boots hit the ground.

I roared at the crowd with arms in the air then whipped around to jog to the group of people sitting alongside of the chutes. Fingers to buckles to loosen the chaps, Marquee was led by the pickup men in front of me. I loved that horse and couldn't wait to draw her again. An 86-point score was announced that put me in the lead.

"Way to go!" High fives were given as I sat in the middle of the group and waited for Brodie.

"Damn you looked good," Ace slid in next to me, with Sammie on the other side.

"Style, man, style!" Someone said from behind us.

"Cramping my style," I turned to Ace. "It's been stuck in my head since this morning."

The gate was opened, and Brodie burst out of the chute on a mare named Business Girl. It was a beautiful ride. When he jogged to us, his grin was wide. Laughter rang out from him when his 86-point score was announced and the fact that we were currently tied for first place in the rodeo. We just had to wait for seven more riders to go.

After the next rider hit the ground before the horn blared, Brodie turned to me, "Why the focus problem?"

"Interview this morning?" Sammie asked.

"Yeah," I nodded with an exhale. "I got that damn 'cramping my style' in my head and can't get it out for some reason."

"I lost a bit of concentration, too," Ace grumbled. "Just enough to lose that damn title."

"You still got thousands added to your standings," Brodie reminded him.

"But it would have been double if..." Ace shook his head.

"Fucking Evilina," I huffed under my breath.

"Evilina? Who in the hell is that?" Tony slid in just behind me as the next chute was opened.

"That's what we've been calling the lady that kidnapped the twins," Ace answered.

"Good name for her," Tony nodded. "They have no clues?"

"Just the fact the night of the sing-along seems to be the beginning of it," I answered.

"So, why since the sing-along?" Tony asked.

"What?" Half a dozen people around us asked and scooted closer.

"When the kidnapper targeted the Houston twins," Tony explained.

Everyone looked from him, to Ace, Brodie, and I.

Destiny's Ignatius busted out of the chute and had his rider on the ground within two jumps. The pickup men swooped in and surrounded the horse.

"Damn," Brodie sighed then turned to look at me with a smart-ass smile.

"Someday," I huffed. "One more rider, then I need food."

The last rider exploded from the chutes and 8 seconds later took the lead with an 88-point ride.

"Well, damn," Sammie stood. "At least you get your food quicker."

"Shouldn't you be on your horse?" Ace smirked.

"There is steer wrestling, team roping, bulls, the Indian dance, the specialty act, and steer roping ahead. I got a little time," she answered and led our group out of the arena and into the hospitality room.

Plates full, we took seats on the couches, chairs, and benches in the hospitality room. There were at least twenty bareback and saddle bronc riders along with Sammie in the room.

"So why the sing-a-long?" Tony asked.

By the time Ace explained the theory another six people had stopped.

"So, the lady in Utah with Ace?" One of the riders asked. "What about you, Granger?"

"I can't think of anyone," I shook my head.

"What about the buckle bunny in Joseph?" Tony asked.

"What?" I huffed.

"I was in the restaurant when the door opened and a good-looking lady came in," Tony smiled. "I was already imagining taking her to bed..." He glanced at Sammie with a chuckle. "Sorry..."

She shook her head, "You guys do that, that fast?"

"Yes," A dozen men answered her.

After a chuckle, Tony continued, "She walked in, I was getting up from the table, but she saw you and beelined for you."

"What exactly do you mean beelined?" I asked.

"Like there was no one else in the restaurant," Tony explained. "You were at the bar, and she walked right to you."

"Yeah," I nodded as the memory of the brunette in the mirror flashed. "I was with my mother so I couldn't take her up on her offer."

"Do you remember anything else about her?" Sammie asked.

"Rockin' body, blue eyes, and a brunette," I answered and looked at Ace. "Didn't you say The Shirt had blue eyes?"

"Yep, and brunette," he nodded. "And Joseph was well after the sing-along night."

"And they found blonde wig strands in the bag you pulled out from her SUV," Sammie nodded with wide eyes.

"She wouldn't need to change her hair if she was coming with you," Tony nodded. "But she would need to during the wedding or kidnapping so you didn't recognize her."

"That is very true," I nodded with a grin.

"If it's the same person, we've narrowed it down to a woman with natural brown hair and blue eyes." Ace grinned.

"That narrows it down to hundreds of thousands," a bareback rider huffed.

"A little more if you consider she would have been in Utah for the Spanish Forks Rodeo and then in Joseph for that rodeo the next weekend." Sammie mused.

"What are the odds of the same woman being in both places?" Tony nodded.

"Pretty high if they are involved in rodeo...breakaway, barrel racer, or family member," A saddle bronc rider added.

"But going after the two men that would have been going to the wedding and been busy on stage together?" Another cowboy said.

I turned to Tony, "You remember anything else about her?"

"No," he shook his head. "She came through the door, basically looking for you, then when you turned her down, she walked right back out again." He chuckled. "Didn't even give me a chance to throw my hat in the ring."

"Shouldn't that have been condom in the ring?" Someone called out and everyone chuckled.

Sammie stood with a smirk and a laugh, "I'm going to find my horse."

I grabbed her arm and stopped her. She looked up at me in surprise.

"Ace and I were both distracted by all this," I reminded her. "Put it all to the side for now and just focus on Grace and your run. Unfortunately, this mess will be here in an hour and there is nothing we can do about it. So, concentrate."

She sighed with a slight smile and nod, "Ok, I will."

"Good luck!" Rang out from the crowd in the room as she walked out the door.

"Detective Fortune is still here," Ace said as I turned back to the group. "I texted him we had a few ideas, so he is on his way here."

When the detective arrived, he looked around the group of cowboys and smirked, "A bit of the Cowboy Nation?"

"Yes, sir," I grinned. "We're about coast to coast in here."

"Florida!" A bareback rider raised his hand and the cowboys all started shouting.

"Texas."

"California."

"Minnesota."

"Wyoming."

"Texas."

"Oklahoma."

"Idaho."

"Montana."

"Texas again."

"Louisiana."

"Oregon."

"California."

"Utah."

"Mississippi."

"New York City."

"Ohio."

"Wyoming."

"Washington."

I grinned at the detective, "Coast to Coast Cowboy Nation."

He laughed, "So, what did you come up with?"

Ace relayed the information we had discussed, and the detective nodded. "I'll keep this in mind and go back through the tips we received. If any of you think of anything else, call the tip hotline and mention Pendleton so I know you were part of this conversation."

After nods of agreement, the cowboys and detectives departed the room.

Taylor, Brodie, Ace, and I were on the back of the bucking chutes when the barrel racers rode into the arena. Sammie turned and waved with a smile then rode the black mare in circles as she waited her turn. Ace's cousin Jamie, as well as Delaney were in the top 12 finalists. We yelled and cheered for all of them with Jamie placing 6th, Delaney was 4th, and Sammie rode out with a grin as she fell .03 seconds short of the championship.

"I guess we're all second best today," she laughed as we caught up with her at the stalls.

An hour later, with goodbyes to my mom and Sammie's parents, Sammie started the engine on her truck and started to pull away but stopped.

"Guys?" She turned to me then looked in the back seat to Taylor and Ace who were each playing with a puppy. "We have to let Detective Fortune handle the investigation. We need to focus on these last two weeks."

"Agreed," I nodded.

"Yeah," Ace sighed. "Today was too much. I'll text Fortune and tell him no communication unless they have something solid."

"We don't want Evilina taking anything more away from you." Taylor added.

"Alright then," Sammie turned back, and the truck started moving. "We have about 10 hours to Marysville, California, so 3 and a half hours driving time split between the three of us."

"Come on, Granger," Taylor huffed with a grin. "You haven't learned to drive this yet?"

"No way in hell on a highway with that trailer and those horses attached." I laughed. "I'm just here for entertainment."

CHAPTER FORTY-EIGHT

GRANGER

Good evening, Everyone, this is Lori Ann Marker with *On The Road Rodeo News*;

Tonight, we catch up with the "Iron Sharpens Iron" Ace Conners part of the traveling trio with Sammie Parkston and Granger Miller. I first met the Connor family a few years back at the high school rodeo level. Ace and his brother Taylor are high school rodeo champions in team roping together as well as Taylor in calf roping. As most of you know, the brothers are sons of the late World Champion Austin Conners who was killed in a tragic accident just prior to his 8th NFR when the boys were 3 and 2 years old.

After Taylor's injury last year at their home in Texas, Ace has been on the road trying to qualify for the National Finals Rodeo while riding Taylor's horse, Quincy. I spoke with Taylor this morning about the final drive for Ace to qualify. After coming in second at the Pendleton

Roundup, they traveled to Marysville California where Ace took the win before traveling to their home state of Texas. That win put Ace 17th in the world standings. Just two spots out of the top 15 where he needs to be to earn the trip to Vegas.

In the last six days they have been in Springhill Louisiana, Amarillo Texas, Poway California, Omah Nebraska, Cumberland Maine, Stephenville Texas, and San Bernadino California. Ace drew a check at all but one of those rodeos which lands him 16th in the standings; only $157 from the coveted 15th spot. A closer look at those standings shows only $2800 separates the 13th to 17th cowboys vying for the top 15. All but one of the five cowboys are on the road fighting their way to the NFR. After his win in Pendleton, Lonnie Banks pulled ahead of Ace by only $400.

There are only two more rodeos left on Ace's schedule; Pasadena Texas and Mona Utah. He not only has to place in both rodeos, but he has to place higher and earn more than those other cowboys still on the road.

As for his traveling partners, barrel racer Sammie Parkston has qualified and is sitting in the 5th position in the world, while saddle bronc rider, Granger Miller, is in 7th. He is just behind his good friend Brodie Rawlins who is currently 6th.

Looking to next year already, Taylor stated that when they weren't traveling to a rodeo, they were home practicing for his return in team roping with his brother.

Stay tuned to this epic cowboy battle to see if Ace can pull off the miracle and join his 'Iron Sharpens Iron' companions in Las Vegas this coming December.

"A miracle?" Taylor huffed as he squatted next to Stomping Dog to put boots on the horse's front legs.

"Just makes it sound more exciting," Sammie smirked as she held the horse's reins.

"More exciting than actually living this nightmare?" Ace slid the back boot on the buckskin horse's leg.

"Damn, Ace," I chuckled. "Remember what your mother said; you're supposed to be calling this an adventure, not a nightmare."

All four of us chuckled.

"She said that because of the Lil Bro's, and they are on the road with Barry taking Quincy up to Utah and she is in the stands waiting for us," Ace pointed out. "The four of us have lived this last week and we can openly call it what it is...a nightmare and I need a nap."

Sammie grinned, "You can nap this weekend...oh, wait, no you can't. We'll be in Rosenberg starting all over again."

Ace glared at her, "Thanks for that."

We laughed again.

"You can nap on the plane in the morning," Taylor grinned. "Or the hour drive from Salt Lake to Mona."

"One thing at a time," Sammie sighed. "Let's get tonight taken care of before thinking of tomorrow."

"Easy for you to say since you're not riding," I teased.

She slapped my arm with a shake of the head, "G-Ranger, you know we hit our rodeo limit, and they need some time off."

"I understand," I assured her. "I'll be taking some time off myself after WACO."

"We all need to rest and heal for a bit," she nodded. "But right now, I'm going up in the bleachers with Charlene."

I watched her walk away then turned to the brothers. Ace was already riding away, and I found Taylor watching Sammie walk away, too. He shrugged with a smartass grin then looked out at the crowd.

"Where's he stand?" I asked.

"Brett has dropped to 18th after his broken wrist. Tom is sitting 13th, Wayne is 14th, and Lonnie won Pendleton over Ace and went from two thousand behind to now sitting 15th ahead of Ace at 16th."

"I saw Lonnie here a few minutes ago."

He nodded and we walked toward the bucking chutes, "Lonnie and Ace here tonight and in Mona tomorrow night. Tom and Wayne in Mona tonight and here tomorrow night."

"Texas is an hour ahead of Utah, so we should know by the time Lonnie and Ace ride tomorrow night what they have to do to get in the top 15."

"And the start is tonight. Ace needs to win...flat out."

"This rodeo starts with bareback riding and moves right into saddle bronc, so I'll be done well before Ace enters the arena."

Taylor nodded and turned toward the bleachers to make his way toward his mother and Sammie. I walked behind the bucking chutes.

An hour later, I was reaching for the pickup man and sliding down to the ground. It was a good ride, not my best, but I was still pleased when the 84 points was announced. That placed me in 3rd overall.

I tossed my bag and saddle in Ace's truck then went in search of him. He was standing at the edge of the warmup arena talking with Lonnie. Ace glanced at me then reached out a hand to shake with his competitor for the 15th position. They smiled at each other with a final respectful nod before Lonnie rode away.

I smiled up at Ace, "Ah, good. Glad I caught you. I have something to discuss with you."

"And what would that be?" He smirked.

I ran a hand down Stomping Dogs' shoulder. "Well, you're riding my horse..."

Ace shook his head, "I don't remember you paying for him."

"Well, I believe that every time you use my horse and earn money, I get 25% and that would be a payment."

Ace laughed, "I think that has to be a mutual agreement and I'm not selling my horse."

"Last year at Lauren's, you said I could choose the horse I wanted, and I chose this handsome buckskin." I huffed with a wide grin and patted the horse again. "So, there is that."

Ace laughed again, "Nah..."

"Oh, yay," I grinned. "So, you just go out there and win more money, so I have a bigger payment on him this month."

I tipped my fingers to the front of my hat, and with a big, wise-ass grin walked away to his laughter.

Lonnie rode out of the arena with a 9.3, fifth place run as I slid on the bleacher next to Sammie. Her hand reached out and grabbed the sleeve of my shirt as Ace walked into the arena. It was her typical move on handling her anxiety. I knew she did the same thing with Ace's shirt when I rode. Taking a deep breath and slowly exhaling, I ignored the ache in my gut. Another deep breath as he walked Stomping Dog into the box and turned. He was barely backed in when he nodded, the lever was pushed, and the horse burst into the arena. Two swings and Ace was already throwing. We barely had a chance to shout before he was off the horse, down the line, and flanking the calf. We held our breath in anticipation as he jogged back and waited for the required six seconds. We jumped to our feet and were cheering after the 7.6 seconds was announced. He did exactly what he needed to do; he took the lead for the whole rodeo.

The four of us shuffled down the bleachers and jogged back to the horse trailers. Ace met us with a wide grin and looked at me with a shake of the head, "I ain't selling him."

After a subdued celebration dinner, we were at the airport in Houston for an early flight to Salt Lake City. Neither Sammie nor I were riding, it was all about Ace this time. He was all grins and teasing with his mother and brother on the short flight and grinned broadly at Liam and Monte when they greeted us in the parking lot.

"You look pretty relaxed," Barry smirked at him.

"I've done what I could do," Ace sighed. "I have one more run, but it all depends on what the other three do also."

"You can only do, what you can do," Barry nodded and drove away from the airport.

We spent the afternoon napping, roping the dummy steer, and eating. After such a long stressful two months, it was a surprisingly relaxing final day.

"I am so proud of you," Charlene pulled Ace into a strong embrace, then leaned back and looked into his eyes. "Have fun," she whispered before she and Barry walked into the crowd to find a spot on the bleachers.

Taylor was helping Ace saddle Quincy while Sammie and Liam were in the trailer watching the Pasadena rodeo and waiting on the tie down results.

Monte and I sat in the lawn chairs in front of the trailer when I glanced at him and found him staring at me with an odd look.

"What?" I asked as my phone dinged an alert.

"I need to talk to someone," Monte whispered and glanced at his brothers.

Text from Sammie to Granger: You placed third.

"Talk."

"I heard Barry talking to Mom on the phone this morning and they were talking about the kidnapping."

I turned my full attention to him. As we had promised each other after the Pendleton Roundup, we had not talked about the kidnapping nor had anyone contacted us.

"What about it?" I whispered in return.

He glanced at his brothers then to the trailer before looking at me with narrowed worried eyes. "Something is going on and there are people coming to the rodeo tonight to talk with you guys."

"It better be after Ace runs," I grumbled in irritation and surprise.

"It is," Monte whispered. "That's what Mom and Barry were talking about. They said they would shoot anyone that distracted Ace and were going to watch for anyone trying to approach him."

"That's why they already left?"

"Yeah," Monte nodded.

"And that's what you needed to talk about?"

"No," his shoulders rose, and he glanced at the ground then back up. "They mentioned something about the lady that approached Ace in Spanish Forks when we were there with him."

"The Shirt?"

"Yeah, her," he smirked then took a deep breath. "Barry said something about wishing they had a better image of her."

"Yeah, that's the last we've discussed about it. That has you worried?"

"Well," he huffed. "Mom said I can only have a phone if I promise to be respectful and not just take pictures of pretty girls."

I grinned at him, "Sounds like your mom."

He nodded with a glance at the trailer then back to me, "I can't say I always did that."

"You're fourteen?"

"Yeah, but, that day when that lady basically threw herself at him and wrapped herself all over him...we were all so surprise and well...for me...pretty excited for Ace."

I turned in my chair and looked at him in surprise, "Are you saying you took pictures, too? Not just the ones Taylor took?"

"I wanted to show my friends at school the pretty girls that hit on cowboys." He nodded with a smirk. "And, now, I'm afraid if I tell

Mom she is going to be mad at me and take my phone but I'm also afraid that if I don't show them to whoever is coming, that it might not help in finding the kidnapper."

"Where is your phone? I'll take a look and see if they would be helpful."

"In Mom's bag...with her," he shrugged. "Everyone I usually text with is here, so I didn't want to carry it."

I nodded, "I tell you what. Once Ace has run, ask your mom for the phone then we'll go look at them and decide if they need to be seen."

He sighed, "Thanks, Granger. I knew you would help."

"No need getting you in trouble if you don't need to be."

"I get in enough trouble for stupid things," he smirked and stood.

Ace was riding to the warmup arena when Sammie walked out of the trailer. Taylor, Monte and I looked at her in anticipation.

"He held the win in Pasadena," she smiled. "Tom won a little money which should keep him at 14th but Wayne missed. According to mine and Lauren's calculations, IF Ace earns more money than Lonnie tonight, he should be 15th."

"It basically comes down to Ace and Lonnie then?" Monte asked.

"Yeah," Liam sighed. "Whoever wins more money tonight will get the last spot and the other drops to the damn crying hole."

"Positive vibes," Sammie smiled at the three brothers. "Do not mention it to Ace if you see him before his run. Just wish him good luck."

"I'm just going to hide out in the stands with Mom and Barry," Monte huffed and with a conspirator nod to me, walked away with Liam following.

"I'm going over to make sure he is in a good mind set," Sammie said.

I followed her to the warmup arena and found Ace and Lonnie talking off to the side again. Both men were laughing and looked completely at ease.

"Let him be," I whispered to Sammie. "I talked with Monte, and he overheard Barry and Charlene talking about someone being here tonight to talk to us about the kidnapping."

"It damn well better be after," Her voice was low, and eyes narrowed.

"It is," I smiled. "That was the same thing I said."

"Any idea what they want?"

"No, just that they wanted to meet."

"Well, if it was good, they would have come to us or announced it already."

"And they came all the way here, to Utah, to meet with us. Must mean it's important."

"Agreed, and this damn night is stressful enough." She grumbled and looked out at the two ropers. "Then I'll just stand here and watch to make sure no one gets near him."

"I'm headed for the chutes. I'll come over and keep watch with you when they are done bucking."

I kept my mind busy by helping the bareback riders and stock contractor, then reluctantly joined Sammie at the arena exit gate.

"Any problems?"

"Nervous stomachache," she huffed. "I just wish this was done."

"Me, too."

We stood quietly watching the rodeo until the tie down was announced. Her hand reached out and grabbed my shirt sleeve...she was shaking.

"He'll do it," I whispered to her.

"He will...because I just couldn't imagine going without him."

Ace rode in behind us while flipping his rope in the air and with a big grin, "What are you two doing?"

"Wishing you would hurry up so we can go eat," I answered.

"I think we should have ice cream tonight," Sammie added with a smile. "Chocolate syrup, sprinkles, maraschino cherries."

"Only if they were soaked in Fire Ball," Ace chuckled. "And I agree."

His name was called, and the arena gate swung open.

"Hey," Taylor appeared next to us. Ace looked down at him as he rode into the arena. "Same thing I've told you the whole year."

"Trust Quincy," Ace, Sammie, and I called out.

Ace laughed and walked into the roping box while Sammie's other hand reached out for Taylor's shirt sleeve.

"What's he need?" She whispered.

"Cole is leading with an 8.4," Taylor answered. "Ace, Matt, then Lonnie finishes it out."

Ace looked behind him as he backed the roan horse into the corner. When he turned, his eyes dropped to the calf, and he nodded.

"Whoahhh," Sammie gasped, and her grip tightened.

My lungs stopped, back tensed, and hands balled into fists as he ran down the rope, flipped the calf, then two wraps and a tie in 8.1 seconds. I exhaled as he trotted back to Quincy.

"He got out clean," Taylor exhaled.

"Stay down," Sammie whispered to the calf.

The official's flag lowered, and we all exhaled in relief.

"He's done everything he could," I turned and smiled at Taylor and Sammie. "Now it is all down to Lonnie."

Ace rode out of the arena with a slight smile to us then stepped out of the saddle. We walked away from the fence and stopped just far enough we could see the arena monitor. Silently, we watched Matt Shiozawa back into the box and nod. As he rode out of the arena with an 8.4, Lonnie rode in.

While Ace's hand slowly slid down Quincy's neck, the four of us stood quietly and watched. That horse could not have worked better for him in the last ten months. The first rides in Lauren's indoor arena the winter before flashed in my memory. Who could have predicted it would come down to one last run and the last day of the year?

Lonnie backed into the box and his horse jumped forward and spun. Lonnie swung the rope around then reached out and patted the horse. The rope was tucked under his arm, he leaned forward with eyes on the calf in the chute. The nod.

It was a perfect throw, dismount from the horse, and run to the calf that had turned perfectly toward him. The flank, one wrap, and the tie.

"One wrap," Taylor exhaled.

"I considered it," Ace said lightly. "Thought I better be safe."

The timer said 8.2 seconds as Lonnie stepped into the saddle. That fast...8.2 seconds and our quest was over...our dream denied.

We turned and walked back toward the trailer.

"I couldn't be prouder of you, Brother," Taylor said softly.

"Are you kidding?" Ace chuckled. "I couldn't have gotten this far and had that chance without this horse you trained."

"Damn good horse," I felt numb...as if my brain did not want to accept that Ace wasn't going to be riding in Vegas with us.

When we approached the trailer, I exhaled in the second dread of the night when Detective Fortune and Detective Monroe were waiting for us.

Whatever they had to say, couldn't be any worse than what had just happened in the arena.

CHAPTER FORTY-NINE

ACE

"Ace." Fortune stretched out a hand to me.

I took his hand then turned to shake Monroe's hand. They both looked concerned. It could be from their news on the kidnapping or the fact they knew I lost the chance to go to Vegas.

Mom, Barry, and the Lil Bros joined us, and it was easy to see the tears in her eyes as she wrapped me in her arms.

"It's all good, Mom," I whispered to her and hugged her tight. As much as I didn't want to talk about the kidnapper, I was thankful for the immediate distraction.

"It was a hell of a battle," Barry took the reins for Quincy and walked him to the trailer. I knew it was a way for him to have time to deal with the disappointment.

Monte walked to Granger and handed him a phone. They both turned away from the group.

"So, there must be some big news if you flew all the way down here," Sammie huffed. The disappointment and irritation were clear in her voice and eyes.

"Your Cowboy Nation meeting at Pendleton has narrowed down a few possibilities of our kidnapper," Fortune nodded.

"I also have a video for you to review," Detective Monroe looked around the group and out to the busy rodeo grounds and arena then to Mom. "Somewhere quieter? You stated there was a monitor in the trailer?"

"Yeah, we can go in there," Mom walked to the trailer and opened the door. She glanced at Monte and Granger who were looking at the phone. "It will be tight, but there is room for all of us." She turned and looked at the two detectives. "Anything questionable that the two boys shouldn't hear?"

"No, ma'am," Fortune answered and with a wave of his hand, invited everyone into the trailer.

When I stepped into the trailer, the sound of the rodeo faded and after taking a deep breath, I let the anxiety and disappointment fade with it.

Granger and Monte were the last to enter.

"It's OK," Granger whispered to him. "This is a good thing."

"What?" I asked.

Granger handed me Monte's phone, "There are three images."

I huffed when I saw the first image of the woman in the Spanish Forks' bar wrapping her arms around my shoulders and lifting a leg up to my waist. The next image was of the woman in complete wrapped mode...just like the image Taylor had sent to Granger and Sammie. The third image the woman had just stepped away from me and looked back at my brothers after I told her they were there. She was looking directly at the phone giving us a perfect image of her face.

"Damn," I gasped and looked at Granger then Monte.

"I didn't know you needed it," Monte quickly said and looked at his mother. "I only took them to show the guys at school the hot girls that throw themselves, literally, at cowboys."

"What is it?" She stepped forward and looked at the phone. "That's The Shirt?" She looked up at me in surprise.

"What?" Was gasped in the room and everyone leaned forward to look at the image.

"Let's get them on the monitor," Sammie reached for the remote.

Within a minute, The Shirt was looking back at us. Long brown hair waved down the sides of her face and to her breasts. Long eyelashes, perfectly shaped brows, and the brown and deep green eyeshadow highlighted the sapphire blue eyes that looked right at the phone. They were as pretty as I remembered.

"She's beautiful," Sammie mused.

"That's the girl from Spanish Fork?" Detective Fortune asked in surprise.

I swiped the phone to show him the other two images.

"Well, I'll be damned," Detective Monroe chuckled and looked at Monte. "Good job."

"So, I'm not in trouble?" Monte's brows rose as he looked at her then to Mom.

"Honestly, Charlene," Granger smirked. "I would have taken the pictures, too and for the same reason."

She rolled her eyes at him then looked at Monte, "No, this turned out to be a good thing."

"Well, this will help narrow down the leads from the Pendleton cowboys," Fortune looked at the image.

Monroe looked at Granger, "You recognize her?"

Granger nodded at the monitor, "She is the woman that approached me in Joseph. I was at the bar and looked up at the bartender; he was looking at the door. In the mirror behind him, I could see that woman come through the door and walk toward me."

"You only saw her from the reflection?" Monroe asked.

"No, she walked up to me, I turned to her, then we spoke briefly until my mother returned," Granger answered.

"So, she knew you? Like she did with Ace?" Barry asked.

Granger's eyebrow rose and he looked at Sammie, "She called me G-Ranger."

"What?" Sammie huffed in irritation.

"Your nickname," Fortune nodded.

"Yeah, that only Sammie calls me," Granger looked at him. "She most definitely walked in that bar looking for me just like she did with Ace."

"The sing-along video shows Sammie calling him G-Ranger," Taylor pointed out.

"So, that beautiful woman is Evilina?" Mom gasped.

"Not necessarily," Both detectives answered.

"This just proves this woman had a fixation on you two and tracked you down," Monroe pointed out. "There is absolutely nothing that links her to the kidnapping."

"Nothing," Fortune repeated.

"There is no doubt in my mind," Barry huffed. "You don't believe it?"

"It doesn't matter what we believe," Monroe stated. "It's what we can prove."

Detective Fortune looked around the group. "We had five names from the leads called in from the Pendleton cowboys. They were all sure the women had been in both towns during the rodeos. Two were barrel racers that we've ruled out. I was going to review the others with you but now that we have a face, I can see if one of those leads takes us to her." He nodded to the image on the screen.

"We can just post it..." Sammie started.

"No," both detectives answered.

"We do not want The Shirt to know that we're looking at her as Evilina," Monroe explained. "There is no evidence, absolutely nothing, that connects them."

"If she even gets a hint that we're watching her, then she could disappear or start covering her tracks before we can find them," Fortune added. He looked at everyone in the room including Monte and Liam. "That image is not to be shared with ANYONE. This theory stays between this group of people."

"It's imperative," Monroe stated. "You can't tell anyone."

"I understand," Mom nodded and turned Monte to her. "Have you sent those pictures to anyone?"

"Nah, I just showed them on my phone," he shrugged with a guilty smirk. "I didn't want you to find out and get in trouble."

"You understand how important it is to keep them a secret now?" She asked him then looked at Liam.

"Yeah," they both muttered.

"I won't tell anyone," Liam said with wide eyes.

"Me either," Monte nodded. "I already sent the images to Granger and Ace so I can delete them off my phone." He looked at the detectives.

Fortune looked at Granger.

"I got them," Granger confirmed.

The detective turned to me, and I shrugged, "I have no idea. My phone is in the tack room. I don't carry it with me when I ride."

He turned back to Monte, "May I have your phone and I'll send the images to myself and delete them from your phone?"

"Sure," Monte shrugged and handed him the phone.

"Everyone understands and agrees that this theory and woman stays within this group?" Monroe asked.

Everyone nodded their agreement.

"You said there was a video you wanted to show us?" Sammie had leaned back against the counter with arms crossed in front of her and legs crossed at the ankles. There was an air of impatient irritation radiating from her.

Detective Monroe nodded, "I just need to connect to your monitor."

We were quiet until an image of the Safeway store where we had found the twins appeared.

"While I was concentrating on the leads coming in, Monroe was working on the vehicles at the parking lot," Fortune nodded to the screen. "Two things that have never made sense to any of us was why did they stop at Safeway and why Redmond instead of Bend where they could have disappeared easier."

"I thought that as we were following them," I nodded in agreement.

"Me, too," Sammie stood from the counter and turned to get a clear view of the monitor.

"And the fact there were no car seats in the SUV," I added.

"Exactly," Monroe smiled. "THAT bugged the hell out of me, but I believe I have the answer. I'll walk you through...I retrieved the video from the store from the moment the grey SUV appeared after the kidnapping." She played the video. "But, then, I went backwards." The video changed and the cars that were visible through the mass of trees were different. "If you watch, right here..." She pointed to a bright blue SUV that was pulling into the same entrance as the grey SUV had. "As you know, the clinic was Sunday and Monday. This blue SUV pulls into the Safeway parking lot and disappears under the trees late Saturday afternoon. I watched every second of the security video from that moment until we saw Ace run in, and Sammie's truck and trailer appear. That blue SUV did not leave that parking lot. It remained in the parking lot the whole time."

"The grey SUV was stolen," Fortune reminded the group.

"You're saying, you think the blue SUV was a getaway vehicle?" Barry asked.

Monroe nodded, "Six hours after the parking lot is cleared of all police vehicles, the blue SUV is finally seen through the trees and then going out the same exit as it came in." She played the video of the car, and we watched it drive away. "There is no clear shot of the driver from the Safeway camera, so I went to one of the businesses across the street and they had an angle from their security camera to get this." A photograph of the blue SUV appeared. "No clear shot of the driver, because of a large black hat this time, but look in the backseat." We all leaned closer.

"Two car seats," Monte gasped and pointed at them on the monitor.

"My guess is they didn't want two car seats in the grey SUV because that would have brought attention to their vehicle at the Rawlin's ranch," Monroe nodded. "They parked the blue one in a parking lot with obstructed security cameras and went there to switch vehicles."

"The grey SUV was stolen," Fortune added.

"Was the blue one?" Granger asked. "Did you get a shot of the license plate?"

Monroe shook her head, "Every shot we got from cameras around the area, the plate was blurry. Even when the car was perfectly clear, the plate couldn't be read."

"We concluded Evilina had placed a cover over the plate, so it looked like it was there, and they didn't get stopped," Fortune explained. "The cover blurred it out just enough it couldn't be read."

"Which could mean that car is actually their car and not stolen," Mom looked between the detectives.

Fortune nodded, "Correct; which means Evilina is detailed oriented. She covered every little detail from covering the plate, finding a parking lot where the vehicles would be hidden, not coming back for the car until well after everyone was cleared from the lot."

"We couldn't find how she got there either...in the black hat," Monroe stated.

The video appeared again and was forwarded to the moment I could be seen running across the parking lot.

Monroe pointed to the monitor, "I timed the grey SUV from this point going backward. If she had driven straight to the blue SUV and moved the bag that had the unique blankets and the twins into it, she would have been pulling out of the parking lot as Ace was running toward the store."

"We would never have known," Fortune added. "We would have seen the grey SUV but without those baby blankets we never could have connected it to the kidnappings."

"We would have thought it was the wrong SUV we followed," I nodded with a frustrated exhale and glanced at Sammie.

"After all her meticulous planning, so detail oriented from the wedding and the clinic, her only mistake was actually going into the store," Taylor huffed.

"The only other thing is the fact she wore a blonde wig," Fortune stated. "As the Pendleton cowboys pointed out, there is no reason to use a wig unless you want to cover your natural color. She didn't want to dye her hair for a reason."

"Because she is The Shirt," Sammie said. "She didn't want Ace or G-Ranger to recognize her."

"BUT there is NO evidence or connection between them," Monroe said. "It's speculation."

"Logical speculation," Taylor shrugged.

"I don't understand how a woman trying to sleep with Ace or Granger has to do with the kidnapping," Liam frowned.

"She was trying to date them so one of them would take her to the wedding and she would have an excuse to be there," Barry explained.

"I didn't think buckle bunnies were dated," Monte looked at him. "I thought you only..." His eyes widened and he quickly glanced at Mom. I quelled a chuckle.

Monroe contained a smile before looking at everyone, "There is absolutely NO evidence that she is the kidnapper."

"And, as we discussed..." Fortune started.

"No looking into who The Shirt really is," Granger interrupted.

Fortune continued, "If The Shirt's image gets out and someone recognizes her, then it's insinuated that she was the twins' kidnapper, you put her in immediate danger."

"And set yourself up for a hell of a defamation lawsuit," Barry nodded.

"Have you shown this to Martin and the Rawlins?" Granger asked.

"Yes," Fortune answered. "We've kept them up to date and they wanted to make sure you three are up to date in case it shook up any other memories."

"You're not going to discuss with us the females the Pendleton group led you to since you now have the image," Sammie said. "And the video didn't shake up anything for me."

"Me either," Granger and I added.

The video on the monitor disappeared.

"Thank you for coming to meet with us," Mom said and walked to the door. "We do appreciate it, but we have a long drive home tonight."

"Understand, I do miss these rodeo road trips." Detective Fortune nodded and looked between Granger, Sammie and me. "We'll get out of your way and let you know if we come up with an identity on either woman."

Mom glanced at me, "Taylor will walk them to their car, and Barry, the boys, and I will go find us something to eat before we leave."

I gave her a 'thank you' hug before they descended out the door leaving Granger, Sammie, and I alone in the now quiet trailer. Sammie was leaning against the counter while Granger sat on the stairs that led to the upper bedroom. I stood quietly for a moment then exhaled deeply.

"Sorry guys," I whispered as the weight of the loss finally hit my gut.

"It's only one year," Granger smirked. "We got lots of years ahead of us."

"Yeah," Sammie nodded with a smile. "Starting Saturday, we have all year to make it happen again. I just want to know one thing."

"What's that?" I sighed.

"Do they really think we're not going to investigate The Shirt?" She chuckled

"No shit," Granger huffed. "What Monte said…"

There was a tap on the door.

"Damn," I whispered and looked at my best friends. "I wanted a few more minutes to let my brain settle."

Another tap.

"I'm guessing they know we are in here," Sammie sighed and walked in front of me to open it.

Lonnie was on the other side and smiled at her then looked up at me, "We were just getting ready to leave but I wanted to stop and see you first."

Sammie glanced back at me then stepped out of the trailer with Granger following her. I knew they were there to help me handle the sudden tightness in my chest.

"Been a hell of a year," I stepped out of the trailer.

"Let's hope next year has us both up in the single digits so we don't have this battle again," Lonnie huffed.

"That is definitely my plan," I forced a smile. "Taylor is roping again so we'll be adding team roping to the arsenal."

"Roping with your brother," Lonnie said wistfully. "Really wished my brother would have gotten into roping, too. That would have been fun."

"It is," I nodded.

"Well," Lonnie hesitated with a look at Sammie and Granger. "I just wanted to say have fun and kick ass."

"What they hell does that mean?" Sammie's back straightened and she stepped toward me.

Lonnie looked at her in surprise then back to me, "My wife crunches the numbers after every rodeo. She said this morning that I had to earn more than you tonight to make it in."

"Yeah," Granger grumbled. "Sammie's crunched the numbers and said the same thing."

"You got the win," I managed to say through a tightened jaw.

Lonnie's brows shot up and he shook his head, "I may have gotten a better time, but the fucking calf kicked free."

There was silence as the air rushed into my lungs and blood raced through my ears.

"What?" Sammie gasped and her hand shot out to my wrist and squeezed.

Lonnie looked at her then over to Granger's surprised expression. "And that," he nodded to Sammie's hand. "Is the only reason that this isn't as heart breaking as it should be," he sighed with a shrug. "I know how hard the three of you have worked for this as a team; iron sharpens iron. I believe in that and highly respect it. If I'm going to stay home, then I can take a bit of solace the three of you get to do it together."

He stretched out a hand and without much thought I gripped it and shook tightly, "I'm sorry, this is just..."

"I know," Lonnie tipped his hat to Sammie. "Like I said, 'have fun'."

As he walked away, the three of us just watched in silence. When he disappeared around a truck, I turned and stepped back into the trailer with Sammie and Granger right behind me.

My hands began to tremble.

Mexican trumpets filled the air and I turned to see Sammie grinning and setting her phone on the counter.

"Fuck yeah," Granger laughed, grabbed her hand and twirled her around.

I grabbed her other hand and twirled her again. Then we laughed, started dancing to Wine, Beer, Whiskey until the door flew open and Taylor was there grinning. He joined the celebration.

CHAPTER FIFTY

ACE

"Why didn't we think of this before?" Sammie stood, hands on hips, and glared at me.

"I don't know," I waved at Liam and Monte as they walked up the steps to our house; each holding one of Sammie's puppies. They were upset they couldn't go with us, but more than happy to puppy-sit for her. "We've been a bit busy the last month...too much to think so far ahead."

"We're fine for Rosenburg and Hempstead," Granger opened the trailer door and tossed in his bag.

"But when we go to Nile?" Sammie huffed. "We're headed to the Circuit Finals in Redmond after that, so I'll have both horses with me."

"What do you suggest?" Taylor smirked.

"I don't know," she grumbled and looked down the length of her truck and horse trailer. "Sergeant , Grace, Stomping Dog, Quincy, and now the team roping horses? We'll need a 6 or 8- horse trailer to be able to haul together. My dad has one with a living quarters section, but I don't think he'll let us borrow it for the whole year."

"We'll have to take two trailers," Granger nodded.

Sammie was near tears, "But I like traveling with all four of us in the truck. It's fun."

"I agree," I nodded. "But we don't really have much of a choice."

"Would you rather I not ride?" Taylor asked with a teasing raised brow.

"Of course not," she glared.

"We'll just have to be strategic in rodeos and traveling next year so we only have to take two part of the time." I shrugged and tossed my bag into the trailer and shut the door. "Let's worry about it when the time comes. We're fine this weekend, so let's just go have fun."

"We have our anniversary party after the rodeo in Rosenburg," Granger told her. "No worrying about the future...just celebrating our first year together."

Sammie smiled, "I agree, and we'll pick up Mason on the way to Nile so he can ride home with me."

"Then, let's get going, Lady Driver," Granger opened the driver's door for her.

It only took ten minutes for the conversation to begin on The Shirt and Evilina.

"Anyone heard from the detectives?" Taylor asked.

"Just a text reiterating not to look into her or share the image," I answered.

"Do you think he really believes we're not going to?" Sammie chuckled.

"No, that's why he sent the text," I grinned. "Just covering his butt when we do."

"I agree with not sending her picture anywhere," Granger added. "But that doesn't mean we can't show it to people while we're at the rodeos."

"Agreed."

I nudged Bear into the back of the box and looked down at the steer in the chute, then glanced at Taylor on his bay, One Spot. Thousands of times we had been across from each other, but no time meant as much to me as this one. The vision of Rob kicking him off the steps, then jumping on his shoulder flashed and I had to turn away from him and move Bear out a step and move him around. A deep breath to contain the compression in my chest and I glanced at Taylor again. He nodded because he felt it, too. This was our chance for a restart; to not let Rob win and take away our dream.

"Just like any other day," Taylor called out and I took another deep breath and looked at the steer.

A nod and we bolted out of the box with my arm swinging the lariat as I had thousands of times before. It was a perfect throw followed by the turn and glancing back at Taylor's throw. Both legs were captured, and we turned quickly. When the official flag went down with a clean run, the anxiety in my chest released with a whoop from both of us. We could hear Granger and Sammie yelling from the exit gate.

We were more than happy to drive away from the arena with a 4.3 second, third place paycheck. Sammie and Sergeant placed second with Granger taking the win. It was a great start to our year. The drain and exhaustion from the last three months melted away as the energy and anticipation for the new year grew.

Not one person we showed the image of The Shirt knew who she was.

Saturday night, when we parked in Rosenburg for the Sunday performance of the rodeo, the horses were stalled, lawn chairs pulled out, and bottles opened. Every person that walked by, we showed them the picture, and no one knew her.

"I've been thinking about what Monte said the other day," Granger leaned back in his chair, crossed his legs at the ankle and took a swig of his whiskey.

"What part?" Taylor asked.

"Me, too," Sammie nodded at him.

"What part?" I repeated Taylor's question.

"That buckle bunnies don't date," Sammie answered.

"Not all of them, some end up dating, and getting married," I corrected.

"True," Granger nodded.

"Nah, that's not what I'm saying," Sammie leaned forward with elbows on knees and looked at me. "From what I've seen, and I'm sure you three can correct me, but most, that are looking for a cowboy, know that they are just passing through and are just looking to hookup for a night."

"I'd say most," Granger nodded.

"Yeah...I guess," I sighed. Sunshine wasn't looking for a hook-up when we met. It just happened...we just connected the moment we met. It was too bad she lived in Georgia, but that didn't stop our having a fun week together. "Excluding competitors because I don't consider them buckle bunnies, I'd agree with you."

"The Shirt is beautiful with a hot body," Sammie continued. "She wouldn't need to come on so strong in the middle of the day."

"You pointed that out before and I agree," Taylor nodded.

"So, what if, she THINKS that's what buckle bunnies do all day?" Sammie looked between us again.

"What is the puzzle queen saying?" Granger frowned.

"We've been assuming she has something to do with rodeo," Sammie answered. "What if she doesn't? What if she was just trying to pass off as a buckle bunny and thought that's how they acted...which some do but most are going to wait until after the rodeo."

"How does your mind come up with that?" Granger shook his head with a smirk.

"Looking at the big picture then putting the small sections together," she shrugged.

"That would be scary," Taylor frowned. "That opens it up to more than the Cowboy Nation."

"Yeah," I nodded. "But, I kind of agree. Could be why the detectives are having such a hard time finding her."

"That woman could walk into any bar after the rodeo and have her pick of the cowboys...even some of the married ones," Sammie leaned back with a sigh. "If she would have approached you after a rodeo, would you have gone Hawaiian?"

"Yes," Granger shrugged. "That's what went through my mind the first second I saw her, and obviously with Tony, too." He looked at me.

"Yep," I nodded.

"Me, too," Taylor added with a grin. "Without a doubt."

"Then showing her picture at the rodeos isn't going to help," I sighed.

"Damn, Sammie," Granger smirked. "I hope you're wrong."

"Yeah," she sighed. "Me, too."

I jogged to the fence by the first barrel and glanced around the arena. Granger was in the first row of bleachers with his phone ready to video Sammie and Sergeant turn at the second. Taylor was set up behind the fence to the side of the third barrel and was kneeling to capture her at a different angle.

My phone was in-hand and ready when her name was called. There were three videos of Sammie's second win in a row at Rosenburg. With Granger placing third and Taylor and I placing fourth in team roping and my tie-down in third, the anniversary party of our first year together began. The first few hours were filled with drinking and laughter with friends stopping by. Then, the rain started and one by one the trucks and trailers departed the rodeo grounds.

"This damn rain is cramping our fun," Sammie grumbled as she stepped into the trailer.

After tossing the last lawn chair into the storage area of her truck I followed her through the door, "I totally agree."

"Cramping our style," Granger chuckled and plopped down on the sofa. Taylor sat on the steps that lead to the upper bed while Sammie opened the door on the stove.

"Just to commemorate last year...." She withdrew a chocolate frosted chocolate cake and placed it on the table, then took four forks out of the drawer and tossed them next to it.

"Awesome tradition," I slid onto the bench seat with Taylor next to me and Sammie and Granger across us.

Chocolate and laughter filled the next ten minutes of our lives. We took a picture of the four of us with chocolate covered teeth, lips, and each taking one last bite of the devoured cake. While Sammie giggled and posted it to our group page, I pulled out two bottles of Pendleton and shot glasses.

"Ain't nobody cramping my Pendleton style," Granger lifted the first fill shot glass into the air then it quickly disappeared. When he set the glass down onto the table, his eyes narrowed as if in deep thought. "Cramping my style..." he whispered.

"I thought cramping your style was just about me getting in the way of you handing out some Hawaiian leis." Sammie's whiskey was quickly tossed back.

"You and Mom," Granger grinned at her then his hand froze in the air as he was about to down another glass. He looked at her with an odd glare.

"What?" Sammie huffed. "Didn't you say something about your mom cramping your style before?"

"Yeah...yeah..." he nodded. "That's just it."

"What?" Sammie, Taylor, and I asked in unison.

"That got stuck in my head in Pendleton and I couldn't figure out why," he mumbled and tossed back the third shot. "Mom said it when she came back from the restroom in Joseph...after The Shirt walked away."

"So, your mom saw her, too?" Taylor slurred.

"Yeah, and, she said that The Shirt looked a lot like a lady she used to work with; said they could be sisters. I'll see if she has a picture." Granger reached for his phone.

"Thanks to Monte, we already know what she looks like," I poured another round.

"And we should just call her Evilina," Sammie tossed another drink down.

"I agree with the detectives," Granger shook his head. "Not until we connect her to the kidnapping." He poured another shot and tossed it back.

"I don't doubt it," Sammie's eyes rolled back, crossed, then she shook her head and giggled. "I think I better stop. We promised to have the horses out of the stalls by six in the morning." She stood and fell against the counter.

Granger's phone dinged and within a minute he was turning his phone to me, "She looks just like her."

The image was of his mother and a brunette smiling at the camera. There was a lake behind them. They looked happy and the brunette looked just like The Shirt.

"Like an older twin," I chuckled and downed another shot. My body was flushed, head feeling like a feather, but brain still focused...a little.

Sammie leaned on the table and over the phone as Taylor glanced at the image.

"Wow, just like her," Taylor slurred.

"I know!" Sammie stood quickly and fell back against the counter with a chuckle. "You should post the image and tell people you're looking for her."

"I'd look like an idiot," Granger grinned. "They would just ask why I don't ask my mom where she is."

Sammie bent over in laughter, bumped her head on the table, fell back against the counter with a grinning gasp, slid down the side of Taylor and then her butt hit the floor then fell back. She kicked her feet in the air in howls of laughter from all four of us.

Her hands came over her stomach and she began taking deep breaths to regain her composure.

"You, OK?" Taylor started to stand but fell back into his seat.

She chuckled and took another deep breath, "Yeah...just gonna lie here for a few minutes."

"Probably a good idea," I laughed and poured another shot for myself, Taylor, and Granger.

"I wasn't talking about the lady with your mother," Sammie sighed. "What if you posted that picture and said you were looking for a younger version of her."

"That you met in Joseph last summer," I nodded and tossed back the whiskey...telling myself it was the last one of the night.

"Isn't that going to look a bit desperate?" Granger drank the shot and popped the glass on the table.

Taylor tossed another back, "Who the fuck cares?"

"If it leads to identifying her, what difference would it make?" I nodded and my head swirled.

"Tell them you met that one time but didn't have time to spend time together," Sammie added from the floor.

"All you need is time," I sang.

"And you couldn't get your mind off her," Taylor turned his shot glass over indicating he was done.

Granger lifted his phone. With his head tipped back, eyes narrowed as he tried to focus, he typed on his phone. After a few moments, he handed me the phone, "How does that look?"

"Read it out loud," Sammie sighed. Her eyes were closed but she had her feet up and swinging in the air.

"Alright," I had to blink a dozen times to clear my focus enough to read. "The blonde in the image is my wonderful, beautiful mother. Please look at the pretty lady at her side. Last summer, in Joseph, Oregon, I met a beautiful woman that looks a lot like her. I was with family and friends at the time and didn't have time to talk with her. I didn't even have a chance to get her name. If you know someone that looks like her that would have been in Joseph the Thursday of the rodeo, please let me know so I can reach out to her."

"Add, 'I can't stop thinking about her'," Sammie's feet hit the ground.

"You couldn't connect that to Evilina," I yawned. "You're just looking for a pretty could-have-been a hookup."

"Sounds desperate," Granger chuckled.

"Romantic," Sammie rolled over onto her stomach and slowly lifted herself to all-fours.

"It might work," I leaned back and my whole body felt like it was going to melt into the cushions. "It would be like Angelina…"

As he had every time, I brought the woman's name up, Granger glared at me, "She has nothing to do with this."

"I'm not saying that," I slowly lifted a hand and waved away his attitude. "I'm saying, other than the cowboys that were around the fire the night you met, would anybody in the rodeo industry know her? As in, be able to look at her picture and know who she was?"

Granger shrugged, "No… and probably not even the guys around the campfire."

"So, this may be the same way if, like Sammie suggested, she really isn't in the rodeo industry."

"You think the detectives will be pissed?" She slowly started crawling to the steps that led to her room.

"You need help?" Taylor chuckled but didn't move from the bench.

"No…and we just ask permission…no forgiveness…or is it…shit…I can't think…" She made it to the steps and slowly crawled up them.

"If it's a good idea, ask forgiveness," I added, but that didn't sound right.

"No, it's better to ask permission not permission," Taylor chuckled with a shake of the head.

"That doesn't even make sense," Granger slid off the bench and placed the empty bottles and glasses on the counter. "It's better to ask permission than forgiveness."

"That's backwards..." Laughing, I slowly typed the words into the phone as Sammie managed to make it to the top of the steps to her bed and Granger stumbled to the couch and fell on it without pulling it down to a bed. Squinting to focus on the tiny phone screen and even tinier words I read the quote, "If it's a good idea, go ahead and do it. It is much easier to apologize than it is to get permission."

"That's not right either," Taylor stood and cleared the top of the table then lifted it to the side. "Get up."

I stood and fell back down twice before getting away from the benches so he could slowly make it into the bed. He fell forward, sideways onto the cushions with eyes closed and breathing already deep. I bounced off the counter until my hand flipped the lights off. My eyes were already closing when I fell next to Taylor and just before the darkness ascended, I wondered if Granger had posted the picture.

CHAPTER FIFTY-ONE

SAMMIE

My hand vibrated and eyes slowly opened to look at the phone clenched in my fingers. 5:15...it was only 5:15. I promised to have the horses out of the stalls by 6:00...forty-five minutes...I hit the snooze button.

It vibrated again and with a deep sigh, I opened my eyes again. How fast could I clean four stalls? I hit the snooze button again. Another ten minutes went by before it vibrated for the third time. Forcing myself to sit up, I looked down and was thankful I still had the clothes on from the day before. I didn't have to spend time getting dressed.

Promising myself a shower before we pulled out of the roundup grounds, I slid off the bed and down into the trailer. Granger was curled into the back of the couch cushions, so I pulled out a blanket and laid it across him. Another blanket was laid over the two brothers that were laying back-to-back and both had a low snore escaping them.

I would take care of their horses; the Lord knows they had helped me plenty of times.

When I opened the door to the outside, the air was fresh, and the ground was covered with puddles from the rain the day before. I changed into mud boots and slid on a hooded coat. One Spot and Bear, the team roping horses, were tied to the trailer first and I cleaned their stalls before stepping into Quincy's stall. He always tucked his nose into the halter. I patted him on the neck as we walked to the trailer. After tying him up next to the other two, I stroked his neck and smiled.

"You are so special," I whispered to him. "Ace couldn't have had a better partner this last year. 'Trust Quincy' How many times did we hear that called out? And you did your job perfectly every time. Maybe I need a t-shirt that says that." I chuckled to myself as he tucked his nose under my arm. "I will always love you, you special roan you."

With a final pat on his shoulder, I walked back to the stalls and cleaned out his before opening the door to Sergeant . The horse greeted me with a nose to the neck and a big exhale of breath across my skin. I laughed and spent a moment giving him attention before walking him to the trailer. He was tied next to Quincy.

I turned to walk away when a truck appeared in the distance. All four horses' heads went up and turned to look at the truck. I quickly took the perfect picture of their well-rounded rumps facing me and heads held high at attention watching the truck.

Post to Social Media:

Meet the "A-Team". On the left is my main guy, Sergeant who, yesterday, gave us our second consecutive PRCA win in Rosenberg and was my leading man in qualifying for the NFR this December. And with the battle call of 'Trust Quincy' you have the roan gelding himself who paired with Ace for an outstanding year that will be taking them to the NFR. Ace could not have had a better horse...no one could have had a better horse than Quincy. Yesterday, they placed third at the rodeo in the beginning of our qualifying for next year's trip to Vegas. Then we have the new crew on the road with us; One Spot and Bear. Taylor has joined us for team roping with his brother on these two horses that just happen to be brothers. Little-known fact; Quincy, One Spot, Bear and my beautiful black mare, Grace, are all out of the same mare, Maggie. She was the last horse the brothers' late father had ridden. How awesome is that?

We'll be on the road soon as we head to 'the next one'.

Love and safe travels.

Just as I finished cleaning the last stall, my phone began to ring but I didn't recognize the number.

"Hello?"

"Sammie, what the hell were you four thinking?"

My mind froze as I tried to think who was on the phone and what the hell did we do?

"Um, what?" I whispered.

"This is Detective Fortune, and I just read Granger's post from last night."

"Oh...." I tried to remember what he was talking about. All I could think of was Angelina was mentioned and something about permission...or forgiveness. "OK...but, aren't you in Oregon? Isn't it a bit early there?"

"No, I'm in Washington, and yes, it is 4:15 in the morning, which gives me a little chance to get ahead of the onslaught that is headed our way."

"I'm sorry, Detective, but I'm not really remembering what he posted. We had our one-year anniversary party yesterday after the rodeo and, well, we were pretty inebriated."

I heard a slight exasperated chuckle.

"Well, that explains the chocolate cake picture," he sighed. "I'll wait while you read it."

"Ok...," I put the phone on speaker and opened Facebook. "But, if Granger posted it, why are you calling me?"

"Because I saw your post on the horses come through and knew you were awake."

I read the post and looked at the picture of the two women again, "She really does look like an older version of The Shirt."

"Yeah, and did you guys get permission from her to post this?"

"Oh, well no. It happened all too fast...and fuzzy."

He huffed a chuckle, "I'll reach out to Shayla and see if I can contact her. I've already had to hide a dozen names that were posted."

"You did?" I gasped.

"You gave Monroe and I administrative rights to be able to monitor the site and we can't have these names out there like that."

"But, it doesn't link to the kidnapping or Evilina at all. The woman would never contact Granger because she would have to explain why she was all over Ace first."

"It just gives us a name we would be able to look into," he sighed.

"You could have deleted the post."

"Yeah, but after the first couple of names came through, and one of them three times, I could see it might help. It's just going to have to be monitored constantly."

"And that's why you're awake at 4:15 in the morning?"

"A detective doesn't have regular 8-5 working hours and I have to work other cases besides this one. I just happened to see it."

"What name came through three times?"

"Cassie Osborn."

"I don't recognize that name."

"Her Facebook page was public, so I went through her past pictures. She definitely looks like the woman from Monte's picture...I'd say it was her. And, six months ago, she posted a picture with a blue SUV and a month ago posted about buying a new green car."

"Wow," I huffed and searched the woman's name on Facebook. "Nothing about a trip to a rodeo?"

"Nothing at all with rodeos, horses, or cowboys. Also, no mention of traveling anywhere."

Three times I searched the name and didn't find a brunette woman, "I can't find her on Facebook. How did you?"

"Just a minute...well, the account is now private, and I can't get in either."

"That's suspicious."

"Or, it's not her and she is already getting hassled by people. Which is why I keep removing names."

I stepped up into the trailer and all three men were still sleeping but I turned on my laptop and the large monitor on the wall. "Did you save her profile picture before it went private?"

"Yes, I'll message it to you." He was still on the speakerphone, so his voice echoed into the trailer.

My phone vibrated so I pulled up the image. The same eyes that were looking into Monte's phone were now looking from mine.

"That is her," I gasped.

"I'd say so," Fortune sighed. "We know who she is and have a bit of confirming information so now we need to remove the post."

"OK, I'm on now and will remove it." I scrolled to the post and screenshot not only the post but all the comments that had been added. "You saved the hidden comments?"

"Yes, remove it."

I clicked the 'delete post', refreshed the page, and double checked the feed. "I did, can you still see it?"

"No, it's gone. I'm going to work on this. You four stop investigating."

"Yeah, we'll do that," I lied with a grin. "When Granger wakes up, we'll check his private messages."

"REMEMBER, there is absolutely NO EVIDENCE that this woman has anything to do with the kidnapping and have a good morning."

The phone call ended, and Granger appeared at my side. I handed him my phone with Cassie Osborn's image displayed.

"Holy fuck, it worked." His voice was full of morning rasp.

I googled the woman's name.

"Fortune wants you to send him any private messages you received."

"I heard that," he turned and retrieved his phone.

"I deleted the post, and you need to touch base with your mom," I glanced at him with a slight smile. "I guess, in our drunken posting, we should have contacted the lady with her to let her know what we were doing."

"Thought never crossed my Pendleton-soaked mind," he chuckled. "Why is Fortune up this early?"

"He said he is a detective and doesn't keep 8-5 hours."

"What the hell are you two mumbling about?" Ace grumbled from the bed.

"Cassie Osborn," I answered and reviewed the dozens of images that appeared on the monitor. Only a couple were the woman we were searching for.

"Who is that?" Taylor huffed.

"The Shirt." I announced and clicked on one of the images that appeared.

"What?" The brothers scrambled from the bed.

The four of us stood and reviewed the images we could find as I told them of the conversation with Detective Fortune. "He wanted us to remember that there is no evidence this woman is Evilina."

"Except the blue SUV that she sold a month ago," Taylor huffed.

"Right after the kidnapping," Ace added.

"Where does she live?" Granger asked and pointed at one of the pictures. "That looks like a business headshot."

I clicked the image and the website for a dental clinic appeared. Her image was part of six images with descriptions of their job duties displayed.

Cassie is a critical part of our administrative team. She is currently working part-time and going to college for her degree at the University of Colorado. Every morning, she will assist you to your private exam room and when you're ready, she will go over the insurance and billing steps with you. You'll be well taken care of by this effervescent, intelligent team member.

"The clinic is in Colorado Springs," Ace pointed to the address on the screen.

"How long will it take to get there?" I turned to him.

He shook his head with a chuckle, "We are almost at the bottom of Texas and that is past the top of Texas. We're looking at about 14 hours of driving."

"Plus, we have to drop the horses off at the ranch," Taylor added.

I turned to walk to the back of the trailer. "You guys load the trailer and get us ready. I'll take a quick shower and the first shift driving."

A half hour later, I was driving out of the rodeo grounds with Granger across from me and the brothers in the back. Our first stop was the grocery store for aspirin, water, energy drinks, and doughnuts.

"Did you get any private messages?" I asked Granger.

"Yeah," he chuckled. "Most asking me if I was desperate, a few ladies volunteering, and then a couple people offering names. The post was deleted by the time most people even woke up to read it."

"You think Fortune called Martin and the Rawlins?" Taylor asked.

"I doubt it," I answered. "I'm not sure if he would have told us if it wasn't for the fact it was our page and G-Ranger's post."

"I think we wait until we know something more," Granger said.

"So, what are we going to do?" Ace asked seconds before his phone began to ring. "Hey, Lauren." He was quiet for a moment before exhaling deeply. "Seriously? That is so cool. Yeah, I'll tell her. When are they going to do it?" Another long pause. "Alright, we're headed to the ranch to drop off the horses before we go kill some time. We have the Nile rodeo next weekend up in Billings then taking some time off. You want us to bring them over after that? OK, will do. See you next week."

"What?" Taylor asked the second he lowered the phone.

"Well, Sammie's post this morning about the horses being related drew some interest," Ace grinned. "A couple companies have called and want to do specials on Maggie and all her horses competing in the NFR and those that were on the road but didn't hit the top 15."

"That's awesome," I cried out in sheer delight.

"That means Delaney and Maestro as well as Sammie and Grace," Granger glanced at me with a wide grin.

"And Jamie with her horses," Taylor added. "As well as Lauren's horses since she made the top 5 in breakaway."

"It's going to be something pretty special," Ace exhaled. "Dad is going to be all over this coverage into the Finals."

"That used to bother you," Taylor whispered. "You OK now?"

Ace's voice shook when he spoke, "After this last year and seeing what it takes to make the NFR? And he did it eight times. I am so damn happy...so damn proud to be his son and have you and him mentioned in every damn thing we do." He leaned his head back and placed his hands over his eyes. "Everything about this last year...how it was almost taken from us...coming back only to get you, me, and Dad mentioned together in the NFR books? I couldn't be..." His voice trailed off.

I had to wipe tears away as I thought of that moment in the fields behind Lauren's barn the winter before when we discussed his father and brother. Pride filled my heart.

After a few minutes Ace spoke again, "Lauren told me to tell you *thank you*, Sammie. She'll call you with the time and date which will probably be late next week."

"I'll be there," I declared. Nothing would make me miss that.

"It's 7:30 here so 9:30 for Fortune," Granger changed the subject. "I say we give him until we drop off the horses then call and decide what to do."

"Agreed," I nodded.

"You good driving Sammie?" Ace asked.

"Yes," I answered.

Within minutes, the brothers were leaned against the doors and breathing deeply as they fell asleep.

At 1:00 our time, just as we were nearing the Conner ranch, Detective Fortune called.

"You sober?" The detective's voice echoed in the cab of the truck.

"Yes," Ace chuckled. "On the road all morning; we're about five miles from the ranch."

I had slowly been waking but sat straight up when I heard the detective's voice.

"You have a few minutes to talk then," Fortune said.

"You're on speaker so we all hear you," Ace said. "Did you get more on Cassie Osborn?"

"Limited amount," the detective answered. "There is only so much we can do without a warrant."

"Then get one," I huffed.

Fortune sighed, "Well, Sammie, I would love to, but I cannot go to the judge and ask for a warrant because a woman tried to hook up with a cowboy or two. Remember, there is no evidence that she is involved in the kidnapping; none, zilch, nada."

I sighed in frustration, "Well...damn."

"I called and talked to the people that identified her on your Facebook page but most of them just knew who she is, but not much about her. But we lucked out because one of them went to school with her last year."

"College?" Granger asked.

"Yes, they are hoping to make movies someday and were taking a videography class together," Fortune huffed.

"Videography?" I gasped.

"That means she knows all about those little cameras," Ace nodded.

"You have to be pretty detail oriented for that, too," Taylor added.

"Correct," Fortune agreed. "But, again, no evidence she's involved. When I could get into it, there was nothing on her page and no one I talked to could say whether she had been in Joseph or Spanish Fork this summer. No matter how hard we are trying to make her Evilina, we just can't place her there. There is a very good chance we're just wasting time with this."

"So, now what?" Granger sighed.

"Monroe and I will continue to monitor the leads you four have coming in. You DO NOT investigate. No more inebriated posting," he ordered.

There was silence in the cab as Ace turned down the driveway of their family ranch.

"Tell me you heard me," the detective grumbled.

"We heard you," the four of us answered.

"I'll call you back when we have something," Fortune said and the call ended.

Ace stopped the truck and trailer in front of the barn, "Do we take the trailer or not?"

"Let's leave it here and just get a hotel," I suggested.

"Where is everyone?" Granger opened the door.

"Lil Bros are in school, Mom is in town," Taylor answered.

Thirty minutes later, our overnight bags were tossed in the truck and we were driving back down the driveway.

"Put the clinic address in the GPS and let's see how far and what time we're getting in," Ace said.

I was sitting cross-legged in the passenger seat with my laptop in front of me as I searched the clinic, put in the address, and stared at the screen.

"How late are we getting in?" Ace asked.

"How far?" Taylor asked.

"Speak, Sammie," Granger chuckled.

I shook my head with a dumbstruck huff, "You're not going to believe this."

All three men leaned in to look at the screen.

"We need to make a plan," Ace exhaled.

"We need to make some phone calls," Granger nodded.

"I need to call my brother." I whispered.

CHAPTER FIFTY-TWO

SAMMIE

"He doesn't look like a cowboy," Granger said softly from the backseat of the truck but leaning over the center console between myself and Ace.

"He did exactly what I said," I lowered down in the front seat and peered over the dash. "He laughed at me and said he didn't have anything that wasn't cowboy, so he had to go shopping."

Mason, dressed in dark green carpenter pants, matching Keen slide-on shoes with no socks, and a black short-sleeved polo shirt tucked in tightly walked to the corner of the dental clinic parking lot. He positioned himself between two cars, so he was hidden from anyone driving into the lot.

Somewhere, hidden in the trees alongside the clinic property was Taylor. "I see her green car pulling in." His voice echoed from the speakerphone on Ace's phone.

The clinic shared the large, asphalted parking lot with the store behind us. A curbed landscaped path divided the main store vehicle lane and the clinic employee parking spaces. A few trees set at each end of the clinic lot but the low bushes next to the curb let us see the green car appear and turn into a space.

"I sure hope this works," Granger said softly as we lowered even farther into the seats.

As her door opened, Mason began a casual walk toward the clinic so that he was next to her when she stepped out in light blue pants and a white sleeveless shirt. Her long dark hair was now trimmed into a straight bob to her shoulders. It was also lightened to a caramel brown with blonde highlights.

"Her car wasn't the only thing she changed," I whispered. "She's still beautiful."

"Good morning," Mason's voice filtered from his hidden phone and into mine that was sitting on the console between us. The speaker phone was just low enough we knew they couldn't hear. "Do you work here?"

Her answer was too far away to hear but she nodded with a very wide smile.

"Oh, she likes him," Ace whispered.

"He is my brother," I smirked. "I've seen a whole lot of pretty girls chase him. That's why I thought he could be our bait."

"Looks like the first step of your plan is working," Granger added.

Mason's voice stopped our chatter, "Do you open this early?"

She shook her head, and we could hear, "...coffee..." as she pointed across the parking lot.

Mason glanced at the building then turned and gave her his most charming smile, "I just moved into town and was going to see if I could schedule an appointment. Can I buy you that coffee while we wait?"

"How in the hell did you guess that?" Taylor whispered over the phone.

"Because if I worked in a clinic across from a Starbucks, I would go there every damn morning before work," I grinned. It just made sense.

Cassie threw what she was holding into the front of her car and shut the door. With a pleased expression she turned to Mason, "We might just have to make it two."

They began a slow stroll across the parking lot with Cassie walking with a swing of the hips and an occasional lean toward Mason.

"Girl is working it," Granger chuckled.

"Well, Sammie," Ace said as the pair made it through the store doors. "You're two for two. We've got her right where you want her. Now what?"

"It's 7:15 and the clinic opens at 8:00 so we see what Mason can get out of her," I rose in the truck and stared at the store door.

"Where did you move from?" Cassie's voice carried into the truck.

It was louder now, as if Mason had been able to get his phone closer to her. We listened to him lie to her about moving from Springfield, Missouri. It was a town a non-rodeo person wouldn't associate with cowboys.

"What about you?" He asked. "Have you lived here long?"

"Here and Fort Collins all my life," she answered. "I've thought about moving, but just haven't done it yet. Maybe after I finish college."

"I've been fortunate to live in a few different states, and my construction job has let me travel the country so I can see how other people live," he chuckled. "Have you?"

"A few times to Yellowstone with my family when I was little," her voice was sweet with a flirty lilt.

"Oh, you need to get out in the world," Mason's voice was warm and caressing. "Especially to the coast."

"Have you been to both? Which do you like more?"

"I love the sunrise in the East and the sunset in the west over the ocean. They both just seem to fill your heart and fill you with energy. Have you been to either?"

"I haven't been East, but I traveled west a few times this summer, but didn't make it to the ocean."

Ace, Granger, and I smiled at each other.

"All the way over there but not to the ocean? That's a shame," Mason sighed. "You must have been there for work."

"I've always wanted to go to New Orleans...Burban Street...see some of the Blue's bands in person." Her voice had risen in volume. "Have you been there?"

"Yes, and I can't say enough about the food," Mason agreed. "You can't beat the food; gumbo, Jambalaya, and some of the best shrimp you can imagine."

"Sounds delicious," she purred.

We patiently waited through another ten minutes of food talk. I looked at my phone for the time...they only had a few minutes left before she would need to go to work.

"A little, but not much," Ace sighed. "So, it's our turn?"

"Let's shake her up a bit," Granger opened the door and the two men slid out and hid behind the truck. The window was open so they could still hear the conversation in the store.

"I do need to get to work," Cassie sighed.

"I understand." Mason answered and they were quiet for a moment until the door of the building opened and they strolled out. "Would you be interested in lunch?"

Her laughter was light, "I'd love to. I won't have much time from the end of my shift here to my first class…maybe just another 40 minutes or so."

"I'll pick you up here then," Mason calmly walked next to her with a glance up the parking lot toward my truck.

Ace and Granger waited until she looked at Mason with a wide smile then nonchalantly stepped out to the vehicle lane between my truck and the clinic. Both in cowboy boots and hat, blue jeans and long-sleeved button-up shirts. They looked like they were walking into a rodeo. Granger turned to Ace with a wicked smile causing Ace to grin. Both men were very good looking, and with the conspiratory humored shine in their eyes, any woman would give them a second or third look. There was no way their target was going to miss them.

Cassie's hand reached out to Mason's arm as she giggled softly. Just twenty feet from the two men walking toward her, she turned and looked at them. Her eyes widened as they shot between the pair and her smile seemed to freeze. She quickly turned toward Mason as if to hide her face.

"Excuse me," Ace stopped and tipped his head to her. "Don't I know you?"

She barely glanced at him, "No."

Mason stopped and she took a step before hesitating.

"We've met," Granger stepped toward her making her step closer to Mason. "At one of the rodeos...Joseph, wasn't it?"

Her eyes widened and chin dropped.

"No, it was in Utah," Ace shook his head.

"I don't know you...either of you," she huffed with a trembling hand tucking her hair behind her ear.

"Are you alright?" Mason asked with concern dripping from the question. His hand reached out to her elbow as if to support her.

"I'm fine, I'll see you here for lunch." She smiled at him then looked back at Ace and Granger. "I don't know you and I have to get to work." She turned toward the clinic, took a step and stopped with a sharp inhale. Taylor was standing at the front of her car innocently looking at his phone and seemingly not paying attention to the small group.

"Your hair was longer," Granger smiled with a nod. "We barely had a chance to talk."

"No, it was Spanish Fork," Ace glared at him then smiled at Cassie. "I was with my brothers, so we didn't have a chance to talk or get to know each other."

"I don't know you," her voice rose. "I have not been to Spanish Fork or Joseph."

"Are you alright?" Mason repeated.

"I don't need to work this morning...let's just go ahead and do breakfast instead of lunch. Shall we go?" She smiled at him with a glance at Ace and Granger.

"Sure," Mason nodded. "I'm riding with my sister, so I'll need to ask her."

All four turned and looked at my truck as I opened the door and stepped out. She couldn't see me until I closed the door and stepped toward the front.

Her hand tightened on Mason's arm and eyes widened in shock, "She's your sister?"

"Well, yeah," Mason smiled at me. "I didn't get the red hair, but..." He stopped and looked down at her. "You know Sammie?"

Cassie tossed his arm away from her and she turned toward her car and Taylor. Monte, Liam and Charlene were now standing next to him. Taylor and Charlene were looking at their phones, while the Lil Bros were kneeling and playing with my puppies. She stopped in her tracks and looked back at the men then to me. Her eyes widened when she saw my parents standing next to me.

"What the hell...?" she exhaled.

"My parents are with us, too," Mason smiled and looked at her. "You look like you know them."

She shook her head and stepped back, "I don't know any of you." When she started to turn, her eyes stopped on Adam and River Westmoreland as they walked down the vehicle lane and passed by her with a slight smile and nod. They walked past the group and disappeared toward the front of the store.

Cassie took a deep breath and after a hesitation, she turned back to Granger and Ace. "I admit it."

I had to contain a gasp.

"Admit what?" Granger asked calmly.

She took another deep breath and smiled at him, "I was in Joseph and hit on you after I had hit on you." She looked at Ace. "I saw you in a video and thought I'd fulfill a cowboy fantasy, but it was ridiculous, so

I came home. There, I admit it, and now I have to get to work." She turned to Mason. "It seems like you are busy with your family, so we'll just pass on the lunch."

Now what? My mind scrambled to come up with a plan. I wasn't sure what we had hoped for but for her to just admit the innocent part and not give us a clue to Elivina wasn't going to work. How could I be so wrong on this? I was sure I was right.

Granger and Ace turned and looked at me expectantly.

A car slowly passed by us with Cassie glancing at the driver. Shayla smiled at her and continued to drive down the car lane, turn the corner, and pull into one of the spaces next to my truck. Cassie had watched her, then turned away from our group. With a glance to the right to make sure there were no cars approaching, she stopped.

I turned to see a long white four-door pickup had pulled sideways in the vehicle lane blocking it so no driver could get by them and to our group. They were forty yards away, but we could see the back door on the side facing us open. After a hesitation, a figure stepped out with boots hitting the ground and then beginning a slow stroll towards us.

I glanced at Cassie who was watching the approach with narrowed eyes and lips rolled tightly. Her face warmed to a deep pink and fingers began to tremble.

The petite, short-haired blonde Lacie Jae slowly walked toward the woman with an unreadable expression, but her eyes didn't leave Cassie's. There was no hurry in her stride. When she stopped ten feet from the woman, Lacie Jae's head cocked slightly, and she gave her slight smile.

"I didn't have anything to do with it," Cassie whispered and took a step toward the clinic then stopped when Taylor, Charlene, and the Lil Bros stopped what they were doing and looked at her.

"Anything to do with what?" I asked calmly.

"I didn't do anything...," Cassie stepped back.

"I'm confused," Mason sighed. "Why would all these people be here if you didn't do anything?"

Her head jerked to him, then back to Lacie Jae whose sweet smile turned into a knowing smirk. Cassie stared at her then turned to watch Shayla walk up next to Granger. Silence ensued as cars pulled into the store parking lot and two cars pulled into the clinic parking lot.

Cassie watched as the people stepped out of the cars at the clinic, hesitantly waved at her then walked to the front of the building. After a few deep breaths, she glanced around the small group then stopped at Lacie Jae's stare. "I guess you were right," she whispered.

My heart nearly stopped, and hands turned to fists in anticipation of her next words.

Lacie Jae cocked her head slightly and her brows rose in silent question.

Cassie took another deep breath then turned back to give the petite blonde her full attention. "Somewhere, somehow I would make a mistake and I would be found."

My heart nearly burst! No one said a word or moved. I was afraid to even move.

Lacie Jae smiled with just a tip of the head forward to give the woman a snarling glare then whispered, "Welcome to the party, Evilina. Meet the Cowboy Nation."

When Lacie Jae's arms rose slightly from her side, people began walking from between cars. Doors to vehicles began to open with even more people joining the growing crowd. Women, men, children all lined the lane from beside us all the way down to the truck that was blocking the parking lot.

"What?" Cassie exhaled in disbelief as she looked at all the people that had attended the wedding and Craig's memorial clinic.

All the people we could reach by phone as we drove through Texas the day before stood quietly and watched her. I was very surprised when the two people that we did not call appeared behind the woman. Detectives Fortune and Monroe stood next to two men I did not know but assumed they were local law enforcement.

"As Lacie Jae stated on the podcast," I said loudly. "It would take an evil person to kidnap the twins of a dead man, so we gave you the name Evilina."

She glared at me with a bit of a snarl but didn't say a word.

Ace chuckled and drew her attention, "The one thing we were really confused about was why did you go to Safeway instead of a store like Walmart? But, when we travel, we always go to stores or restaurants we know...where we feel like we are home." He looked at the Safeway sign above the building that had the coffee shop inside.

"The grey car was stolen from Spokane, so you would have gone by the Safeway in Redmond and known where it was and how easy it was to get to," Granger added.

Cassie sighed and her shoulders lowered.

"But, why in the hell would you kidnap the twins of a dead man?" I huffed and could feel my own cheeks warm in anger. "How would you have even known about them?"

"That would be my fault."

We turned to a man that stepped forward toward Lacie Jae. I didn't know him, but I had seen pictures of the woman that approached with him. She was the twin's biological mother.

"I met Cassie at college," the man continued. "She was part of a group conversation when I was telling them about the twins and Martin's generosity and heart for paying for Gail's college tuition so she could go to school and still be part of the twins' lives."

"So, you weren't going to keep them, you were going to ask for ransom? You thought he was rich?" Granger growled at Cassie.

"I wasn't going to ask very much..." Cassie started then stopped when the echo of vehicle doors being shut reached us.

We turned to see Martin, Evan, Logan, Brodie, Delaney, and Camille standing by the truck that blocked the parking lot. Granger lifted his phone and ended the call that had allowed them to listen to the conversation.

Martin held the twins in his arms as he walked toward the group. The closer he got to us, the angrier his eyes glared, and his chest was rising and lowering as if trying to keep control. Cassie's breath caught and she took a step back, but Mason blocked her retreat. Adam and River appeared behind her.

Martin walked past Lacie Jae and stood within feet of the woman that had kidnapped his grandchildren. His body was visibly trembling.

"Do you know why I have them in my arms?" He growled. She shook her head as she looked between the babies then back to Martin. "Because holding them, is the only way I can keep my hands off your throat."

Cassie's arms wrapped around her waist as if to protect herself.

Goosebumps had risen on my arms from the threatening tone, and it must have affected the four detectives too as they stepped forward. I had no doubt that Cassie didn't even know they were there. The people that had appeared from behind the vehicles in the parking lot, filled the lane behind the family.

"I can't and won't physically tear you apart like I would like," Martin hissed. "But do you know what I can do?"

Cassie slowly shook her head with eyes wide and watched him closely.

"I'm going to go to your trial," he continued in a low menacing growl. "I'm going to sit through every minute of it. I'm going to stand up and testify to the jury on what a true pleasure and joy it was to raise Craig. To spend thousands of hours and miles together traveling to rodeos and clinics, to friend's ranches, or just sitting at home watching TV or cooking dinner together. I'm going to tell them how much my son meant to me. Then, I'm going to tell them about the sheriff at my door telling me he was killed...telling me that my son, my heart, the reason I looked forward to getting up every morning, was dead...that he wasn't coming home to me ever again. I'm going to tell them how it nearly destroyed me, how lost I was, how my heart had been torn out of my chest...how each day after he died, I thought of him...I mourned him every damn minute.

Then, I'm going to tell them of the second I learned of these two miracles I'm holding. I'm going to tell that jury about the first time I saw them, touched them, and how devasting it was when I realized that my son didn't know about his babies, and that they were going to grow up without knowing the love he would have given them." He paused and lifted the two babies higher in his arms. They curled into his shoulder and neck with eyes darting from each person around them. "I'm going to tell them what Ellie and Caleb mean to me and the entire family. How much love we have for them…how much seeing them every day gives us a little of my son back to us. They are healing my heart and my soul. Then, I'll let the jury know the shock, fear, anger, disbelief that someone would come to our home and take these miracles from us. And do it on the day we were honoring their dead father…how meticulous it was planned to do it that day." His head lowered and his voice trembled. "Then, do you know what happens next?" Her eyes glistened as she barely managed to shake her head. Fear radiated from her. "Craig's mother is going to take the stand and she's going to break every heart in the room." His menacing glare changed slightly to a warning. "By the time we are done testifying, every jury member, the judge, and every person in that room will hate you. They will despise you, and you will spend most of the rest of your life in a little cement room."

Her whole body trembled as the tears began to slide down her red cheeks.

Martin turned and handed Caleb to Lacie Jae and Ellie to Gail. When he turned back to Cassie the woman gasped and stepped back into the arms of Detectives Monroe and Fortune. They turned her away and walked her into the mass of cars.

Much to my surprise, Martin turned to me, took my arm, and pulled me into a strong embrace. I held him as tight as I could as his body trembled. Tears flowed from both of us.

The rising chatter from the hundreds of people around us had Martin finally taking a breath and rising away from me. His smile held relief and thankfulness.

"I don't even know what to say," he whispered to me. "I have lived every day wondering if she was going to try for them again. If it wasn't for you and that intelligent mind in solving puzzles, I don't know that we would have ever known."

My father wrapped his arm around me, "Don't mess with a stubborn, analyzing, red head."

Martin and my parents laughed as my whole body sighed in relief.

The next two hours were filled with an impromptu brunch at the back of the parking lot with everyone that had driven or flown in for the confrontation. There was laughter filling the air, especially from Martin. He was bent over walking slowly as each twin had a hold of his fingers balancing as they carefully walked to each side of him. Pride radiated from him as he grinned at the family in front of him. Once it was clear the twins were leading Martin to Evan in the wheelchair, Granger and Ace swooped in to lift them up and away from their laughing grandfather. They squealed in delight.

When everyone had slowly departed except for the Rawlins, Martin and our families, I crawled onto the tailgate of my truck and cuddled Jack and Jose. The two puppies always seemed to bring smiles to everyone and had entertained all the children at the party. They quickly curled around each other on my lap and fell asleep. Petting them softly, their sleeping made the energy in me begin to drain. The anxiety of the last twenty-four hours was catching up with me.

"Sammie?"

I looked up to see Lacie Jae and Logan walking up to me. "Hi."

Lacie Jae smiled at the exhausted puppies then up to me, "We wanted to thank you personally for all this."

"To putting closure to the kidnapping," Logan clarified.

"I'm so glad it is behind us," I sighed.

"Except for the court stuff," Lacie Jae shrugged. "But we know what happened, she's in jail and...now, our wedding is no longer a horrible event."

"It was never horrible," Logan shook his head.

"But having that woman use the wedding...," Lacie Jae said then took a deep breath. "That is past and now all those people at the wedding came here and made this even more impactive and now, looking back, I see the wedding as the beginning of Evilina's end."

"Good way to look at it," I smiled.

"And now," Logan grinned. "We can just rodeo."

"I'm with you there," I chuckled.

Mason slid onto the tailgate next to me and lifted a puppy onto his lap and smiled at the couple.

"We would like to thank you, too, Mason," Logan stretched out a hand to him. "You sure don't look like that cowboy I met at the birthday party last spring."

We all laughed.

"I had to have the clerk help me shop," Mason admitted. "But I have to say, they are comfortable."

"Well, you're very handsome," Lacie Jae grinned.

Mason glanced at the 6' 5", very wide steer wrestler, making him laugh.

"She does that on purpose," Logan grinned and slid an arm around her waist. "It's time to sweep her away...we're about to get back on the road."

Lacie Jae giggled and waved as he led her away.

Mason and I sighed and looked down at the puppies curled in our laps.

"I think they should go home with me," he glanced at me.

"Not happening," I yawned.

"Well, it looks like you won't be taking the first shift driving back down."

"I need sleep." I sighed. "I saw you talking to the twins' mother."

"Gail, she's a nice girl, kind of funny and smart. Giving Martin custody was pretty selfless."

"Who was the man that was with her? That blamed himself?"

"Her brother, Eric."

"So, he would have known," I nodded with another deep sigh. Liam came into view as he strode with a determined march right at us.

Liam stopped and grinned at Mason, "Mom said I could do it."

"Awesome," Mason nodded.

"Do what?" I looked between the two.

"Mom said I could go to Mason's ranch and take cutting lessons from him," Liam gushed.

"I thought you were going to try bucking horses," I chuckled.

"Nah, I liked riding the steers, but Monte liked the horses. He's going to try that, and Mom said I can try cutting or reining cow horse."

"That's a pretty good mom that will let you try out different disciplines," Mason said.

"I have the best mom ever," Liam grinned then turned and looked at our mother. "Yours is pretty good, too."

"We agree."

Taylor was taking the first shift of the drive back to the Conner Ranch while Ace sat in the passenger seat.

"That was a hell of a morning," Mason sighed as he relaxed into the seat in preparation for the long ride back.

I turned enough to lay my legs over his and lean back against Granger's arm.

Ace's phone shrilled into the cab of the truck, "It's Fortune."

"Think he's going to yell at us?" Granger chuckled.

"Only one way to find out," Ace grinned. "You're on speakerphone."

Fortune's voice echoed from the speakers of the truck, "You inebriated?"

We all chuckled in response.

"Probably the most productive inebriated post ever made," Fortune grumbled. "We got there as she and a gentleman were walking out of Safeway. Even though I'd seen his picture, I didn't recognize him and was as surprised as Cassie was when Mason said he was Sammie's brother."

I chuckled and opened my eyes to look at Mason's grin. "He's in the truck with us."

"Who called you?" Granger asked.

"No one," Fortune grumbled. "I had no doubt what you were going to do when you saw the store that shared the parking lot with the clinic. We flew in overnight and parked about five minutes before they walked out. I was so focused on you that I also didn't pay any attention to all the other cars that were filling up the parking lot. That was a pleasant surprise."

"Has she said anything?" Taylor asked.

"Nothing more than what she said at the store, but it is enough to get that warrant," Fortune answered. "Martin scared the hell out of her, and she just asked for a lawyer and wouldn't talk. It's going to take a couple hours before the attorney can meet with her. I honestly don't think she considered what would happen when she was caught."

"She had convinced herself she covered every detail," Ace added.

"And, except for a certain red head, she probably would have gotten away with it," Mason said.

"Was she on the list?" I closed my eyes.

"What list?" Fortune asked.

"The list you gave Ace and Granger in Pendleton," I explained.

"When we met championship morning," Ace said. "The people that had liked our social media pages after the sing-along night."

"Well, I didn't look at that," Monroe said to the ruffling of papers. "Let's see...yes, she was."

"We just hadn't gotten to investigate her yet," Fortune added.

"Then you would have seen her image and matched it and also seen the vehicle she sold," Granger said.

"But still wouldn't have had any evidence to match her to the kidnapping," Fortune clarified. "So, if it wasn't for that red head..."

"We all did it," I closed my eyes again, turned into Granger's arm, tucked in a little closer and let the exhaustion begin to take hold.

"No, you started us down the road at looking at her as Evilina," Granger smirked.

"Sammie?" Fortune said.

My mind was beginning to fade, and I just sighed.

"She's a bit comatose," Mason chuckled.

"Well, girl, if you can hear me," Fortune said. "You need to consider applying for the FBI."

I chuckled into the dark.

"Now, we can finally concentrate on that rodeo in December," Granger leaned back to the door.

"Well, look at that," Ace cried out.

I couldn't get myself to crawl out of the dark enough to know why he yelled.

CHAPTER FIFTY-THREE

GRANGER

"What?" I turned enough Sammie's head wasn't so kinked as she fell asleep.

"The back numbers have been posted," Ace answered.

"Perfect timing," Taylor chuckled. "Now that you can concentrate on the rodeo instead of the kidnapping, we can focus on all those fun details."

"Granger, you are #34," Ace announced. "Sammie is an even 60, and I am…#89."

"Which means the official standings are posted, too," I added.

"And again, Granger, you ended #7, Brodie is #6, Sammie is #5, and I am…well, son-of-a-bitch," Ace chuckled.

"What?" Taylor and I called out.

"I ended at 14th by $74," he chuckled then sighed. "Lonnie hit the crying hole by $76."

"Damn, close race" I sighed.

Mason glanced down at his sister then took his jacket off and rolled it into a ball then handed it to me. I wiggled enough to move Sammie's head and tuck the coat under her head then slid my arm up and over her which tucked me into the corner comfortably. I glanced at Mason, and he was already leaned back with eyes closed.

Last thing I remembered before my eyes closed was the brothers talking about Maggie and their dad.

Somewhere in the distance I heard, "We're going in to eat."

My eyes barely opened when the slam of the doors shot them open.

"What the hell?" Sammie muttered as she sat straight up.

"Where are we?" I yawned.

"Since my truck is right there, I'm going to say Amarillo, at Youngblood's Café." Mason opened his door and stepped out.

Sammie threw his coat at him and wiggled down the seat to follow him. "I'm freaking hungry."

Mason grinned at her, "Of course you are, but do something with that hair before we go in the restaurant. I don't want you to embarrass me in front of my friends that were nice enough to let me leave my truck here."

I laughed and opened the door.

Ace was on the phone when we entered the restaurant.

"He's checking with Mom to make sure the flight got them home," Taylor explained and watched Mason walk to the waitress.

She gave him a hug, a nod, and a full pot of coffee for him to bring to the table.

"I've ordered," Mason stated as he slid onto a chair and started pouring the coffee.

"For all of us?" Sammie asked.

"Yes, couple orders each of fries, nacho fries, stockyard burgers, chicken fried steak, and mash potatoes." Mason ran a hand down her hair to try and control it.

She giggled and pushed his hand away, "A cup of coffee then I'll go wet it down."

"Hungry much?" Taylor chuckled.

"What we don't eat is coming home with me so I don't have to cook tonight," Mason shrugged.

"Any word from Fortune?" I asked Taylor. "It takes 5 hours to get here so they should have something by now."

"I'll message him," Ace answered as he lowered the phone then started tapping on it.

Sammie disappeared to the restroom and returned with damp hair swept back. Her blue eyes shone with happiness.

"Well, that's a bit of an improvement," I smirked at her.

"G-RANGER!" She feigned irritation and slapped me on the shoulder. "Just for that, I want a group picture." She lifted the phone overhead and the four of us leaned in behind her. After lowering the phone, she giggled, and sent the image to social media.

"Fortune said he would call in fifteen minutes," Ace said as the first group of plates were placed in the center of the table.

Within those fifteen minutes we nearly finished every plate that had been delivered.

"So much for leftovers," Mason chuckled.

When the phone rang, Ace looked around at the nearly empty restaurant then set the phone in the middle of the table and hit the speaker button.

"You're on speaker with all of us and we're in a nearly empty restaurant," Ace warned.

"Good to know," Fortune said. "Detective Monroe and I are in an office at the police station...just the two of us."

"Did she talk?" Sammie asked.

"Like I said before," Fortune answered. "Martin scared the hell out of her, after having a meeting with an attorney she told us most of it."

"Most?" Mason asked.

"She had someone steal the car in Spokane and they helped her escape then get back to her car at Safeway," Fortune explained. "Then they ditched the car in the river. She told us, in our opinion, all of it except who that accomplice was because she won't get them in trouble. She said she would spend more time in jail than put them in one."

"Somewhat honorable," Taylor sighed.

"She's a bit...different," Fortune stated. "She isn't like most people, she lacks empathy."

"What does that mean?" Taylor asked.

"She thinks out the process and details," Fortune answered. "She only thought of the money. She came up with a 'fool proof' plan and just did it without thinking about the twins or how the family would react or how they would feel losing the twins because, in her mind, they weren't going to get hurt and they would only be gone for a few days. It wasn't until she heard Lacie Jae's podcast that she realized how bad it was with the family. When Martin made his speech, she realized how other people were going to react."

"She didn't even connect she was taking the babies on the day that was for honoring their father until she heard it on the podcast," Monroe said. "It was just how the opportunity played out in her plan."

"Very cold…" Mason huffed.

"She was an interesting interrogation," Monroe said. "We'll figure out who the accomplice was without her help; that person is just as responsible as she is."

"Agreed," we all nodded.

"So," Fortune said. "We are leaving the final sentencing agreement with Martin to approve but for now she will definitely be incarcerated for years, and we'll not have to worry about a court case. However, we have the warrant and will be investigating everything she has told us and getting evidence just as backup in case she changes her mind down the line. It will also help lead us to her accomplice. Eric was right, she did get the information about the twins from him and decided to take the twins because she knew Martin would pay anything for them. She said she was only going to ask for enough to pay off college and help her buy equipment and get set up for the future. Once she read about the wedding then the clinic she came up with a 'fool proof' plan. Just as Sammie had said, she saw the sing-along video and targeted Ace and Granger for the reason Sammie said."

"Why did she go into Safeway instead of leaving?" Sammie asked.

"The twins woke up and were crying so she went in for Benadryl to help make them go back to sleep," Monroe answered. "And, so you know, she has no idea how we connected her to the kidnapping."

"Which means," Fortune said. "Before Lacie Jae showed up, no one mentioned or accused her of anything. It was all in her own mind. When Lacie Jae walked up to her, Cassie had no idea that we had no evidence, at all, that connected her to the kidnapping. We also have no intention of telling her or her attorney. It's a detail that will keep her cooperating."

"She openly gave you a confession without anyone even questioning her," I pointed out.

"Which will go down in history, and no one will believe it," Fortune chuckled. "But, for now, put all this behind you and focus on getting ready for Vegas."

"That's our plan," Ace grinned.

"My wife and I have already purchased tickets and we'll be in the audience cheering you on," Fortune announced.

"I'll drive." I grinned at the group as they turned to me with wide eyes. "There is no long-ass trailer or champion horses attached so I can finally take a turn."

"A turn?" Sammie smirked. "You can drive the whole damn way."

As she said goodbye to Mason, I checked my phone for messages and saw her post with the image she took. It was a good picture of the five of us, but her words made me chuckle.

Sammie's Post:

How lucky am I? I have these handsome cowboys in my life as my best friends! And how lucky are they to have me as one of their best friends? I just love traveling with the four of them, I wish my brother, Mason, could travel with us more often.

This last year was quite the adventure and the next two months are going to be the icing on the cake!

It's time! Let's rodeo!

CHAPTER FIFTY-FOUR

Good Evening Everyone, this is Lori Ann Marker with *On The Road Rodeo News*;

We are just days away from the opening night of the National Finals Rodeo here in Vegas and I just spent a few hours with the "Iron Sharpens Iron" team of Ace Conners, Sammie Parkston, and Granger Miller. Ace's younger brother, Taylor, has now joined that team.

We discussed their last couple months of preparation for the rodeo and taking some time off.

Ace and Taylor have been roping, roping, roping! When they aren't on the road roping everywhere they can, then they have been home practicing. They are already in the top 20 of team roping for the year and are determined to make it to the top 10 by summer and stay there so they don't have a repeat of Ace's race this last September. Ace is also continuing with tie-down during the break with his buckskin, Stomping Dog. He gave Quincy November off from competition, but they are fired up and ready to start Thursday night.

Sammie also let her horses rest a few weeks after taking second in the Columbia River Circuit Finals. Then, she spent time with her family's cutting horse herd in Oregon and with her brother in Oklahoma.

After winning the average at the Circuit Finals, Granger has been fencing at the Westmoreland Stock Contractor's ranch and keeping himself tuned in with practice with the other saddle bronc qualifiers.

I asked who in their families would be joining them this week. Sammie's parents and brother are here. Granger's mother is here with him. Ace has his mother, all three brothers, and his late father's team roping partner, World Champion Heeler Barry Wilder. Barry has been Ace and Taylor's mentor since they started roping. Also, his cousin Lauren Conners is in the Breakaway Finals competing this Tuesday and Wednesday for the title.

Sammie and Ace brought their horses in early for check-in and health checks. That includes Sammie's main horse Sergeant and the black beauty known as Grace. Ace brought the gorgeous roan Quincy and Stomping Dog. The buckskin happens to be the horse Granger will be using for grand entry. Sammie will be riding one of her father's horses for the entry while Ace is riding his team roping horse Bear. That means they checked in six horses.

They have special dinners tonight then Tuesday is the big night when they receive their back numbers, jackets, and a large number of prizes. It's going to be just the beginning of the next fourteen days of event practice, entry practice, autograph signings, dinners, and the 10 days of rodeo action.

The one thing you will not hear this team talk about is the heroic rescue of the Houston twins and the capture of the woman who took them. They have already announced on social media their focus will only be on the rodeo and their families. Don't even ask, because they will just walk away. I understand, because it takes a lot of grit, determination, and focus to compete in this rodeo.

I'll be checking in with the trio all week long and will be one of the loudest in cheering them on each night.

CHAPTER FIFTY-FIVE

SAMMIE

Text from Sammie to Granger and Ace: WHERE ARE YOU?
Text from Ace: Coming around the corner.

I stepped away from the large doorway into the Thomas and Mack Arena and saw Ace and Taylor striding towards me. Behind them was Granger running at full stride and when he passed the brothers the two took off after him. The race was on toward me with wide grins and laughter ringing in the air.

"Glad you're hurrying; I've only got 5 minutes," I turned to the opening of the building and took Ace's arm to my left and Granger's to my right. Taylor stood just behind us with camera raised as we strode into the arena for the first time. When we stepped onto the arena dirt, I slid my hands from their elbows down to grip each of their hands. We squeezed tightly and took deep breaths.

"Well, we did it," Granger looked up to the mass of red seats, and then his eyes fell on the bucking chutes across the arena from us. "Those chutes are going to be much better than sitting in recliners and watching on TV."

We chuckled and nodded in agreement.

"Spur shot," Taylor said as he knelt on the ground.

We arranged our boots so all three spurs we had received for our birthdays were visible and he took a dozen shots.

"That's a special one for the parents," Ace turned back to the arena and our gazes wandered.

"Delaney said to take it in now, during practice, and cherish the grand entries. Then, it's all work each night and to tune it all out." I whispered and looked around the building at the people preparing for the rodeo.

"Barry said basically the same thing," Ace exhaled. "But, damn, all I can think about is Dad riding into this arena with him."

Granger nodded, "You and Taylor go over to the roping chutes and have your moment. We'll get your pictures then you have to focus."

A man standing at the gate that led to the roping box watched the two brothers walk toward him. It was clear he recognized them and nodded before swinging open the gate. They walked into the box and stood where their father had ridden for seven years, that should have been eight and more.

I couldn't hold back the tears and hands shook as I held the digital camera up. Granger took pictures with the brothers' phones.

"Let's give them some time," I whispered, and we walked away from the brothers as I looked at my watch. "I love we had that moment together, but I have to go get Sergeant ready for practice." I looked at the brothers still standing in the box, then turned to Granger. "I don't want to rush them, so I'm out. I'll see you guys before the ceremony tonight."

Granger nodded then grinned, "Wear something pretty."

I laughed, "You, too, G-Ranger."

After a full day of practice and meetings, I dressed in something pretty. The dress was black, stopped at the top of the knee with a fluff of lace at the hem. It was highlighted with a chain belt with multiple buckles and matching ankle boots. I finished the look with the steampunk top hat I had worn to the costume ball the spring before. Red hair in ringlets and gold gear earrings that matched the gears in the hat band. It was fun, unique, and made my parents and brother laugh when I modeled it for them.

"You look beautiful and just as quirky as your personality," Dad laughed and hugged me tight.

"I can't wait for your friends to see this," Mom said and adjusted the ringlets over my shoulder.

"Yeah," Mason smirked. "Wait until you see them."

"Oh! You're killing me!" I laughed and rushed them out the hotel room door. The ride to SouthPoint for the back number ceremony was full of teasing and laughter. I love my family.

When we drove into the front of the hotel casino, I saw Shayla and Granger first. Her blonde hair was styled straight to her shoulders and tucked behind her ears showing the turquoise earing Granger had bought her before he went on the rodeo road. The necklace that matched was visible through the open collar of her gold knee-length dress.

Granger's shoulder-length blonde hair was brushed out full in all its glory, mustache was combed and tweaked at the ends, and his goatee seemed fuller than normal. His light brown hat was a perfect match to Paul Newman's character Buffalo Bill. The jacket was the same tan with white elaborate applique on the shoulders and front yokes as the characters had been in the film. Fringe hung across his back and down the sleeves. Underneath was a white collared shirt with a black bolo tie with a buffalo head broach holding it together. He looked like he had just stepped out of the Buffalo Bill movie.

I squealed in excitement as I stepped out of the car and waved at him. His bright blue eyes lit with laughter when he saw me.

"I love it!" He called out.

"This is so fun! We need lots of pictures," I giggled.

Mom took our picture then we searched around the mass of vehicles for the two brothers. They and the Lil Bros were standing by the valet stand with their mother and Barry. Taylor and the Lil Bros wore black jeans, white button-up western shirts and black cowboy hats.

Ace wore the same but covering the shirt was a dark navy-blue jacket that I recognized "Oh, my," I whispered.

"What?" Mom asked.

"That's the jacket his dad wore at one of his back number ceremonies," Granger answered. "There is a picture of his father, mother, and Lauren in the award room at the 3.3 ranch from that night."

My eyes were glistening when the brothers saw us and strode over with wide grins. After laughter, hugs, and greetings we made our way into the casino to the media carpet for our official arrival photos.

The first picture was of Ace, Lauren, and Charlene as a replica of the portrait of his dad. A dozen group poses later, the last image taken was of Ace, Granger, and me.

The evening was full, fun, and more than I could have dreamed.

I was sharing a room with Mason and when we finally fell onto our beds he rolled on his side and looked over at me.

"I need to tell you something."

I looked at him and smiled, "It better be good, because if you tell me something that bursts this bubble I'm going to beat you to death."

He grinned, "I consider it a good thing."

"Then what?"

"I've been in a bit of a long-distance relationship with someone and I'm really happy with her…more than anyone else."

"Who is it?"

"Gail."

"Gail who?"

"Gail Masters."

"I don't know who that is."

"You do. She's Ellie and Calebs mother."

"Oh," I gasped in surprise.

He rolled onto his back and looked at the ceiling, "After the rodeo, she is coming to Oklahoma to spend a week with me."

"Isn't she going to college?"

"Yes, she wants to be an OR Nurse and assist with heart surgeries."

I thought of the small blonde woman that had stood next to Lacie Jae when confronting the kidnapper. She seemed strong, protective of her babies. "You said that day she was funny and smart."

"She is."

"Well, don't screw up her college plans."

He chuckled, "I won't."

Thursday night, I leaned against Sergeant's shoulder and took deep breaths as we watched the live feed on Dad's phone from Mom's phone as she pointed it to the large monitor that hung over the arena. Granger was leaning over the chute measuring the rein on his horse Vain Reflections with Brodie and Brody Cress at his side. The official and cameraman moved next to him. Another deep breath as he stepped over the panel and slid onto the saddle.

"You can do this," I whispered.

I gripped the reins in one hand and Dad's shirt sleeve in the other as Granger leaned back. He nodded and the gate was flown open with Cress and Rawlins both yelling at him. Granger's ride took him in a large circle with high lunging kicks. He was in full stretched, picture perfect position when the horn blared.

"He did it," I exhaled as the 86-point score was announced.

"Got the first one down," Dad nodded. "Get in the saddle and keep him warmed up. I'll let you know when Ace is up."

When the last horse was escorted out of the arena, Granger had placed second for the night.

I was back at Dad's side when Ace and Quincy rode into the arena and backed into the box. The horse's rump barely hit the pads when Ace nodded. They rode out of the arena after an 8.8 second run. He finished seventh for the night.

"Ride around a bit and relax," Dad said as he waited next to me as I remounted. "Remember," he placed a hand on my leg making me look down at him. "I am so proud of everything you have done and the grace you have shown as you made your way here. You go out there and just get the job done. Nothing else matters except this outstanding horse, you, and those three barrels."

My heart pounded in love, pride, and anticipation. "Thank you for everything, Dad." I whispered.

"I'll see you down the alley," he smiled proudly and walked away.

Sergeant loped three laps then Gaston rode in next to him as we walked toward the arena.

I smiled at the horse then to his rider.

"Remember," Delaney said softly. "It's work now, just focus on the run and let everything else melt away."

"Thanks, I've worked on that since I was young in cutting competitions."

"Ah, I forgot you were well practiced at this."

I chuckled, "At cutting, but this barrel journey has been a roller coaster. Who would have thought that day we met for you to buy Memphis and I rode Sergeant for the first time, and you rode around the arena giving me all the advice you could that we would be here together two years later?"

She laughed, "I would! You have no idea how hard it was to sell him, and I just wanted to make sure he didn't go to a pretentious little brat. Once I met you, I had no doubt we would be here together."

"Thanks, Delaney. I couldn't have had a better mentor. You've taught me a lot; that day until now."

She smiled warmly and we drew quite as we rode into the lane. She was the first racer of the night, and I was the second. Camille walked next to her as Dad appeared to lay a hand on my horse's shoulder then tapped my leg. There were no words. All his love, belief, encouragement, and understanding were in that little tap. It had been like that since my first cutting competition when I was nine.

I thought of the nights the year before lying in bed at the 3.3 Ranch bunkhouse praying that I would have the chance to win a go round buckle and get on the stage to thank my family. They were proud of me even if I didn't get there...even if I didn't get to Vegas. I was fighting for my dreams. Mom had always said that was the most important thing...not giving up on your dreams. Mason and I always had their love and belief as well as we believed in each other and always encouraged our dreams.

I missed Mason not being at the fence as I rode closer to the entry gate. He would always stand and encourage me, but I knew he was in the red seats watching down and mentally sending me good thoughts.

I also missed Granger, Ace, and Taylor. How odd was it that my best friends, which included my brother, would all be men?

My mind cleared as Delaney and her horse Gaston ran into the arena. A calm took over me and I could feel Sergeant 's body relax. Dad patted him on the shoulder as Delaney ran out of the arena. I heard nothing but could feel my heartbeat slow as I stared at the gate. It opened and I nudged the bay horse forward.

A run, three turns, then another run...that's all I had to do. I'd done it thousands of times. I trusted my skill and the horse's ability and when I leaned forward, he took off at a run. There was no sound...just the barrel...we turned once...twice...and the third and final turn the roar of the crowd vibrated through my concentration. Hands high on his neck until we reached the tunnel when I sat back and took a breath.

The clock said 13.71...it was a good run. My back relaxed as we walked out of the gate and out into the night. Dad appeared at my side with a grin and a pat on the leg.

"Beautiful," he beamed.

Granger and Ace were waiting for us, so I slid off Sergeant and wrapped them both in a big hug. "We did it."

"Seems real now," Ace chuckled and looked at Granger. "Were the chutes better than the recliner?"

"Absolutely," Granger laughed.

Another racer trotted by us and smiled at me, "Great run."

"Thanks!" The excitement was bubbling through me as I turned to Dad. "What did she run?"

"Delaney was 13.79, she was 14.54," he answered.

We were quiet as each racer trotted by us.

"Oh, my God," I whispered and looked at Dad as the last rider ran into the arena. My heart began to pound as he took the reins from me while Ace and Granger stepped in next to me. I gripped both their arms. My breath shook as I stared at the tunnel and the woman waiting for the round winner to be announced.

The crowd roared and the woman turned and looked right at me. "Let's go. On the black horse up front..."

A bit numb and stunned, I ran to the horse she indicated and followed the flag girl through the arena gate. It was a blur of faces, applause, and the announcer yelling my name. When I was out the gate again, I slid off the horse and with Ace and Granger right behind me we followed the woman to make our way through the tunnel-like hallways of the building.

When I saw Amy Wilson looking at me as the cameras were ready to capture the interview my whole body was calm...as if living in a dream. I wouldn't remember what I said during the onslaught of interviews to follow until I watched them that night. I was still in that dream as we made our way to the South Point Hotel for the buckle ceremony.

The calm remained when my name was announced and I led my family, my best friends, and my mentor onto the stage.

Later, when I watched the recording of the interview, I was surprised at how calm and professional I sounded. After praising my best friends who partnered with me for the journey and heaping huge love and respect on Sergeant and Grace, I was given the opportunity I had dreamed of for so many nights.

"I want to thank my family...my brother, mother, and father who are all champions in the cutting industry and know how hard it is and how much work it is to fulfill dreams. They have done nothing but encourage me, love me, yell at me when needed, and be by my side. Although I will be keeping the whiskey for my best friends and myself, this buckle is for my parents for believing in me enough to bring Sergeant Pepper into my life."

CHAPTER FIFTY-SIX

GRANGER

Friday night, in the tunnel behind the chutes, I climbed the panel to lay my saddle on the back of the large bay horse, Burban. Two team ropers trotted past as they left the arena.

"Toes out," Brodie said as he walked behind me and carried his saddle to the pretty wild-maned horse, Business Girl.

I answered with a chuckle, "Lift."

Eight horses were already loaded in the chutes by the arena and ready to start.

Leaning over the saddle to attach the cinch, a rider that had exited the arena stopped right behind me. I turned to see Delaney's husband Ryle Jaspers smiling at me.

"How was the run?" I asked.

"Best we've done in here," he answered with a grin and his partner Jess stopped next to him.

"3.9," Jess grinned.

"Damn, nice, congrats," I reached out and shook their hands.

"I just wanted to stop and say how much Delaney loved Sammie asking her to go on stage with her last night. It meant a lot to her." Ryle turned and looked over his shoulder as the gate was opened for the next team to exit the arena.

"It meant a lot to Sammie, too," I nodded. "It was a hell of a night."

Ryle grinned, "That it was. We all need to work on getting more stage visits and celebrations this week."

"Agreed," Jess and I nodded.

I turned and sat on top of the panel and scratched Ryle's palomino horse's ears. Three more teams passed by us until the last team of ropers beat the pair with a 3.7 second run.

"Shit," Ryle huffed and with a wave the pair trotted out of the building.

I turned back to the horse with a sigh for the pair. I sure would have liked to see them win a round. There were eight more nights to go for them. Their confidence was up so I had no doubt they would do it.

The roar of the crowd echoed down the tunnel as the first bronc rider burst from the chutes. I closed my eyes and visualized the ride the night before. It was almost a blur. If it wasn't for video replays, I'm not sure I would have remembered it. My mind went back to the first ride at the clinic in Pendleton with Craig. I could feel the energy from his bright smile and laughter after I fell from the red horse...my first bronc. It felt like the day before and yet so long ago at the same time.

I missed Craig; wished he was here with us on the podium behind the chutes.

I sighed again at his loss...then shook my brain back to reality. The last thing Craig would want, or what I wanted, was to dwell on him not being here. Instead, I thought of Leo, Spence, and Dale at that first trip to the clinic; meeting Evan and Martin, the excitement and disbelief I had that riding bucking horses could be fun...addicting AND you could get paid for doing it. All the trips Leo, Spence, and I had through the years...laughter, jokes...just the whole damn adventure.

Then there was Ace and Sammie. Life changing friends. I don't know how I got so lucky as to meet them and have them lead me back to Mom and drive me to my dream...to this building. I stepped back and looked down the tunnel and at the people and horses. The anticipation for the ride rose again.

The slam of gates and chute slides had my heart rate rising. My bronc, Burban, walked forward. I jogged ahead and up onto the platform to meet him at the chute. For just a moment, I let myself take in the expanse of the building, mass of crowd, and the enthusiasm of the announcers.

A chute opened to my right with Lefty Holman on Zoaria Hills bucking out into the arena. The crowd roared and my heart rate increased.

Someone patted me on the shoulder, and I turned to Adam grinning at me. "Get 'em."

"Yes, sir," I smirked, and my attention went back to Burban.

After traveling last year with Ace, I took on his technique of just concentrating on the details...the steps to making a successful ride.

When I stepped over the panel and slid onto the horse, the sound from the announcer faded. The official and camera man appeared over me, but my mind was focused on the horse, rein, stirrups, cinch, and flank.

"We good?" I called over my shoulder.

"Ready," the flank man answered.

Lean back, lift the rein, toes out, bite down on the mouthguard, deep breath, and then nod...the gate was opened.

Burban went straight up in the air and muscle memory had my feet planted above his shoulder. A lunge and the spurring began, and it felt good. The whole ride felt good and just rode it out until the pickup men appeared at my side. It was a picture-perfect dismount and as I jogged back to the chutes, I thought of the year before when Sammie came up with the idea for practicing the dismounts. My grin was wide from the memory as I made my way out the gate, up the stairs, and to Brodie's side.

My score of 85 points matched Lefty's and after Brodie's successful ride he received a matching score. We ended in a three-way tie for 3rd place.

After dropping off my gear in the locker room, I ran back to the chutes to wait for Ace's run. His 8.3 second run landed him in the 5th spot for a paycheck.

We were both on the bucking chutes when Sammi's name was called out. She flew into the arena with Ace and I leaning with her as she turned each barrel. The second she was out, we climbed down to celebrate her fifth-place finish. All three of us had earned a paycheck.

Late Saturday morning, we met at the back door of the Convention Center and walked into Cowboy Christmas together. There was already a lineup of people waiting for our autographs when we arrived. The walls behind us were filled with the images we had taken the spring before with the swords and dramatic skies behind us.

"That is so cool," Sammie grinned as she looked at each image and slid onto a chair.

For two hours we signed, talked, laughed, took pictures, and relaxed. It was the longest time we had spent together in four days. We followed it with lunch before going our separate ways again.

Saturday night was another good night for us. After finishing in fifth and in the money, Ace matched his run from the night before with 6th place in the money finish. Sammie was 7th...just out of the money but still left the arena with a wide grin. After tucking Sergeant away for the night, we met our families at the steak house for dinner.

Martin was already there standing with Little Caleb in his arms while a beautiful woman with long dark hair stood next to him holding Little Ellie. The woman wore skin-tight blue jeans, knee-high black boots, and a red shirt that emphasized her curves very well.

"Who in the hell is that?" I exhaled.

Taylor answered, "Lauren's best friend is Andrea...Andrea's brother is Greg, and that is his ex-wife, Jodi."

"Lauren and Jodi are really good friends," Ace added.

"She's freaking gorgeous," Sammie whispered.

"From the look on Martin's face, he agrees," Taylor chuckled. "Jodi flew in last night and they met at breakfast this morning."

"And have been nearly inseparable since," Lauren stepped in next to us. "I do believe they are both very infatuated with each other...and she adores babies."

"Yeah, they are both beaming," I nodded and walked in to be greeted by a grinning Evan and his girlfriend, Sawyer.

The evening was full of good food, friends, and laughter.

Mom sat next to me with River then Brodie on the opposite side of her. Sammie was to my right then her parents and brother.

My phone, Brodie's, and River's all rang out and we immediately reached for them and read the emails with the Sunday night draws posted.

"Well, look at that," River grinned at me. "You get to try your luck with Henry the First tomorrow night."

I laughed as I read through the list of horses and riders, "At least I've drawn one of your horses this year."

"Iggy is 5th and 10th round so you still have a chance," Brodie added. "Unless I draw him again, but first, Birch Bubbles tomorrow night."

I leaned back and lifted an arm over the back of Mom's chair while looking around the table at our family and friends.

"I love we ended up with such a wonderful group of people," Mom smiled up at me.

"Me, too," I sighed. "And I love this rodeo life."

Sunday night, as I pushed myself off the arena dirt and watched Henry the First buck away from me, I still loved the rodeo life. I quickly made my way through the gate and up the stairs to stand next to Adam. His smartass grin greeted me.

"He almost got you."

I laughed, "Let's say I was relieved when they said I made it to the eight. He's fun to ride."

"That is his 5th outing in this arena, and if that stands, you are his 5th second place ride," Adam sighed. "Someday, that damn horse will get his buckle."

The gate to Brodie's horse was swung open and he rode to a 3rd place 85-point score. Brody Cress won the night on Cancun Moon, and we were all pleased when we set our gear in the locker room before running out to watch Ace.

"How's he doing so far?" Cress asked.

"He's Mr. Consistent," I answered. "All fifteen are within fifty-thousand of each other, so every night has a whole new leaderboard. No one is going to runaway with the title here."

"The average win will probably be the deciding factor," Cress predicted.

"And nobody will have a clue on that until Saturday night," Brodie added.

Ace was the third rider to walk into the arena and back into the box. As he had the previous nights, once Quincy's rump hit the pads, he nodded.

"Come on...," I whispered. It was clockwork...near perfect. When he jogged back to the outstanding horse, I could see a visible sigh from him as he smiled at the judge. The official time of 8.2 seconds had him in first place. By the end of the night, he walked away in second.

"Nice run," I told him when he made it up onto the platform.

"Felt damn good," he smirked. "If I can just do that the rest of the week."

"Just look at each night, not the whole week," Cress told him. Since he had won three average titles, it was well learned advice.

Delaney was the third barrel racer to enter the arena and ran the fastest time of the whole rodeo.

"Damn that looked good," I grinned. I could imagine the whole family yelling for her and looked up to the suite I knew that her dad and Evan were watching from. Then my eyes wandered to the area I knew Mom was sitting. I found her just as Sammie's name was called out and her whole body leaned forward in anticipation of the run. It made me smile at how much she liked my friends, and how much I enjoyed having her with us.

Sammie and Sergeant raced into the arena, and the run looked identical to the other three she had completed already.

"I swear, if you overlapped all four runs on video, there wouldn't be a stride different," Ace chuckled as we made our way to the back.

By the time we found her, Sammie was standing next to the horse and hugging her dad. They had placed third with Delaney winning the night.

Sammie grinned as we approached, "I'm having so much fun!" She looked at Ace, "Nice run, Cowboy!"

"You, too," he wrapped his arms around her in a strong hug.

"What about me?" I pouted at her making her laugh and giving me a hug, too.

"I can't imagine this week without you two here with me," tears filled her eyes.

"Oh, that's enough of that," Jeremy shook his head at his daughter. "You're not even halfway done with the week and you're going to be a blubbering mess by Saturday."

She threw her arms around Sergeant and just laughed.

I stood at the horse stalls with Sammie and Ace as they took care of their horses. Taylor was scrolling through the results as we waited.

"I don't remember seeing you at the book signing today."

He shrugged, "I was at the convention center but hanging out with a friend instead of standing around watching you three sign autographs. Gets kind of tiring after a while."

"I imagine so. I'd be bored to death."

The alert from my phone rang out and I reached for it as the three turned and looked at me in anticipation of the draw. They all knew Destiny's Ignatius was part of Monday night's group of horses.

The list appeared and the anticipation made my heart beat a little bit stronger.

"Brodie drew Destiny's..." I started.

"No fucking way," Taylor grumbled.

"He had him last year," Sammie whined.

"...Inferno." I finished.

"Oh, damn," Ace chuckled. "Who got Iggy?"

"You?" Sammie's eyes widened until I shook my head.

"No, I drew Glory Hawk," I answered with a sigh. "River and Adam have got to be so disappointed."

Taylor's brow rose, "Why? Because you didn't draw him?"

"No," I exhaled. "Because he's in the re-ride pen."

"No, freaking way," Ace shook his head.

"Yeah," I nodded. "And two deep."

"How does a horse like that end up in the re-ride pen?" Sammie's shoulders fell.

I shrugged and slid the phone back in my pocket. "Glory Hawk is a 90-point horse and Inferno has taken all the riders that managed to stay on him this year to the pay window. They are both good."

"Well," Sammie shut the door on the horse's stall. "You still have Saturday night."

"And all of the next few years," Taylor chuckled.

I nodded in humored agreement, "I think I'll stalk him next year and go to every damn rodeo he goes to."

Text to Brodie: Great draw for you, River disappointed?

Text from Brodie: Disappointed on Iggy, excited about Inferno's first ride here. She's a bit up and down. I told Adam she can stay with them tonight.

Text to Brodie; LOL, how did she take that?

Text from Brodie: Thought it was funny until Adam said no way in hell.

Text to Brodie: We still have Saturday night, odds of him in the re-ride pen both draws must be low.

Text from Brodie: That's what I told her.

Text to Brodie: Nothing we can do to change it, so let's kick some ass tomorrow night.

Text from Brodie: I BELIEVE we will!

Text to Brodie: I BELIEVE!

Another full day of autograph signing, meeting with sponsors, and interviews and Taylor handed me the reins for Stomping Dog.

"Who are we going to have do this next year when you're riding with us?"

He just grinned and shook his head, "Did you hear what happened today?"

"When, where, about who?" I stepped up onto the horse.

"Martin and Jodi had their first official date."

"No, kidding? Damn, she is one of the most beautiful women I've ever seen."

"She owns a fitness center and is a palates instructor."

"Rocking body but the hair, eyes, smile...she is gorgeous. But I know Martin...respect and admire him...he's like a dad to me. Beauty is one thing...it's the heart and how she would be to him."

Taylor nodded with a smile, "Lauren doesn't let just anyone into her world. If Jodi is there as one of her good friends, then she is going to be a good for him, too."

I nodded and rode away with a good feeling about Martin and the night. Sammie rode in next to me on her father's horse and my night got even better. It was fun to watch her excitement for the entry and standing next to her as we took in the crowd. Only thing that would make it better was if Ace was riding with the Oregon group instead of the Texas group.

I was standing on the panel adjusting my saddle onto Glory Hawks' back when Ryle and Jess rode out of the arena. I turned and sat quickly when they stopped.

"And?" I asked.

They both grinned.

"3.5 this time," Ryle announced.

"Damn close to that 3.3," Jess added.

"You'll get it," I said and had no doubt they would. "How was the party last night?"

"You should have come out with us," Ryle answered. "You all have a standing invitation any time we make that stage."

"So, I can join you tonight?" I smirked.

They both turned to watch the last pair of team ropers ride into the arena. When they rode out, Ryle and Jess grinned at me then rode back into the arena for their victory lap.

"We'll see you at SouthPoint," Ryle called out as they rode past me on their way out of the aisle.

And my mood rose, anticipation peeked, and my belief in it being a very good night climbed.

I stood behind the large Glory Hawk and watched Brodie slide down onto Inferno. Adam was tightening the cinch and watching Brodie for the nod.

"You're two out," the chute boss pointed to me.

The gate swung open, and Inferno bust out of the chute with one leap then instant high kicks with his nose pushing the dirt in between. With Brodie's black shirt, hat, and chaps, and the black mane of the horse and nearly black hair of his hide, they were beautiful together. Picture perfect as the horn blared.

His 91 points confirmed to me it was a very good night.

When I slid onto the back of Glory Hawk, I had no doubt in my mind that I could ride her for more than 90. She had a strong powerful kick, and she was rhythmic. I just needed to get that first mark out and we'd have a great score.

Brodie jogged up the platform as the next rider's gate opened.

"Good ride," I grinned at Brodie. "Did you lift?"

He laughed, "I did. You should try it, too."

"I might just do that."

As if trying to tell me I wasn't being serious enough, Glory Hawk bucked forward then lowered her butt down. My mind went right back to her as I adjusted myself in the saddle and waited for the horse to stand back up. The rope was tied around the gate with the man staring and waiting for my nod. The official was there, and the camera was just at her head and pointed at us.

The horse shifted back up, I leaned back and with the full belief it was going to be a glorious ride, I nodded. The gate opened and she took a grand leap into the arena. Toes out, lift, mark out was perfect and then we bucked across the arena dirt.

When the horn blared, I knew it was not glorious but just a practice ride instead.

I leaned over to the pickup man and over the top of the horse's rump knowing that it wasn't even a good enough battle to place for the night. At least I had ridden and was going to get a score to stay in the chase for the average...probably dropping down to fourth or fifth.

When I turned back to the chutes, I saw the red flag on the ground next to a flank strap. The official was pointing at his clip board.

"Flank came off at the first jump. Want the reride?"

"Yes!" It was a glorious night. I didn't just get to ride one horse, I got to ride two. "I like Shadow Jacket."

The official grinned, "He's already been taken."

"He's first in the reride," I looked at the clip board he held to me.

"While you were focused on resetting for your ride, Trey's horse underperformed so he gets the first re-ride." He pointed at the clip board; right next to the name of the next horse.

Destiny's Ignatius

"Serious?" I inhaled.

"Yeah, you have 20 seconds to decide," he grinned.

"Oh, I'm all in!" I patted him on the shoulder with a nod then turned to run to the gate.

I was met by Brodie and Adam. Both were grinning broadly.

"I've got to get my saddle." I told them.

"Yeah, you do," Adam huffed.

"He's already in the chute. If we can get you ready while the next four are going out, you can ride now instead of waiting for the bulls," Brodie said.

"Which means, your stable mate is waiting for you," Adam waved his arm to the side to invite me onto the platform.

I made a noise that made everyone laugh, then I rushed by Adam to retrieve my saddle. Cress was already lifting it off Glory Hawk when I ran up to him.

"Make it good," he grinned at me as he handed down the saddle.

I didn't think of anyone or even the horse, except Ace and his routine of telling himself the basics...the steps.

"Take your time," Adam said as he met me at chute behind the horse that filled up the whole damn thing. The excitement was gone now, it was all focus and work from him. "They still have three ahead of you. You've waited for this moment for a long time...take it in."

With a focused mind, I settled the saddle on the horse then began the routine of adjusting the cinch while Adam adjusted the flank strap.

"He doesn't like to stay in the chute for long once you're on his back," Adam added.

All other sounds faded away until all I could feel was my heartbeat in my veins.

"Two out..."

I measured the rein...once, twice...and zipped up the vest...routine...don't think...tap the hat down tighter.

"Next out..."

Deep breaths then I stuffed the mouthguard in and bit down. Another deep breath...I stepped up onto the rail and stepped over to the in-arena panel, so I was straddling above the horse.

"Don't forget that shake of the head," Brodie leaned down to turn the stirrup for me.

Another deep breath and I looked at the horse. He was turned slightly looking out into the arena then his large nose rose above it. His long thick forelock lay over the white stripe I knew was there. My mind went to the moment I arrived at the Westmoreland's ranch the year before and rode the buckskin next to his fence where Destiny's Ignatius allowed me to glide a hand over that long nose and down his broad jaw.

Then, my mind went to Kennewick...to the moment I stared at the horse in the pen and made up my mind to honor Craig and turn-out. I wasn't ready then, but I was more than ready now. It was time again to honor Craig but this time by riding him.

I ran a hand down the side of Iggy's neck, "You and me..." I whispered so low I knew the men at my side couldn't hear it over the announcer.

My racing heart eased, veins numbed, breaths deepened...one more stroke down the horse's neck and I lowered onto the saddle. Routine had my feet sliding into the stirrups.

"Believe."

I had no idea who said it, but I could feel the word as if it was inside of me; in my heart and mind.

I did believe it. With everything that was in me, I believed I could ride this horse.

After another deep breath, I hesitated. Having been in the calm serene space in my mind, I wasn't sure everyone else was as ready as I was. My gaze went up to the official leaning on the panel in front of me, the camera man next to him, then Brody and Brodie, and finally I turned to speak over my shoulder.

"Adam?"

"We're ready. Do NOT loosen your grip. Ride to 12 seconds."

The song in the building filtered into my concentration and I grinned. Imagine Dragons' song: Natural

And you're standing on the edge face up
'Cause you're a natural
A beating heart of stone
You gotta be so cold
To make it in this world
Yeah, you're a natural
Living your life cutthroat
You gotta be so cold
Yeah, you're a natural

"Yeah," I whispered. "Yeah, Craig, I got this."

I lowered in the saddle and Iggy's body rose in anticipation. Rare up, high buck, shake of the head...it played in my mind then my hand rose to tighten the rein, and I nodded.

Destiny's Ignatius lifted on his back hooves and launched us into the air to fly into the arena. He was a good fifteen feet out before his front hooves hit the ground with back hooves so high in the air I had to slam my own feet forward and brace in the stirrups to remain in the saddle. My head was nearly touching his rump. He rose in the front, and I spurred as fast and hard as I could in preparation for the next kick...three, four, five times with each so high I bumped on his back. I knew the shake was coming but was ready for it and stayed upright in the saddle. Then, he launched us into the air again. For that second, I felt like I was flying and leaned back to match the long stretch I knew he was showing...then he was down and back up in the air again. His hooves were at least six feet in the air, with our bodies stretched out flying mid-arena when the horn blared. I didn't loosen my grip until I saw the pickup men ride in next to us.

When my hand lowered to get a double grip on the rope, my fingers relaxed just enough I was launched over the back of the pickup man's horse. I landed on my feet and my arms flew in the air...the crowd roared…and the song filled the arena again.

Yeah, you're a natural
Living your life cutthroat
You gotta be so cold
Yeah, you're a natural

Again and again, I punched the air to the beat of the music until I saw Ace standing on the panels by the roping chute. He was screaming and punching the air with me.

"YEAH!" We growled at each other.

Then I turned and my eyes sought out my mother in the stands. She was jumping with arms waving in the air. Right next to her were Caleb, Gloria and the, standing on her seat yelling, River.

The record tying score of 93 was announced. I had matched Brodie's ride on him the year before.

The large bay stallion and the pickup men ran in front of me, and I twirled to point to the suite where Martin and Evan were watching. When Iggy ran past me again, I tipped my hat to him, fist pumped the air again then I ran for the gate. Brody and Brodie met me first, then Adam was there and we wrapped each other in a strong embrace.

He leaned back, gripped both of my shoulders and laughed, "I knew you could do it."

Someone grabbed my arm and drug me away from the group, "Interview..." The lady pulled me down the hall.

Then I heard her.

"G-RANGER!"

I turned back to see her running toward me with the widest smile and pride shining in her eyes. When she neared, she jumped in the air and landed in my arms. We wrapped each other in a celebratory hug.

"I am so happy for you!" She laughed, leaned back, and placed a hand on each side of my face. "I had to come, but you need to interview, and I need to get back to my horse." Then she turned away.

As she ran back down the hall, she skipped high in the air with her laughter floating back to me.

I was pulled and escorted through the halls to the interview by the arena then down to the media room. After finishing the last interview, I turned to leave when Ace walked into the room with wide strides and a big grin. Brodie was right behind him.

"You done already?" I laughed.

"7.7 and landed in third place."

"Hell, yeah!" We embraced again. "We need to get out there for Sammie."

We were at the roping chutes when she ran into the arena. There was no sign of that excited and happy racer that had ran after me in the hallway. Her face was complete concentration as she turned each barrel then raced out with the clock stopping at 13.59. By the time we made it back to greet her, it was announced a third-place run.

I watched the video of my ride three times by the time we arrived at SouthPoint casino for the buckle ceremony. Martin, all the Rawlins, Charlene, Taylor, the Lil Bros, Sammie's parents and Mason were there to go on stage with us. The only people missing from my life were Spence, Leo, and his dad, Dale.

As we waited at the back door while the other round winners took to the stage, I felt a tap on my shoulder and turned. There they were with wide mischievous grins. I hugged Leo and Spence then Dale.

"I didn't know you were here," I finally stepped away.

"We wanted to surprise you, so your focus stayed on the horse," Dale said.

"It was Leo's idea that we agreed with," Spence added.

"Man, I couldn't have been prouder and couldn't have yelled any louder." Leo chuckled.

"The last time I saw that horse was when I was flying over his shoulder," Spence smirked. "YOU definitely made up for that."

When I walked out onto the stage my heart was full. When the Westmoreland's joined us to pick up the buckle for Destiny's Ignatius, I was asked to introduce who was with me.

"Relatives are in your blood, family is in your heart," I started with the corny but heartfelt statement. "Everyone here from Leo and Spence who got me into this dream to Sammie and Ace who helped me achieve it...everyone in between...my mom, Dale, Evan, and Martin who are all like fathers to me and the rest who are like brothers, sisters, cousins, aunts, and uncles...they are my family."

My hands shook when I was handed the bottle of Pendleton and the boxed buckle, and my arm was firmly around Mom as we smiled in pure happiness when we smiled at the camera.

CHAPTER FIFTY-SEVEN

ACE

"You know," Granger yawned. "I don't think, since the time we met last year, that we have gone more than 30 minutes without talking."

"And there you go and break the streak," I twisted my neck back and forth then rolled my shoulders. "Late night, early morning, even got an hour nap in and I feel like shit."

"Between Ryle and Jess winning last night and our celebration, I'd say we were lucky to get in the rooms before 2:00."

I glanced at the large tent that served as the hospitality room, "You want to stop and get something to eat?"

"No, I have a bar in my bag. Anything more would make me throw up right now." On our way to the stalls, we walked past riders already mounted on their grand entry horses. "As late as we are today, it's a good thing we have Taylor saddling for us."

"I don't see him...where is he?" For the last five days, Taylor already had Quincy, Bear, and Stomping Dog brushed and ready to go by the time we arrived.

"No clue," Granger yawned again. "I don't think he drank as much as we did last night."

Taylor appeared from around the corner, "Sorry, got caught up with something."

"No big deal, we have plenty of time," Granger shrugged and opened the stall to Stomping Dog. "I don't see Jeremy either."

I ignored their chatter as I walked Bear out of his stall. Taylor was walking towards us with the pad and saddle when I tied him up. With a low grumble I turned back to the stalls.

"Just leave Quincy there for now," Taylor slid the brush across Bear's back. "I'll get him ready while you guys are doing grand entry."

I knew my irritation was unwarranted, but it still creeped into my gut. I liked routine...steps to get things done. Now we were out of order, and I felt rushed; even though we weren't.

Sammie and her dad appeared and their light banter with everyone caused my back muscles to tense. Jeremy was usually alone with Sammie coming later...it was out of order. I took a breath and combed Bear's mane.

"You're awfully quiet tonight," Sammie laid a hand on my arm and smiled that perfect little happy smile. That irritated me, too.

"Just trying to focus," I mumbled.

"Relax, Ace," Taylor tossed the saddle pad onto the horse. "You're getting yourself…"

"I'll do what I do," I grumbled and walked to the tack room to pull out the exercise bands. I stretched, pushed, pulled, and did everything I could do to relax my back.

Every night I enjoyed running in the grand entry, even if I couldn't ride with Sammie and Granger. But when we ran back out of the building, I was still tense.

Per our routine, Taylor was just outside the building to take Stomping Dog so Granger could go into the locker rooms. I was so lost in my thoughts I didn't notice he wasn't riding beside me until I reached the stalls.

"What the hell?" I grumbled and glared around me to search for him but only saw Sammie's dad walking toward me.

"I asked him to give us some time," Jeremy explained.

"What for?" I stepped off the horse and had to keep myself from swearing. It irritated me that everyone was changing my routine and throwing me off.

"Look at me, Ace," he came to a stop in front of me and begrudgingly I did as he asked. He smiled slightly, "I am 43 years old and have competed nearly all my life. I train now for other people and have the added stress of trying to make the best horse for them. Sometimes, it is tough." He hesitated and nodded to the horse. "You are feeling that stress."

"Yeah," I huffed and started taking the saddle off Bear. "And throwing me off my routine is not helping."

"And that is why I am here," Jeremy smirked. "You need to do what you do at home or on the road. Catch your horse, brush your horse, saddle your horse, and ride your horse. Routine, just like home."

I exhaled as my back muscles tensed but I just nodded.

"Like I said, I've been there. You have time, so just relax and get that routine...think it through...one step at a time." With that, he nodded at me, patted the horse's rump and walked to the stall where Sergeant waited.

I took a deep breath and put Bear's saddle away, brushed him, then put him in his stall with hay and grain. I took a moment, like I always did, and ran my hand down his neck and shoulder. A bit of the tension in my shoulders eased.

Sammie had joined her father when I stepped out of the stall and grabbed the halter for Quincy. She smiled but didn't approach.

By the time I had the horse haltered, brushed, and saddled my back was relaxed, and mind was at ease. It was simple, it was routine...that's what I needed. I knelt to put the boots on him and looked around. The area was busy with horses and riders, but neither Sammie, Jeremy, nor Taylor was in sight.

"I guess it's just you and me," I scratched the horse's nose, rubbed down his neck and stepped up into the saddle just to lean over and rub his shoulder.

Instead of going into the building, I watched Granger's ride on the monitor at the hospitality tent. After the excitement from the night before with him finally having the chance to ride Iggy and having a record-tying ride...a spectacular ride, this one seemed a bit normal for him. He scored 81 points; well out of the money. Brodie rode after him and landed in 5th place with an 84.5.

By the time Quincy and I walked into the building for the run, my body was relaxed and mind clearer. I stopped the horse, ran the process in my head and twisted my arms in front of me to practice the two wraps and a hooey. Routine...

I was the fourth rider of the night and as I walked into the arena my mind processed the steps again. I adjusted the string in my teeth, twirled the rope and tucked it under my arm, then rolled my shoulders. I walked into the box with a glance at the calf. It was standing straight and looking down the arena. Quincy turned in the box as normal, and I glanced back to see his rump hit the pad. When I turned back to the chute, the lever was pulled, and the calf took off.

"Holy hell, rope!" My mind yelled and I took off. We were way behind the calf, but my muscle memory had the rope swinging, flying, falling over the calf's neck and I was stepping out of the stirrup...the normal routine.

As I flanked the calf, I visualized the walk into the box and turn; I knew I didn't nod. I could have challenged the release, but it was too late...two wraps and a hooey and my hands went in the air. Damn. We were so far behind the calf when we came out of the box it took too much time...15 seconds flat.

I shook my head in disgust at myself for not declaring that I didn't nod. I grimaced, my stomach ached, and I shook my head again as I stepped back up on Quincy who immediately stepped forward...his routine. My eyes went to the official...his lips were rolled into a line. He knew it, too.

I looped the rope back then took the piggin' string that was handed back up to me.

"Damn it," I whispered to myself and walked Quincy out of the arena, down the aisle and out into the night without saying word. No money added to the standings, too much time added for the average time, and not being fast enough to call the challenge. No one would be proud of that run.

"Happens too damn fast," Taylor met me at the door and took the reins as I stepped off. We walked back to the stalls together.

By the time we returned the tie-down was over, barrels set and the first two barrel racers had run.

"Four guys missed tonight including Chris," Granger said as we walked up next to him. "That was a rough go-round for everyone."

I took a breath and nodded but continued cussing myself out in my head. It wasn't the first time the chute had been open without my nodding, but damn, on such a big stage and when so much was on the line? Damn...

Sammie ran into the arena, we all leaned for her as she turned the three barrels, and she ran out in 13.81 seconds and out of the money.

When we met up with her and Jeremy, she was still all smiles, laughing, and stroking her horse's shoulder.

I let her exuberance roll off my shoulders and nodded at Jeremy, "Thanks for earlier. You were right, it helped."

"Wish the run would have worked out better," he sighed.

"Yeah, me too," I grumbled.

"Look at it this way, Ace," Sammie said as she stepped out of the saddle. "You still have a time for tonight. You have a time in all six nights and are in the running for the average. It could have been worse...you could have missed."

"How can you be so positive all the time?" Taylor laughed as my stomach grumbled in irritation that I agreed with her.

Silence answered him as we all looked at each other. Granger finally smirked, "Princess and her pretty ponies haven't ALWAYS been positive."

The tension began to dissolve with memories of Sammie's furious tantrum at Granger in Rosenberg.

"Is this a story I should know?" Jeremy asked with raised brows to his daughter.

Sammie blushed then chuckled, "No."

He gave her a hug, "Then I'm going in to find your mother. We'll see you in the morning."

Sammie was behind the wheel as we drove away from the arena. I was staring into the dark night with my mind still replaying the chute opening when she stopped, and the doors opened. My eyes focused on her trailer.

"What are we doing here?" I gasped in surprise.

"Going home and recharging for the night," Granger said.

"I need a night here instead of a hotel bed," Sammie unlocked the door, and we eagerly followed her inside.

Ten minutes later, we were in sweatpants and t-shirts with bowls of ice cream and Tombstone playing on the monitor.

Sammie was sitting on the steps to her room with her head turning from the TV to the three of us on the couch. Her eyes filled with tears with lips rolling in a tight line.

"What?" I asked in concern.

Taylor and Granger turned to look at her with raised brows and spoons being dropped into their bowls.

"I was just remembering the night my parents bought this trailer," she chuckled softly and wiped away a tear. "I was sitting right in this very spot, looking at the empty trailer and couldn't wait to see what memories my three friends and I were going to make in here." She glanced at the memory wall that was filled with hundreds of pictures taken throughout the year.

"Some pretty damn good ones," Granger grinned.

"Unforgettable memories," I added.

"But," Taylor nodded with a slight smile. "We weren't the three friends you were thinking of at the time."

She giggled and rolled her eyes, "Thank heavens! I would never have gotten here if I was still riding with them."

"Just shows you," Taylor grinned. "You have to watch who is in your crowd."

"I didn't even know you three at that time," Sammie sighed and lifted her bowl in the air as a salute. "I feel so blessed you three and your families are in my crowd."

We raised our bowls and agreed with her.

I didn't think sleep would come and that I would be haunted by that damn chute opening but, in the bed I'd called home all summer, I slept better than I had all week.

When I woke, I could hear Sammie and Taylor's muted voices from outside and Granger's deep sleeping breaths inside. I didn't open my eyes, I just laid quietly and thought of Dad. In the replays I had watched of his runs at this rodeo, not one had the chute opening without his nod. There were misses in the first years, but he and Barry were nearly perfect the last two.

I knew his parents, my grandparents, had both passed by the time he had competed in his first National Finals Rodeo. Lauren and Mom had both talked about how proud they were of him. The interviews showed their beaming grins as they spoke of him. I wanted that. I wanted Dad to be proud of me. I wanted this rodeo for him. I wanted...him.

Even before my opens opened for the day, my chest was hollow, heart aching again for what should have been. My hands balled into fist and tapped the cushions of the bed.

The sound of the door opening finally had my eyes opening with Sammie greeting me with a wide morning smile. Her hair had been curled the night before, but now it was flattened to her head on one side and pushed well above her head on the other. "Did you even look in the mirror before you ventured outside?"

"No," she giggled and glanced toward the bathroom door that had a mirror attached. Then she laughed; that innocent but contagious laugh. "Taylor, what the hell! Why didn't you tell me."

Taylor grinned from behind her, "I thought you knew and didn't care."

"Glad there were no cameras out here," she chuckled and walked through the trailer to the restroom. "I'm going to take a shower here then I'll meet you guys at the convention center for the autograph signing then after we have lunch with Detective Fortune and everyone."

"You need a ride?" I swung my legs over the side of the bed and stretched.

"No, Dad's coming to get me." She closed the door behind her.

Granger had stood and was converting his bed back to the couch. "Brodie is coming to get me, so you two are on your own."

"Are we coming back here tonight?" I asked and stood.

"I needed this," Granger nodded. "Let's decide after the rodeo."

I nodded and slid on my jeans and looked at Taylor, "We can change at the hotel."

He just walked out of the trailer.

"We'll see you at 10:00," I said to Granger and followed in irritation.

He was quiet on the drive to the hotel. It wasn't until we parked and began walking to the entry doors that he finally glanced at me, "You doing OK this morning?"

"The good night's sleep helped, but I'm still a bit...I don't know." Lost? Heartbroken? Missing Dad...I didn't say it because I knew he did, too. We had talked about it the first morning when we had our pictures taken in the box where Dad and been 18 years before.

He nodded and remained quiet until we were walking down the hall towards our room. "I guess I should warn you that we're not alone."

CHAPTER FIFTY-EIGHT

ACE

Lauren, Barry, and Mom were waiting for us. Taylor walked next to them and turned to look at me with a bit of a glare.

"What's going on?" I hugged Mom good morning. "Where are the Lil Bros?"

"Having breakfast with the twins…which is also Evan, Martin, and their girlfriends," she answered.

"I wanted to talk to you about the last few days," Taylor said in a flat tone. "And I wanted them here when I did."

"About what?" I exhaled in irritation. "I screwed up last night…I…."

"Stop," Taylor put a hand up. "Shit like that happens, we've all been there, done that."

"Then, what is this about?" My back tensed.

"While we were competing in high school rodeo and the last year or so, you've always felt the pressure of being Austin Conners' son. We've both tried to keep people from comparing and expecting us to be like him...as good as him."

"I got over that...I..." My back straightened but his hand shot up again.

"I know," he nodded. "We talked about that and the fact you want the three of us mentioned in the NFR record books together."

"That's what you said when you started toward this dream with tie-down last year," Lauren nodded in agreement.

"What's that got...?" I started but stopped when Taylor's hand went up a third time. "I'm going to break your damn arm if you keep doing that."

He just gave me a smartass smirk, "I know how you feel about Dad because I feel the same way. I also know you have been focused on trying to make him proud of you this week."

My throat and heart tightened because I knew I was failing and him mentioning it confirmed it.

"You're putting a lot of pressure on yourself," Barry nodded in agreement.

"Any son would," I managed to exhale.

"Ace," Taylor stepped toward me with eyes narrowed. "I asked them here when I talked to you so they can confirm what I'm about to say."

My shoulders rose and head tilted to him in a silent warning about what he was about to say. "What the hell does that mean?"

"No one in this world knew Dad better than them," Taylor stated firmly. "All three in different ways. Lauren as his niece...more like daughter and training partner. Barry as a hundred thousand mile traveling partner and team roping partner, and Mom as his wife...his soul mate in life."

I looked at the three and nodded my agreement.

Taylor smiled slightly at them then looked back at me, "Dad would be very happy and proud of you for being here this week. No matter how you ended up in the world standings."

"Agreed," the three said.

I took a deep breath to loosen my lungs that had suddenly tightened.

"But and they will agree with me again," Taylor started but didn't look at them, he looked directly in my eyes. "What would be more important to him, what would make him the proudest a father could be, is the man that you have turned out to be."

I swallowed hard and gritted my teeth together.

Taylor continued without a glance to the three people nodding, "He would be, and is very proud of you, and it doesn't have anything to do with roping or competing. It has to do with the fact you would, and have, dropped everything you were doing to help one of us or the Lil Bros. Last year after the attack, you stayed with me the whole time. You were there to support and help Mom through it. You did everything you could do to protect Monte and Liam from what their father had done. Your first thought was how to protect them from hearing about it before you and Mom could tell them. You worked with the police to make sure it didn't get out, so they didn't have repercussions at school and in the media.

When I was healing, you pushed me through physical therapy and the process of starting to rope again. Because of that, because of your fighting for me, I do have a chance to be at a high competitive level again.

Without hesitation, you helped a woman you barely knew...Sammie to get to the next rodeo when she made a big mistake, and you encouraged her through the problems she was having. You brought Granger in as our fifth brother and taught him how to be a better, well-rounded cowboy. He got the job with the Westmoreland's because of what you taught him. With that, he was able to practice more, learn horses at a different level, which made him become an even better saddle bronc rider. And most importantly, your love for our mother, led him back to his."

I took a deep breath as Mom's hand covered her heart.

"And," Taylor continued. "Without a thought to how dangerous the situation could be, you ran into that store to save those babies from a kidnapper. A person...or as far as we knew it could have been more than one person that could have been armed and dangerous."

I huffed, "I hadn't thought of that."

"Exactly," Barry said. "You were thinking of nothing but saving those twins without a second thought of how dangerous it could have been to you."

"There is no doubt in my mind, that Austin would have...is proud of the man you are," Lauren smiled softly with tears glisten. "He always encouraged me and told me that it was more important to be a good person in life than being a good roper."

"Your father was a VERY good man," Mom whispered with a tear escaping. "He was a man that everyone could depend on for help. He wanted everyone to succeed, which is why the Idaho ranch became a training center."

Barry nodded. "When we were on the road, if someone needed help, even if it put a hardship on us or we missed a roping, Austin was there to help."

"Just the fact that, at twenty-one, he took me in when I was only twelve years old and fought to make sure no one could take me away from him...as if I were his own, tells you how good he was," Lauren wiped away a tear. "What Taylor says is the gospel truth. No matter how you do this week...even if you won that gold buckle, he would be prouder of the man you are than anything else."

"I miss him," I finally managed to whisper. "I wish he was here."

"We all do," Barry sighed.

"We miss the man...the good man that he was," Lauren cried. "Not the champion roper, but the man."

With a deep breath and a hand wiping away the tears gliding down my cheeks I released the stress, fear, anxiety that had overwhelmed me the last week.

"You understand," Taylor exhaled with a knowing, relieved smile.

"I do," I nodded. "I guess, when I have a son or daughter, I would feel the same way."

Mom stepped forward and wrapped her arms around me, "You must stop trying to prove yourself this week. You're here, you battled to be here and proven you deserve to be here. You need to start enjoying it now."

"Ropin' is no fun if it's just work," Barry nodded. "You have to put the fun back in when you can. Enjoy the adventure."

I took another deep breath and squeezed Mom until she squeaked with laughter. "Alright, I got it. I know what you're saying." I smirked at Taylor. "Even if it came from my little brother, I'll take your advice."

"You know why last night happened?" Lauren asked.

"Because the first four nights when I backed into the box, I didn't hesitate and nodded," I answered her with a smile.

"He just anticipated what you were going to do," Barry added. "Just an honest mistake."

"I know," I grinned. "Shit happens."

"Motto of a team roper," Taylor chuckled.

"No," Barry shook his head. "That would be 'where's the beer'?"

"Where's Taylor?"

Granger turned to look at me as we walked toward the restaurant for the group lunch, "Didn't you ask me that same thing yesterday?"

I grinned, "Seems to be the theme for him this week."

"You look like you're in a better mood," Sammie chirped. "You were having a lot of fun at the signing."

"I am and I was," I stopped to wave her through the restaurant door before us.

Detective Fortune and his wife were already seated when we arrived. They stood and greeted us with wide grins and congratulations. We chatted about the rodeo until Fortune's eyes went to the door and filled with pure delight.

Martin walked through the door with Little Ellie in one arm and his other around his new lady friend, Jodi, who was carrying Little Caleb. Evan and Sawyer were right behind them, followed by Taylor and Shayla.

"I finally get to meet those adorable babies," Fortune grinned and stood to greet them.

"Oh, my gosh," Sammie gasped. "You haven't met them!"

At the sound of her voice, Ellie's eyes found her and she began squirming out of Martin's arms.

"Sammie," Ellie shouted as Martin set her on the ground.

"Gra, Gra, Gra," Caleb clapped at Granger.

Jodi set Caleb down and the two one-year-olds began toddling to Sammie and Granger.

As introductions and greetings were exchanged, I couldn't help but casually take in Martin and Jodi together. I glanced at Granger, and he seemed to be doing the same thing until he turned and looked at me.

"They look very comfortable together, but they've only known each other for five days," he whispered.

"But it looks more like five months," I forced myself to quit looking at the duo and turned to see Brodie, Delaney, Camille, Logan, and Lacie Jae enter the restaurant.

The next hour was filled with talk of rodeo, traveling, and raising babies. The twins were the hit of the restaurant.

It was only after the table was cleared that the conversation turned to the kidnapping.

"I'll only say this," Fortune addressed the group. "I am here talking with you for final details before we arrest the accomplice on Monday morning."

"You found them?" Martin exhaled.

"We did," The detective nodded. "He was a high school friend of Cassie's that did her the 'favor' of getting the SUV then dumping it in the river. Even had an Airbnb rented for a couple weeks after...somewhere to hide until the ransom was paid."

"Why haven't you arrested him already?" Evan asked.

Fortune smirked, "Wanted to wait until this week was over so it wasn't in the headlines and overshadowing anything here. He isn't going anywhere...thinks he got away with it. I told the bosses I wanted to touch base with all of you before we do anything. He agreed."

"Thank you," Martin looked around the table at all the relieved faces. "Thank you, Detective, for everything you've done."

"My pleasure," the Detective nodded with a smile to the twins. "And from this point forward, my name is Dwight."

"Third time is a charm," I grinned at Granger as we walked toward the stalls. "Where's Taylor?"

All three horses were already saddled and waiting but Taylor wasn't in sight. Jeremy was sitting in a chair; leaned back and tapping on his phone.

He glanced up as we neared, "Taylor said he would be right back. I told him I'd watch the horses."

"I appreciate that," I said and ran a hand down Bear's shoulder and Quincy's nose.

Taylor still hadn't appeared when we left for the grand entry, but he was standing outside the door to take Stomping Dog from Granger when we came back out.

"Kick ass," he told Granger as he disappeared into the building. Then he mounted the horse, and we rode to the stalls.

I switched horses as Taylor remained on the buckskin then rode with me as I warmed up the horse. It was different, it was not our routine, and it didn't bother me at all. It felt...normal.

When I finally rode away to get ready to run our 7th run of the week, Taylor stepped off the horse.

"Hey, Ace!" he called out.

I glanced over my shoulder at him.

"What am I going to tell you?" he grinned.

We both laughed, "Trust Quincy."

And that was something that had been missing from the last week; our battle cry from the last year. Leaning down to run a hand over the horse's shoulder, I knew I did, there was no doubt.

When we finally walked into the arena, I glanced at the calf in the chute, he was looking straight ahead. For the first time all week I looked around the area outside the panels at all the men watching and waiting. Then, I looked at Joe Beaver, the announcer standing just on the other side of the box. I had tuned everyone out all week, but this time I listened to what he was saying.

"This cowboy right here has had a decent week until last night. But now, he just has to shake it off. I knew and roped with his dad, Austin Conners, and I tell you, this cowboy is as good as his dad was and has the chance to be even better. He just has to get out of his head and get back to the basics...the fun of roping."

I couldn't help but smile as we walked into the box. No doubt he had been talking to Mom and Barry. Tonight, there was no reciting of steps I needed to do; I already knew and so did Quincy. When we turned and his rump hit the pad, I looked at the calf, down the arena, then back to the calf and nodded.

Thousands of times I had ridden out of the box and this one was all muscle memory and automatic. The calf ran straight, Quincy positioned me perfect for the throw and it was right on the mark. 7.4 seconds later, I was jogging back to the horse and mounting. He stepped forward and I ran a hand down his neck, scratched between his ears, then patted his rump before looping the rope and smiling at the man handing me the piggin' string.

When the round was done, I was first for the night, which raised me to fourth in the average, and sixth in the world standings. When we made our way onto the buckle ceremony stage, Joe gave me a quick embrace of congratulations with a "I knew you had it in you. You just had to get out of your own head" grin.

Then we celebrated. At the end of the night, next to a large bottle and three glasses of Pendleton on the rocks, Granger, Sammie, and I took off a boot, set them on the table so the spurs showed then placed our Round Win Buckles next to them. A dozen pictures were taken then posted.

Post with image: Proverb 27:17, *'Just as iron sharpens iron, a person sharpens the character of his friend.'*

Thursday night we all made it 'in the money'. Delaney won the round with Sammie in third. I took fifth, Logan placed second, Ryle and Jess were second, and Brodie and Granger tied the night in third. It was another night on stage supporting each other and this time ending at the steak house.

Friday night, after a third place run and quiet night in Sammie's trailer with Sammie, Granger, and Taylor, we received a text from Lauren just as the lights were turned off:

Text: Going into final round

Ace 8th in world standings and 3rd in average

Granger 5th in standings and 2nd in average

Sammie 4th in standings and 4th in average

Brodie 2nd in standings and 3rd in average

Delaney 1st in standings and 1st in average

Ryle/Jess 3rd in standings and 7th in average

Logan 2nd in standings and 5th in average

Sleep well cousins and friends. We finally get to go home in 36 hours.

"Home..." Granger whispered.

"Home is going to be so weird," Sammie giggled softly.

"I can't wait," Taylor sighed.

CHAPTER FIFTY-NINE

ACE

"Mathematically, you could win the championship," Taylor said as he leaned back in his chair and looked around the cafe. It was off the strip and quiet. Just what we needed before the very long day ahead of us.

"Seriously?" I shoved a forkful of pancakes into my mouth.

"Chris came into the Finals leading the standings and has led most of the way until he missed Tuesday night. If you catch in a decent time tonight, you'll probably take 2nd in the average. You just need to have a faster time than him...more money in the standing and add the average earnings you could take the championship."

"Basically, it doesn't matter what anyone else does? Just get faster than Chris," Granger said as he handed the waitress his credit card.

"Well, I'm not a mathematician," Sammie sipped her coffee. "But who would have predicted coming in at 14th and walking out in first?"

"Not me," I said honestly. "Not even going to ponder it. Just going to go rope. We've had a hell of a year and walking away with a round buckle each. It's time to just enjoy our last day before we have to start all over again."

"And enjoy your last ride on Quincy before I take him back," Taylor grinned.

"You should use Stomping Dog tonight," Granger said to me as he took his credit card back from the waitress. "That way, if you win all that money, I get 25% to pay him off."

We all laughed.

"I have not and never will agree to sell him to you." I shook my head.

"We already talked about that," Granger stood.

"Yes, we did," I agreed and followed him out the door. "He's mine but we can start looking for you another horse."

"You've won enough here and throughout the year," Taylor said. "You can afford to just go buy one."

"Nah, can't do that," Granger shook his head. "Right now, all I have is what fits in my truck, so it would have to stay with Mom and her back yard isn't big enough for a horse."

"At least you're thinking it through," Sammie smiled as she opened the truck door.

"Yeah, well, that does happen now and then," Granger grinned at her.

I stood in front of the monitor at the hospitality tent and watched Logan walk his horse into the box. Taylor and Jeremy were at my side as Logan nodded then burst from the box. His 3.6 second run won him the night, third in the average, and reserve world champion.

We were back in front of the monitor to watch Ryle and Jess place second for the night and the average. They were third in the world standings.

When it was Granger and Brodie's turn, we were in the building at the panels across from them. Ten great rides later, Granger slid onto the back of one of his favorite horses; The Black Tie. The gate swung open and high kicks and quick spurring had them coming right at us. When the horn blared Granger jumped from the horse and landed on the ground ten feet in front of us.

We were yelling at him when he grinned and pointed at us then turned to jog back to the gate. His 89-point score would give him third for the night, third in the average, and third in the world standings.

The next ride had Brodie on Major Huckleberry take second for the night, second in the average, and the reserve world champion.

When I rode into the building for our run, the battle cry echoed into the building from behind me.

"TRUST QUINCY!" Taylor and Jeremy yelled.

A smile escaped as we walked into the arena the second to last run of the night. When I glanced at the calf, his head was down. I glanced at Joe Beaver talking into the microphone but this time his voice was low enough I couldn't hear him.

We walked into the box and the barrier was stretched. Another glance at the calf and his head was up and he was looking down the arena. His previous run in the building he had bolted out of the box and raced to the end. He was going to be fast, and we needed to come out of the box right behind him or it would be another 15-second run.

A deep breath, adjustment of the piggin' string in my teeth, a twirl of the rope then I tucked it under my arm. I backed into the box and the second Quincy's rump hit the pad, I nodded. In 7.4 seconds, my hands were flying in the air and the air blasting from my lungs as the calf began struggling against the string. For the last time, I jogged to Quincy and stepped in the stirrup. When my butt hit the saddle, Quincy stepped forward and we stared at the still struggling calf. The official nodded barely a second before the calf kicked the rope off and stood. I leaned forward and scratched between Quincy's ears as the crowd roared.

"Close one," the official rode in next to me with a smile.

"Yeah," I exhaled in relief that he didn't struggle free, or outrun me, and that I didn't have to run another one this week. I'd finished better than I had expected coming into the week.

As we walked out of the arena, I thought of Dad and smiled. I knew he would have been proud of me before that run, but I also knew he would have been damned elated with it, too. I did my job and that's all I could do.

I stepped out of the saddle and ran a hand down Quincy's nose, "Thanks for getting me here, Boy. I'd trust you every day of the week."

Chris nodded as I turned to watch the monitor hanging from the ceiling mid-arena. When his hands flew up, the clock stopped at 7.4 seconds. We had tied. With a mixture of happiness and disappointment I turned and ran into Taylor. His arms wrapped around me.

"So, damn proud of you," he growled then stepped away and we made our way down to the exit doors.

"ACE!" We turned back to see a guy in a white shirt yelling. "Get out here!"

"What for?" I hesitated.

"You got it!"

"Got what?"

"The title, Man. The damn title."

I turned and looked at Taylor, "Didn't I have to be faster than Chris?"

He shrugged, "I think, he just couldn't earn more than you."

"ACE!"

"I don't think they're right," I turned and walked back in with Taylor right beside me.

"Go do your lap and you have interviews." The guy in the white shirt grinned.

I glanced at Taylor. He seemed as confused as I was but shrugged. "Go, do the lap before they change their minds," he chuckled.

In a bit of numb disbelief, I stepped back up on Quincy and looked at the guy. "You sure they got it right?"

"Yeah, get in there," he laughed.

I made my way into the arena with hat in hand and loped around at the cheering crowd until I approached the bucking chutes. Granger and Brodie were there yelling and cheering. Granger's arms were extended to me, pointing at me and his grin couldn't have been wider.

We growled, "Hell, yeah," at each other as I passed them.

It didn't seem real, as if in a very vivid dream. Even as I was interviewed, I kept waiting for someone to step in and say they made a mistake.

Granger was waiting for me in the media room, and we stood in front of the large monitor watching as Sammie raced into the arena. There was concentration in her eyes, but she had a wide smile as she turned the three barrels in her fastest time of the rodeo: 13.68.

No one matched her time, and she won the night, with Delaney winning the average and the title. Her second year in a row.

We were still in the room when we heard Sammie yell down the hallway, "Out of my way!"

She rounded the corner and squealed in delight when she saw both of us. Cameras were firing as she jumped into my arms then quickly pulled Granger into the hug.

The white fog rose from the arena floor and blocked the path to the stage that was sitting in the arena.

I was staring at the ground taking deep breaths when I felt someone walk up to me and bump my shoulder. Delaney's wide grin greeted me.

"Has it soaked in yet?" she asked softly.

"I'm waiting for someone to walk up and tell me they made a mistake," I exhaled. "It really can't be true."

"It is...I felt the same way last year when they told me." She glanced around at the commotion around us. "When you walk out there, take it all in. Enjoy it because there are thousands of ropers out there that want to be there."

I nodded, "Thanks...how long before you realize it really happened?"

"In a couple days when you start seeing the pictures all over social media," she chuckled.

"Ace," Someone yelled and waved me through the door and into the white fog.

In that disbelieving haze I walked through, up the steps, shook hands then made my way to the announcer.

The microphone was suddenly in front of me.

"Ace Conners, our tie-down champion. Not since Tyson Durphy in the 2016 NFR has someone come from 14th place to win the championship. Ace, you have had a tremendous year from fighting to get here to battling each night to get on this stage."

"Oh, yes ma'am, it has been a heck of a year. But, this isn't just my achievement. I have to thank my brothers, my mentor, Barry Wilder, and my mom. But, even they will agree, that I would not be here at the rodeo or standing on this stage without my "Iron Sharpens Iron" team of Sammie Parkston and Granger Miller. They supported me and battled with me all year. I may have this buckle and title, but they earned it with me. No one can have better partners than them." He took a deep breath and grinned. "Although, they would say the reason I am here is because of my partner, Taylor's horse Quincy, bred from my father, Austin Conners' last horse, Maggie. I was told to trust Quincy and I did…he, Sammie, and Granger are why I am on this stage tonight."

CHAPTER SIXTY

Epilogue

The Rawlins truck and horse trailer slowly pulled out of the equestrian park and toward the highway leaving only Sammie's truck and trailer and Ace's truck with camper and horse trailer remaining.

With a last pat on the shoulder and hand sliding down the back of Quincy, Ace stepped out of the trailer and Taylor shut the door.

"I think that's it," Ace told him.

"New NFR qualifier and championship saddles locked in the tack room, new buckles secure in the back seat, drinks in the cooler, and snacks in the console," Taylor grinned. "We're ready to hit the road."

Sammie wrapped her arms around Ace's waist, "All the important things," she giggled. "If I didn't say it enough last night and this morning, I am so over the top happy and proud of you."

Ace squeezed her tightly, "You did, but until the whole thing sinks in, you can just keep saying it."

Sammie stepped away from him to give Taylor a hug goodbye. "Did you decide if we're driving straight through or stopping somewhere?" She asked Ace.

"Right now, we'll just push through. If we get tired, I know a couple ranches where we can stop and rest," he answered and checked the tack room door on his trailer.

"If you get tired of driving, just let me know and we can trade," Taylor told her.

With Sergeant, Grace, and her father's horse already loaded in Sammie's trailer, Granger checked the back gate then the tack room door. Both were secure.

His phone rang and he pulled it from his pocket with a grin, "It's River…hello?" He was quiet a moment before he laughed, and his eyes radiated pure joy. "That is awesome! I couldn't be prouder, happier, thankful, and so damned honored to have ridden him here. I'll be buying every picture I can find of that ride. Yeah, safe travels to all of you." He hung up the phone and grinned at the trio looking expectantly at him. "Destiny's Ignatius won the Saddle Bronc of the Finals."

"Oh, yay!" Sammie clapped.

He leaned a hip onto the trailer wheel well and smiled at the brothers. "I'm glad you're headed to the Idaho ranch instead of Texas," Granger said to Ace and Taylor.

Sammie wiggled her way to sit on the wheel well next to him.

"I'm not sure exactly where the saddle and buckle will land in the future," Ace stood in front of them and decided they looked very comfortable together. "But, for now, it will be in Dad's trophy room."

"I love that idea," Sammie grinned.

"Maybe when we get them in there, it will all seem real," Ace chuckled, then sighed as he looked at his watch. "Let's get on the road."

He turned to the truck then stopped, looked back to Sammie and Granger, hesitated, then turned back to the pair who were still sitting and leaning on the trailer.

"Before we do," he stepped to Granger and lifted a hand. Granger reached out to shake it, but Ace held it tightly. Then, he reached out with his other hand and held it to Sammie. With a confused smile, she slid her hand into his.

"Before anything else happens, you two need to get this thing going," Ace slid Sammie's hand into Granger's. They both looked at him in surprise. He looked at Granger, "Maybe once, you thought you didn't have anything to offer her, but that's changed now, and you can offer her the world." Granger's brows rose as Ace turned to Sammie. "I agree with Taylor. You will never look at anyone the way you look at him." He nodded toward Granger, then stepped toward his truck. "Get that going and we'll see you tonight."

Sammie and Granger didn't move. They just sat quietly, hand- in-hand, and watched the brothers drive away. When they disappeared and they were the only ones left in the whole parking lot, Granger looked down at their hands.

"Do you really like me...that way?" Sammie whispered.

"Remember that day in the Costco parking lot and you locked the truck door even though the window was open, and you made me promise never to tell anyone how we met?" He didn't look at her, he just focused on their hands.

"Yes," she whispered with a light giggle.

"When you smiled at me, that devilish grin…" he finally looked into her shining blue eyes. "I fell for you then and more every day since."

She gasped, "Oh...I didn't know." She looked out in the direction the brothers had disappeared, to their hands that remained motionless, then up into his blue eyes. "Do I look at you differently than everyone else? Did I then?"

He smiled slightly, "I honestly don't know. But since we've spent most of our time this last year with Taylor and Ace and they saw it...I guess so. Either way, I guess the question is, do you like me...that way?"

Her gaze went back to their hands, and her fingers began to curl around his, "When Ace and Taylor drive away, it's OK because I know we'll talk, text, or video chat all the time…daily most of the time. But, when you drive away, all I want is to be in the passenger seat next to you. The phone, texting, and video just isn't enough with you. I want you, in person, by my side." His fingers curled around hers. "I can't imagine life without you, and I don't want a life without you."

Their eyes met and they smiled.

"So, G-ranger, now what?" She whispered.

"Well, I'd say the best way to start is with a kiss." He turned so he was still leaning against her, and their fingers tightened even more.

Sammie's free hand went to his belt to grip it tightly as he leaned down toward her. With their lips just inches apart, her eyes closed in anticipation. She waited but he had stopped.

Her eyes slowly opened, "Are you going to kiss me?"

"At least a million times," he whispered. "But this one...the first one? I've dreamt of this one for over a year so I'm just taking my time."

They smiled at each other then she leaned up and pushed their lips together.

When they finally parted, she leaned back and looked into his happy blue eyes, "Who knew picking up a cowboy off the side of the road could lead to such an adventure?"

ABOUT THE AUTHOR

I was raised with Shetlands and ponies and have loved horses since I watched a Shetland colt born when I was four.

Growing up, the TV show Bonanza was my favorite. I loved that western life and wanted to be Little Joe and Hoss' little sister. I wanted to live at the Ponderosa. Watching rodeos on television and attending when I could was the closest I could get to the cowboy way of life.

That changed when I purchased my first 'big horse' when I was twenty-one and living in Alaska. I now have the great-granddaughter of that horse in my pasture.

I am also a Professional Rodeo Association Photographer and specialize in the equine industry; shows, races, jackpots, and rodeos. With my photography, I create my own covers.

The Tagger Herd Series was my first venture into fictional writing and I love the family and horses in the series.

My first 'stand-alone' novel was Hoofbeats in the Wind which ventured into rodeo.

My next book, Coffee With Cowboys delved deeper into the rodeo world and researching for the book was an adventure. I have met wonderful people from fans, stock contractors, and competitors. I thank every one of them that have helped make that book a possibility. It will always be special to me because of the people I met.

Bijou Bay was inspired by Black Rock Ranch and the story of Clyde and Paul.

Writing, researching, photography, my two dogs, Morgan and Tagger, and Kit in the pasture, fill my world and keep me busy.